BEST SPORTS STORIES 1982

BEST
SPORTS
STORIES
1982

A Panorama of the 1981 Sports World
With the Year's Top Photographs

Edited by The Sporting News and Edward Ehre

E. P. DUTTON
NEW YORK

The publishers and editors of this anthology are deeply indebted to those who have served as judges over the years, particularly John Hutchens, an editorial member of Book of the Month Club, Inc., John Chamberlain, a nationally syndicated columnist and book editor, and Jerry Nason, former sports editor of the BOSTON GLOBE. Their adjudications in choosing the prize-winning stories have been an important facet in the continuing success of BEST SPORTS STORIES.

Published in the United States by E. P. Dutton, Inc.,
2 Park Avenue, New York, N.Y. 10016

Library of Congress Catalog Card Number: 45-35124

ISBN: 0-525-24126-4

Published simultaneously in Canada by Clarke, Irwin & Company
Limited, Toronto and Vancouver

10 9 8 7 6 5 4 3 2 1

First Edition

Table of Contents

The Prize-Winning Photographs

BEST ACTION PHOTOGRAPH

BEST FEATURE PHOTOGRAPH

Other Photographs

PREFACE

Our contributors received a notice in 1980 from E. P. Dutton that the publication of *Best Sports Stories* would be suspended in 1981 because of the illness of both editors. Both Irving Marsh and I believed that the 1980 edition would be the last and thus mourned the passing of a "Best Friend," a project to which we had dedicated ourselves since 1944. And that, evidently, is what John Schulian felt, also, when he wrote a touching valedictory piece for *Inside Sports* magazine.

The story was labeled, "Saying Goodbye to a Best Friend," and was carried in the "Culture" section. That's where the demise of our book wound up. CULTURE! And suddenly sports writing was in the same class with "Lady Windemere's Fan," "Fanny Hill," "Black Beauty," and other classics. I purchased a beret and bought two more strings for my classical guitar.

It was our editor at Dutton, William Doerflinger, who felt that the book should not languish in moldy libraries next to Gibbon's "Roman Empire." He set out to find somebody like Lazarus, somebody who could bring the anthology back to life. He found *The Sporting News.* The editors there sent out the announcements, screened the material and sent the best stories to Mr. Marsh and myself for judging.

Mr. Marsh, unfortunately, at this time lost his dear wife, Eva, and felt he could no longer continue with the project. Bereft of a dear colleague for the first time in 36 years of collaboration, I, with the aid of *The Sporting News,* decided to go it alone.

Best Sports Stories 1982 had a very short pre-publication period. Entries had to be submitted by December 15, 1981, and most of them arrived the last week and a half before deadline.

In past years, Irv and I spent long hours reading, captioning, typing biographies, sorting and balancing the book. We had to rush the typing, get manuscripts to the judges who sometimes were in different parts of the country, and often had to resubmit the articles in case of ties. We felt this aspect of the book should be changed.

The new editors and Mr. Marsh felt that I should assume the judging of the articles for the 1982 edition. I had had almost four decades of reading and judging of sports writing. The book has been very successful and has continued to receive warm critical notices through the years.

And now to the 1982 edition of *Best Sports Stories.* With a melange of hesitancy, shyness and forebearance, I make my first announcements:

WINNERS OF BEST SPORTS STORIES 1982

News	Joe Gergen	Newsday
Magazine	Tom McIntyre	Sports Afield
Magazine	Roger Kahn	Sport

BEST SPORTS STORIES PHOTO CONTEST

Best Action Shot	Richard Darcey, The Washington Post
Best Feature Shot	Norman Sylvia, Providence Journal-Bulletin

After worrying and fretting over the final decisions, I wanted to acknowledge the merit of some of the other articles that contended for the prizes right up to the end. Therefore, following some of the stories that you soon will be reading appears a short commentary on the writer and how he handled his material. The entire selection process was difficult and left me with gnawing doubts. In my mind, every story appearing on these pages was well written and deserving. But everybody can't be the winner.

So out of its internment comes the new and improved child of top sports writers and talented photographers from around the country. Enjoy!

Edward Ehre

Walter (Red) Smith

In 1944 we sent out our first flyers to solicit sports articles for "Best Sports Stories." One of the first pieces submitted was from a 39-year-old sports writer in Philadelphia named Walter Red Smith.

His story was concerned with the lambasting his alma-mater, Notre Dame, had taken from the Davis-Blanchard-led Army team. It was delightfully humorous. His major worry was for the stricken ghosts that were somersaulting under the epitaphs in Shamrock country.

For the next 44 years, six of which he served as a judge for *Best Sports Stories,* his writing and attitudes always held that the principle of sportsmanship, not the score, was the ultimate mission. He loved athletic competition, but was troubled in his later years by the duplicity and ambiguity that marred the athletic arenas.

But Red never moralized. When irked by an infringement of the rules, or the wretched ignobility of sports stars and the establishment, a touch of his sardonic pen, or wry twist of Irish amenity, took care of the situation. He was, without doubt, the most popular sports writer of our time—maybe of all time.

The world is diminished by his death.

Best News-Feature Story

The Hit Man Became the Target

BOXING

By *JOE GERGEN*

From Newsday
Copyright © 1981, Newsday, Inc.

The message on the back of Thomas Hearns' robe set down the challenge: "Winner Takes All." Left unsaid was the rejoinder: "Loser Takes Fall." It would have been appropriate for Hearns' handlers to turn the robe inside out when they half-carried the former World Boxing Association welterweight champion out of the ring.

Two knights in white satin shorts met on a makeshift ring set above the tennis courts at Caesars Palace last night. When the 14-round war in the desert ended, Sugar Ray Leonard's left eye was nearly closed. Hearns' eyes were wide open, but they were as expressive as Little Orphan Annie's. Let's assume for posterity that Leonard's bad eye was but a frozen wink.

He had done it. Not just beaten the previously undefeated Hearns, but accomplished it in the manner of Hearns. The dancer turned stalker. The boxer turned slugger. That was Thomas Hearns, a/k/a The Hit Man, backpedaling, slipping and sliding off the ropes, running for his wits.

It was a graphic display of role reversal. Hearns ran but he couldn't hide. In the end he caught every bolt of Leonard's fury and sagged to an invisible seat on the ropes. On this steaming night, in the most lucrative prizefight in history, it could be said of Hearns: Good field, not enough hit.

There was nothing undignified about Hearns' performance. He withstood a savage attack in the sixth and seventh rounds and came back from the wobbles to counter beautifully. Hearns pounded on that left eye of Leonard's until it looked like raw meat. But Leonard stood fast and then shelled Hearns in the 13th. The 14th was batting practice until referee Davey Pearl decided at 1:45 that the match no longer was sport.

And in stopping Hearns, in rousing his weary legs from the stool when they seemed heavier than the night air, Leonard proved one very important thing: Not only did he have talent and flair and charisma, but he had heart.

After Leonard's lone loss of his professional career, a 15-round decision to Roberto Duran 15 months ago in Montreal, Duran was asked why he had won and he pounded on his bare chest. Later that year, of course, Duran would walk away from his World Boxing Council welterweight title in the middle of the eighth round. The victory left Leonard dissatisfied. No one knew how tough he could be when he had to be.

Leonard had talked frequently about his distaste for boxing. And he sometimes appeared more interested in putting on a show than putting up a fight. But last night when Thomas Hearns put the question to him, at a time when all three judges had inexplicably decided that Hearns was leading on points, Leonard summoned something deep from within.

"In the middle rounds I knew the fight was very close," Leonard said. "I think he had an edge because he was scoring and I wasn't throwing many punches. I brought it up from my guts, from the bottom of my heart." And it was breathtaking, even shocking to see.

Only the previous day, Leonard's attorney, Mike Trainer, had cautioned that Leonard's image was not in tune with his ring personality. "Everyone thinks he's a nice kid," Trainer said. "That's because he looks too cute, too sweet, too nice. If you had been with him the last four weeks and had watched someone thumb him and seen what he did to that person, you'd know he's not a cute little kid in the ring."

In the 13th and 14th rounds last night, he was a monster. Forget the 7-Up commercials with his 7-year-old son. Last night, peering at what some considered the hardest-hitting welterweight in history through half an eye, he drank from the same potion that transformed Dr. Jekyll into Mr. Hyde.

A right hand staggered Hearns just when he appeared to be coasting backward to victory in the 13th round. A kitchen-sink combination deposited Hearns on the ring apron, although Pearl called it a shove. Seconds later, Hearns was sitting on the second strand of ropes and Pearl, counting through the bell, stopped at nine.

Nothing could save him in the 14th. He was defenseless. He didn't say, "No mas," as had Duran. Instead, Pearl mercifully and wisely said it for him. Standing next to the ring, Don King shouted, "They shouldn't have stopped that fight. The man was on his feet." It should be noted that King was shut out of this promotion. And when Hearns did get to his feet, he was supported by two seconds.

Pearl had done the right thing. The TKO should not even have been necessary had the judges been watching the same fight as 25,000 fans, including such celebrities as Bill Cosby, Richard Pryor, Burt Reynolds, Jack Nicholson and Cher—plus tennis stars John McEnroe and Vitas Gerulaitis, who were sitting on a court on which they frequently have played. Cosby, incidentally, wore tennis shorts and sneakers; McEnroe wore a jacket, white shirt and tie.

The real star of the night, of course, was Leonard, who is determined to leave a mark as one of the great fighters of our time. Last night he took a giant step in that direction. In 101-degree heat under the ring lights, Leonard frustrated a very tough opponent, occasionally enraged him into punching after the bell, and then sent him to never-never land with a terrible, vengeful force.

There was only one official knockdown, according to the referee, although Leonard swore there were three "since my vision was impaired." It was one of the few laugh lines of a brutal night. Leonard wore dark glasses as he spoke it, but there was no mask to hide the injury to Thomas Hearns. His reputation had suffered a terrible beating.

Judge's Comments

Joe Gergen's coverage of the Sugar Ray Leonard-Thomas Hearns fight is a laidback, lucent report of two fine athletes honoring each other both in the ring and out. The editors of this collection of sports articles always have felt that coverage articles lose their vitality in a short space of time. The logistics of time, space, memory and impact are the tyrants that inhibit a writer's successful story—one that will not remain with the reader very long after the initial reading.

Gergen's report is both convincing and colorful. The tension and ambivalence in his account rivet the reader to the pages.

The description of the beating that Leonard took in the seventh, eighth and ninth rounds was vivid. Hearns kept pounding on Leonard's eye until it looked like raw meat. Gergen continues:

"But Leonard stood fast and then shelled Hearns in the 13th. The 14th was batting practice until referee Davey Pearl decided at 1:45 that the match no longer was sport. And in stopping Hearns, in rousing his weary legs from the stool when they seemed heavier than the night air, Leonard proved one very important thing: Not only did he have talent and flair and charisma, but he had heart."

The height of the drama comes when Gergen destroys the "Mr. Nice Guy" image that has come to be associated with Sugar Ray Leonard:

"In the 13th and 14th rounds last night, he was a monster. Forget the 7-Up commercials with his 7-year-old son. Last night, peering at what some considered the hardest-hitting welterweight in history through half an eye, he drank from the same potion that transformed Dr. Jekyll into Mr. Hyde."

Here is a fine example of what A.J. Leibling once described this way: "Some of the finest writing in America comes off the sports pages."

Gergen has been awarded first prize by the editors of this edition for the best news-coverage story.

Best Magazine Story Co-Winner

Buff

OUTDOORS

By *THOMAS McINTYRE*

From Sports Afield
Copyright © 1981, Sports Afield, a Publication of Hearst Magazines

They saw the buffalo after killing the elephant. The professional hunter switched off the engine and eased out of the battered olive Land Rover, carrying his binoculars. His client got out on the other side without making any noise, and one of the trackers, without needing to be told, handed his 300 down to him. The client fed the 200-grain Noslers into the magazine, put the 220-grain solid into the chamber and locked the bolt as the professional hunter glassed the buffs.

It was nearly sunset, and already in the back of the Land Rover lay the heavy curves of ivory, darkened and checked by decades of life, the roots bloodied now like a pulled tooth. They had found the old bull elephant under a bright acacia late in the afternoon, having tracked him all day on foot. He was being guarded by two younger bulls, his askaris; *and when the client made the brainshot, red dust puffing off the side of the elephant's head, and the old bull dropped, the young ones got between and tried to push him back onto his feet, blocking any finishing rounds. But the bullet had actually just missed the bull's brain, lodging instead in the honeycomb of bone in the top of his skull. As he came to, he regained his feet, and they had to chase him almost a mile, firing on the run, until he went down for good. By then it was too late to butcher out the dark-red flesh, so they left that task until the next morning when they would return with a band of local villagers and carry out everything edible, even marrow in the bones. They took only the tusks that afternoon. Still, when they finally reached the Land Rover again they were very tired, pleased with themselves, and ready only for a long drink back in camp.*

So when on the way to that drink the professional hunter spotted a bachelor herd of Cape buffalo (with two exceptionally fine bulls in it), it was all a bit much, actually. But he motioned his client to come around behind the Land Rover to his side, and crouching they worked behind the low cover toward the mbogos.

The first rule they give you about dangerous game is to get as close as you possibly can before firing—then get another 100 yards closer. *When the professional felt they had complied with this stricture, to the extent that they could clearly see the yellow-billed oxpeckers hanging beneath the bull's flick-ing ears and feeding on ticks, he got his client into kneeling position and told him to take the one turned sideways to them: put the solid into his shoulder, then pour on the Noslers. That was when the client noticed that the profession-al was backing him up with a pair of 8X German binoculars instead of his cus-tomary 470 Nitro Express double rifle, but the professional just shrugged and said, "You should be able to handle this all right by yourself."*

Taking a breath, the client hit the buffalo in the shoulder with the solid and staggered him. The bull turned to face them, and the client put two quick Noslers into the heaving chest, aiming right below the chin. The buffalo col-lapsed. As the client reloaded, the second fine bull remained where he was, confused and belligerent, and the professional hunter urged his client to take him too, Oh my yes, him too. *This bull turned also after the first solid slammed into his shoulder and lifted his head toward them, his scenting nose held high. Looking a wounded Cape buffalo in his discomfortingly intelligent eyes is something like looking down the barrel of a loaded 45 in the hands of a mean drunk. That is the time when you have to be exceptionally mindful, how-ever, of what you are doing out there in Africa and make your shots count—particularly when your professional hunter, who is backing you up with a pair of 8X German binoculars, leans over and whispers calmly, "Look: he's going to come for us."*

Another careful breath and the client placed two more bullets neatly into the bull's chest beneath his raised chin, just the way he had on the first one, except this bull did not go down. That left the client with one round in his rifle, and as he was about to squeeze it off he wondered if there would be any time left afterward for him either to reload or make a run for it. But for now there was this enraged buffalo that had to be gotten onto the ground somehow. All the client could be really concerned about was holding his rifle steady until the sear broke and the cartridge fired and the bullet sped toward the bull—but just before the rifle fired its last round the buffalo lurched forward and fell with a bellow, stretching his black muzzle out in the dirt. Then he was silent.

Standing up slowly, the client and the professional hunter moved cau-tiously toward the downed buffalo (the rest of the small herd now fled) to find them both dead. Only then, in the dwindling light did they see that one of the first bull's horns, the horn that was turned away from them when the client first shot, had been broken away in recent combat and a splintered stump was all that remained. He had been a magnificent bull at one time, but at least the second bull's horns were perfect, beautifully matched sweeps of polished black horn, almost 50 inches across the spread. And there glittered a burnished half-inch steel ball bearing buried in the horn boss covering the bull's head like a gladiator's helmet. The ball bearing had once served as a musketball fired out of an ancient muzzleloader. Whoever the native hunter who fired it was, he must have had one overpowering lust for buffalo meat, and for buffalo hunt-ing. What became of him after he shot and missed with his quixotic weapon at a ludicrously close range is probably best not speculated upon, however.

When I first heard that story I was a boy of nine or ten. It was told by a gentleman of my acquaintance (a man who taught me how to hunt then, and with whom I have had the pleasure of hunting ever since), who had experienced it on a safari to Tanzania 20 years ago. Like most hunting tales, it has been twice and three times told since, yet unlike some others it has aged rather well and never grown tedious with the telling. Every time I hear it, and see the massive head on the wall with the steel ball shining out of the horn, it explains something, mysteriously, of why a person could get daffy about hunting Cape buffalo. And, mystery or not, its power as a legend sent me off to East Africa once to hunt the buffalo myself.

Black, sparsely haired, nearly a ton in weight, some five feet high at the shoulder, as smart and mean as a muleskinner's whip, and with a set of immense but elegant ebony horns which sweep down then up and a little back, like something drawn with a French curve, to points sharp enough to kill a black-maned lion with one blow— horns which can measure almost five feet across the outside spread —the African Cape buffalo is, along with the Indian water buffalo and the Spanish fighting bull, one of the three great wild cattle in the world today. Of these three, though, the water buffalo has now been largely domesticated, although a few animals transplanted to Australia and South America have reverted to the untamed state. The fighting toto's wildness is the product of over 2,000 years of men having restricted his breeding to keep the aurochs' blood still running through his veins. The Cape buffalo alone has had no dealings with men, other than of the most terminal kind.

With his ferocious temper, treacherous intelligence, and stern indifference to the shocking power of all but the most outlandishly large-caliber rifles, the Cape buffalo is routinely touted as the most dangerous member of the African Big Five (which also includes the lion, leopard, rhino and elephant). Whether he is or not all depends, as does almost everything under the sun, on what you mean. He is certainly not as sure to charge as a rhino or as quick as the carnivorous cats. And in the words of Grits Gresham, "Nobody ever got *wounded* by an elephant." But the buff is quick enough; and when he makes up his mind to charge, especially when wounded, there is no animal more obdurately bent on finishing a fight. In open flat country he may present no serious threat to a hunter properly armed, but you seldom encounter him in baseball-diamond surroundings. More often, he'll be in a swampy thicket or a dense forest. He is clever enough to go to cover and fierce enough to come out of it.

The best measure of the Cape buffalo's rank as a big-game animal may simply be the kind of esteem professional hunters hold him in. It is a curious fact of the sporting life that tall, strapping, red-faced chaps who make their livings trailing the dangerous game all come in time to be downright maudlin about which animals they feel right about hunting. Most first lose their taste for hunting the big cats, so that while they will usually do their best to get a client his one and only lion, their hearts will not be entirely in it: the predatory cats in their appetites for meat and sleep and sex are simply too close to us for comfort. Then there is the rhino, the hulking, agile, dumb, blind, sad, funny, savage, magnificent Pleistocene rhino who every day is getting hammered just that much closer to the Big Jump we term extinction—under present conditions only a raving sociopath could feel good about destroying one specimen of that fleeting arrangement of molecules we term rhino.

Out of the Big Five, then, that leaves only the elephant and the Cape buffalo to feel at all right about hunting, and to my knowledge hardly any real professional hunter, unless he has lost interest in hunting altogether, ever totally loses his taste for giving chase to these two. There is no easy way to hunt elephant and Cape buffalo—you must be able to walk for miles on end, know how to follow animal signs well, and be prepared to kill an animal that can just as readily kill you—and this makes them the two greatest challenges for taking good trophy animals, and the two most satisfying. Something about hunting them gets into a hunter's blood and stays. To offer one further bit of testimony on behalf of the buff, consider if you will the widely known piece of jungle lore that the favorite sport of *elephants* is chasing herds of Cape buffalo around the bush, and the buff's position as one of the world's great big-game animals seems secure.

Which is why I wanted to hunt buff and went to do so in the southwestern corner of Kenya (still open to hunting then) near Lake Victoria, in the Chepalungu Forest on top of the Soit Ololol Escarpment and above the Great Rift Valley, to arguably the loveliest green spot in all Masailand, and one which I dearly hated—to begin with, anyway.

To find buffalo there we had to put on cheap canvas tennis shoes (because they were the only things that would dry overnight) and slog every day into the dim wet forest (filled with butterflies and cobras, birds and barking bushbucks, gray waterbucks and giant forest hogs, rhino, elephant and buffalo), penetrating a wall of limbs and vines and deep-green leaves woven as tight as a Panama hat, and through which one could see no more than ten feet in any direction. On going in, the advice given me by my professional hunter, John Fletcher of the late lamented Ker, Downey & Selby Safaris, Ltd., was that, in the event of my stumbling onto a sleeping buffalo (as well I might), I should shoot the animal dead on the spot and ask questions later. It took only a momentary lack of resolve at such a juncture, he assured me, to give a buffalo ample opportunity to spring up and winnow you right down. And that was the root cause of my hating this beautiful African land: It scared the hell out of me, and I hated being scared.

As we hunted the buffalo, though, a change began to come over me. We had had unheard-of luck on cats at the outset of the safari, so that at dawn on my fifth morning of hunting in Africa, while concealed in a blind constructed out of cut brush, I had taken a very fine leopard as he came to feed on the hanging bait—the cat toppling from the tree as a long yellow flame sprouted from the muzzle of my 300. And on the evening of the same day, we had incredibly gotten up on an extremely large lion, *simba mkubwa sana* in the words of the trackers, crouched in long grass which shaded his tawny hide to a lime tone, and I had broken his back with my 375, establishing what may very well have been some sort of one-day East African record for cats. So when our hangovers subsided two days later, we moved off from that more southern country near Kilimanjaro to Block 60 above the escarpment, assuming we would quickly take a good buffalo (a bull with a spread over 40 inches wide—ideally 45 or better, with 50 inches a life's ambition—along with a full, tightly fitted boss), then move on again to the greater-kudu country we had, until the cats, not hoped to have time to reach.

Instead of a good buffalo in short order, however, we had to go into the forest every day for two weeks, first glassing the open country futilely at daybreak, then following into the cover the tracks the buffalo left when they had moved back in before dawn, their night's feeding done. In that forest, where the light sifted down as if into deep water, we picked our way for two weeks over rotting timber and through mud wallows, unseen animals leaping away from us on all sides creeping forward until we could hear low grunts then the sudden flutter of oxpeckers (more euphoniously known as tickbirds) flaring up from the backs of the buffalo they were preening, and then the flutter of alarmed Cape buffalo flaring up as well, snorting, crashing so wildly away (yet also unseen) through the dark forest that the soggy ground quivered, and the trees were tossed about as if in a wind storm, and the report of wood being splintered by horns could be heard for hundreds of yards through the forest.

That was the sound a breeding herd of cows, calves and young bulls made as they fled; but other times there would be the flutter of oxpeckers and no crashing afterward, only a silence that the booming of my heart seemed to fill, and we knew we were onto a herd of bulls, wise old animals who were at that moment slipping carefully away from us, moving off with inbred stealth, or maybe stealthily circling back to trample us into the dirt! For much of those two weeks, then, I saw things in that forest through a glaze of fear as ornate as the rose window in a medieval French cathedral.

I discovered, however, that you can tolerate fear roaring like a train through your head and clamping like a limpet to your heart for just so long; and sometime during those two weeks I ceased to be utterly terrified by the black forms in the forest, and instead became excited by them, by the chance of encountering them, by the possibility that my life was actually on the line in there: my heart still boomed, but for a far different reason now. What was going on in that forest, I saw, was a highly charged game of skill: if you played it wrong, you might be killed; but if you played it just right, you got to do it over again. No more than that. But when something like that gets into your blood, the rest of life comes to lack something you never knew it was supposed to have before.

Then one evening we chased a breeding herd in and out of the forest for hours, jumping it and driving it ahead of us, trying to get a good look at one of the bulls in it. Finally we circled ahead of the buffalo into a clearing of chest-high grass where they had to cross in front of us. We hunkered down in the grass and watched them as they came out. The bull appeared at last, but he was only a young bull, big-bodied but not good in the horns. As we watched him pass by, a tremendous cow buffalo, the herd matriarch, walked out, maybe 60 yards from us, and halted. Then she turned and stared directly our way.

If she feels her calf or her herd is threatened, the cow buffalo is probably as deadly an animal as there is; and at that moment I thought that was just the most wonderful piece of information in the world to have. It meant she might charge, and, may God forgive me, I *wanted* her to. Very much.

"All right," John Fletcher whispered, his William G. Evans 500 Nitro Express carried across his body like a laborer's shovel, "we'll stand now, and she'll run off. Or she'll charge us."

So we stood up, John Fletcher, me, and the trackers behind us, and the buffalo cow did not budge. We could see her thinking, weighing the odds, her nostrils twitching. John Fletcher and I brought our rifles up at the same time without a word and took aim: as soon as she started forward I knew I was going to throw a 375 into the center of her chest, exactly where my crosshairs were, and if she kept coming I would throw in another, and another after that, but I would not run. As the seconds passed, I felt more and more that, for perhaps one of the few times in my life, I was behaving correctly, no fear clouding my vision now.

Then the cow snorted and spun away from us, following the herd, her calculations having come up on the negative side for her. I took my finger off the trigger, then, and carefully reset the safety. And all the trackers came up and clapped me on the back, smiling their nervous African smiles, as if to say, *You did well.* I was glad we hadn't had to kill the cow after all.

Yet, when at first light on our fourteenth day of buffalo hunting we reached the edge of a small dewy field and spotted three bulls feeding in it 100 yards away, I did not kill my first Cape buffalo at all well. Though he was the smallest-bodied buffalo of the three, old and almost hairless, his horns swept out nearly 45 inches, much farther than those of the other two, and when I fired—low, near his heart, but not near enough—he began to trot in a slow circle as the two younger bulls came past us at an oblique angle, just visible in the edge of my scope. I shot him again and again, anywhere, and again, and John Fletcher fired once, and at last the bull went down and I had to finish him on the ground. There was still, I had to admit, after the bull lay dead and all my ammunition was gone, enough fear left in me to prevent my behaving in a completely correct manner.

We went on hunting Cape buffalo after that right up to my last day on safari—John Fletcher looking for an even better trophy for me, and me looking to make up for the first kill, hoping there was still time. On the last morning of hunting we flushed a bushbuck. I had only the briefest second to make one of the toughest running shots I have ever tried and took the sturdy little antelope through the heart as he stretched into top speed. Suddenly I was very anxious to try another buffalo before leaving Africa.

We found the herd that evening when John and I and my non-hunting friend William Cullen were out alone, the trackers back helping break camp. The buffalo had been drifting in and out of the forest all that gray highland afternoon with us behind them, a bull's cloven print, as big as a relish tray, standing out from all the others. It seemed that we had lost them for good until a small boy, no older than four or five, wearing a rough-cotton toga and carrying a smooth stick, appeared startlingly out of the bush before us and asked in Masai if we would like to kill a buffalo.

The child led us along a forest trail to the edge of the trees, where he pointed across an open glade to the bull. The Cape buffalo bull, his tight boss doming high above his head, stood in the herd of 10 or 15 other animals in the nearing dark, only a few yards from heavy cover—in which, in no more than half-a-dozen running steps, he could be completely concealed. John Fletcher, for one, was something more than slightly aware of this. He remembered too well how I had killed my first bull, and though he'd said nothing, he knew how much the buffalo had spooked me. If I wounded this bull now and he made it into the forest with the light going, and the second rule they give you for dangerous game being that you follow all wounded animals in . . . well . . . John Fletcher looked at me carefully. There was no denying it was a good bull, though, and the trackers and camp staff would want some more meat to take home, and there was still a little light, and—*and oh bloody hell!*

I glanced at him, then back at the buffalo. I was, at that moment, as all right as I was ever going to get. This was where it counted; this was what it was all about; this was exactly what I'd come here for. It was in my blood now, only John Fletcher might not know that. I told him.

"Where," I whispered, easing the 375's safety off, "do you want me to shoot him, John?"

John Fletcher stared at me even harder then, but this time he whispered only, "There, in the shoulder."

You can see where a Cape buffalo's shoulder socket is under his hide, and if you travel through his body from there you will reach his spine where it dips down from his humped back to become his neck. That was where I laid my crosshairs, and when the 270-grain Nosler hit him there it broke his shoulder and shattered his spine. Suddenly the bull was down, his muzzle stretched out along the short grass and the buffalo's bellowing death song (what the professionals call "music" when they hear it coming from a wounded bull laid up in cover, because it means he's done for) coming from his throat. The rest of the herd wheeled on us then, their eyes clear and wide and most uncattlelike, the smell of the bull's blood in their nostrils. I finished the bull with one more round to the neck, and the herd was gone, vanishing as quickly as that bull could have vanished had my nerve not held and I had not behaved correctly.

That last night in camp, while the African staff jerked long strips of buffalo meat over the campfire to carry back to their wives and children, John Fletcher, William Cullen and I sat in the dining tent and ate hot oxtail soup and slices of steaming boiled buffalo tongue and drank too much champagne and brandy, and laughed too loud too. We finished breaking camp at dawn the next morning and returned to Nairobi.

It seems I may have gone on at too great a length here already, but I wish I could go on even further to tell you all the other Cape buffalo stories I know, like the time John Fletcher was guiding a famous Mexican *torero* who meant to kill a bull buffalo with his curved steel sword—brought with him from Mexico for just that purpose—and what made him change his mind. Or how when you awoke in the middle of the night, needing to seek relief, and stepped outside your canvas tent, you might make out, just there on that little rise at the edge of camp, the silhouettes of feeding buffalo against the cold stars. Or how one of the many herds we chased out of the forest and across the green country led us into a spectacular cloudburst, and the storm wind began to swirl around so that our scent was swept in front of the 50 or 60 funereal-black animals and turned them back *on* us, and as they started forward I asked John Fletcher what we did now, and he said lightly, "Actually, we might try shooting down the lead buffalo and climbing onto its back."

But what I wish most of all is that I were back in those African highlands I grew to love, hunting the Cape buffalo I grew to love too —probably still scared, but only enough to make me sense my true heart curled inside my chest and beating, telling me of what I am capable.

Judge's Comments

"Nearly a ton in weight . . . as smart and mean as a muleskinner's whip . . . the Cape Buffalo has had no dealings with men, other than of the most terminal kind."

If the reader detests guns, loaths the killing of animals for sport and eschews reading that deals with this subject, he might not find too much pleasure in this story.

However, the author, a neophyte, presents a grisly, riveting picture through his own feelings and actions that sometimes leaves the reader terrified. When he finally spots his quarry glaring at him in a tense, clutching moment, he says:

"*Then, I saw things in that forest through a glaze of fear as ornate as the rose window in a medieval French cathedral.*"

He continues, "*I discovered, however, that you can tolerate fear roaring like a train through your head and clamping like a limpet to your heart for just so long.*"

And finally, "*What was going on in the forest, I saw, was a highly charged game of skill: if you played it wrong, you might be killed; but if you played it just right, you got to do it over again. No more than that. But when something like that gets into your blood, the rest of life comes to lack something you never knew it was supposed to have before.*"

It is this kind of imaginative writing that holds the reader on the edge of his seat.

Best Magazine Story
Co-Winner

He's a Yankee Doodle Dandy

BASEBALL

By *ROGER KAHN*

From Sport Magazine
Copyright © 1981, by Sport Magazine

He stepped from the 1981 Cadillac, immaculate in white and blended shades of blue, and the earth rose slightly to meet his feet. "It's him," people said in the sunlit afternoon. "It's George. It's him. Hiya, George."

As he strode toward the little minor league ballpark at Pompano Beach, a retinue materialized and grew. A crew from the television program *60 Minutes.* Yankee officials. Policemen. Ushers. But most of the swarming people were fans.

"Hey, George, would you sign this?" "Hey, George, how about an autograph?" "You really gonna fine Reggie?" "Hey, George, are the Yankees gonna win?"

He slowed his pace, the better to sign his name on scorecards and the backs of tickets, and uttered pleasantries to the idolaters. His path crossed that of a ballplayer, Bob Watson, the Yankee first baseman, who was headed toward the field. "Isn't anybody under 38 working today?" George asked. Watson, actually a lad of 35, trudged on, ignored by the fans and the television people.

"I'll sign," George said. "I'm glad to sign. Thank you for asking. Hello, son. How's the schoolwork going?"

About him people chattered and beamed, the way people beam in the presence of a superstar, a sun King. George Mitchell Steinbrenner III, principal owner of the New York Yankees, basked in his own glory, a happy, restless man.

He is fun and business, charm and fury, a remorseless tyrant in the boardroom and a particularly compassionate friend. "I work 12-hour days," he says, "and I never ask anybody I hire to work any harder than I do. But I guess I am a sonofabitch to work for. I don't know if I'd want to work for me."

His rages at poor performance have left at least one major league pitcher weeping in the clubhouse and have driven former business associates to move a thousand miles away. Talking about Steinbrenner's full, ranting wrath, Reggie Jackson cringes like a battered child. "When he really rips me and Gossage and Nettles." Jackson says, "you know how I feel? Screw it. I don't care if we win or lose. I just want to get away." But after Elston Howard, the first of the black Yankees, died last December, Steinbrenner quietly, indeed secretly, paid all the medical bills.

Like all men of powerful passions, Steinbrenner evokes powerful passions in return. When Al Rosen was president of the Yankees —a limited presidency under Steinbrenner's absolute monarchy—he was afraid that one of their baseball arguments would explode into a fistfight. Although he admired George, Rosen could not continue working for him.

Steinbrenner's anger can be severe and charged with personal expletives, and it knows no time clock. One former Yankee staff man, fired several times during Steinbrenner outbursts but always rehired within hours, eventually resigned. Steinbrenner later invited him to lunch and made him a generous offer to return.

"I just can't take those 3 a.m. calls from you anymore," he said.

Steinbrenner pointed to his own World Series ring. "That," he said, "is the price you pay for this."

The man did not return. The price, he thought, was too high.

"Look," Steinbrenner says, "I'm like a fan. I live with the Yankees and I die with the Yankees. I'm an involved owner and one way baseball bought itself trouble was with owners who were *not* involved." His talk is quick, sometimes gruff, always urgent. "I'm an involved owner and we've finished first four times and won the Series twice since I've been here. Our attendance has gone up for eight consecutive seasons. That's a record."

He is a master at milking the media, at keeping the Yankees in the news. It apparently took him weeks to decide to retire Manager Dick Howser last fall. Meanwhile, Yankee stories won space away from New York's dreary pro football teams, the Giants and the Jets. Last March, when Jackson reported to spring training two days late, Steinbrenner fined him $5,000. Stories about *that* won space away from the Rangers and the Knickerbockers. Of course, milking the media, like milking a cow, exposes a man to knifing hooves. The press file on Steinbrenner is a harvest of wormwood.

The case for Steinbrenner is nicely made by William Denis Fugazy, a New York entrepreneur best known for the huge limousine service that bears his name. "I call him the Commander," Fugazy says, "and sure he's a powerful guy with strong opinions. But he's a tremendous civic asset, even beyond bringing the Yankees back to life. He's always working for causes, good government, a dozen charities. The charitable work is private with no publicity. The Commander is one tremendous man."

Steinbrenner tries to be careful with the media. By decree his family—a wife and four children—is off limits to the press. He cooperated with Harry Reasoner on a segment for 60 Minutes, but a friend says George would not have agreed to appear had the interviewer been Mike Wallace. "George," the man comments, "doesn't need Mike the Knife." It is, however, a bit late for Steinbrenner to lower his strong-jawed profile. He has become a thundering presence, a water buffalo in Bowie Kuhn's patch of summer flowers.

"George Steinbrenner," Dave Winfield mused on a pleasant spring afternoon. "I read more than I know from experience, but I've picked up this. Some love him. Some hate him. Most fear him."

It is surprising to learn that the object of so much intense feeling was once an English major at Williams College, among the maples and white pine trees of western Massachusetts, and that he wrote his senior thesis on the heroines of Thomas Hardy's novels, whose lust always lay between the lines.

"We're going to be wired for 60 Minutes," Steinbrenner said in Florida. "They want to pick up a little of our banter. It'll be great exposure for you."

Not everything had been proceeding according to plan. I'd wanted to spend a few days with George, watching him at play and at work in three or four of his businesses. I'd have to settle for a few full hours, George had said cheerfully. He really couldn't conduct his business with readers listening in. Now some of the time we did have would be wired into the second most popular television program (after Dallas) on earth.

"We'll respect anything you want to keep for yourself or use for background," Harry Reasoner promised.

"We work with little wireless transmitters," one of the technicians said. "You'll forget you have them on. We've even used them with First Ladies, and four of them, four presidential wives, actually wore the transmitters into the bathroom. You ought to hear those tapes." (This was about the time some in the media were criticizing Steinbrenner's taste.)

George and I settled into a box. On the field the Yankees and the Texas Rangers went through final warm-ups.

"This seems to be the spring of moaning millionaires," I said. "Ruly Carpenter can't afford the Phillies. Is Ray Kroc going broke in San Diego?"

"The day Kroc goes broke, the country goes broke," Steinbrenner said. "And don't worry about the Yankees. We don't need a benefit luncheon."

"Some blame you for the high cost of free agents."

"I didn't start free agency, but as an involved owner I've had to figure out how to live with it. How do I know how much to offer a Jackson, a Winfield? There's some talk with my financial people, some talk with my baseball people and there's a little bit of intuition.

"Too many noninvolved owners treated baseball like a hobby. Now, understand Marvin Miller of the players association. When he was with the steel union he didn't get publicity because he was a second-row guy, a mastermind. But Miller is more than capable. He's brilliant. What happened when baseball bargained with him? They gave away the house. They locked the barn door after both the horse and wagon were gone. You can't leave the business of baseball to baseball people. What does a brilliant baseball man necessarily know about business, about who to hire to bargain with Miller?

"The owners, the businessmen, should have been more involved. I'm a damn-involved owner with 25 years' experience in labor negotiation. The current baseball situation, where certain clubs do have money problems—well there are ways in which free agency negotiations could be reopened, but you have to know what you're doing." He did not say it, but clearly George's choice as baseball's best renegotiator with Miller is George M. Steinbrenner III.

He glanced up. Doc Medich was starting for the Rangers. "What a fine young man," Steinbrenner said. "I was really pleased to have him on the Yankees." Oscar Gamble reached the young doctor for a soaring three-run homer to right. "Hey, Oscar," George bellowed in delight. "Attaway, Oscar."

A young Yankee righthander named Gene Nelson began blowing away the Rangers. George watched and signed more autographs and went from topic to topic with great agility. On shipbuilding: "How much is a pound of steel going to cost? If I make a mistake it can cost a million dollars."

Bowie Kuhn. "He's growing to become a good commissioner. Sometimes he acts pompous but he's a smart man, a good leader. There's been talk that some people want to replace him and that they expect me to help. Wrong, I am a supporter of the commissioner."

The Yankees. "I walk out of a hotel in New York and my energy gets going. It's a battler's city, battles all day long. My ego feeds on that competition. I love it. I want the team to be like the city. I didn't think they battled hard enough in the playoffs against Kansas City last year, and that's why I got worked up. After we lost the third game I called a staff meeting for 8:30 the next morning. Work! Battle!

"And owning the Yankees is just unique. I've had offers, big offers, to sell the team. No way. Owning the Yankees is like owning the Mona Lisa."

I was beginning to run short of breath. That happens, of course, when you talk long and hard and fast. With Steinbrenner, you run out of breath listening.

The roots of all this hammering intensity lie in a prosperous Cleveland suburb, Bay Village, where Steinbrenner was born into comfortable, sedate circumstances in 1930. The family business, Kinsman Marine Transit, a Great Lakes shipping company, dates from the 1840s. Fireworks, loud and flamboyant as a Yankee press conference, accompanied George's arrival. His birth date: July 4.

As a boy, George went without an allowance. His father, Henry, a graduate of MIT, was severe and disciplined. He bought his son a variety of chickens and ordered him to look after them. "You can make your spending money selling the eggs." The boy worked tirelessly and prospered. He called his egg business the George Company.

To this day Steinbrenner can and will describe the differences that distinguish a guinea hen from a Plymouth Rock and from a Buff Wine Dot. At 13, when he was shipped to Culver Military Academy in Indiana, Steinbrenner was ordered to sell the George Company to his two sisters. "I don't remember the price," he says, "but it must have been pretty good. My sisters still don't talk to me." Other sources report that it was $50 cash.

At Culver, George played end, ran hurdles and won an award for all-around excellence. He still expresses abiding respect for military men. "He's the only guy I know," says Bill Fugazy, "who walks around humming the theme from *Patton*."

At Williams, one of New England's prestigious Little Three colleges, George ran varsity hurdles and developed a fondness for Hardy, Shelley and Keats and a passion for Shakespeare. He became president of the glee club. He wrote a sports column for the Williams *Record*. "As a columnist I was not a knocker," he says.

He spent his service hitch in peacetime as a general's aide in Columbus. After that, had George stayed with family tradition, he would have gone into the shipping business and settled into a life of disciplined, affluent obscurity. But sport tugged at him as strongly as it tugged at Stan Musial or, for that matter, Reggie Jackson. It was something clean and exciting that attracted crowds. It was a way to break new ground, to establish, in the current phrase, an identity. For George, who actually favors blue, sport seems to be something like that beckoning green light Gatsby saw and sought on a dock he could not reach.

He briefly coached high school football and basketball in Columbus and in 1955 signed as an assistant to Lou Saban, then head football coach at Northwestern and now Rosen's successor as president of the Yankees. Steinbrenner moved on to Purdue as backfield coach, but life as a Big Ten assistant was limited, insecure and poorly paid. Besides, his family was calling him back to the Great Lakes.

As the giant steel companies acquired fleets of their own, Kinsman Transit ran into buffeting days. After three years "when my father and I really beat the bushes for business," Kinsman signed a contract with Jones & Laughlin guaranteeing a considerable annual tonnage.

George had helped rescue the family business; he was then 30.

Still, sport beckoned. Against family advice, Steinbrenner borrowed and scratched and organized a $125,000 partnership that bought an industrial basketball team, the Cleveland Pipers. But with pro basketball beginning to rise, the industrial league was doomed. The Pipers won two championships and went bankrupt, with George shouting and scrambling to cover the payroll.

He turned his energies back toward the waters and became part of a group that purchased the American Ship Building Company, a sprawling enterprise with shipyards in Tampa, Cleveland and a half dozen other cities. American Ship prospered, but it wasn't sport. "Actually, George was trying to buy the Cleveland Indians," recalls his longtime associate, Marsh Samuel, "but Vernon Stouffer, who owned the Indians, was taking his time deciding on selling. Patience has never been George's long suit. Then the Yankee thing came up."

On January 3, 1973, it was announced that a group headed by George M. Steinbrenner of Cleveland had purchased the Yankees from CBS for $10 million, or about $3 million less than CBS paid in 1964. No one has found a better bargain in sports. The Yankees, purchased for a reported $10 million in 1973, showed a net profit of about $7.5 million in 1980.

Why would CBS sell at a loss? The late 1960s had been an inglorious Yankee era. The team finished 10th in 1966, and on one September day that year the Yankees played the White Sox at the old Stadium before a crowd of 413 paid.

The finest achievement of Michael Burke, who ran the team for the CBS conglomerate, was convincing New York City politicians to rebuild Yankee Stadium. Cost overruns were enormous, but today we have the New York Yankees, not the New Jersey Meadowland Yankees.

"About a year before the sale," Burke says, "it became apparent that Willie Paley (the chairman of CBS) would want to sell the club. He asked if I'd be interested in putting together a syndicate, and I went about New York talking to people, including some financial exotics. The interest was zero. Absolute zip. But Gabe Paul learned what I was doing and put me in touch with George. We had lunch and we agreed to try to buy the team together. George spoke to certain people, Bunker Hunt, Lester Crown, and we came up with the $10 million."

Burke and Steinbrenner also agreed to run the club together. "But it was early apparent," Burke says, "that George and I could not be compatible, so we elected to part in adult fashion." Burke, who retains a nine-percent interest in the Yankees, announced his withdrawal from the day-to-day operations of the club with great style. He quoted lines from a William Butler Yeats poem called "An Irish Airman Foresees His Death."

In the plays of Shakespeare, Steinbrenner's favorite dramatist, triumph and tragedy work in magical alternation. So it is in Steinbrenner's life. Before he had time really to enjoy the ballclub he had won, the Mona Lisa he had found in the South Bronx, he was caught in a backwash of Watergate.

Steinbrenner is an independent Democrat. Among his good friends today are Ted Kennedy and Tip O'Neill. At Cleveland in 1969 and '70, Steinbrenner organized fund-raising dinners for Democratic Congressional candidates and, George being George, raised almost $2 million. Then as the 1972 presidential election approached, President Nixon's infamous men, angered by his fund-raising for Democrats, sprang at him from all sides. They threatened an antitrust investigation of American Ship Building. His steamers might lose vital port licenses. Steinbrenner, his companies and all those close to him would undergo Internal Revenue audits that would be "memorable."

Steinbrenner decided to buy his way out. He personally gave $75,000 to CREEP—the Committee to Re-elect the President—and gave "bonuses" of $25,000 each to eight American Ship executives. The bonuses, also, were donated to CREEP. That sort of forced contribution is illegal, although not unheard of in American executive suites, according to Steinbrenner associates.

The $275,000 was not enough. Nixon's people wanted whatever dirt Steinbrenner had discovered as a Democratic fund raiser. George kept silent. In April of 1973 he was indicted on 14 counts alleging conspiracies to violate the campaign-funding law. Still silent, he pleaded guilty to two of the charges a year later and paid a $15,000 fine. Kuhn suspended him for the season of 1975 but let him return to baseball in 1976. Coincidentally, that was the year in which the remodeled Yankee Stadium opened. Less coincidentally, that was the year in which the Yankees won the pennant for the first time since 1964.

Under the benign Florida sun, I said to Steinbrenner: "The conviction means that you can't run for president."

Steinbrenner's response was so quick that the same thought must have previously crossed his mind. "Unless," he said, grinning, "I get a pardon."

His performance as Commander of the Yankees has been innovative, tireless, impulsive, loud and most of all, effective. He was the first man to react to the possibilities, as opposed to the perils of free agency. He has expanded the Yankee scouting program and brought a measure of intelligence to the farm systems. By irrational tradition, minor league clubs have generally been supervised by one man, the manager, who pitches batting practice, teaches hitting, works with infielders and outfielders and in some instances drives the team bus. All Yankee farms now, from Triple-A Columbus to Paintsville, Ky., in a rookie league, employ at least two full-time coaches, in addition to a manager. Yankee minor leaguers, who are supposed to be learning the professional game, now have reasonable teaching staffs to help them. No fewer than six of the Yankees' seven farm teams won a pennant in 1980.

How do you get results like that? You learn the game. You hire the best people and you drive them as you drive yourself; drive, drive until your staff works harder than anyone else's staff.

Up close some consequences are unsettling. A Yankee secretary, asked recently what kind of sandwich she wanted at her desk for lunch, abruptly paled. "I can't eat," she said. "He's here. Mr. Steinbrenner is here."

A new backwash threatens Steinbrenner these days. Those who see baseball as an American art form profess to be offended by his fortissimo chatter. I believe that baseball is an art form and I believe that major league baseball is a business. Ten years ago the business was in trouble. So William Paley felt when he elected to sell the Yankees at a loss.

Now, among the moaning millionaires, franchises sell for ever-greater sums. The one executive who shows us all what you can do with a franchise is George Mitchell Steinbrenner of Bay Village, Ohio, Tampa, Fla., and the South Bronx.

At Pompano the Yankees defeated the Rangers 9-2. George signed a final autograph. Next day Reggie Jackson would ask what Steinbrenner had said. "He didn't knock you, Reggie," I said. He looked surprised—and disappointed.

"I have some ship business in Tampa tomorrow," Steinbrenner told me, "but I'll be back the next day and we can spend more time together. Don't be a stranger. Is your hotel room okay? I really like your books. Don't forget to bring your kids to the Stadium. They'll be my guests. It will be great spending more time together."

I am trying to give a sense of what one feels sitting beside him. Unfettered energy. A whirlwind. An earthforce, lightly filtered through a personality.

The winter had been bitter cold, and my new novel was proceeding at a slow, strangely exhausting tempo. Now the world excited me anew. If Steinbrenner survived bankruptcy in basketball and Nixon's troops and still found his Mona Lisa, is there any reason, any reason in the world, why the rest of us can't find our Mona Lisas, too?

Meeting tomorrow, 8:30 a.m.

Neckties. Jackets. Pressed Pants. (No jeans, please.)

Have your presentation cogent and complete.

Be prepared to work harder than you've ever worked before.

Work! Battle! Or be prepared to work for someone else.

Judge's Comments

There are reams of newsprint dealing with such colorful characters as Howard Cosell, Reggie Jackson, Casey Stengel, Sugar Ray Leonard, Bowie Kuhn, Pete Rose, Magic Johnson, etc. Their newspaper images range from clean-cut and sensible to just plain lousy. Nobody, however, evokes more love-hate reviews than Yankee Owner George Steinbrenner.

In this instance Roger Kahn, a free-lance writer of national renown, has worked with a wide frame for his easel in painting a vivid picture of the unpredictable Yankee boss. He pictures Steinbrenner as a complicated, multifaceted individual who will offend the public in one breath, perform charitable acts in another. He is well educated and bright. He is canny, abrasive, pugnacious and egotistic. Kahn's assessments often are regaling and imaginative. ". . . With Steinbrenner you run out of breath listening." Or "He has become a thundering presence, a water buffalo in Bowie Kuhn's path of summer flowers."

Provocative, expressive writing.

Best Feature Photo
Journey's End. The Trophy is Ours!

by Norman A. Sylvia, of the *Providence Journal-Bulletin* shows what a football season is all about. The hands straining to touch the cup, the ragtag arm coverings and the fingers wildly gesticulating the ubiquitous "We are No. 1" tell the whole story. Copyright © 1981, The Providence Journal Co.

Best Action Photo
Pas De Two

by Richard Darcey of the *Washington Post* shows University of Maryland's Albert King popcorning Virginia's Ralph Sampson en route to two points during Maryland's 85-62 victory in the ACC tournament semifinal. Besides winning the action prize in Best Sports Stories, it also garnered the blue ribbon in the 1981 White House News Photographers Association's annual contest. Copyright © 1981, The Washington Post.

The Rozelles: PR & Pizzazz at the Super Bowl

PRO FOOTBALL

By *TONY KORNHEISER*

From the Washington Post
Copyright © 1981, The Washington Post

He is in a deep-blue suit, and his skin tone, which has always been Pete Rozelle's finest feature, is copper. Against it, his teeth are pearls.

She is in a gold-sequined blouse above a long, black skirt, and on the replays from all the different angles, from the front, the back, the sides, Carrie Rozelle sparkles.

They don't just walk; they glide.

They don't just smile; they beam.

They don't just greet people; they embrace them.

It goes on for hours here in New Orleans at the National Football League party that provides 4,000 pounds of food for 3,000 invited guests at a cost said to be $400,000. "Super Bowl XVI ... And All That Jazz." Oysters, crab fingers, creole-stuffed peppers and strawberries served XV, count 'em, XV different ways, jazz bands, Dixieland bands, dancing waterfalls and two young, beautiful women swinging gently in perches made to look like musical notes, tossing miniature football helmets to the crowd.

His league. Her theme. Their night.

The people never stop coming at them and for each there is a special clasp, a personal question, a warmth in the Rozelle manner that suggests cashmere. It is one thing to know your role; it is quite another to be perfectly natural at it, to never be gratuitous, to be sincere. To believe in it.

It may well be that it is hollow at the core of Super Bowl Week, that when you get there, there is no there there. But first, last, and always Pete and Carrie Rozelle thank you for coming.

The Job This Week:

"The first thing Pete does when he gets to the Super Bowl city is he makes sure the league people have done what they've supposed to," says Jim Kensil, who was executive director of the NFL before becoming president of the New York Jets. "Then, he shakes hands with everybody who wants to shake his hand."

And then?

Kensil laughs.

"That's it."

Be visible. Be available. Be accessible.

Pass among the people. Thank them for coming.

From the Governor's Suite on the 27th floor of the New Orleans Hilton, there is a view of the Mississippi River that belongs on a travel brochure. This is where Pete and Carrie live this week, and Pete has just come from his annual Super Bowl tour-deforce press conference where once again ("that's XV in a row") he struck just the right tone and said just the right things to leave 1,300 accredited journalists marveling at his skill. Having taken off his tie and put on slippers, he is sitting with his feet up on an oak table, and in his left hand is his ever-present Carlton cigarette. As always, he seems perfectly calm. Nothing to hide. Nothing to get hung about. He wouldn't spill his drink in an earthquake.

"To a great extent I accept what Jim says as valid," he says. "It's probably the most superficial week of the year because of the ceremonial responsibilities."

Parties. All over, parties. Musts.

Three on Thursday, including a black-tie dinner given by Mayor Ernest "Dutch" Morial, two more on Friday including the big one; no less than six on Saturday including a reception hosted by the Rozelles' close friends, the Kemps, as in Joanne and Jack, the former quarterback turned All-Pro Republican in Congress; three more on Sunday. Public relations. Classic case.

They're tiring, but Pete and Carrie have made a separate peace with that; in fact, Carrie says, they rather like them now that they've learned how to do them well.

"Look," she says, "I like people. I love to talk to people. I'm lucky to have been that way all my life. Cocktail parties can be dreadful; I'd much prefer having dinner with six or eight people. But if I couldn't make small talk at these things, I'd be a total loss to Pete. I'd stand there looking like a jerk. I know I'm on stage this week, and I see myself as a hostess. For this week especially I'm the commissioner's wife and I want to look good. It's kind of frivolous, and at times, it's excessive, like the Mad Hatter's Ball. And it's a good time. It's like having a magic wand. I can help make a lot of people feel really good for a few days, and Pete, well, this week it's as if Pete were an orchestra leader."

Rozelle shrugs.

"Carrie's better at it than I am," he says.

The Swarm:

The game was sold out; the hotels were filled; the joint was jumping.

All week long the French Quarter swelled to become the French Half. In a city built on food and music, restaurants on Bourbon Street routinely told eager gourmets that the wait was no less than 90 minutes and jazz joints were so jammed that people had to do their toe tapping on the streets. Must-go bars like The Old Absinthe House were so crowded that reaching for your wallet was a delicate surgical procedure. If you drank enough—and a lot of people made that their mission—it could take all night to realize that the topless dancers with the large, bare breasts in the honky-tonk weren't women at all. Mondo Bizarro . . . And All That Jazz.

New Orleans officials estimated that The Swarm deposited $40 million on the city last week in anticipation and celebration of America's Game, and that doesn't count the profit made by ticket scalpers who got as much as $500 a pop for one of the 75,500 tickets clearly marked with a face value of $40.

After XV years surely mere "hype" can be discarded as an explanation for all this. The Super Bowl has gone far beyond the hype stage, far beyond the "ultimate game" stage. For most of the people who went riding on the city of New Orleans, the game was just the last event in a siege party. Last call, if you will. Super Bowl is now a holiday week, an American celebration. It moves of its own pace.

"I had no idea it would get like this," Rozelle says. "That it would become such a total package. People are coming for a full week and the game is played on only one day."

It may be that the "how" and the "why" are beyond us, that the snowball has become a glacier, frozen and fixed in the mid-winter conscious.

Still, you can try.

Why are we here?

"Hmmm, that's so strange," Carrie says. "I've never been asked that before . . . You don't think, in part, that it's a media event? . . . It's funny, but I hear so many people say the game is meaningless compared to the parties. I know a lot of people say the game is a letdown when it finally comes. People seem to talk about where they went and who they saw. You know, celebrities, athletes, movie stars. Isn't that very American, though?"

She pauses to consider all of it.

"Maybe it's no longer a sports event," the wife of the commissioner says. "Maybe it's part of the American scene."

The Hostages:

The NFL executives started talking about the hostages two weeks ago, when it appeared they might be released before the inauguration. Rozelle knew from last year that the hostages were particularly interested in the Super Bowl and he made available 100 copies of the Super Bowl program for Air Force One to carry to West

Germany, enclosing a personal note he'd written to all 52.

Had they been released earlier, the NFL might well have invited them to the game (NBC actually did), but coming when it did—just five days before the game—Rozelle chose not to push it.

"To me," he says, "it just didn't make sense for them. We'd never bring them here just as a showcase for the NFL—only if they wanted it."

Still, there was concern as to "how do we commemorate the release without being corny? How do we do it tastefully so it isn't viewed as taking advantage of the media and the hostages and deifying the Super Bowl? You try to strike a fine line in what's tasteful or appropriate as opposed to overkill."

The solution was to make a brief, commemorative announcement of the release before the singing of the national anthem. And to give each ticket holder a yellow bow as they entered the Superdome.

And to fasten a massive yellow bow—80 feet by 30 feet with 180-foot streamers—to the face of the Superdome.

So you could see it from Mars.

Pete and Carrie:

He is 54. She is 43. They have been married almost eight years, the second marriage for both. He had one child. She had four. She was married to Ralph Cooke, son of Jack Kent Cooke, the owner of the Washington Redskins. The commissioner of the NFL is hired by the owners.

"So Pete was an employee of my father-in-law, if you will," Carrie says. "The circle is very curious."

Carrie says she was in the process of divorcing when she and Pete, both avid tennis players, were paired as doubles partners after Super Bowl VII in Los Angeles.

"I thought Pete was terrific," Carrie says. "It was instant on my part. I ran right after him."

She was born in Canada to a banking family. (She is still a Canadian citizen, though she promised Jack Kemp that if Ronald Reagan became president she would file for American citizenship.) The family had money and her father opted for becoming a college professor and told Carrie—the oldest of his three daughters—that it was important she have a profession. She spent a year in medical school, but dropped out and became a nurse instead. "I was never going to hack it," she says. "It wasn't the time to pioneer." She modeled off and on —she has the classic up-turned nose and slight overbite that produces a clean, wholesome look in magazines like Seventeen—then married.

He was born in California to the working class. He went to high school with Duke Snider, and they became close friends. What he really wanted to be was a sportswriter. But when he was a student at junior college, he began hanging around the L.A. Rams' training camp as a gofer for the team's publicity man and discovered he was a natural at PR.

He did sports PR for the University of San Francisco while an undergraduate there, then PR for a brewery, then PR for the Rams and later became general manager of the Rams. In 1960, when he was just 33, the NFL, apparently in desperation on its 23rd ballot, named Rozelle as its commissioner. He was in the men's room washing his hands when Carroll Rosenbloom, who then owned the Baltimore Colts, came in to give him the news.

To say the league has prospered under his leadership is to say you can get wet under Niagara Falls. The league has grown from 12 to 28 teams, each of which makes $5.8 million a year from a television package worth $650 million over four years. In 1961, the Cleveland Browns were sold for $3.8 million. Today a franchise in the NFL— any franchise—is worth $35 million.

The league pays Rozelle $430,000 a year. There are some who say it's crumbs given his record.

They seem very much in love. They often hold hands when they walk, and one never leaves or enters their home in Harrison, N.Y., without a kiss from the other.

The day they married they vowed never to spend a night apart, and they never have. In fact, it is written into Pete's contract that Carrie goes wherever he goes. She drives him whenever he needs a car, and she does all his secretarial work on the road.

"My payoff," she says, "is that I'm married to him."

The Food Tasting:

Because she knows that people are looking at her and because she wants to look "as feminine and as stylish" as she can, Carrie Rozelle has brought different outfits for each of her public appearances. Today, for the ceremonial food-tasting of what will be served at the big NFL party, she is in a deep purple dress with thin gold earrings, a gold necklace, and gold bracelet. Gold becomes her, she wears it well. Some women don't. Some women wear so much of it they look like a branch office of an import-export firm.

"Carrie has great style, grace and personality," says Don Hewitt, producer of "60 Minutes." "If you went to central casting for a commissioner's wife you'd come up with Carrie."

Accompanying her to the food-tasting—thinking all the while it would be an informal lunch—are some of her best friends: Joanne Kemp, Edie Wasserman and her husband, Lew, head of Universal and MCA, and Joan Tisch and her husband, Bob, head of the Loews Corporation. Notables.

As it turns out, more than 30 people including camera crews and reporters are waiting for them. Now *this* qualifies as hype, especially when the NFL man takes five full minutes to introduce the chef and all but invokes the memories of Washington and Lincoln in singing the praises of American cuisine.

Through it all, Carrie is cool.

She doesn't miss a name.

"Total recall," Joan Tisch says. "She's good at it, and she likes it."

As the chef leads her from course to course to course to course, explaining each one, she asks questions.

"How many avocados will you use?

"Is this a traditional New Orleans dish?

"Are the recipes available?

"What happens to the leftovers?"

It is a small touch, but a nice touch. Rather than make the chef act like a trained seal, she has involved him in conversation and eliminated whatever tension he might have felt. It does not go unnoticed by Joanne Kemp, a politician's wife.

"She's a pro," Joanne Kemp says.

When it is all over, Carrie has taken just one bite of a main dish and one spoonful of a strawberry and whipped cream dessert, yet she has paid such attention to the contents in each of the 11 chafing dishes that it seems she surely tasted enough food to feed Bulgaria.

"I've known her for almost eight years now," says a friend of Rozelle, "and I've never seen her make a wrong move."

On her way out, Carrie Rozelle thanks everyone for coming.

The Reputation:

"He has no conscience, no point of view, no philosophy," says Ed Garvey, head of the NFL Players' Association. "His whole effort is public relations. If you ask about contractual negotiations with the players, he tells you to take it up with the management council, a body he created so he could stay above the real issues. If you ask him why there aren't more blacks in coaching or management, he says, 'Well, gee, golly, gosh, it's not because of anything I've done.' He's a disaster on the social issues, but when it comes to asking the press, 'How's the lobster Newburg?,' he's terrific."

"He's a great salesman," says a writer and social friend of Rozelle. "You can't lay a glove on him. Each time you think you've got him, he comes up with another film, another angle you haven't seen."

"The world's greatest PR man," Al Davis has called him. Al Davis owns the Oakland Raiders and is, by the way, suing the NFL and Rozelle to move his team to Los Angeles.

P.R.

They're even his initials, thanks to an uncle who called him Pete rather than his given name, Alvin.

Good old Pete, slicker than Teflon.

"He's slick," Carrie says. "Of course, he's slick. He does his homework. He knows what he's talking about. That's slick. He is a PR man. That's how he started. And he's very good at it. And that's why, in part, the league has been so successful."

And courting the press? Providing millions of releases, mountains of worthless information, arranging tennis and golf tournaments, a 24-hour free bar, enough free food to fill the Taj Majal during Super Bowl week?

"He doesn't try to buy the press," Carrie says. "He respects the press. He likes the press. Remember, he wanted to be a sportswriter."

P.R.

"I imagine it's my long suit," Rozelle says. Nothing to hide, nothing to get hung about. "Life, to a great extent, is public relations . . . my reaction to being classified as a PR man depends on how it's written. In defense of the inference, in 21 years on the job I've learned more than just public relations . . . I come to the floor on controversial issues, and I'm constantly in the role of authority. The general public could have no awareness that I'm really a sensitive person."

What it comes down to is the tone.

Do we mean "slick" as in "calculating and conniving?" Or "slick" as in "smooth, confident and without deceit?"

Given the choice, Rozelle chooses "smooth."

After you shake his hand, you don't have to count your fingers.

The Press Conference.

The Rozelles normally find Super Bowl Week tiring, but exhilarating and satisfying; this year Carrie was apprehensive.

The Davis Business.

Al Davis had not only become partner to a lawsuit threatening the NFL constitution and socialistic revenue-sharing that is the legacy of the Rozelle Era, but Davis has gone so far as to accuse Rozelle of personally scalping tickets, a low, common crime.

"It's been a long, tough year," Carrie was saying. "The business with Pete and the Raiders has been hanging over our heads and making us uncomfortable. Neither one of us has been sleeping well; Pete's getting up in the middle of the night, chain-smoking, pacing. I worry about his health. He's tired. You can see it in his face. He has deep circles under his eyes."

People who hadn't seen him in a year were saying the boyish commissioner was finally looking his age. The press conference, they said, would be a real test. Surely Rozelle would look out at so many Indians that if he wasn't 100 percent he might pull a Custer. The press conference is legendary among those who cover Super Bowls. It is conceded to be Rozelle's finest hour. "He's absolutely in command," said a writer who'd seen VIII of them. "He manages to be witty, charming and substantive. Watch him with the cigarettes, watch how he'll light one whenever he wants to buy time."

For almost two hours before, Rozelle huddles with his aides and attorneys, preparing for what will surely come. They fire questions, suggest responses.

When he takes the podium, he has his game face on.

He is in a light blue suit, and his eyes are crystal.

"Visine," Carrie says.

He lights a cigarette, puts it in an ashtray and looks out at more than 1,500 people.

O.K., shoot, he says.

As reporters raise their hands with questions, Rozelle often calls on them by name, as in, "Okay, Brent?" For years it has been part of his game plan to cultivate familiarity, and the first-name identification is a metaphoric arm around the shoulder of an old friend. It always scores points.

The first eight questions and 16 of the first 20 questions are about Davis, and Rozelle's answers are in effect a public deposition. His voice is strong, his manner authoritative, but his tone is nonthreatening. He never wavers, never ducks. He looks each questioner in the eye for the whole of the answer.

Somehow he manages to call the proposed move of the Raiders from Oakland "unconscionable" and Davis "an outlaw" without making a personal attack. And Rozelle's famed wit shows through when he is asked, "Where will Oakland be in eight months?," and he answers, "Across the bay from San Francisco unless the San Andreas fault interferes."

It goes on for 80 minutes.

He's breezing. Never lights a cigarette.

Then, probably from habit, he lights one before taking a question, and that question—not about Davis—is the last one.

"Anybody else?" Rozelle says.

No one.

"Thanks very much. I hope you had a good time."

Carrie has watched and listened attentively to all of it, and now she is smiling as her friends come up with their reviews.

"Marvelous," Lew Wasserman says.

"Super job," Joanne Kemp says.

"Politicians should be so candid," Jack Kemp says.

Then, noticing a reporter scribbling, Kemp adds, "Well, some of us are."

Later, Rozelle will review his performance with the attorneys, but for now, he is pleased. "I think I hit the tone I wanted to project," he says, "one of candor and honesty. It's not just a slick hype. I knew I'd have to spend most of the time on the Raiders' situation, but I didn't want to take on Al. It's not between Al and me; it's between 27 owners and one owner."

It is pointed out that he lit only two cigarettes, took a total of three puffs.

"Don't tell Carrie," he says. "My God, she'll be all over me, insisting I can quit."

Laughing, he lights another.

The Game:

The commissioner's box is stocked with food and drink and good friends—the Kemps, the Tischs, the Wassermans, among others. There is a TV set inside and another outside, so you can see replays while facing the field. There are headsets with TV or radio feeds, and two telephones, one for the commissioner to call NFL control, the other for him to call NBC control. As command posts go, it is a little bit of Park Avenue.

Pete and Carrie arrive early, some two hours before game time; they take seats in the second row, immediately behind Jack and Joanne Kemp. It may be impossible for Pete Rozelle to root, but he can still talk football and who better to talk it with than Kemp?

Fifteen minutes to kickoff and Rozelle is on the phone. It's Don Weiss, the NFL executive director, calling.

Rozelle is beaming.

"The hostages are watching," he says. "We just got word."

He looks up at the monitor.

The face he sees in his own.

He had taped an interview with NBC two days before, and he listens to the audio feed through the headset. "I'm mainly interested in how it appears I'm answering," he says. "I want to come across as candid and honest."

What surprises him is that his appearance is not followed by Davis. Instead, there is only a commentary piece on Davis by NBC's Pete Axthelm.

Though he shows no emotion while listening to the commentary —not even when it is reported that Davis had called him "corrupt"— he places a call to Weiss as soon as the segment ends.

"The only reason I agreed to the interview is because they said Davis was going on, too," Rozelle says. "I'd have preferred not to go on, but I'd have looked bad if I didn't."

Rozelle feels used.

"That burns me," he says.

As the game goes on, Rozelle continues to watch the field and listen to the feed. Carrie just watches. "I prefer the visuals," she says. It is especially hard on her not being able to root. "Awful, just awful," she says, "I like to yell and scream." She opens her hands to reveal two gold ear rings. "I sit there holding these like Captain Queeg," she says. "Sometimes I actually even sit on my hands."

By the middle of the third quarter it becomes obvious that Oakland is by far the superior team today and that Rozelle will have to present the Super Bowl trophy personally to Davis. The friends in the box—and they are good friends—say nothing about it, but it is clear they feel for him.

"He's prepared for it," Bob Tisch says. "He's set for it. I'm sure he'll handle it well."

Pete and Carrie watch the game quietly.

Often they look at each other and smile. If they share a joke, it is a private one.

With 5:30 left in Super Bowl XV Rozelle leaves his seat to confront the inevitable. "I'll point out that it's a tremendous organization," he says. "They did it the hard way," coming in as a wild-card team and having to win four games. "I'll credit Al for putting it together and Tom Flores for a great coaching job."

Nothing to get hung about.

"There might be some reaction from the players," Rozelle says. "But not from Al." On his way out the door he says, "The one thing I'm sure he won't say is that he's happy to win this one for the fans."

Then, cigarette in hand, he is gone.

Carrie watches it on TV. While the others crowd around the set inside the box, she sits facing the field, watching the monitor, listening through the headset.

She sees Pete graciously give the trophy.

She sees Davis graciously accept it.

And now, her Super Bowl Week done, Carrie Rozelle is alone with her thoughts and smiling.

Not Every Day a Kid Loses All

BASEBALL

By *JERRY GREEN*

From the Detroit News
Copyright © 1981, The Detroit News

REQUIEM FOR A BIRD...

"Got a dime?"

The clubhouse guy handed him a dime and Mark Fidrych dialed the phone number in Massachusetts.

Collect.

"Mom, Dad, I made it."

It was April 6, 1976. Ralph Houk, the manager of the Tigers, had just told him he was going north to pitch in the major leagues.

"It's not every day a kid makes it," said Fidrych. "I'm one in a million. I'll tell you man, it's the rush of my life. I'll never have another high like it. I went to stand up and my legs shook so much I couldn't stand.

"You married? Like when you got married. That's a rush."

The game was on national TV and Mark Fidrych beat the Yankees. "We want the Bird, we want the Bird." In the grandstands 48,000 screamed their lungs out. Fidrych returned to the dugout and waved his baseball cap. They cheered and cheered and cheered.

"Wow, it was like Tom Jones or something," said Fidrych.

It was June 28, 1976, a Monday night. Around the country magazine writers booked plane reservations to Detroit. Fidrych was 8-1 and talking to the baseball.

"You got a lot of things going for you now, don't you Mark?" somebody said.

"Well, my car is still going good," said Fidrych.

In Detroit, you could buy Mark Fidrych T-shirts, Mark Fidrych bumper stickers. You could watch Mark Fidrych TV specials. A dozen magazines reported on Mark Fidrych's antics. The ball park was filled to near capacity three times a week.

"I want to be the same Mark Fidrych who came to this game,"

Mark Fidrych said about keeping his curly head on straight.

It was July 4, 1976—and he was 9-1. Somebody asked him if he'd ever had a high to compare with the hysterics at the ball park.

"Yeh," he said, "when I first got my mini-bike. I paid for it myself from caddying."

"The Bird," said the tall man from over Mark Fidrych's shoulder.

"I thought we had a game to play," responded Fidrych.

This was Philadelphia, it was July 13, 1976, and Fidrych was going to be a starting pitcher in the All-Star Game.

He turned around and glanced at the man he had brushed off.

"Did you send me a thing in Texas?" Fidrych asked the man.

"I tried to call you," the man said.

"Yeh, yeh," said Fidrych. "Where's your son? I'd like to talk to him."

"He's around," the man said. "Now don't talk to those young fellows. Talk to the old man."

"Okay," said Fidrych. "I was just wondering how he was doing with those dates."

"You come to Washington, he'll fix you up," said the man.

"I may do that," said Fidrych, standing to shake hands with Gerald Ford, president of the United States.

This was going to be a wingding. It was December 7, 1976. Baseball was blending with the movie biz in Hollywood. Frank Sinatra, Cary Grant, Don Rickles—with baseball's best, including the rookie of the year.

That morning Mark Fidrych had gone jogging along the L.A. freeways and returned to the hotel to shower. With blond curls dripping wet, clad in blue jeans and a T-shirt, he went down to check the ballroom.

"What am I supposed to do at the banquet?" Fidrych asked a baseball muckamuck working on the seating arrangements.

"Who wants you?" said the muckamuck, a man in a baggy suit. "You got nothing to do with baseball."

"I'm Mark Fidrych," Fidrych said, turning to walk away.

"Oh, oh," said the muckamuck. "Come to the dinner. You'll be on the dais."

"What's a dais?" asked Mark Fidrych.

The whole group entered the disco in Northboro, Mass. The music blared and all of them dropped onto their backs and wiggled across the dance floor in time to the music.

"It's a dance we invented," said Mark Fidrych. "It's called the Fried Egg."

He tried to vault a fence at spring training to take a shortcut into the clubhouse. He came down funny. Next day he leaped for a fly ball in the outfield and came down funny again.

His knee ached like the devil.

"I was scared," said Mark Fidrych. "I was so scared I didn't even tell my father on the phone. Can you believe that?

"I had eveything and now I might have lost it. I thought my arm would go before my legs. It's better to go out and lose every game than lose it this way."

It was dark in Zimmerman's Bar in Lakeland, but you could tell Mark Fidrych was holding back tears. The date was March 22, 1977.

The telephone rang in the house in Northboro, Mass.

"Mark," said the voice of Jim Campbell, "I'm sorry. We've put you on waivers. If nobody claims you, we're going to have to give you your unconditional release."

Mark Fidrych put the phone down and went out of the house.

Campbell did not have to borrow a dime. He did not call collect. The date was Oct. 5, 1981.

Judge's Comments

Jerry Green tells the heartbreaking story of a young pitcher, Mark Fidrych, who took a city and the entire baseball world by storm in 1976.

For one entire baseball season, Fidrych had the city of Detroit at his command. Strangers invited the young celebrity over to their homes. Young people in crowded night spots rolled around on their backs on the floor. The dance was called the "Fried Egg," a tribute to "The Bird," as the young phenom was affectionately called by Tiger fans. He was even visited by the President of the United States, Gerald Ford, in the locker room prior to the 1976 All-Star Game. Fidrych was the American League's starting pitcher.

But fame, as Green painfully points out, is fleeting. Fidrych hurt his knee the following spring as he attempted to vault a fence when he took a shortcut to the clubhouse. The next day, he leaped to field a ball in the outfield. Again, his knee began to hurt. Fidrych feared the worst when it happened, but it turned out even worse than that.

Mark Fidrych worked his whole life to prove he could pitch in the major leagues. And for one season, he pitched with the best of them.

Green quotes Fidrych as saying he was "one in a million" when the Detroit manager, Ralph Houk, told him that he made the big-league roster in the spring of 1976. After his misfortunes on two consecutive days only one year later, Fidrych's chance to return to the majors some day was at least that unlikely.

One Year Since the 'Miracle'

OLYMPIC HOCKEY

By *DAVE DORR*

From the St. Louis Post-Dispatch
Copyright © 1981, St. Louis Post-Dispatch

I suppose I shall never completely forget it. To have been a part of that sweet, sweet moment; to have been there in a tiny Adirondack village with kings and queens and the rest of the world breathlessly looking in; to watch an entire country—my country—weep with joy and be proud once again, that was it.

To see it, feel it, taste it. How many times in one's life does that chance come along?

One year ago, it happened. At 5 p.m. Friday, February 22, the U.S. Olympic hockey team skated onto the ice for a game with a Soviet Union team considered so superior that kings and queens and all of the National Hockey League could do no more than bounce off its armor. They were 20 Merited Masters of Sport from Kremlinland who had won the world's championship 17 times in 19 years.

The day before the game, I had spotted U.S. goalie Jim Craig standing outside the security entrance to the Olympic Village, waiting for a ride into Lake Placid. We talked.

"Maybe it's history in the making," he said, kicking at the snow. "We might all be making history. You never know. When I was watching them play Canada (on Wednesday) I found myself rooting for the Russians. If anyone is going to beat them, I want it to be us."

This was not just an Olympic hockey game. Given the tenuous world political climate—the U.S. hostages in Iran, Afghanistan, the pending boycott of the Summer Games in Moscow—it was us against them. The daily reports from Iran were disheartening. All of America needed a lift.

The U.S. hockey team was what most Americans perceived themselves to be; part of the American ethic that says honest effort is rewarded. They were 20 college players and unknown minor leaguers who made themselves into a team. They were not afraid to work and not afraid to succeed. They were having fun.

For 61 exhibition games over a period of six months, they had been welded into a unit by a scowling coach, Herb Brooks, who was on their case constantly and praised them so little there were times they hated him. But he had their attention. From the beginning he prepared the team to win the Olympic gold medal with Soviet tactics —superior physical conditioning and a system of criss-crossing patterns, speed and puck control.

He gave the players psychological tests and he intimidated them, but they knew he could coach. They nicknamed his merciless wind sprints, red line to red line and back again, "Herbies." Ah, but look here. In the seven Olympic games they played they outscored their opponents in the third period by 16-3.

They were barraged by his aphorisms. When he would recite them the players would look at each other and roll their eyes.

—"Passes come from the heart and not the stick."

—"Gentlemen, you don't have enough talent to win on talent alone."

—"You've got a nickel brain and a million-dollar pair of legs."

Thirteen days before the teams met at Lake Placid, the Russians ripped the U.S. squad, 10-3, at Madison Square Garden in New York. Later, it was learned the game had been arranged by the U.S. Olympic Committee to help the U.S. team pay its bills. Brooks was not at all displeased with the outcome. The man had something up his sleeve. On to Lake Placid.

At 4:15 p.m. Friday, February 22, I walked across the street from Lake Placid High School, the press center, to the Olympic Fieldhouse, a spider-legged arena that appeared as if it would leap into the air at any moment. I showed my ticket (a $67.20 seat if I had paid for it) to an usher at the door and walked up the stairs.

For those accustomed to the tundra climate of upstate New York, walking could be a complicated chore. That was because you were dressed in several layers of clothing and huge boots that we called "moon shoes." You did not walk, you waddled. I had further compounded my problems by misplacing my mittens on the second day of the Games.

Inside the arena, the Russian press corps and gold medalist pairs skaters, Irina Rodnina and Alexandr Zaitsev, arrived wearing long Siberian fur coats and fur hats. The outfits looked like uniforms of the state. A few of the American spectators were belligerent, taunting the Russians by shouting, "Get out of Kabul!" The Russians ignored the cries.

In the U.S. locker room, Brooks was reading from a crumpled piece of yellow paper: "You were meant for this moment. You were meant to be here. So let's have poise and possession of ourselves at this time."

Buzzy Schneider gave the United States a 1-1 tie in the first period on a 50-foot shot past Vladislav Tretiak, the Soviet goalie. With one second left in the period, Mark Johnson tied it again at 2-2, on a rebound of Dave Christian's 100-foot slap shot that bounced off Tretiak's shinpad.

When the Russians came out for the second period, Tretiak had been yanked and Vladimir Myshkin was in the nets. Going into the third period the Soviets led, 3-2. Johnson tied it at 3-3 on a power play. With 10 minutes left in the game, Mike Eruzione, shooting off the wrong foot, got the go-ahead goal. United States 4, Russia 3.

In the stands, Eugene Eruzione, Mike's father, celebrated so boisterously with friends his glasses were knocked off.

Go, clock.

Craig was making one amazing stop after another. My God, can he hang in there?

Hurrrrrrrrrry up, clock.

The Russians began changing lines every 45 seconds in an attempt to wear down the U.S. players. No way. Herbies, remember?

I didn't dare breathe. Was it really going to happen? I recall hearing the final 20 seconds being counted off by the crowd and then pandemonium. The U.S. players mobbed Craig. Sticks and gloves were everywhere. U.S. players were diving on each other on the ice in jubilation.

I couldn't believe what I was seeing. My mind was spinning. Eight years earlier, at Munich, I had watched an identical scene when the Soviets defeated the United States in that controversial Olympic basketball game. The Soviet players hugged and rolled on the floor. One of their coaches poured a bottle of mineral water on them.

The fieldhouse was shaking to the screams of "YEW-ESS-AYY!" Hundreds of flags were being waved. In the U.S. locker room, the players sang "God Bless America." In the hallway, New York State troopers were standing crying.

On Lake Placid's Main Street, people were bunched in front of the stores that had televisions. They were squeezing and shoving, anything to see. They were on tip-toes on boxes and sitting on each other's shoulders. They counted down the final seconds, shouting, and then people were streaming out of the bars and restaurants, all running for the fieldhouse.

When I finally worked my way outside, the scene was crazy. Thousands of people were singing, dancing, crying. They were climbing on cars and buses and yelling, "YEW-ESS-AYY!" The flags. Everywhere, the flags. From Mirror Lake, where medal ceremonies were being held for the skiers, fireworks illuminated the sky. My God, I thought, was all this preordained?

It was late when I sat down to write. I finished at 5 a.m., transmitted two stories to the Post-Dispatch and walked out into the morning. The celebration on Main Street was diminishing, but only slightly. There was enough beer sold that night to drown Syracuse.

I was in luck. I found a bus with a driver who spoke English and got a ride to my motel in Saranac Lake, 12 miles away. While at the Winter Olympics, I developed a distaste for buses. That can happen when you wait for hours in freezing weather, toes numbing, for the sight of one bus. It arrives, finally, and you climb aboard with a question. The driver, imported from Canada, shrugs and says, "Je suis francais."

My motel, Keough's, was a conglomerate of old summer cottages by Lake Flower and never before had been used in wintertime. I had one lightbulb, but lots of blankets. I knew a writer from Colorado Springs, Colo., staying at Wilmington, another small village near Lake Placid, who slept the entire Olympics in his longjohns, his tube of toothpaste in the crook of a knee to keep it from freezing.

By Sunday morning, word had filtered back to Lake Placid that the country was in love with its hockey team. We heard stories of how drivers, yelling, had pulled to the side of the road and honked their horns when the score of the victory over the Russians was announced. An American ship, a sentry vessel in the Atlantic, had flashed the score to a Soviet sub. Strangers danced with each other. A basketball game in Kansas City was interrupted and spectators sang "The Star-Spangled Banner." Unbelievable.

A telegram to the U.S. team said: "Congratulations for kicking the Soviet butts. What's your secret? The Afghan Rebels."

The United States met Finland for the gold medal at 11 a.m. Sunday. The day promised magic. The scene was exhilarating. Three goals in the final period (Herbies, remember?) gave the Americans a 4-2 victory.

In the final five seconds I remember seeing Schneider fling his stick—it left his hand spinning like a helicopter blade—and with open arms collided with Craig. They embraced. The flags. Craig, wrapped in an American flag, his eyes searching. You could read his lips. "Where's my father?" Then Eruzione, the gold medal being placed around his neck, and the other players rushing to stand there with him.

On January 26, as I watched the buses with the freed hostages, engulfed in a canyon of yellow ribbons, flags, bells and sirens, that same feeling returned.

The Lake Placid Olympic Organizing Committee is $22 million in debt and bankrupt. I don't want to hear it. I only want to stand and hear what I heard that Friday night, the happy shouts that drifted across the lake and up into the mountains.

"YEW-ESS-AYY!"

Believe in miracles?

The Human Side of a Soviet Goalie

HOCKEY

By *PAT CALABRIA*

From Newsday
Copyright © 1981, Newsday, Inc.

The straight, grim row of Soviet players filed silently toward the ice until Vladislav Tretiak recognized the face ahead of him. He dropped his skates to the pavement with a clatter and smiled. He saw Bobby Clarke.

"Interpreter," Tretiak pleaded.

An official of the Soviet delegation quickly was summoned, and Clarke and Tretiak exchanged short sentences and warm embraces in a corner of the empty rink. The words came haltingly for both players. No one was needed to interpret their smiles. "Any Flyers on the team?" Tretiak asked.

"Ken Linseman," Clarke said.

"Oh," Tretiak said. "Small guy." He held his right palm at his knee.

Clarke laughed, then asked about Valery Kharlamov, the great Soviet left wing who was killed with his wife last month in an automobile accident. Suddenly, Tretiak's smile disappeared.

"He left two young children," Tretiak said. "It's sad. He was my friend, and I miss him very much."

Tretiak quickly changed the subject. "You are not in the tournament?" he asked.

"No," Clarke said. "Canada didn't want me." Together, they shrugged.

For a precious 15 minutes yesterday, Clarke and Tretiak traded stories and firm handshakes. On the eve of the game between the Soviets and Team USA in the Canada Cup tournament, they renewed a friendship that has endured for nine years under circumstances that often do not allow for even a passing remark.

The Soviets are instructed to keep to themselves, unlike the Canadians and Americans. Clarke had to travel 20 minutes outside the city for a reunion he knew would be brief, if permitted at all.

"It's just 10 or 15 minutes every time we see each other," Clarke said. "But it's worth it."

When the Soviet team's bus driver impatiently gunned the motor, Tretiak slowly moved to catch up. He hugged Clarke again, then turned when he reached the door and waved. Clarke never looked so gentle or vulnerable.

Later, Tretiak said: "I know a lot of players in Canada— (Larry) Robinson, (Guy) Lafleur, Bobby Hull. With Bobby Clarke, it is something special."

Tretiak, perhaps the world's best goaltender, and Clarke, who has frustrated goaltenders for so long, met in the 1972 Canada Cup. During the next tournament, four years later, Tretiak was on a shopping trip in Philadelphia when he asked a Flyers official to drive him past Clarke's sprawling home in Cherry Hill, N.J., the one with the swimming pool constructed in the P shape of the club logo.

Clarke and Tretiak once had lunch for more than an hour, with an interpreter alongside. "We talked about family, sports, almost anything," Clarke said. "We didn't talk politics."

Tretiak is one of the few Soviet players who has earned—and uses—his privilege of rank, freely expressing himself, while solemn teammates and coaches hurry by.

He has been the Soviets' premier goalie since he was 17. He led the Red Army team to title after title, and now, at 29, he has been called upon to help re-establish the Soviets in world hockey after their loss to the United States in the 1980 Olympics. The upset still is a source of irritation for Soviet officials.

"Why bring up Lake Placid?" said Boris Mayorov, the deputy head of the Soviet delegation. "It happened almost two years ago. This is a new tournament. I don't want to talk about it."

Then he said: "No more interview."

Tretiak grinned at the mention of Lake Placid, although he was blamed for the Soviets' loss. He allowed Mark Johnson's sloppy goal at 19:59 of the first period, and the Soviet team left the ice tied, 2-2, with one second left.

When the Soviets were waved back onto the ice by the officials to complete the period, Tretiak no longer was in goal. The United States went on to win, 4-3, and Tretiak's place on the team seemed uncertain. Yet, the Soviets have failed to develop a suitable replacement, and Tretiak is said to have returned to top form.

"We want revenge," he said. "I played one period. If I played two (more) periods, we would not have lost."

A poor performance in this tournament could speed Tretiak's retirement to a coaching position with the Red Army team. The job will have its advantages. At least, Tretiak can be with his wife and two children in Moscow. He now sees his daughter, 4, and his son, 8, only between tournaments.

"Whenever I am away, I want to be home," he said. "But you

have to do what you have to do."

"He told me he has the same problems I do," Clarke said. "His wife never sees him; she gets mad, she wants him to quit and stay home."

It is hard for Tretiak to stay home. The Soviet team has been preparing for the tournament since June. Tretiak says as he has grown older the work has become more tiring. His face still is fresh and smooth, and his brown hair is combed short and neatly behind his ears, but his waist is rounder than Clarke remembered it.

"It is hard, all the travel and the work," Tretiak said. "But that is the life of a sportsman." He said to ask Clarke—he would understand. Of course, Clarke did.

"He seems like an awfully nice guy," Clarke said. "I wish I really could get to know him."

So Long, Swede Risberg

BASEBALL

By *NELSON ALGREN*

From Chicago Magazine
Copyright © 1981, Robert M. Joffe, estate executor of Nelson Algren

"Who is he, anyhow, an actor?"
"No."
"A dentist?"
". . . No, he's a gambler." Gatsby hesitated, then added coolly:
"He's the man who fixed the World's Series back in 1919."
"Fixed the World's Series?" I repeated.
*The idea staggered me. I remembered, of course, that the World's
Series had been fixed in 1919, but if I had thought of it at all I would
have thought of it as a thing that merely happened, the end of some
inevitable chain. It never occurred to me that one man could start to
play with the faith of fifty million people—with the single-minded-
ness of a burglar blowing a safe.*
"How did he happen to do that?" I asked after a minute.
"He just saw the opportunity."
"Why isn't he in jail?"
"They can't get him, old sport. He's a smart man."

—F. Scott Fitzgerald

Major leaguers were our gods. We weren't worshipful. We knew
they were merely men like our brothers and fathers. Yet with a difference. When a father or a brother died, he left no record of himself
for remembrance. But a major leaguer, even though up for only a
season and most of that spent on the bench, left a batting, fielding, or
pitching record for All-American time. Major leaguers possessed im-
mortality.

Every neighborhood has its golden boy. Ours was a scrawny,
pug-nosed, freckle-faced 13-year-old, Jake "Lefty" Somerhaus, who
was already pitching to 18-year-old semipros and whipping them.
He possessed a deadly eye on a basketball court, was a dazzling
open-field runner, and, the first time he picked up a cue, played rotation like a pro. None of his four older brothers had ever excelled in
anything. Jake had it all.

In a neighborhood of tough kids. Jake wasn't tough. He didn't have to be. Whatever sport he turned to he knew, beforehand, that he would be better at it than anybody. Even in pitching baseball cards he was better than anybody.

The cards were 10-for-a-penny colored strips of major leaguers. Every kid on our street carried a pack of them, waxed and bound with a rubber band. Baseball cards were our currency. The wax was to stiffen them for gambling.

We'd play five, 10, or 15 up, but would pitch only one card. Each player would finger-snap it off the top of his pack, at a line three sidewalk squares away. The kid whose card drew closest to the line then took cards from the others and tossed them over his head. Those that came down face up were his. Second closest followed.

Jake's, as often as not, slid right *onto* the line. Mine usually came in third or fourth. The last kid was lucky if he got a single card back from his investment.

Every kid had to pick a favorite player. I couldn't pick Lefty Williams because I threw righthanded. Moreover, he already belonged to Jake. I couldn't have Shoeless Joe Jackson or Happy Felsch or Ray Schalk or Urban Faber or Buck Weaver or Eddie Collins or Nemo Leibold or Dick Kerr either. It looked like I might have to settle for McMullin, a utility infielder. Then the kid who owned Swede Risberg moved off the block and Risberg became mine. My name immediately became Swede and remained so for many years.

Risberg played shortstop deeper than any other player of his day. He was tall, rangy and lantern-jawed. James T. Farrell remembers him as "snaring a grounder deep over second base and getting the ball to first base like a bullet."

He would have looked dazzling anywhere, except playing beside Eddie Collins, because Risberg possessed prescience. He'd begin moving to his left with the pitch, knock down a drive through the middle and cut the runner down with that iron-handed peg. But everything Risberg did, Collins did with more flash. When Risberg singled, Collins doubled. When Risberg doubled, Collins doubled and stole third.

Himself a grammar-school dropout and strictly a boy for the girls and the booze, it hurt to be perpetually outplayed by a college graduate who didn't drink, smoke or chew. What hurt even more was getting less than $3,000 for the same plays the graduate was being paid $14,500 to make.

The Swede was a hard guy. He took to fighting as easily as he did to baseball and occasionally confused these crafts. At Oakland he'd protested a third strike simply by stepping up to an umpire and knocking him cold with a short chop to his jaw. "Call *that* a third strike," he'd commented while the other umpire was trying to bring his colleague back to life. And he walked back to the dugout in disgust.

The cards were a variable currency, their value depending upon a player's prestige. I had to give two Hod Ellers and one Dutch Ruether to Jake to get just one Eddie Cicotte.

Cicotte was a 35-year-old French Canadian who had grown up believing, as Eliot Asinof has observed, that "it was talent made a man big. If you were good enough, and dedicated yourself, you could get to the top. Wasn't that enough of a reward? But when he'd gotten there he had found out otherwise. They all fed off him, the men who ran the show and pulled the strings that kept it working. They used him and used him, and when they'd used him up they would dump him. In the years he'd been up, they'd always made him feel like a hero to the American people. But all the time they paid him peanuts. The newspapermen who came to watch him pitch and wrote stories about him made more money than he did. Comiskey made half a million dollars a year out of Cicotte's right arm."

Cicotte had brought the pennant to Comiskey Park in 1917 by winning 28 games and had brought it there again, in 1919, by winning 29. When Comiskey had benched him, toward the season's end, he explained that he did so to avoid risk of injury to his star with the World Series coming up.

The real reason was that Cicotte had gone to Comiskey, before the season opened, and had asked him for a raise. After 12 years at the top he was still earning only $5,500 a season. Dutch Ruether, for one example, after pitching only two seasons, was earning twice that sum.

Comiskey turned him down. "However," he assured the pitcher, "I'll do this for you. I'll pay you a bonus of $10,000 if you win 30 games for me."

Cicotte had accepted. When he'd won 29 and there were enough days left for him to pitch twice more, Comiskey had benched him.

"Comiskey throws money around like manhole covers," was all Cicotte said.

I had to give Jake two Edd Roushes to get one Shoeless Joe Jackson. Edd Roush, the Cincinnati center fielder, was hitting around .350 and earning $11,000. Jackson, hitting 50 points higher, was earning half as much. Harry Grabiner, Comiskey's front man, went to see Jackson at his home in Greenville, S.C.

Jackson couldn't read or write, but his wife protected him. When Grabiner assured her that the contract he offered guaranteed Jackson $9,000 a season for three seasons, she wanted to know whether it contained a 10-day clause: the clause that entitled an owner to fire a player with 10 days of notice. This protected the owner from having to support a player who'd been seriously injured. It didn't do much for the player. Grabiner assured her his contract contained no such clause; but he did not show it to her.

Instead he maneuvered Jackson out of the house, put the contract up against the house's wall and handed Jackson a pen.

Jackson signed. The contract contained a 10-day clause.

I traded Jake three Heinie Grohs for one Buck Weaver. Weaver was the third baseman whom sportswriters had nicknamed "Error-a-Day Weaver" when he'd first come to the White Sox from Pennsylvania mining country. His hitting was as weak as his fielding. Kid Gleason, Comiskey's manager, had made a .300 hitter of Weaver by switching him at the plate. He had developed him into the finest-fielding third baseman in either league.

Buck Weaver had a habit of grinning while inching up on a batter, which so unnerved Ty Cobb that he refused to bunt against Weaver. Weaver was a joyous boy, all heart and hard-trying, who guarded the spiked sand around third like a territorial animal.

He was one of eight players who met with the gamblers. Then he dropped out of the conspiracy. His only guilt was that he possessed guilty knowledge. At the trial he was denied the right to take the stand and defend himself.

He took no money. Nonetheless, he was banned from professional baseball by Judge Landis, an enraptured Puritan. The judge's statement read:

"Regardless of the verdict of juries, no player who throws a ball game, no player that promises to throw a ball game, no player who sits in conference with a bunch of crooked gamblers discussing ways and means of throwing a ball game, and does not promptly tell his club about it, will ever play professional baseball."

Weaver was the sort of man who could wear a pitcher down by fouling pitch after pitch until the pitcher blew sky high; but he was not the kind of man who would inform. He was outlawed because he did not.

"Landis wanted me to tell him something I didn't know," he explained to Jim Farrell in his last interview, in 1954. "I didn't have any evidence. A murderer," he added, "serves his sentence and is let out. I got life. I never threw a ball game in my life. All I knew was win. That's all I know."

Fourteen thousand fans signed a petition requesting that Weaver be reinstated.

Year after year, long after his playing days passed, Buck Weaver tried for reinstatement, to prove his honesty. Year after year his petitions were turned down.

He wound up coaching a girl's softball team, and died of a heart attack on the street, in 1956, on Chicago's South Side.

Arnold Rothstein, a multi-millionaire gambler who never gambled on anything until the fix was in, walked into the Green Room of the Ansonia Hotel, in New York City, a few minutes before the opening game of the 1919 Series began in Cincinnati.

Tokens, representing the players, would be moved, by telegraphic report, on the big green diamond-shaped chart suspended on the wall. The chairs were all filled. Rothstein didn't care. He had no intention of watching the full nine innings anyhow. Arnold didn't care for the game.

He had left his instruction—indirectly—to Cicotte: "If you hit the first man up, in the first inning, with a pitched ball, I'll know the fix is in." Cicotte had found $10,000 beneath his pillow the night before, in the Sinton Hotel in Cincinnati.

Cicotte's first pitch was a called strike right across the plate. His second hit Rath between the shoulder blades. Before Rath had reached first base, Rothstein had left the hotel on his way to do some heavy betting against the White Sox. His betting would not be on individual games, but on the Series. He was not a man to take chances.

It was a 1-1 ball game until the fourth inning. Then, fielding an easy grounder off the bat of Larry Kopf, with a man on first, Cicotte turned too slowly and threw too high to Risberg on second, so that Kopf was safe at first. Greasy Neale singled and Ivy Wingo did the same, scoring Kopf. Then Cicotte fed a ball to Dutch Ruether, a weak hitter, that Ruether smashed for three bases, bringing in Neale and Wingo. Final score: Reds 9, White Sox 1.

The biggest cookie on the White Sox pitching staff was Lefty Williams. He was a Southerner, in his mid-20s, who kept a mental book on every player in the league. He'd won 23 games for Comiskey in 1919. He pitched with great deliberation, studying his man head to toe before every throw. He could cut the outside corner at the knees or break a curve below a batter's chin. He'd often complete a ball game without giving a single walk.

With the score 0-0 in the fourth inning of the second game, Rath got a base on balls off him and got into scoring position on a sacrifice bunt. Groh walked and Roush singled to center; Rath scored and Groh slid safely into third. Williams gave Duncan a base on balls and Kopf slammed a triple into deep left. Final score: Reds 4, White Sox 2.

The players had been assured, before the Series began, that they would have $100,000 to divide among themselves if they went along with the gamblers. Cicotte had been paid $10,000, Jackson $5,000, and Williams $5,000 by the time the third game was to be played.

An ex-pitcher named Burns, acting as go-between between gamblers and players, distributing Rothstein money, asked one Abe Attell for the balance. Attell, at the moment, was preoccupied, with two other gamblers, in counting and packaging their winnings off the first two games. Every corner and crevice of the room was stacked with greenbacks. Attell flat refused to pay off the players.

Burns became so enraged he started to go for Attell, who'd been featherweight champion of the world. The two assistants stepped between, spoke urgently to Attell, until he finally handed $10,000 to Burns and said, "That's enough for them bums—that's all they get."

Burns, now awestruck by Attell's demonstration of consummate stupidity combined with unlimited arrogance, picked up the money. He had to wonder how in God's name he was going to explain to the players. Not to mention how he was going to get his own cut.

"Tell them bums to win the third game," Attell called after him. "It'll be better for the odds."

Were the players scapegoats? That's putting it too lightly. Worse, far worse. They were as solid a group of horse's asses as were ever tricked into playing crooked in any sport on earth.

With a single exception: Weaver.

Weaver sat in on the first session with the gamblers, with seven other players, and made the only decision, later, that made good common sense:

"Take everything they offer us. Then we go out and whip Cincinnati four straight. What do we care about *them*? As much as they care about us."

He batted .324 for the Series and played errorlessly.

James T. Farrell, who saw Dick Kerr pitch the third game, descibes Kerr as "small and frail." Because of his lack of height and heft, Kerr was 26 before he got into the majors. He'd won 13 in his rookie season of 1919 and had lost seven.

The feeling of the players behind him was that, if they couldn't win behind veterans like Cicotte and Williams, why give support to a busher?

Kerr didn't require their support. The Reds could hit nothing off him but feeble infield grounders. "His curve ball dropped, that day, with startling suddenness," Eliot Asinof assures us, "all his pitches had eyes. Perfectly placed, perfectly timed." Everything that Schalk asked for, he delivered. Final score: White Sox 3, Reds 0.

Roush came to bat in the fifth inning of the fourth game, with the score 0-0, and tapped a slow grounder to Cicotte, who knocked it down, then threw wildly to Gandil, who let it get away. The runner went to second. Kopf lined a single to left and Jackson rifled a perfect throw to the plate that didn't get there. Cicotte got a glove in its way and deflected it. Two runs, two hits, two errors by the pitcher. Final score: Reds 2, White Sox 0.

Again, in the sixth inning of the fifth game, neither side had scored. Eller popped a fly ball between Jackson and Felsch, and Felsch picked it up but threw badly to Risberg, who let the ball roll away from him. Final Score: Reds 5, White Sox 0.

The players had finally caught on that they were being played for a group of idiots. Risberg and Gandil had waited, together, for one Sport Sullivan, also handling Rothstein money; but Sullivan had not shown up. He was using Rothstein money to make his own bets.

Nothing was said between the players, but all understood that the fix was off. After the Reds had scored four runs, in the sixth game, Jackson slashed a single to center; Felsch followed with a hit on which Jackson scored from first. Schalk drove a single to left scoring Felsch. With the score tied 4-4 in the 10th inning, Weaver opened with a double, Jackson advanced him to third with a single, and Gandil singled, bringing in Weaver. Final score: White Sox 5, Reds 4.

The White Sox got a run in the first inning of the seventh game, another in the third, and the Reds began making errors. In the fifth inning Jackson crashed a hard double to left, scoring two men. Final score, Cicotte pitching: White Sox 4, Reds 1.

To Arnold Rothstein, any man of talent who worked for peanuts was a dumb brute. He didn't like dealing with dumb brutes. Now, with the games standing 4-3 and the White Sox playing like themselves, he became genuinely frightened. He'd bet over $100,000 on the Series, and Rothstein did not lose lightly.

The fix, apparently, had come unglued. He called in Sport Sullivan.

Their talk was quiet, Rothstein revealed neither anger nor anxiety. He was, in fact, cordial.

It wasn't until after he had left that the full impact of what Rothstein had been saying struck Sullivan: If the White Sox won the Series, Sullivan could not live.

Sullivan suppressed his inner panic and phoned the number of The Man in the Bowler Hat in Chicago.

The Bowler Hat's trade was murder.

"Does Williams have children?" he asked Sullivan. No. "Is he married?" Yes.

"Good enough. Send five hundred. Will make contact upon receipt."

Lefty Williams and his wife were confronted, the evening before the eighth game, in the entrance to their hotel, by a man in a bowler hat. He was smoking a cigar and asked for a private conversation. Mrs. Williams excused herself.

She did not know, and may never have known, that the conversation centered on her.

When the man in the hat informed Williams that he was to lose, the following day, Williams turned away. An iron grip on his shoulder turned him back.

It was no longer a question of money, the Hat assured Williams. It was a matter of his wife. She could get hurt. She could get hurt bad.

Williams stood enraged, wanting to strike out. Yet he was afraid. He was deadly afraid of this Hat.

Not only was he going to lose, The Hat told Williams, but he was going to lose in the first inning. Or else.

Then he walked away.

Williams put his first pitch over for a strike, the next afternoon, on the Reds' leadoff man, Rath. Rath took a cut at his second pitch and fouled it. Then he popped out to Risberg.

Daubert, the second batter, singled. Williams put two strikes across on Groh; then Groh singled sharply to right.

Edd Roush, the Reds' heaviest hitter, came into the batter's box. Gleason signaled to the bench for James and Wilkerson to start warming up. Schalk walked out to the mound to talk to Williams.

Roush smashed Williams' first pitch to right. Daubert scored easily, and Groh stopped at third. Schalk was now bellowing at Williams and shaking his fist.

Christy Mathewson, in the press box, observed to a sportswriter that, so far, Williams had thrown nothing except fastballs.

Duncan, following Roush at the plate, sent a screaming foul into the left-field seats. Williams' next pitch went high and wide of the plate. Schalk had to leap desperately to prevent a wild pitch. Duncan then singled to left, Groh and Duncan scoring easily.

Gleason shouted something at Williams, but Williams ignored him. He threw hard to Kopf for a strike. "Nothing but fastballs," Mathewson repeated.

Gleason called to Bill James to replace Williams. James let in one more run. The Reds had gotten four hits, on 15 pitches by Williams, and three runs.

In the eighth, with the score 10-1 against them, the Sox put on a four-run rally.

Final score: Reds 10, White Sox 5.

So long, Swede Risberg.

No rumors of the fix had yet reached us by midsummer of 1920. The White Sox were still white. Swede Risberg was still my favorite player. I began to walk pigeontoed because Risberg was pigeontoed. I did this for a full year before my mother asked me why I was walking "like that." I couldn't explain. I still walk like that.

Chicago, New York and Cleveland were in a triple tie for first place in August of 1920, when the Yankees came to town. Neither Jake Somerhaus nor I had ever seen a major league ball game. We rode the el out to Comiskey Park to see Cicotte pitch against Babe Ruth. Carl Mays, the submarine-ball pitcher, was going for New York.

By the time we got there, that Sunday morning, bleacher seats had been sold out two hours before the game time. A crowd, predominantly black, was milling around the bleacher walls, which were still of wood.

We followed a throng onto a rooftop a block from the park, and saw the first half of the first inning, in which Cicotte struck out Ruth. We also saw that the cops were beginning to have trouble with the mob pressing the bleacher walls. They were riding here and there, striking blindly at heads, but fans were already beginning to clamber over the walls. We headed for them; by the time we got there it was a small-scale riot. Somebody gave me a boost and over the wall I went into the park.

I didn't run. I joined the fans sitting on the grass behind the left fielder.

Some left fielder.

He was Shoeless Joe Jackson.

I *saw* him.

I was almost close enough to *touch* him.

He hit over .400, had the greatest throwing arm in baseball and he could run. What's so important about learning to read and write after *that?*

In later years I saw Grover Cleveland Alexander and Jack Johnson in Hubert's Museum. But that was after they had had their day. This was the living man in his prime. I'll never see his like again.

In the seventh inning, Cicotte struck out Ruth again and shut the Yankees out, 3-0.

Our love of the game was not shaken by the exposure that followed. But we stopped pitching baseball cards and took to shooting dice. The men whose pictures we had cherished were no longer gods.

Jake Somerhaus went to the University of Wisconsin on a scholarship and pitched winning ball there for four seasons. He never grew heavy enough, however, to make the majors.

Once I was walking with a young woman, who turned to me and said, "You're favoring your leg. Does it hurt?"

"It's an old injury," I said.

"How did it happen?"

"A big Swede hurt it when I was a kid." I invented a story to gain sympathy—"The Swede was a hard guy."

Courtside Microphone John McEnroe's Worst Enemy

TENNIS

By *GARY NUHN*

From the Dayton Daily News
Copyright © 1981, Dayton Daily News

So *The Angry American* won Wimbledon.

And came on the television screen afterward and said something that sounded like, "I am not a bad guy."

NBC should have cut immediately to a tape of that other famous American saying, "I am not a crook."

No, John, you're a beautiful person; a gem. After all, NBC kept listing your scores under "Gentlemen's Singles," right?

There is a theory that *The Angry American* is misunderstood, that since John Patrick McEnroe II apologizes afterward and admits he is a boor, that makes him not a boor. That is *Gobledy Logic;* forget it, please.

There is another theory—the *Violent Society Theory—that "Junior," as he is called, should have been spanked more (or perhaps even foot-faulted) when he was a child. The same theory wonders if we're sure it's too late.*

In truth, the problem, as anyone with a TV knows, is the presence of courtside microphones; they are McEnroe's worst enemy. We are willing witnesses to this man-child's whining. TV has made tantrum voyeurs of us all.

When Jimmy Connors and Ilie Nastase were at their worst, in the early and mid-70s, the state of the art—television—was less refined. Sometimes you could hear snippets of those two blowhards' act, but rarely could you grasp them in their entirety. For better or worse, you get Johnny Mac *au naturel.*

Those who saw Connors and Nastase in person know they were so far beyond McEnroe, they shouldn't be linked in the same paragraph. Connors and Nastase were frequently profane. Both used their middle finger without hesitation. Their consistently classless behavior had much to do with bringing on the system of fines that is now haunting McEnroe.

Many of Connors' attempts at "humor" revolved around his crotch. It was not fun; it was not funny.

In comparison to that, McEnroe's behavior is positively civilized. His vocabulary is all from the dictionary. He calls people "Mr. Incompetent" or a "fool" or a "disgrace to the human race." In all of McEnroe's snits, I have yet to hear a foul word.

From the reactions, you'd have thought McEnroe shot these umpires and linesmen. This is to assure you he didn't.

To take the *Courtside Mike Theory* to its conclusion, if every argument in sports were miked, McEnroe would end up on the angelic side of the species, mild-mannered even. Sure, "Junior" insulted a couple of men. But in sports, sad to say, men insult men.

Football players, especially linemen, routinely harass each other with four-letter expletives. You think football officials are scared? Nonsense. How many times have you seen the ref turn off his hip-switch mike when a player approaches?

In baseball, creative profanity is a daily ritual. Sit behind a dugout and hear the reaction after a close play at first. Umps look straight ahead until someone uses "the magic word." Next, read Billy Martin's lips. I've seen him two inches from an umpire's face, screaming. "You're full of . . . ; you're full of . . . ; you're full of . . ." Let's not even mention the dirt throwing, Billy's imitation of a 3-year-old in a sandbox.

The last couple of seasons, there have been floor mikes in the NBA, too. Cussing is commonplace after close officials' calls; the key to not getting a technical is to not press the issue.

In boxing, how many times have we heard Ali issue racial slurs?

It is one thing to consider McEnroe's behavior abominable. It is quite another to think him alone, even in his own sport. What McEnroe has, unfortunately, is visibility. While fellow tennis cry-babies like Butch Walts, Fritz Buehning and others never make TV, McEnroe is a fixture.

None of that excuses John McEnroe. He is a case unto himself.

John McEnroe is insecure. During interviews, he has an involuntary habit of shrugging his shoulders, not just with every sentence, but with every pause. It is his substitute for the "you know" so many athletes use. I counted once; he shrugged 17 times in the space of a three-sentence answer.

The "disgrace to mankind" confrontation was telling. He quibbled. He tried to weasel out of it, insisting he was yelling at himself. It was a pathetic attempt to gain sympathy. It told something about Johnny Mac's character.

There is no comparison between Connors and McEnroe. (Reformed now, you may call him *Jimmy The Good,* if you like.) Connors' schtick was just that, an act; even in the noisiest moments, you always knew. Also, Jimbo loved himself; he never would have lost if there had been a full-length mirror at center court.

McEnroe is different. He is a fragile person, never in control. He is exactly what he seems, a pilotless aircraft about to crash. He does not like himself, thus the dime-store, day-after apologies.

What is most worrisome is that McEnroe's spells might ultimately be self-destructive in a personal sense. Obviously, they aren't in a tennis sense; he routinely plays above his rancor.

Too many geniuses have been swallowed by their own single-dimensionness. I worry for John McEnroe.

The Annual Fall Frolic

by Jayne Kamin of the *Los Angeles Times* shows first baseman Steve Garvey (background), relief pitcher Steve Howe and catcher Steve Yeager in the triumphant moment after the Dodgers had defeated the Yankees in Game 6 of the 1981 World Series. Copyright © 1981, Los Angeles Times, Jayne Kamin.

Public Depression

by Dan Dry of the *Louisville Courier-Journal*. A player on the Lexington Bryan Station high school basketball team covers his head in dejection after his team's loss in the Kentucky state championship game. This action was caught in the foyer near the dressing room and the player seemed oblivious to the sympathetic glances of the departing fans. Copyright © 1981, The Courier-Journal and The Louisville Times.

The Ump Bump Has Gone a Little Too Far

BASEBALL

By *BLACKIE SHERROD*

From the Dallas Times Herald
Copyright © 1981, Dallas Times Herald

Perhaps you noted, as the Rangers reeled along their mysterious path on the West Coast, that their Oakland tormentors were without their fearless leader. Alfredo Martin, who has made BillyBall a byword where only pidgin baseball was spoken, was unpresent on the field.

Actually, Ballbilly was several rods away, hidden from view, steering the warfare from his clubhouse like A. Hitler in his Berlin bunker. Feet propped, pipe stoked, eyes fixed on the toob, dugout telephone to ear, he relayed instructions to his little heart's content and the Rangers' discomfort.

Only thing missing was Ballbilly's presence. Which is considerable.

Actually, all a manager's suspension amounts to *these* days is a physical banishment from the premises. He is not barred from calling the shots, only from being caught in the act by the naked eye. He can use telephone, Morse code, blinker lights, tom-toms or carrier pigeon as long as he doesn't show his face. In Martin's case, most umpires would settle for that. BillyBall is not one of their favorite conversationalists for he is apt to introduce such fringe topics as eyesight, relatives and personal hygenic habits.

Martin drew his penalty from American League President Lee MacPhail for one of those childish fits last May, in which he kicked some nasty old dirt on umpire Terry Cooney.

This is a routine that most managers feel they must go through occasionally and, frankly, it has always been one of the great mysteries of baseball to me. Why should a grown man go through the kindergarten act—stomp, kick dust, throw cap in air, stick nose $\frac{1}{8}$ inch away from umpire's beak and see how much tobacco spray he can distribute?

Oh, I know the baseball rationalization. It's a part of the tradition handed down by McGraw and Frisch. Such displays supposedly intimidate an umpire, embarrass him, maybe sway the *next* close decision he faces, in order to avoid a similar tantrum. Also, the temper seizures allegedly stir a manager's players, inflame them, inspire them to emotional efforts above and beyond. What a bunch of unmitigated balderdash. Nowadays, players are too busy reading The Wall Street Journal or working out their deferred payments on a pocket computer even to notice.

What's Ole Crazy doing out there?

Oh, nothing. Another of his fits. He's good for another five minutes, so tell me, what does E.F. Hutton say about this new money market?

Dallas Green is normally a cold, composed guy with the emotion of a tableleg. But he pulled one of those explosive raindances recently in a dispute with umpire Steve Fields.

The Phillie manager added a new twist. Goodness, was he angry. He knocked Fields' cap off and then kicked it for three points. Now Green is a well-preserved man with average eyesight and normal muscular control. If he were actually mad enough to *hit* the umpire, he could have managed it. He didn't *have* to miss and settle for the cap. You may note that even though managers seem to go completely berserk with rage, I mean *completely*, they don't get berserk enough to pop the ump on the pump.

You've seen Frank Lucchesi, when he managed the Rangers, go absolutely wild. Eyes big as teacups. Hair like Don King. Foam. Voice rising to a jungle scream. You would swear a man consumed with such unholy rage would be capable of crimes of great violence. Yet he somehow winds up just short of strangling his enemy, or even touching him, and succeeds mostly in looking like something from Captain Kangaroo.

Anyways, Green not only was suspended but strapped with a $5,000 fine. He and Martin, of course, in the manner of the day, appealed to the civil courts.

You may remember that Earl Weaver, one of the really exemplary volcanos of our time, was suspended for a temper exhibition during *spring training!* Now that, friends, is a dedicated temper.

In no other sport, save that of a champeen rassle match with Hyena Hank Hugo vs. The Peruvian Hunchback, must we witness such temper exhibitions.

John McEnroe and Nasty Nastase and Jimmy Connors have been universally chastised for their displays on the tennis court, yet their outbursts are, excuse the expression, child's play compared to the frenzied shows of Weaver and that crowd.

Bobby Knight is known for his volatile basketball nature, but he is a pussycat alongside Tommy Lasorda.

George Halas, on the Chicago Bear sideline, was an NFL scandal. Billy Martin would make Papa Bear clap hands to ears and flee for the nearest cathedral.

Umpires are not a placid lot, but for years they were considered serfs, devoid of public rights. Oh, they could send a player or a manager to the showers, but league bosses frowned if this happened *too* often. Now, in the style of the day, umpires are asserting themselves as they should. They even staged a labor strike, even though most of baseball pretended not to notice.

And they have protested recently. As Danny Thomas used to say years ago "I'm a citizen! I got my rights!"

The New York Daily News' Bill Brubaker interviewed several umps after the Martin-Green detonations. Ed Montague, six years in the National League, explained why he frequently glances into the stands between plays.

"Some managers get fans so mad at the umpires that someday some nut up there with a rifle is going to take a pot shot at us," said Montague. "I've talked to some of the players and they feel the same way. They think it's going to come down to that. I mean, they're shooting the Pope. What the hell's wrong with an umpire?"

It could happen and someday, if the trends keep up, it probably will. In the meanwhile, the great managerial temper act will remain merely amusing but not very.

The Shot and the Dynasty Come Up Short

PRO BASKETBALL

By *MIKE LITTWIN*

From the Los Angeles Times
Copyright © 1981, Los Angeles Times
Reprinted by Permission

Kill the book. Unless you want to call it "The Gang That Couldn't Shoot Straight."

The dynasty that was to be the Lakers on a Sunday afternoon at the Forum. Rome fell to the Huns, China to the Mongols. The Lakers fell to the Houston Rockets, 89-86, and history will not remember them well for it.

They fell when Magic Johnson's shot launched 10 feet from the basket with five seconds left didn't. The ball, unmolested, traveled maybe four feet, and into the waiting hands of Moses Malone.

Malone was fouled immediately and made two free throws, building the Rockets' fragile 87-86 lead into victory.

"I blew it," said Johnson, who had a day he'll never forget—but will spend a summer trying to. He had 12 rebounds and nine assists but connected on only 2 of 14 shots. That wasn't exactly typical of the Lakers, but it was symptomatic of the disease to which they succumbed.

The defending NBA champions are suddenly only a memory. No glory, only confusion. The Rockets stripped them of their title in an upset that rivals the most stunning of sports upsets.

The Rockets, who were 40-42 in the regular season and had to win four of their last five games just to make the playoffs, had to beat the Lakers twice at the Forum in a best-of-three mini-series. All that's left is to wonder how it could happen.

There were few explanations in the Lakers' locker room. "There's no way it should have happened," Jim Chones said.

"Maybe it was just the pressure of not wanting to lose," Jamaal Wilkes said.

It wasn't a pretty game. More like a brawl, really. The Rockets controlled the tempo throughout, despite the Lakers' speed lineup. More surprisingly, they held together when the Lakers didn't.

The Forum floor, especially in the last few minutes, could have been called the land of opportunity. The Lakers owned the floor and the fans and figured to have more poise. But try finding that poise in the final score.

The Lakers sure couldn't.

There were turnovers and missed shots and missed free thows. One thing to lose to a Philadelphia or Phoenix in a classic game. But another to lose to Houston, especially on a day when the Rockets shot but 35 percent.

The Lakers shot 39 percent. In the last three quarters, they scored only 57 points. No, it wasn't pretty. Yes, there was win-or-play-no-more defense. The intensity could have started a brush fire. But where was the Lakers' talent edge?

"We didn't play well," said Chones, who didn't play much at all.

Most of the other Lakers wanted to credit the Rockets. But it wasn't that easy. The Rockets beat the Lakers without an awesome game from either Moses Malone (23 points, 10 rebounds) or Calvin Murphy (14 points on 4-for-15 shooting).

"If you knew how good a job we would do on Malone," Lakers Coach Paul Westhead said, "you would have to think we had a pretty good chance to win."

The Lakers thought so, too, when in the fourth quarter they took a 77-73 lead on a hook shot by Kareem Abdul-Jabbar, who was one Laker to have a big day with 32 points and 18 rebounds.

But Robert Reid, who scored 16 before fouling out, hit two straight jumpers and Murphy finally hit one to put the Rockets ahead, 79-77, and set the stage for the tight finish.

Two foul shots by Abdul-Jabbar tied the score at 85-85 with 2:22 to play when the Lakers and Rockets exchanged misses.

And even when the Lakers finally scored with 30 seconds to play to break the tie, they botched it.

Johnson drove to the baseline and was fouled by Reid, his sixth. Johnson, with three chances to make two, missed his first two before finally hitting one.

Instead of a two-point deficit, the Rockets were down by only one, 86-85. The Rockets wanted the ball in the hands of Malone or Murphy. Both got it, but neither had a chance to shoot.

Murphy slipped the ball to Mike Dunleavy instead, and Dunleavy hit from 16 feet with 15 seconds to play.

Westhead put the game, the season, in the hands of Johnson. Who else? He drove the court with the option of passing or taking the shot himself. He guided the ball straight down the middle, as he's done so many times in so many key situations, but his shot didn't fly. It barely fluttered. Earvin Johnson obviously left his magic at home.

Johnson couldn't remember missing a shot half as important as that one.

Someone asked him when the last one was. "This was the first," he said. "I just missed it. I'd take that shot again. I'd take it 10 times out of 10, and I'd make it 8 or 9."

There were no tears from Johnson. "I quit crying over basketball games in high school," he said.

There weren't many tears in the Laker dressing room. There may have been some distractions, however, on the day on which their season would end. Recent newspaper stories had quoted Johnson as saying some of his teammates might be jealous of him.

Before the game, some Lakers were seen grouped together discussing the issue.

"There was a lot of pressure added by the press," Johnson said.

"It couldn't have helped," said Wilkes, who scored 12 points in the first quarter but only 16 in all.

There had to be some explanation—dissension, distractions, something. No NBA champion has repeated since the Boston Celtics in 1968-69. But to lose to the Houston Rockets in the mini-series?

It's unprecedented. No defending champion has done it.

The Rockets played well. They played a half-court game and never allowed the Lakers to run. They did a much better job of exploiting mismatches. They made 21 of 22 foul shots while the Lakers hit 22 of 35.

"If we'd made a few more foul shots . . ." Nixon said. "No, you can't say that. If we'd made a few more shots from anywhere. I don't know. Give Houston some credit."

The Rockets were ready to take some. Malone thought they'd won a championship already instead of the right to play San Antonio in the Western Conference semifinals.

"We knew we would be the champs," Malone said. "We knew if we played together and hard we could win."

Malone also thought that the Lakers should have gone to Abdul-Jabbar for the last shot. "Magic took it," he said, "but they should have gone to the big man."

Abdul-Jabbar, who played 46 minutes, stood as tall as he is. And you know how tall that is. He blocked four shots and had four assists. He did all he could.

And with him playing well and Mark Landsberger coming off the bench to shut off Malone—who didn't score a basket in the final period—it didn't figure that the Lakers could lose.

But the game, the way it was played, dictated that neither team could pull away. Westhead, who said he felt "a deep emptiness," thought it would come down to the last minute.

"We just didn't get it done," he said.

Judge's Comments

I have felt for a long time that sports writing has come a long way since the days of Westbrook Pegler, Hype Igoe, John Kieran, Grantland Rice and many others who set the pace for the new breed of today.

Today's sports writers no longer adhere to the stiffly disciplined, circumscribed styles that graced the sports pages after World War II.

The writing has become a melange of colorful, exciting reportage that did not exist. The athletes have become the headliners, the score an incidental that, once given, returns to the wings. Mike Littwin's NBA playoff story is a fine representation of modern coverage.

The headline reads, "The Shot and the Dynasty Come Up Short." The score does not make its appearance until the second paragraph. After that, Magic Johnson takes over as the tragic hero. Before he's through, Littwin covers the Lakers' explanations, shooting percentages and gives a good evaluation of the winning Houston Rockets. Good heady stuff for a deadline story and far more dramatic than in the olden days.

A $35 Ride Bought a Nightmare

HORSERACING

By *DAVE KINDRED*

From the Washington Post
Copyright © 1981, The Washington Post

Not far from the Laurel race track, there is a night spot of the urban cowboy persuasion. Paul Nicolo chose it as the place to corrupt his best buddy, Sammy Boulmetis. They are an odd couple, both jockeys but one a street tough kid from Boston, the other the boy next door who at 24 still won't use profanity in front of his parents. Nicolo said no one ought to be that nice, and so a month ago he watched happily as the boy next door, after an unprecedented two beers, paid $2 to ride the mechanical bull.

"I can bust this bull's buns," Sammy Boulmetis said loudly, putting down his beer and taking a hard look at the saddled robot.

"Cut the crap and get to it," Nicolo said. The race track has a lot of folks called common, meaning lowdown, but the kid from Boston knew Boulmetis was uncommon and loved him for it. Only Sammy could get away with teasing Nicolo about the nice chaps he wore for morning workouts; "tah-tah chaps," he said, as if speaking to a British dandy, not a Boston tough. Now, because Nicolo would leave Maryland soon, moving his tack to Kentucky for the spring, this might be his last night out with Sammy for a while. "You gonna ride or not?" Nicolo said.

It took only five seconds for the bull to toss Boulmetis on his ear. Nicolo thought it was the funniest thing he had ever seen when Sammy, staggering up, looked at the bull and said, "I've got him now."

The second time around, Boulmetis rode the hair off the bull.

And then, celebrating with a third beer, he said to Nicolo, "Your turn."

"Nope," Nicolo said. "I get paid to ride; I don't pay to ride."

Sammy Boulmetis was paid $35 for the ride that broke his back March 22. A rider seven years and better each year, he worked for the $35 as a substitute rider on a filly named Val Des Portes in the ninth race at Pimlico that day. The jockey who had ridden the filly in her only other race, Ken Black, had to ride for another trainer in the ninth. Sammy worked the filly in the morning two weeks earlier, and the owner liked the courteous, clean-cut kid. So Sammy's agent, Bobby Vaughan, got the assignment for his client.

As the field turned into the stretch, Val Des Portes was far behind. The book on Boulmetis is that he sits still on a horse, keeps out of trouble and finishes strongly. Even with the filly out of it, Boulmetis did an honest day's work. He passed Noble Jade, the horse Ken Black rode, and was running next to last when, with a report like a gunshot, Val Des Portes' right foreleg shattered.

Had there been warning, it might have been different. A jockey knows the signals of pain from a horse, the half-steps of indecision that come in an animal bred both for running and courage. Given warning, a rider can pull his horse's head up to slow down.

That is why the Jockeys Guild, the riders' union, has campaigned for strict enforcement of medication rules. Because tracks all over America run day and night nearly every day of the year, the demand for horses increases annually. To keep horses running, and so to make money, some horsemen have abused medications and sent animals to work so drugged up their brains could not receive warning signals of pain from their legs.

In the old days, unscrupulous trainers "nerved" their horses, which is to say they took a knife and cut the foreleg nerves that deliver the messages of pain. Nowadays they use laser beams instead of knives.

Val Des Portes was a sound horse, making only her second start. She was a victim not of man, but of her breed. Thoroughbreds are 1,000-pound animals running 30 miles per hour on legs half the thickness of Pete Rose's forearm. As all that force came down on the filly's left hoof, the leg exploded.

The horse took a header. With no warning of danger, Sammy Boulmetis was perched atop the filly's shoulders, pushing her to work harder. He might have sat back and coasted home for the standard $35 a rider gets for running out of the money. But Sammy did honest work, and so he balanced himself over the filly's neck as if this anonymous ninth race were the Kentucky Derby. Always vulnerable, jockeys never are in more danger than when driving their horses to a better effort.

Race trackers talk of spills. A jockey doesn't fall, he doesn't have an accident; he takes a spill. It sounds dainty, almost harmless. The half-ton animal tips forward and the 100-pound man is spilled off its back. These brave little men are spilled so often they don't keep count. Three weeks earlier Sammy Boulmetis had X-rays taken of his shoulder after a spill at Bowie. The shoulder still has two pins in it from a spill in '78.

This time, in a meaningless race that would earn him $35, Boulmetis was thrown violently to the ground.

Maybe he broke his back right then, or maybe it was broken when Ken Black's horse, coming up from behind, stepped on him.

The first time he saw the X-ray picture of his son's spine, the old rider let his eyes go shut.

Sammy's spine was broken in two. The top piece ran straight and true to about waist level. The piece in the pelvic region was twisted at an odd angle with the broken-off end pulled maybe an inch and a half away from the rest of the spine. Jockeys see a lot of X-rays, but Sam Boulmetis Sr. had never seen one this bad. There was, on the picture, a snowstorm of bone fragments along the broken twig of a spine.

A printer's devil in Baltimore after World War II, Boulmetis took a job at the Laurel race track because everybody kept telling him that he was little enough to be a jockey. For eight months, at $50 a month, he mucked stalls and hot-walked horses, occasionally wangling his way on top of a horse for a morning workout.

He won his first race May 10, 1949, and he won nearly 2,700 more before he retired in 1966, a Hall of Fame rider. Only 37 then, he said he quit because he had four children from 6 to 13 and he wanted to go out on top. Wise guys at the tracks, though, said he no longer was the daring gambler of his youth, that he preferred safety to risk. Given a choice of taking the outside or flying into a closing hole on the rail, he took the long way. Any horse Boulmetis rode would have to be much the best to win, a handicapper said.

Jockeys don't admit fear because to admit it is to betray the hero's code of the bravest little men in sports. "You don't think about going into a hole," Sam Boulmetis said of his daring youth, "you just go. You're there before you realize there is a hole. It's reflexes. What happened to me was reflexes. That, and competitive desire. I could feel it wasn't the same. Before, if I got beat, I was annoyed. Later, I wasn't."

It wasn't fear, he said. Maybe 20 times in 20,000 races in his 17 years, Boulmetis went down with a horse. He was never hurt seriously, just broken arms and legs and the collarbone a few times.

"Being scared? No. Getting hurt? No. I didn't have that fear. It was just certain things I wanted for my family. And I had a good job waiting as a patrol judge."

Now a state racing steward in New Jersey, Boulmetis, 51, was putting sealer on a new kitchen floor at home when the phone rang just after 5 o'clock March 22.

Four hours later, in Baltimore's Sinai Hospital, he looked at an X-ray that made him close his eyes against its story.

Julie Snellings quit her race track job in Florida and drove two days to get to Sinai. She believed she knew what Sammy wanted to hear. Only she knew.

Julie's sister, Cyd, is Sammy's fiance. His parents never left the hospital. Nicolo was there, and so was Bill Passmore, a jockey who at 48 had ridden with Sam Boulmetis Sr. and then taken Sammy as a race track son. Two years ago Passmore broke his back, cracking two vertebrae in about the same place Sammy did. Passmore had seen a lot of X-rays, including his own, but Sammy's pictures caused a chill to pass across his shoulders.

They all cared, but Julie drove two days because only she knew what Sammy had to hear. Only she was in a wheelchair.

For six months in 1977, Julie Snellings may have been the best woman jockey ever. She won 46 races on the Maryland-New Jersey circuit. Her agent, Chick Lang Jr., said Julie looked like the woman who would make it big because she had built credibility without going to bed with trainers. She came from a race track family; her mother was a trainer for 25 years and her father, Aubrey, was a top rider in the '50s until he broke a leg in a spill at Charles Town. Eighteen years ago, when Julie was 5, Aubrey Snellings committed suicide.

Always a strong kid behind soft brown eyes and a smile that could melt a steward's cold, cold heart from a furlong away, Julie wrote a letter in July of '77 to an old boyfriend, the jockey Jackie Fires, who had been paralyzed in a spill at River Downs.

"You're the toughest guy I ever met," Julie wrote. It had taken her a month to find the right words, she said. In that month she tried to put herself in Jackie's place. She would hold her legs motionless and try to get out of bed. She wanted to know how it felt to be paralyzed before she wrote anything. "If anybody can do it, you can," Julie wrote.

Her spill happened the next month at Delaware Park when a careless rider cut in front of her horse, tripping it.

As Sammy Boulmetis would be four years later, Julie Snellings was a pickup rider on her last mount. She didn't want to ride Roc Ruler, because she already had six jobs on a 100-degree day, including a ride for the nation's leading trainer then, King Leatherbury. Working for Leatherbury, she said, was the biggest thrill of her life. But when Roc Ruler's trainer begged her to help him, she did. A new rider needs friends.

This was a race for 2-year-old maidens, the kind of race no rider likes because the horses are unpredictable and sometimes unmanageable. If they don't pin you screaming against the gate, they may toss you over the rail. It is all a rider can do to keep these babies going straight. Julie Snellings sensed she was in trouble as soon as a horse passed her on the outside. She knew the jockey as a punk with no brains.

She knew, somehow, that he would cut back in front of her too soon. She tried to get her horse's head up, to slow down. It was too late, and her horse's reaching front legs clipped the heels of the other horse.

Catapulted from the saddle, Snellings landed on the back of her neck. She broke the fifth, sixth and seventh thoracic vertebrae and severed the spinal cord.

The doctors were brutally direct. They told her immediately she would never walk again. She hated them for not lying to her. All she wanted was some kind of encouragement, even false hope. Without hope, she told them to let her die. Pull the plugs, get these tubes out of my throat. Kill me, she said. When a nurse said, "Young lady, you better get used to it, you're never gonna walk," Snellings grabbed a pitcher of water at her bedside and threw it in the nurse's face.

One day Jackie Fires called.

"Remember that letter you wrote to me?" he said. "I put a return address on it and it's coming back to you."

So four years later, by now lighting the world again with her smile, Julie Snellings believed she knew what Sammy Boulmetis needed to hear. Only Julie, of all the people who loved Sammy, really knew. Her sister was engaged to him, but her sister wasn't a rider and her sister wasn't in a wheelchair. Only four months before Sammy's spill, Julie watched him sneak her four years' worth of medical reports out of the house. He sat in his car three hours reading about Julie's physical and emotional problems.

Sammy often pushed Julie in her wheelchair, teasing her by suddenly tilting the chair up, and Julie, laughing, would say, "One of these days, just wait, when I'm walking and you're in this thing, I'll scare the hell out of you."

Julie shared with Sammy an intimacy of dreams and fears. Julie would know what to say, and Sammy would listen.

"There are a lot of people crying outside this door, because they think you're not going to make it," she said.

She had sneaked into Boulmetis' hospital room, entering only after the rider's parents had left the building. They were worried that seeing Julie in the wheelchair would hurt their son.

"But I'm not crying," Julie said, "and do you know why? Because you're going to walk out of here. As low in your back as the break is, the spinal cord can't be severed."

"Julie, they told me it was," Boulmetis said. "But, Julie, I've got this tingling in my leg. Did you have that?"

"Sammy, listen to me. That's good. If your leg is tingling, the spinal cord isn't severed."

"Really?"

"I wouldn't be telling you if it wasn't so."

Racing killed her father and put her baby sister in a wheelchair, but Cyd Snellings wasn't worried when she met the jockey Sammy Boulmetis. She is 24, a race tracker, working at the mutuel windows some, in the photo department some, and she wasn't worried about falling in love with a jockey. With his shoulder ripped up in a spill that summer of '78, Sammy had his arm bandaged for their first date. But that comes with the territory. Nothing serious.

This past Christmas Sammy gave Cyd an engagement ring. The boy next door and the tiny girl with the China doll beauty are building a home in Baltimore. Something worse than a ripped-up shoulder can't happen to Sammy, Cyd thought. It happened to her sister and that was a guarantee against it happening again to anyone close to her.

At Sinai Hospital about 6 o'clock March 22, a doctor told Cyd Snellings that her man had the worst broken back he had ever seen. I hate to be blunt, the doctor said, but Sammy probably will be paralyzed from the waist down forever. Everybody was crying in the hallway, Cyd said, and then she screamed, "No no, this can't be happening, this doesn't happen twice in a lifetime. I have to see Sam."

She ran into his room, pulling away from doctors, and the first thing Sammy said to his fiance was, "Now I'll be able to keep Julie company."

"Oh, God, Sammy, don't say that," Cyd said.

They had him doped up against the pain. "I love you bad, Cyd."

"I love you, too."

"Just be strong for me," he said.

Sammy Boulmetis traded in his black Riviera for a silver Peugeot diesel because the black car showed all the race track dirt. Next to riding, he loves working on that car the most, tuning it up, making oil changes. Most race trackers' cars look like a horse slept in the front seat. But Sammy's Peugeot, Bill Passmore said, is the world's cleanest race tracker's car. That car is just like Sammy, the rider said: clean, bright, handsome, economical.

If you ask around about Sammy, all you hear is how great a guy he is. His agent, Bobby Vaughan: "He's the greatest kid you could ever imagine. You want to know about Sammy? The horse he took the spill on, they called it a nickname, Pickles. The first thing Sammy said to me when he came out of the sedative was he winked and said, "Robert, how's Pickles.' " His peer/father confessor, Passmore: "He's a super fella, a real stand-up fella who never said a bad word about anybody and if he heard you say something bad about somebody, he would stand up for them."

Paul Nicolo, his jockey buddy, went to Sammy's hospital room in Baltimore. Everyone was quiet, worn down by melancholy.

"Sam, does this mean you can't do my oil change?" he said.

On the first Sunday after Boulmetis' spill, doctors at Thomas Jefferson University Hospital in Philadelphia gave the rider's family good news.

The spinal cord, as Julie Snellings had said, was in fact not severed. The break in the spine occurred below the cord and affected only a bunching of nerves known as "the horse's tail." The nerves were bruised badly, but Boulmetis did have feeling in three spots down his right leg and high on his left thigh.

Doctors would do surgery the next Thursday, April 2, in an attempt to realign the pieces of the spine. The injury was a "bad fracture dislocation of the lumbar spine, a relatively common injury in high velocity car crashes," said Dr. Jewell L. Osterholm, chairman of the department of neurosurgery at Jefferson and a project director of the Regional Spinal Cord Injury Center of Delaware Valley, one of only 14 such specialized centers in the U.S.

"The prognosis," Osterholm said before the surgery, "is better than with a cord injury. There is some possibility to recoup use of some muscles."

Paul Nicolo, upon hearing this back in Baltimore, delayed for a day his move to Kentucky's Keeneland Race Course. He would celebrate.

He put on his tah-tah chaps. He went to the urban cowboy place. This tough kid who doesn't pay to ride, paid this time.

"I'm gonna ride that damned bull for Sammy," he announced.

Nicolo rode the hair off that thing, going around five times, stopping only when blisters came up on his hold hand.

To prepare Boulmetis for surgery, the Philadelphia doctors first put him in traction for five days. They drilled four holes in his skull to attach a metal ring. From pins through his knees, they hung bags of sand. Now Sam Boulmetis Sr. saw a new X-ray picture. This time he kept his eyes open, for now he could see hope. Slowly, the pieces of the spine were moving together.

The doctors finished the work Thursday when they inserted two steel rods along the spine, clamped them and a metal plate together next to the spine and grafted bone from the hip to the point of the break—all done to stabilize the spine, once shattered into snowstorm fragments but now a pretty X-ray picture of the orthopedic surgery work of Dr. Jerome M. Cotler, Osterholm's partner in the Jefferson acute care department.

That first night at Sinai Hospital in Baltimore, Sam Boulmetis Sr. thought his son would be yet another of the dozens of brave little riders he has seen go from the track into wheelchairs. One of them, Ron Turcotte, who rode the great Secretariat, called the hospital the other day. Another of them, Julie Snellings, is writing Sammy a letter just as she wrote Jackie Fires four years ago.

Now the old rider thinks his son will walk with braces.

"The good news," Boulmetis said, "is that a lot of Sammy's nerves were not damaged. The doctors are very optimistic he will get more feeling back in his legs. There is even a little bit of movement in the right leg. In the left leg, he doesn't have any movement, but when they asked him to move it, you could see the thigh muscles trying to move. That's a good sign because he couldn't do that before.

"There was lots of pressure on the nerves and they were badly bruised, so it will take a long time, maybe a year, for the nerves to be okay. But the doctors right now feel Sam has an excellent chance of walking with braces."

Osterholm wouldn't go that far in talking to a newspaperman. "The injury is to the cauda equina—the horse's tail—and those nerves have the potential for recovery. The patient is recovering, improving all the time in terms of sensation. The prognosis is reasonably favorable, but this was a very severe injury and I am hesitant to say how much will return."

Next week Sammy Boulmetis will be fitted with a "tortoise shell," a molded, removable plastic vest used for support in place of the maddening body casts so many riders have endured. As soon as he gets the shell, Boulmetis will go downstairs at Jefferson to the rehabilitation center.

"He can't wait to get started," his father said. "And as soon as he can sit up, Sammy wants to see everybody who wants to see him." He didn't want to talk yet, while on his back, but he told his father to tell the newspapers to thank the Sinai hospital people and the Jefferson spinal cord unit.

"Some of our prayers have been answered," Sam Boulmetis Sr. said.

Because Sammy is allergic to plants, the family has asked that no one send flowers to the hospital.

Paul Nicolo knows that, but he intends to ignore the family's wishes the first Saturday in May when he is at Churchill Downs for the Kentucky Derby.

"I'm going to get a rose from the winning jockey," the tough kid said, "and send it to Sammy."

The Tube That Won't Let You Up

GENERAL

By *LEIGH MONTVILLE*

From the Boston Globe
Copyright © 1981, The Boston Globe

A guy named Leroy Witherspoon came dribbling across my eyes at 3 in the afternoon. The clock was ticking down. The crowd was going wild. I was going wild.

Five . . . four . . . three. Leroy let it go. Two . . . one. The ball went through the hoop. A definite swish. A 30-footer.

"Did you see that?" I asked.

Silence.

"Did you see it!" I demanded.

I was alone. I was sick.

I was screaming about something that had happened almost two days earlier. I was screaming about the fact that Potsdam State had tied Augustana College to send the Division 3 NCAA basketball final into overtime. I don't know where Augustana is located. I am a little hazy about Potsdam. I knew none of the players involved. I did know that Potsdam won in overtime. I knew that tape-delayed fact already, having read it two days earlier on the scores page of a newspaper.

I still was screaming.

Never in my worst sports junkie moments, not even on a spectacular fall afternoon, the family out in the leaves, me in the living room with a football game involving the nondescript Kansas City Chiefs or the St. Louis Cardinals or the Detroit Lions, had I felt this bad. This was Florida. People in Boston would kill to be 20 feet outside my motel room door, sitting at the pool on a workday Wednesday afternoon with a pina colada and a smile in the 80-degree sunshine. I was watching Leroy and Potsdam on my glow-in-the-dark little television, located two feet from the flyswatter and the Gideon Bible.

Help me, Father, for I have sinned.
I was hooked on ESPN.

I never had seen it before, you know? I had heard rumors. *They have it in Malden. My brother has it in Springfield. Twenty-four hours of televised sports every day of the week.* I always had said I wanted it. I demanded it. Bring me the cable. Bring me 24 hours of sports every day. Bring it and bring it now. I was outraged that my area of the United States was so tardy in receiving this greatest technological breakthrough in the history of mankind.

I found now that I couldn't stand it.

Or, worse yet, that I couldn't handle it.

ESPN, which went onto the air in September of 1979, just pumps those sports at you. Sports you never knew existed. Sports you never cared existed. Ask me if I would walk across the street to watch Potsdam play Augustana and I would laugh. Ask me if I didn't have to walk anywhere, just turn the knob . . . I watched track from New Zealand, auto racing from Bristol, Tenn., Division 2—or was it Division 3?—swim championships from some steamy pool, a taped tennis match from Rotterdam that I saw three separate times, Jimmy Connors against Sandy Mayer.

It was just so easy. Get up in the morning and turn on the set. A fight is on! Freddie Roach of Dedham, no less. Sit and watch. Go somewhere, do something, return to the room to shave, turn on the set again. Gymnastics! Do something else. Prepare to go to bed . . . no, turn on the set. Just to check. SportsCenter! Every score of every game ever played! Followed by soccer from England, Crystal Palace against Tottenham Hotspurs. By God, that's old Mike Flanagan of the Tea Men out there! Fall asleep as the action fades to more New Zealand track.

I began to feel as if I were on a diet of honey-dip glazed doughnuts.

Excuse me.

I began to feel physically ill. If too much is not good for you, as mother always said, this definitely was too much. The set controls you. There is no time, nor inclination, to watch the rest of television anymore. Not even the news. There is no inclination to read books, newspapers, anything. Turn the knob. Watch the games. No need to talk.

I called ESPN yesterday to see what I would be missing today because my week in that motel room has ended. I will be missing: midnight, Martin Luther King Games, decathlon I; 1 a.m., Auto Racing 1980, A Look Back, A Look Ahead; 2:30 a.m., SportsCenter; 3 a.m., Top Rank Boxing from Philadelphia; 5:30 a.m., NCAA Volleyball, Golden Dome Classic semifinal; 7 a.m., SportsCenter; 8 a.m., Professional Rodeo from Mesquite, Texas; 10 a.m., SportsCenter; 11 a.m. NCAA Gymnastics, Div. 2. That's just half the day, with shows like Arizona State baseball and Superstar Volleyball Cup and the

Virginia 500 to follow in the afternoon and night.

"How many homes are you in now?" I asked the ESPN man.

"Eight-point-nine million," he replied. "We project we'll be in 30 to 35 million by the middle of the '80s."

"And the long-distance future? Do you expect you'll be in every home before 1990 as the cable moves down every street in America?"

"We would think so."

My palms sweat at the thought.

I have seen the future and it is Leroy Witherspoon on a sunny Wednesday afternoon.

The Yankees' $20 Million Gamble

BASEBALL

By *PHIL BERGER*

From the New York Times Magazine
Copyright © 1981, Phil Berger

The locker room of the Yankees' spring-training quarters in Fort Lauderdale, Fla. David Mark Winfield sits at his dressing cubicle, wearing a size 44 pinstripe jersey and not much else. Around him, reporters, photographers and sportscasters mill, waiting for baseball's highest-paid player to go to work for the New York team.

Because Winfield is suddenly the game's richest performer—a contract estimated at $20 million for the next 10 seasons—his every move is recorded in notebooks and on film. This day, when the 29-year-old player reaches to the floor for his Adirondack Big Stick bat, pencils move, cameras click. When, for luck, he spits into his brand-new fielder's mitt, attention is paid. His pat answers to questions are reflexively entered on note pads:

"I feel great. The weather's great."

"I'm proud to be in pin stripes, proud to be a Yankee."

"Pressure? Not really. I'm taking it low key."

"Reggie? I won't have any problem with Reggie (Jackson). I'll get along with everybody."

All the hubbub is in keeping with a game in which money—big money—is the message these days. Until last year, Dave Winfield was tolling for the San Diego Padres at a relatively piddling $350,000 a year and was just another star in the baseball galaxy, a player virtually ignored by the national press, except when he might be criticized for not yet living up to his vast potential.

All that has changed and Winfield, whose opening game as a Yankee is scheduled for April 9, is now in the spotlight. But as closely as he is scrutinized, one senses an ease and even a detachment in him, as if he were coolly assessing how to parlay new fame into the grand figure—extending beyond baseball—that he would like to be.

As just a player, he is imposing enough: 6 feet 6 inches, 220 pounds and the lean, sinewy frame of a superior athlete—"athlete" as distinguished from a mere player. It is a distinction that counts among scouts in any major sport. An "athlete" has the God-given speed, power and reflexes to overcome rough edges and inexperience.

So it is with Winfield, who was drafted in 1973 by the Padres as an outfielder, though his experience at that position was limited to his final year at the University of Minnesota, where he was better known as a pitcher. His basketball career at the university was just as unlikely, coming about when an assistant coach saw him in an intramural game during his junior year and had a hunch he might be varsity material. The coach, Jimmy Williams, was right. Not only did Winfield make the team, he ended up a starter. Following his senior year, he was drafted by the American Basketball Association's Utah Stars and the Atlanta Hawks of the National Basketball Association. (The Minnesota Vikings of the National Football League also drafted Winfield, though he had never played football in high school or college.)

It is the record of a prodigy, but the trouble San Diego had when Winfield began talking last year of a long-term multimillion-dollar contract was the gap between the prodigy's potential and his everyday performance. In eight years as a Padre, Winfield had a career batting average of .284 and just under 20 home runs a season—figures that did not add up to million-dollar wages by San Diego's reckoning.

To put Winfield's salary request in historic perspective, imagine 1950s players like, say, Andy Pafko, Sid Gordon or Del Ennis—reliable pros with statistics similar to Winfield's—asking to be paid the same salary as a Ted Williams or Stan Musial. Such gall would have been unheard of back then.

But Winfield's bonanza is the product of a spending trend that has sent player salaries soaring and shaken up the baseball business in the process. It follows the dramatic structural changes of the mid-1970s that tipped the bargaining advantage to the players after decades of team owners holding the upper hand.

The need for vast amounts of capital in today's game has made owning a baseball team a more risky proposition. In the recent past, a number of franchises—Seattle, the Chicago White Sox, Baltimore, Texas, Oakland, Houston, Boston and the New York Mets—have been sold to new owners, and another team, world-champion Philadelphia, is for sale. It is an unprecedented turnover rate for baseball. As before, the teams are mostly privately owned, but the new owners tend to be heads of conglomerates looking for diversification—and some fun—rather than individuals whose only business is baseball. Some represent fortunes earned in well-known corporate ventures like the McDonald's fast-food chain (Ray Kroc, owner of the San Diego Padres) and Doubleday publishing (Nelson Doubleday Jr. bought the New York Mets in 1980).

Even in today's inflationary baseball times, Yankee Owner George M. Steinbrenner III's $20 million outlay for Winfield is a high roller's play. It also exemplifies the kind of spending that has brought about the current impasse between owners and players—at issue is compensation for free agents—that threatens to lead to a baseball strike if it is not resolved by May 29. No matter. Steinbrenner has taken the plunge. He is betting that Winfield, in left field, will be able to reach the potential he showed only occasionally at San Diego—in 1978, when he hit .308 with 24 home runs and 97 runs batted in, and the following year, when he batted .308 again, with 34 home runs and a league-leading 118 runs batted in. "My baseball people told me he's a premier player," says Steinbrenner of his new purchase. "He can run, throw and hit with power." A Winfield at the top of his game just might help the Yankees regain the American League pennant—and World Series—they last won in 1978 and justify Steinbrenner's expenditure.

On such hopes are millionaire athletes born. It is a curious fate for Winfield to be the current symbol of the heavy money that has worked into the game, for he is a man whose own instincts perfectly match the larger commitment of today's baseball. Like many of the sport's owners, Winfield aspires to be bigger, too—his vision directed toward the corporate world from which the Steinbrenners come to baseball. In Winfield's case, it has led him to launder his personality so as more nearly to resemble the corporate ideal of a sports hero, one who is virtuous, homogeneous and will not make waves.

Of course, whether he reaches heroic proportions will depend on what Winfield accomplishes with the Yankees. San Diego was a chronic loser while he was there, and it affected his competitive fire, Winfield says, preventing him from building flashy statistics. He expects to do better in New York, inspired, as he was not in San Diego, by players who can keep pace with him. "It's very hard," he says, "for one ballplayer to carry his team."

Even with the Yankees' winning tradition, though, Winfield may find problems here, too. Yankee pennant races have been known to turn into three-ring circuses. In recent years, Steinbrenner, star slugger Jackson and departed Manager Billy Martin, among others, produced enough controversy to qualify the Yankees as the longest running soap opera in baseball.

Should things go wrong this year for New York, Winfield, with his $20 million price tag, will be a conspicuous target. But his past reveals that he is cool under pressure. From the peewee and midget leagues of his native St. Paul to the major leagues, teammates and coaches have described him as immune to nerves. And Winfield himself would have you believe he is above the pressure of $20 million. In truth, he holds a grander view of what all that money buys, saying, "The Yankees didn't pay me just to play baseball. They saw a man who's going to contribute to the team, the city and to a lot of young people in the area."

Winfield is widely known for his good works—a philanthropist in spikes. He has sponsored free medical examinations for some of the thousands of underprivileged youngsters who have been his guests at major-league games. In addition, for several years running now, he has been the host of a party for children at baseball's annual All-Star Game. In Minnesota, he has contributed money to recreational facilities and has worked to raise funds for programs run by the university.

"People have done a lot," he says, "to help me get where I am. And in return, I've always given back a little of what I've earned. Even in 1973, when I was making a rookie's salary, I started a scholarship program for ghetto kids. I've been doing things like that for a long time. So in 1977, I went to my attorneys and created a non-profit operating foundation (the David M. Winfield Foundation for Children) with tax-exempt status. . . . Section 501 (C) 3 to be precise."

The insider's tax jargon—from the Internal Revenue code—shows the sort of image Winfield likes to project: a well-spoken, urban man who just happens to be a ballplayer as well. Winfield is a man with goals. As a senior at the University of Minnesota—he concentrated in political science and Afro-American studies, finishing his four years several credits shy of his degree—he filled out a questionnaire for the sports-information department there. In response to a question about his occupational ambition, he wrote "Mayor of Minneapolis," an entry that may no longer reflect his distant goals—about which he tends to be vague—but surely jibes with his outlook back then.

"Dave kind of emerged in his last years at the university," says assistant basketball coach Williams. "Very responsible. He went to class, worked hard. Was a young man who wanted to be somebody. If he met an individual who was a 'somebody' to him, he would listen hard. David was always impressed by successful people. He saw these people as models."

The model he has chosen for himself seems carefully cultivated—part Shining Example, part entrepreneur. His vocabulary is a mix of polysyllabic words and politic circumlocutions. The effect is of an affable smoothie moving straight ahead and not inclined to reveal himself.

When he does let his guard down, the contradictions of Winfield's character come into focus. In mid-February, for instance, Winfield traveled to two resorts in the Catskill Mountains for "sports forums" —a question-and-answer format for adults and children—that he handles with the ease of a borsch-belt performer.

After his first session, a pair of female schoolteachers commended him for the articulate image he offers youngsters, one of them adding: "I hope you make the point that it's important to do schoolwork." At the next Catskills site he responded to a question by saying: "To anybody who's interested in making it in baseball, I still say, 'Go to school and get an education.' "

It is a stock image he is presenting: the athlete as a forthright soul, a swell fellow to emulate. No harm in that, particularly if the individual happens to be—corny or not—what he is depicting.

But Winfield is not always the stalwart figure he portrays in public; he can be manipulative. Cornering me in the lobby of a Cat-skills hotel, Winfield refers to an earlier remark he had made about a woman in his bachelor life and asks that it not be used in my story. It is a harmless item—one I had not intended to use—but Winfield feels obliged to negotiate to keep the woman's name out of print. He winks, he smiles. Then, to clinch his case over a nonexistent issue, he says: "I mean, I'm going to be around here a few years. And I assume you are, too. So we're"—he smiles—"going to be doing business for a long time, right?"

With Winfield, contradictions multiply. Spend any time with him and his efforts at calculated image-making become apparent. No sooner does an idiom like "talking stuff"—meaning, roughly, "ki-bitzing," or "shooting off the mouth"—get voiced than he is wondering how it will go over in a family newspaper. Yet in the same con-versation he will use a saltier phrase about chasing women without hesitation. Or he will tell you he was known at Minnesota as "the D.S."—Designated Superman—for his abilities to pitch and hit, then ask the writer not to reveal his source. It is as if he sometimes loses track of the Winfield he means to put on public display.

The problem comes in trying to assemble the various pieces of the Winfield jigsaw puzzle, to determine whether the Shining Exam-ple is as lustrous as the player would have you believe. While a check of the record shows Winfield's philanthropy is no token gesture—he has invested time and energy, and helped people—still, something seems off. There is a sense that he is working the image, priming it to suit his purposes, and in the end, sanitizing the Shining Example.

For instance, early on, I wonder whether Winfield has ever been in trouble with the law. He tells me no. Yet, later, I learn of a police incident he was involved in during his freshman year, one he spoke about several years ago to a San Diego sportswriter, Bill Weurding. Weurding quoted him as saying: "I had everything going for me. Then I almost blew it all, my scholarship, my chances at a pro ca-reer, everything."

"What happened," Weurding wrote in the San Diego Evening Tribune, "was Winfield became friends and began running around with a couple of the wrong kind of guys. And the rent was about due. And there was this warehouse not far away filled with things of value.

"So one night the warehouse was broken into and the three thieves got caught. Suddenly, Dave Winfield, All-American boy, found himself an accomplice to grand theft.

" 'I spent three nights in the slammer,' remembered the Padres right fielder. 'And I was looking at spending three years there.' "

When I check with Winfield on the episode, for which, according to Weurding, he was sentenced to three years' probation, Dave acknowledges it tersely, dismissing it, not out of any detectable embarrassment, but out of what seems a conscious resolve not to muddy the image.

Even his brother, Steve, older than Dave by 14 months, asks me to downplay his civil-rights activity from college days, out of concern, he says, for the reaction of the corporations brother Dave expects to deal with.

But Winfield's struggles and his failures, while not in keeping with the Shining Example, provide insights into an individual with deep reserves of talent, feeling and drive.

Take his senior year with Minnesota's basketball team. Others on the squad, intent on pro careers, saw Winfield as a threat to their ambitions. "And what happened," says Williams, "was they tried to mess him up, calling him 'that baseball player,' saying he shouldn't be starting, accusing him of shooting the ball too much, picking on him for no good reason."

One afternoon, during a practice drill, Winfield suddenly stopped running and, with tears in his eyes, dropped to one knee. "He was," says Williams, "used to being appreciated in baseball. He wanted to be liked here, too, and was not. It kind of bothered him."

Winfield did not give in to hostile teammates. At one practice he and his teammate Ron Behagen, who later played professional basketball, came to blows, and Winfield, according to Williams, got the better of it. From then on, the pressure abated. "I'm easygoing," says Winfield, remembering the incident. "But if something's unjust, all I can say is, watch out!"

Dave Winfield was born in St. Paul on October 3, 1951. From a preschool age, he and his brother, Steve, were raised by their mother, Arline, who had divorced their father, Frank, a waiter on the Great Northern Railway.

Mrs. Winfield worked for the audio-visual department of the St. Paul school system. The family was poor, with no car and sometimes hand-me-downs for clothing. But, as Steve recalls: "There was enough good feeling that we didn't spend a lot of time thinking about not having. And somehow the Christmas tree was never bare and there were presents on our birthdays."

There was also discipline. "If I'd do something wrong," says Dave, "my mother would say, 'Go get a switch.' It was like the Richard Pryor routine. She'd be hitting me with the switch in rhythm with her words—'Don't . . . you . . . ever . . .' Eventually, I got hip to that. And rather than get the kind of switch that'd go 'whoosh whoosh' in the wind, I'd bring her back a small one."

The Oxford Playground, half a block from their home, was where the boys learned baseball, often with the guidance of neighborhood fathers. The two of them imagined themselves as the next big-league brother combination, like the Deans (Dizzy and Daffy) or the Alous (Matty, Felipe and Jesus). "We heard," says Steve, "that a rookie could make $5,000. In those days it sounded like a whole lot of money."

The Winfields dominated St. Paul's baseball scene until Steve's freshman year at the University of Minnesota—Dave was a high-school senior then. In 1968, the elder Winfield was motivated by the shooting of Dr. Martin Luther King Jr. to become part of the protest movement. Though a member of the freshman team, he drifted away from baseball and into coaching youngsters.

Dave Winfield's baseball career at Minnesota met with more success. Through three seasons there, Dave was a major-league prospect as a pitcher. He played no other position regularly, though he wanted to. Then, in his junior year, he injured his pitching shoulder. Recuperating that summer in a league in Alaska, he was used as a pinch-hitter. "First time up," he says, "I hit a grand-slam home run out of the park and onto the roof of a bowling alley. I began to play regularly in the outfield."

Suddenly, in his senior year, he was a pitcher *and* an outfielder. Winfield batted .385 in 43 games, had eight home runs and 33 RBIs. But he still expected to be drafted as a big-league pitcher. Instead, he was selected as an outfielder by San Diego in the first round of the free-agent draft in June 1973 and signed for a $15,000 rookie's salary and a $50,000 bonus. The Padres were not contenders and could afford to give Winfield on-the-job training. "I'd play," Winfield says, "only against pitchers they felt I had an opportunity to get a hit off."

Early in his career, Winfield met Albert S. Frohman, a 55-year-old caterer, who had migrated west from North Woodmere, L.I., on the advice of doctors treating him for a heart condition. In New York, Frohman had befriended Mets like Ed Kranepool and Cleon Jones, whom he had hired to shake hands and sign baseballs at his catered affairs. After moving to Encino, Calif., he stayed friends with the Mets, and through them met other players. In time, Frohman came to represent catcher Joe Ferguson, then with Houston, and outfielder Jerry Turner, of San Diego. Eventually he became Winfield's agent, too.

Al Frohman is the man who negotiated baseball's most lucrative contract.

Nearly a foot shorter than Winfield, at 5 feet 8 inches, he is a man whose moods can swing from torpidity to chain-smoking effervescence—his words, and ideas, emerging with a fluency that troubles some who have dealt with the pinky-ringed businessman. Among his detractors, Frohman is viewed as something of a con—a fast-talking operator who is using the good-fellow Winfield to his own ends.

The two men themselves see their relationship as a multidimensional experience that combines nearly paternal closeness (Frohman: "David saw my grandchild born. My children call him brother.") with an unorthodox business collaboration. For example, they say that no contractual agreement binds them as player and agent, nor is there any "understanding" about Frohman's cut on the contracts he negotiates. *Doo-vid*, as Frohman sometimes calls Winfield—using a Yiddish equivalent of his name—gives what percentage he wants. Their relationship, he says, is based on trust. For his part, Frohman has divested himself of other player clients. And in his unstinting allegiance to Winfield, he has moved back to New York, despite the ill effects the climate might have on his health.

The unlikely bond may have its roots in the kind of extended family Frohman says he grew up with back in Brooklyn: "With my father, Louis (a rabbi turned caterer) you never knew who you'd find at the dining-room table. He'd pick up people like stray cats. There was a young Puerto Rican fellow, Victor Cruz, he found eating out of a garbage can on Pitkin and Herzl in the snow. He invited Victor home for dinner, and Victor stayed for 23 years. My father put him to work at home and later in the catering business. We moved once or twice. Victor always went with us. There was another fellow, a black man named Al Washington. He stayed 20-odd years with the family. They both lived on the premises. They were not treated like hired help. They didn't eat separately. They were part of the family. If there was a party or a wedding, you couldn't invite the Frohmans unless you invited Victor Cruz and Washington. My father died in 1953. Victor Cruz disappeared. They found him at my father's grave. He stayed there for four days. About three months later, Victor died, too. When my mother passed away 10 years later, she left Washington part of the estate."

On a casual basis, Frohman helped Winfield in negotiations that raised the player's salary from $16,000 in 1974 to $40,000 in 1975. He took a more active role in later contracts, as Winfield's value grew: $57,000 in 1976 and a four-year deal for $1.4 million in 1977 that expired last year.

Along the way, Frohman worked with the Winfield Foundation and discussed various business ideas with the player. One of them, a family-style health resort, did not pan out in San Diego—it even got embroiled in litigation. Another idea of theirs would have team and players jointly pursue available fringe revenues (endorsements, speaking engagements and so forth) and split their revenues. The concept, seen as a partial remedy for baseball's soaring cost of doing business, is to be launched this season with the Yankees. Top Hat Promotions Inc.—with Winfield and Steinbrenner as its first clients —will do business for any Yankee who asks to be represented. Steinbrenner says, "Top Hat will be helpful to the Yankees. It's something coming back our way. It's a breakthrough in baseball."

In guiding Winfield to his breakthrough contract, Frohman has been ever watchful, ever concerned about his Doovid, and sensitive to any slights. San Diego, he says, was not big enough to accommodate the visions Winfield had for the foundation and other ventures. The Padres, he claims, didn't do much better. "I told (San Diego's President) Ballard Smith after David won the RBI crown, 'Give him a watch to show your appreciation. All these years he's been here, give him a day.' The Padres were negative. I guess they felt if they gave him something extra, he'd get high and mighty."

There is a San Diego version, of course: It makes Frohman out to be a gadfly responsible for removing much of the glow from Winfield's Shining Example.

Bill Weurding, San Diego sportswriter: "Dave was always confident. But in the early going he didn't have the ego that later developed. In the last few years, his ego went sky high. In my opinion, this happened soon after he hooked up with Al Frohman, who served as his ego stroker, kind of like Bundini Brown did to Muhammad Ali. If things went bad with Dave, it was always somebody else's fault, according to Al Frohman. You'd constantly hear Frohman telling him, 'It's the ball club around you. If you had some good players here, you'd be great.' Dave heard it so often, he eventually came to believe it. It was as if—'Well, Al says it, it must be right.' "

Rollie Fingers, ex-San Diego pitcher now with the Milwaukee Brewers: "Look, Dave had ego. But everybody in this game does. The thing is you've got to keep it under wraps. He didn't. He'd come across as if he was better than everybody else on the team. Like he'd say he needed someone hitting behind him—other teams pitched around him and whatnot. Or that there was no one on the team who could bring out his ability. Well, who wants to hear that—particularly from a guy who didn't always go to the wall to catch fly balls or didn't always dive for the ball? I don't care if the Muppets are batting in front of you, you still gotta go out there and put out. Shoot, he'd just come across as better than everybody. He'd go on radio-TV after a game and everything was I-I-me-me. The guys started singing this song: "Old McWinnie had a farm, me-I-me-I-oh.' I sang it many times myself. One of my favorite tunes."

Bob Chandler, publicity man, Padres: "Dave was basically a nice guy, but he had a distorted view of the world from Al Frohman. An example: There was a banquet in San Diego about two years ago for San Diego's outstanding man. Dave was one of the 10 finalists. The guy who eventually won was involved in minority jobs. After the banquet, I congratulated Dave for being one of the finalists. He told me, 'What an honor to be in this company. The guy who won deserved it.' Then Al Frohman—I actually saw this—went to work on him. Told him: 'What a rotten city. Any other city, Dave Winfield would have won.' I said to my assistant, Be Barnes, 'You watch. After Al Frohman talks to him, he'll think he got a raw deal.' Next day, that's just what Winfield told Be."

Weurding: "I'm official scorer in San Diego and late during the 1979 season Winfield, after a great start, was in a slump and seeing his batting average dip to around .300. In one game, against the Dodgers, I ruled an error on a ball Winfield hit to Ron Cey. That night, Frohman called me at home to ask me to change it to a hit. He explained how important to Dave it was that he hit over .300 and that my call might kill his chances. He even suggested Winfield would never speak to me again if I didn't change my decision. I didn't yield to the pressure; our relationship (mine with both Frohman and Winfield) was a bit strained for many months after that. From that point on I began to realize that they were not above using people if they could get away with it. This, of course, is a direct contradiction to the image they are always trying to project publicly, so I couldn't help but become suspicious about Frohman as Winfield's financial and business adviser after that. Al Frohman can be utterly charming; that's his long suit. But. . . ."

Dave Winfield: "The people at San Diego will say anything to make Al and me look bad. People will even take the Pope and find something wrong with him. I'll tell you this: There's one team that's happy to have me. And the Yanks will be even happier when the year is over."

Even if Steinbrenner finds happiness in his $20 million gamble, it will not likely change the current mood among baseball owners, who seem bent on a showdown with the players.

To understand how this came to be, roll back in time to those days of yesteryear when baseball's old order reigned. Back then, general managers could afford to be tightfisted in salary discussions: A dissatisfied player was bound by the standard contract's reserve clause to play for his team until it chose to trade or release him.

In 1970, a St. Louis Cardinal outfielder, Curt Flood, challenged the reserve clause in an antitrust suit. Flood lost his case, but the issue did not disappear. Failing to anticipate the players' eventual victory in the reserve-clause battle, and hoping to pacify them, the owners agreed to arbitration in salary disputes. Their tack failed: The reserve clause was knocked down in 1975, replaced by the concept of free agency. Today, a player with six years of major-league experience can declare himself a free agent and offer his services to other teams.

As a result of these changes—arbitration and free agency—as well as everyday inflation, the average salary of players jumped from a reported $31,543 in 1971 to a high of $143,756 in 1980, according to the Major League Baseball Players Association. Given the freer movement among clubs by players, some team owners have tried to stabilize their rosters by offering long-term lucrative contracts. In 1976, for instance, Steinbrenner signed Reggie Jackson to a five-year, $2,660,000 contract, which was considered a baseball fortune then.

Winfield's contract is the new standard. His base salary for 1981 is a reported $1.5 million a year—the highest in baseball. A signing bonus, incentive clauses and cost-of-living adjustments are said to boost the total 10-year package to about $20 million. Winfield is not alone, though, among players getting rich today. Others have profited in a big way at the bargaining table.

In an apparent effort to discourage spending on free-agent salaries, the owners are asking that a team losing a free agent be compensated with a player from the other club's roster, rather than with an amateur draft choice, as is now the case. This proposal, which would inhibit owners from bidding on free agents and consequently diminish the players' bargaining ability, has met with resistance from the players, and an in-season strike looms. (If there is a strike, Winfield will not be paid for its duration, according to both Steinbrenner and Frohman.)

No matter how the labor dispute is resolved, the way baseball does business will never be the same. Not only has big money driven out owners who cannot or will not spend on the present scale, but it has forced teams to expand their revenue base. The Yankees have done just that. In 1973, when Steinbrenner headed the group that bought the Yankees from the Columbia Broadcasting System, the purchase price was $10 million. The team is worth triple what it was bought for, if the $21.1 million sale price of the Mets in 1980 to Doubleday is any gauge.

Exact earnings of teams are not usually known because most major-league clubs do not as a policy open their books. In today's game it is not just ticket sales that count. The Yankees and Steinbrenner have built other income sources. "What Mr. Steinbrenner has done," says David Szen, the Yankees' assistant director of press relations, "is create a very big radio-television network." That network will bring the team an estimated $4 million in 1981, according to Broadcasting, a trade magazine. By contrast, other teams will bank much less—Kansas City, $500,000, and Milwaukee, $800,000. "Take radio," Szen continues. "We're not on just WABC here in New York. There are 52 stations this year, including ones in Connecticut, Vermont, Pennsylvania, Massachusetts, Florida, Texas, Alaska and Louisiana, including Lafayette, La., which picks us up on days when Ron Guidry, who's from there, is pitching. In 1973, it wasn't anywhere near this extensive.

"As for television, we've got stations in Albany, Rochester, Syracuse, Hartford and New York. WPIX, our flagship station in New York, is showing 106 games this year. In 1973, it showed only 83 games."

Other Yankees revenues come from concession sales, which the team splits with the city; a merchandising operation that markets Yankee products—from a pin-stripe Toyota to warm-up jackets, T-shirts, notebooks, scorecards and yearbooks—and the licensing of the team logo.

Even before Winfield's arrival, the Yankees were an attraction. The team drew 2,627,417 fans at home in 1980, which broke the American League record of 2,620,627 set by the 1948 Cleveland Indians. (By contrast, in 1972, the club drew only 966,328 fans at home.) On the road, 2,461,240 fans watched New York play—a major-league record. With the Yankees' $20 million man in the line-up, interest in the club figures to be even higher this year. But, as

Szen says, "Dave's real value is in sustaining the Yankee tradition, in keeping us where we are."

Fort Lauderdale again, on that media-intensive day. Winfield stands in the batter's box, hitting against a live pitcher. Or trying to. Several of his swings result in foul balls into the cage netting above him. On one pitch, he misses the ball completely. A fan hollers out, "Reggie, where are you?"—a humorous dig, for Jackson is not due in camp for two days.

But it is Reggie's example that has become the Yankee standard. And, in its facetious way, the remark shows what is at stake here—the expectations from Steinbrenner on down to the ticket-buying public. For the Yankees' $20 million man, the erratic years at San Diego are behind him. And, as the Padres' Ballard Smith says: "For Dave Winfield, there are no excuses now."

Punchoff After Faceoff

by Bruce Bisping of the *Minneapolis Tribune*. A brave referee sepa-
rates Minnesota's Steve Christoff and Buffalo's Larry Playfair during a
fight in last year's Stanley Cup quarterfinal round. Copyright © 1981,
Minneapolis Tribune.

Tongue Not in Cheek

by Stormi Greener of the *Minneapolis Star*. Buffalo's Jim Schoenfeld
looks in disbelief as a Minnesota fan expresses his feelings during a
Stanley Cup quarterfinal game in Minneapolis. Schoenfeld took the
gesture in good humor and skated back into the action with a smile on
his face. Copyright © 1981, Stormi Greener, The Minneapolis Star.

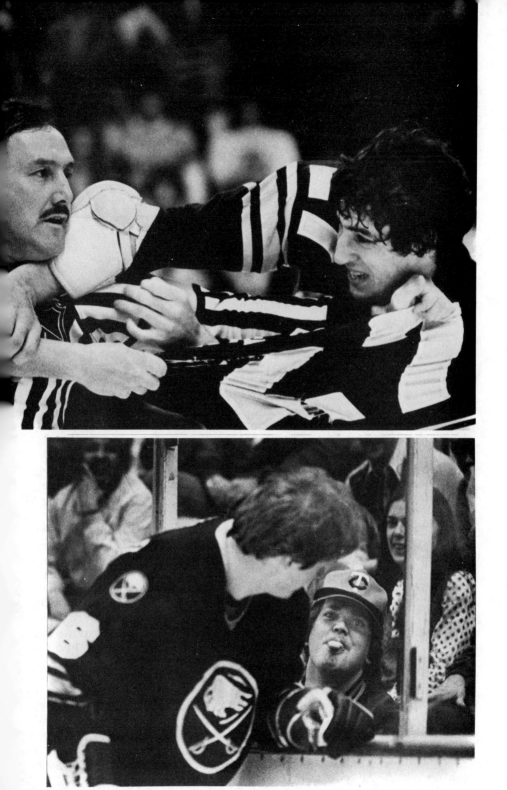

Watson Masterful

GOLF

By *DENIS HARRINGTON*

From the Pensacola News-Journal
Copyright © 1981, Pensacola News-Journal

It was a day that would not die.

Even when the sun still lolled sleepily in its heaven the pulse of the day could be detected, a slow, steady throb that would rise to a feverish tempo within a matter of hours. It was the day of decision at the 45th Masters Championship. A day that saw Tom Watson withstand the challenges of two of golfing's greatest—Jack Nicklaus and Johnny Miller—to win his second Masters by two strokes with an eight-under-par 280 total.

Nicklaus and Miller tied for second with 282 totals. Pensacola's Jerry Pate closed with a 70 to finish four strokes back at 284.

At the start of play Watson, who received $60,000 for the victory, owned a one-stroke lead over Nicklaus and but a few over the likes of Greg Norman of Australia, John Mahaffey, Bruce Lietzke and Ben Crenshaw.

The eyes of golfdom were fixed fat on this group and none were turned to Miller, a man who felt that an impossible dream once achieved in the 1973 U.S. Open at Oakmont could be repeated.

Starting seven shots off the pace, he struck early with birdies at the first and second holes. Then he stumbled at the fourth with a bogey and again at the sixth, but quickly regained his momentum with back-to-back birdies at 8 and 9.

Again, he tripped over a bogey at the 10th hole. Grimly he rose once more and clicked off birdies at 13, 14 and 17 to rush home in 68 for a six-under-par 282.

"I didn't think I had much of a chance when I began today," he told reporters following his round, "but then I thought back to Oakmont in 1973 so I didn't entirely rule out the possibility, either."

While he spoke in the press building the pulse of the day pounded with a febrile beat, its cadence measured in the intermittent roar of a surging crowd.

"I knew I had a chance of winning when I made that putt at 9," Miller said. "I've played a good tournament regardless of what happens. I didn't go down like a choking dog. I fully intended to let Watson know I was there."

Out in the angry sun Mahaffey was making a move to the fore while Nicklaus faltered and Watson proceeded methodically in pursuit of par.

"I just went for the pins today," Miller concluded quietly. "It may have been nuts, but I never once went for the center of the green. I am happy to do as well as I did and if a playoff comes, I'm not afraid to tee it up with anybody."

The pulse of the day beat relentlessly now, driven by the frenzied pitch of the battle that obsessed it. Mahaffey's bulldog countenance, now flushed with the strain of the fight, began to fall. Slowly, irrevocably, his hour slipped past, hurried by an outpouring of bogeys.

Now, Nicklaus came on, a grimace tapering his lips in a wan sneer. After staggering out in 38 he birdied the 13th hole, slipped back with a bogey at 14 then renewed his charge with birdies at 15 and 16. He finished at six-under 282 to deadlock Miller.

Immediately in his wake came Watson, the pulse of the day thumping in his ears, the shouts and cheers that hailed Nicklaus' last-ditch deeds. Put to the test, he did not flinch. A scrambling par out of the ditch at 13, a had-to-have birdie at 15 and a gut putt for par at 17 sealed the victory he so desperately sought.

Ultimately, finally, the pulse of the day became his own, carrying him to a height that no other contender could mount.

"Well, inside I felt I should have won," a deflated Nicklaus said after the trial. "I gave away too much, too early. I got a couple of breaks early and it really turned my mental attitude positive. I just didn't take advantage of it."

In response to questions about Watson's play, Nicklaus was as gracious in defeat as he had always been in triumph.

"Inside, I feel I should have won," he said, "but Tom just beat me on the back nine. He's an awfully good player and he's going to win a lot of majors. The strongest part of Tom's game is his mental toughness. He makes putts when he has to make them."

Then Nicklaus was gone into a fast gathering dusk that still heaved with the pulse of the day, the excitement of many voices yet serving as an erratic pacemaker.

"Nobody put a real solid move on me all day," Watson said, sitting on his throne in the interview lounge. "Whenever I had a bad shot I said to myself, forget it and go on."

What had crossed his mind when he saw Miller on the board with a six-under-par total?

Smiling, Watson said, "I told myself at 15, you got the championship if you par the last three holes. And when I made that par putt at 17, I said to myself, the championship is yours."

He thought a moment then said, "I won the tournament. Nobody lost it. I went out and won the tournament."

Memories of a National Resource

BOXING

By *FURMAN BISHER*

From the Atlanta Journal
Copyright © 1981, Atlanta Journal

Joe Louis became Barrow again Tuesday. In death they returned the name by which he began life and returned the body to the soil. The beginning and the end were of contrasts as broad as a chasm, and reflect the American legend. Joe Louis Barrow came out of a sharecropper's cabin in east Alabama and was buried in Arlington National Cemetery, a ground sacred to Americans who come here to honor their military dead. Just a few days ago, Gen. Omar Bradley was put to rest here. Just up the hill from the old heavyweight champ's grassy plot is the tomb of the Unknown Soldier. In death, he'd be keeping good company.

When he came into the world the odds were about as long as they can get. He left with millions watching. The services were nationally televised by Cable News Network from the Memorial Chapel, an oddly shaped creation that looks as if it may not be finished yet.

This was the second service. The first was in Las Vegas and was akin to a carnival. The casket was placed in a boxing ring in the sporting annex of a gambling casino, performers featured Frank Sinatra and Sammy Davis, and at the end they gave the corpse a standing ovation.

The service here was left to the clergy, representing a broad spread of faiths. Catholic, Protestant, Jewish and Muslim participants were advertised and all performed except the Muslim, who was a no-show. The interior was lighted up by the frequent flashes of photographic bulbs, most of them belonging to free-lance fans responding to the appearance of anyone of fame.

In that sense, it was like a Hollywood premiere set to the score of "Amazing Grace" and "Rock of Ages." Several hundred gathered along the street, in parking lots and across the way in front of the Fort Myers Base Exchange, straining the gallery ropes for a glimpse of anyone of notoriety. They were disappointed.

Muhammad Ali arrived about noon, unusually stoic, but wherever he went, the center of attention. He never became quite convinced that this wasn't his show. Jersey Joe Walcott entered quietly. Joe Frazier came later and equally as noiselessly. Billy Conn came in the company of Edward Bennett Williams, lawyer, franchise owner and butterfly of Washington society.

They would have been late, but this was one time the corpse was late for its own funeral. Services were scheduled to begin at 1. It was 1:15 before the honor guard wheeled the casket in from McGuire's funeral parlor where it had been on display during the morning.

A few old cornermen and fight handlers were there. You can always pick them out, bent and gnarled, looking out of place without a towel on one shoulder, a water pail in one hand and mouthful of cotton swabs. They were like sponges for a kind word or recognition.

Before any of them, a fellow in a jacket that said "World Champions 1958" on the bosom stood around the church door as any onlooker would. He turned out to be Lenny Moore, the old Baltimore Colt, who had driven over.

"I never met him, but I wanted to be here," he said. "He was the black man we could all look up to, before Jackie Robinson, before Campanella, before any of them."

Joe Louis didn't have to go around calling himself "The Greatest." "Brown Bomber" said all that needed to be said of him. He never had to pound himself on the chest or his ego on the back. He held the world heavyweight title longer than any other man, and that said enough for him.

He was solid American gold. It may read like solid American corn, but here was a man who loved his country and put it where his heart was. Out of the purses of two championship fights he peeled off $100,000 for the Army and Navy Relief Fund. He had 96 exhibitions for fighting troops around the world during WWII, and that can't be translated into a cash figure.

The money he earned in the prime of his time was frittered away by people he trusted. Leeches were onto him. It was never accounted for. The disgrace of it is that he wound up living on the house in Las Vegas. "Greeter," they called him at Caesar's Palace. It had a nice ring to it.

It was there that I was able to sit on the periphery of one of Louis' richer moments in later life. They threw open the hall and put on "A Testimonial to Joe Louis" at Caesar's one night. From all up and down The Strip they came in for a gig, the big and the loud and the small and the grasping. Of all the guests of the evening, one in particular stood out. He had come all the way from Hamburg, West Germany, to pay tribute to Joe Louis.

Americans have made much of the triumph of Louis over Schmeling in 1938, gaining much, much more of a political nature in time than was relevant. It was a blow for democracy over Nazism, or so it became. Above the fact that it was the launching of Louis.

On this night in Las Vegas, Max Schmeling, now a gentleman of distinction and affluence, had come to speak his testimony to the Brown Bomber who had knocked him into humiliation. They stood on the stage and embraced and they spoke like brothers of each other, and that was a moment to remember. Really, more so than this day they put Joe Louis to rest on a hillside at Arlington National Cemetery with a 21-gun salute. Then they lowered him into the ground, and that is all that remains of the great fighting man, except a memory that shall become a national resource.

Judge's Comments

Furman Bisher does more to honor one of the greatest fighters who ever lived, Joe Louis, after Louis' death than many of the fighter's so-called "friends" did when the Brown Bomber was still alive.

Louis had one of the most devastating knockout punches of all-time and held the world heavyweight championship longer than any other man. But Louis never went around telling everyone that he was "The Greatest." He didn't have to. Those who saw him in his prime, before his pathetic comeback attempts of later years, knew how good he was.

Bisher was one such person. In this tribute to Louis, Bisher tries to forget all the sad moments of Louis' life—like when the old fighter had to serve as a "greeter" in Las Vegas night clubs just so he would have a place to sleep at night and enough money for food. Louis won a lot of prize money from his many championship bouts, and even donated $100,000 for Army and Navy funds during World War II. But he was taken advantage of during his career by unscrupulous "leeches" who probably were incapable of earning a living on their own. Louis died an almost penniless man.

There should be absolutely no doubt to the reader how Bisher feels about Joe Louis. He is critical of the "carnival" atmosphere that surrounded Louis' first funeral—when a group of celebrities paid their last "respects" to the Brown Bomber by giving the corpse a standing ovation. He calls Louis "solid American gold." But his admiration for Louis is best seen when he calls the man from eastern Alabama a "national resource."

Few other Americans are worthy of such praise.

Picking Up the Pieces at Indiana U.

COLLEGE BASKETBALL

By *MALCOLM MORAN*

From the New York Times
Copyright © 1981, The New York Times Company
Reprinted by Permission

As the bus headed south on Highway 37 on that giddy Tuesday late last March, the basketball players from Indiana University squinted out windows with eyes that had seen more celebrating than sleep, and saw something that remains as vivid as the memory of the game they had won the night before. At nearly every crossroad from here (Bloomington) to Indianapolis, a distance of more than 40 miles, the people of southern Indiana had gathered spontaneously. The morning after the Hoosiers defeated North Carolina in the national collegiate championship game at Philadelphia, schools emptied and children stood along the road and cheered; farm work was put aside, and farmers stepped down from their tractors for something more important, to say thanks.

The team reached Assembly Hall, the huge campus arena where the students waited, and where the players took the microphone, one by one, to give their own thanks. When the microphone was handed to Isiah Thomas, the sophomore All-America who was voted the outstanding player of the championship, the thousands of students spoke first:

"Two more years ... Two more years ... Two more years ... Two more years ..."

Ray Tolbert had already thought of that. Tolbert, the only senior among the starters, had been thinking about the players who would return. "The true Indiana team from my era was really going to be this year," Tolbert says.

But at the start of a new season, Coach Bob Knight has had to begin the construction of a new team. In the eight months since the celebration, Thomas' decision to leave changed a successful combination, and a tragedy has brought on feelings that these Hoosiers had never known. Last season's triumph is now a basketball on a shelf in the coach's office, a trophy in the lobby, a mental snapshot of Thomas and his mother weaving through the mob on the Spectrum floor to meet in a long embrace.

Less than a month after he had helped cut down the nets in Philadelphia, Thomas decided to pass up the two more years in order to provide his mother with the financial security that professional basketball could bring. He applied for the National Basketball Association draft and eventually signed a four-year contract with the Detroit Pistons that was reportedly worth $1.6 million.

Three months after Thomas' decision to leave, on July 25, came the shocking news—Landon Turner, the junior who had been the difference in the championship season, was in an automobile accident on State Road 46, eight miles east of Columbus, Ind. As the day went by, the news became more frightening. Turner was unconscious, with a fractured spine and paralysis in his arms and legs.

Until late last season, in Knight's estimation, Turner had been, all at once, the most talented athlete he had recruited at Indiana and the most consistently inconsistent. For two and a half years he had been an unsolvable puzzle.

Suddenly, with five games left in the Big Ten season, Turner was starting and drawing the most difficult defensive assignments, and adding power that complimented Tolbert's. Thomas had been voted the most valuable player during the tournament, but Turner had made the most remarkable contribution. At last, he was more than just a remarkable physical specimen at 6 feet 10 inches tall and 240 pounds. He had become, in his coach's mind, the best player in the tournament.

Thomas did not know about the accident until late Saturday night, when he arrived home in Chicago from a trip to the Virgin Islands. That night, he took a plane to Indianapolis, met a teammate, Randy Wittman, and went to Methodist Hospital, where Turner had been transferred.

All night, the feelings came in waves. "I kind of didn't believe it," Thomas said. "Then I just wanted to be close to him. I should be there. Then I started feeling maybe kind of guilty that I had left Indiana. I felt like I lost a sense of loyalty that I owed to the team."

Wittman remembered, "He said to me, 'If I knew this was going to happen, I wouldn't have left.' "

Several hours after the two arrived at the hospital, they were allowed into Turner's room. Turner was unconscious, and Thomas had been prepared to see the worst. "But when I got in there," Thomas recalled, "he looked like Landon. He had a tube in his mouth, and he had a neckbrace on, but there were no scars.

"I hollered, 'Landon, Landon,' and his eyelids kind of fluttered. But they were probably fluttering just to be fluttering. It probably didn't mean anything."

Thomas kept talking, even if Turner could not hear. For two hours, Thomas talked to his friend, and held his hand, and knelt at his bedside, and prayed.

What Turner and Thomas had shared, among other things, was an address: Doghouse, c/o Robert M. Knight, Bloomington, Ind. 47405.

Thomas laughs when he thinks about those times. "If coach wasn't hollering at him," Thomas said, "he was hollering at me."

But surely Thomas was not in the doghouse as much as Turner. That was impossible, because no one was. "He owned it," Thomas said, laughing. "He bought the place."

Success had come easily for Turner in high school. He averaged 21.4 points and 15.8 rebounds in his senior season at Arsenal Technical High School in Indianapolis. He was the best center in the state and already there was talk that he could play in the pros. But Turner was not prepared to play for Knight.

He has soft eyes, an easy disposition and a gift for being able to make people laugh, but those things did not help him on the court or in classrooms. He needed an ability to escape from sticky situations. Once, that subject was not very funny. Now, his teammates smile at the comic relief. Thomas said: "I'd ask myself: 'How does Landon always come through? How does he always weasel his big self through?'"

Turner was only 17 when he enrolled at Indiana in the fall of 1978. His grades were not good, and Knight's tirades at practice sometimes drove him to tears. That December, Turner was one of eight players who were disciplined for training violations. Five—including Turner, Tolbert and Mike Woodson—were placed on probation, while three others were dismissed.

The following March, in the National Invitation Tournament championship game victory at Madison Square Garden, Turner scored 13 points and had five rebounds, and held Purdue's Joe Barry Carroll to 14 points and eight rebounds. It was a glimpse of what could be.

But all through his sophomore year, and into the conference season last year, the pattern was the same. Concentration would be followed closely by carelessness. Turner's performance in the classroom became poor enough that Knight ordered him to run at 7:30 in the mornings as punishment.

Turner's talent was hidden behind the black curtains of closed practice sessions. "Sometimes," Thomas said, "coach would get mad at him, and Landon would have to practice for the whole practice. He couldn't come out. He'd get mad sometimes. He'd be on the white team, playing against Ray. He'd just own Ray when he really got mad. Anything he wanted. It was just incredible."

"Hey," Tolbert said, "I'm telling you, when Landon gets mad, he can do anything he wants to. He took me and whoever guarded him apart."

But when the crowds appeared and the ball was tossed into the air, there was something missing. Knight was running out of tactics and patience. Whether he reasoned with Turner or pushed him, the results were the same.

Finally, at the end of a practice before a game against Northwestern last February 12, Knight tried something new. "I told him he should go to the NBA," Knight said, "because he'd have a better chance of playing in that league than he ever had playing for us. We'd gone through this for two and a half years. I said, 'I just don't think you're ever going to play here.' It was the first time I told him, 'Landon, you can't play.' "

On a cold Thursday night, Turner's game began to change. He was sent into the game, dropped a pass, traveled, committed another turnover, and quickly came out. But when Turner went back in, he made four of five shots, scored nine points and committed just one foul. For those few minutes, Knight said, "He played as well as I had ever seen him play."

Three games later, Turner became a starter and Indiana won 10 straight. From the night against Northwestern, in the 23rd game of the season, until the Monday night in Philadelphia more than six weeks later, Turner was as good a player as he had ever been. He had played well in all but two games in that stretch. He was voted to the all-Final Four team. His grades were the best he had made at Indiana. Just as Tolbert had helped him, Turner appreciated the idea that he would be expected to help younger players.

The coach had developed a special satisfaction for what Turner had achieved, just as a teacher develops a fondness for the difficult student who finally responds. "You've got more emotion tied up in that kid," Knight said.

"There's a bond that grows," Tolbert said, "between him understanding the teacher or the coach, and the coach understanding him. If somebody cares about your future, it shows. I think you could see that with Landon and Coach Knight. You could see the bond growing."

In some ways, nothing has changed. The leadership process has continued, and the sense of humor is still as wild. Less than two weeks ago, Tony Brown, a junior guard, received a letter from Turner. The letter thanked Brown for his care, asked him to work hard in basketball and in class, and reminded Brown of his talent. "He told me that if I use it correctly, that I can be one of the top guards in the Big Ten this year," Brown said.

And when Brown walked into Turner's hospital room on Halloween, he found his friend wearing a three-foot long cowboy hat and eyeglasses with lights that blinked on and off.

By the time the Hoosiers had their celebration last March, Knight had begun the process of leaving the coaching business. As the Hoosiers advanced through the tournament, shortly after CBS won the television rights to the NCAA tournament, Knight informed the network, through a friend, that he would be interested in talking to the network about its coverage and his future.

After the Hoosiers won the tournament, Knight began discussions with CBS about a multi-year position that would begin this season. He came to meetings with notes and ideas. "Bobby is intrigued by the influence that the business has," said Kevin O'Malley, the executive in charge of college sports. "I think he sits there on Saturday afternoons and listens to what people say, and bridles at what they say. I think there was a time when he was ready to make the move. That was my impression."

Knight would only say that the discussions were a private matter. It was not until late August that he called the network and said that he had decided to stay at Indiana. "Ultimately," O'Malley said, "I think the accident was one of the very strong influences in his saying, 'I really must remain where I am.' I think he began to see this season as a challenge."

The challenge of helping the Turner family meet its medical costs has also become an important part of Knight's job. Just as he has been at the center of storms during his 10-year tenure at Indiana, Knight has been at the center of the fund-raising effort, authorizing and publicizing benefits, speaking at dinners, even pitching to former Hoosiers in a home run contest before a minor league baseball game at Indianapolis. "I said, 'If anybody hits one hard, I'll knock you down,' " the coach remembered, and smiled. Tom Abernethy found out, the hard way, that his old coach had not been kidding.

At the start of a work day nearly two weeks ago, Knight sat behind his desk and softly dictated letter after letter, thanking someone who had done something for Landon Turner. "I'm a coach," he said. "I think that's a coach's responsibility. That just happens to be one of those responsibilities."

His players say they have not detected any change in Knight. His practices sound no less demanding. When he went to Indianapolis recently, to speak at a convention of the Indiana Trial Lawyers Association, there was the same deadpan stand-up act. Knight was having fun, playing the room, throwing non-poisonous darts at his favorite targets: Puerto Rico, Purdue University and sports writers.

On the outside he seems the same.

On the inside? "Nothing has ever affected me like this," he told Billy Reed of the *Louisville Courier-Journal* shortly after the accident. "To see that kid there in that bed . . . I've watched this kid four years now, counting his senior year in high school. All that potential, trying to figure out how to get it to explode for him. He was as close to being a totally effective person as he has ever been."

On the way to his speaking engagement, there was a stop to make.

Knight pulled his car up to Methodist Hospital, took the elevator to the third floor, stopped at the nurse's station, walked past the sign that read SPINAL CORD, and sat next to Landon Turner's bed.

Turner's grip was firm when he shook hands as he was lying

down. He wore a new, less uncomfortable neck brace. He weighed 219 pounds. He spoke of getting a degree and a job, and maybe playing again someday. Turner had gradually regained the use of his hands and arms; he had played ping-pong in a wheelchair and had caught a basketball during his twice-daily physical and occupational therapy treatments. He visited home for the first time last weekend, and his mother, Rita, hopes to have her son home for Thanksgiving.

The coach asked if Turner had the tickets for his visit to the game played against the Yugoslavian national team last Saturday. "I get four comps, being a senior," Turner said, and smiled.

"What the hell have you done this year to get that?" Knight said, straight-faced.

"If I wasn't here, I'd be busting my gluteus maximus."

Knight smiled as he remembered the old enigma. "Well, we're not so sure about that, are we? I've been there before."

"And I've been there before," said Ernie Cline, Turner's high school coach, sitting on the other side of the bed.

Turner laughed. "I must've been pretty good. I covered Albert King, Al Wood, Kevin Boyle. . . ."

For nearly 30 minutes, they went back and forth, Knight sitting forward in mock seriousness, Turner leaning back to laugh. When Turner, in a serious moment, thought out loud about not knowing when he will return to school, Knight said: "You'll go back when we decide you'll go back. You have no say." And Turner was laughing again.

The coach noticed the small growth of hair above Turner's upper lip. "Hey, Turkey, you better shave that off before the Yugoslavia game," he said. "You were going to test me, weren't you?"

Turner told the truth. He had intended to shave his chin, but not the hair on the lip. Knight offered to send a razor. It didn't matter what Turner wore, but that hair would not be welcome. "I might even wear a uniform and report in," Turner said. He was clean-shaven last Saturday when he was wheeled onto the court and surprised by the public-address announcement that he had been named a team captain.

At the end of Knight's hospital visit, when it was time to go and the coach was standing at the foot of the bed with his hands stuffed in his front pants pockets, he told Turner something he had said at practice that day. The team had looked so awful at one point that Knight had offered the opinion that Landon Turner, wheelchair and all, would be an improvement.

Turner laughed and laughed. "I'll be back next week," his coach said as he turned to leave for a dinner and another ride down Highway 37.

It's Champagne With a Twist of Lemon

WORLD SERIES

By *MARK HEISLER*

From the Los Angeles Times
Copyright © 1981, Los Angeles Times
Reprinted by Permission

Wednesday night in the South Bronx, where they'd been used for a punching bag for the last half-decade, the incredible, battling Dodgers got it all back.

Behind Burt Hooton, who won his fourth postseason game, and Pedro Guerrero, who drove in five runs, they simply flattened George Steinbrenner's pride of New York, the Yankees, 9-2, before 56,513 in Yankee Stadium and that gave them the 78th World Series, four games to two, after having trailed, two games to none. For the first time since the era of Sandy Koufax, the Dodgers are champions of the world.

"There'll really never be another moment like it," Steve Garvey said afterward.

Sixteen minutes after the game's end, copies of a statement by Steinbrenner, the Yankee owner, were passed out in the press box, meaning the statement must have been prepared while the game was still on. It read:

"I want to sincerely apologize to the people of New York and to fans of the New York Yankees everywhere for the performance of the Yankee team in this series. I also want to assure you that we will be at work immediately to prepare for 1982. . ."

Before this one, the Dodgers had lost their last four World Series, in '66, '74, '77 and '78, falling in four, five, six and six games, respectively. In '77 and '78, they lost to these same Yankees, and in '78 the Series was the exact reverse of this one. The Dodgers, the favorites, won the first two games at home and then lost four straight. Their infield played badly, they spent a lot of time complaining about the New York fans and they were remembered for all of that for a long time afterward. All the way up until this week.

After their three-game Dodger Stadium sweep, an off day Monday and Tuesday's rainout, they fell behind, 1-0 Wednesday night on Willie Randolph's third-inning homer, but tied it an inning later when Steve Yeager knocked in his fourth run of the Series with a ground single between short and third, out of the reach of the diving Graig Nettles.

And then, in the bottom of the fourth, in his most second-guessed move of a second-guessed Series, Yankee Manager Bob Lemon sent Bobby Murcer up to hit for his starting pitcher, Tommy John.

There were two runners on and two out, Tom Lasorda having just had Larry Milbourne walked intentionally. A TV camera caught John in the dugout, looking unhappy. His lips moved. "Unbelievable" is what it looked like John said.

Murcer lined out to Rick Monday in right field, ending the inning. George Frazier entered in the fifth and the Dodgers bombed him again. There was a bad-hop hit and a bloop, but before Frazier got the side out, the Dodgers had scored three runs, the first on Ron Cey's bad-hop single, the second and third, breaking the game open, on Guerrero's two-run triple to the wall in distant left-center. Frazier was on his way to becoming a three-time loser in this Series. Only in the World Series that ran longer than seven games had any pitcher ever lost three games before Frazier did it.

"I wanted to get some runs," Lemon said. "I didn't think it was a gamble."

"How had John looked to you?" he was asked.

"I've seen him better," Lemon said. "I've seen him worse. He'd given up six hits in four innings. I just thought I'd make a move then, get some runs."

Lasorda: "If they wanted to take him out, that was fine with me."

An inning later, Lemon tried Ron Davis again and that didn't work out so hot, either. Davis got bombed for his third time, too. He faced four batters, one of whom he retired, two of whom he walked. The fourth, Bill Russell, singled between third and short again to make it 5-1.

A moment later, Derrel Thomas went up to hit for Cey. Cey had returned to the lineup after his Sunday beaning by Goose Gossage and was 2-for-4 at this point, but now he was feeling woozy. Thomas drove in a run with a fielder's choice.

Dusty Baker hit a grounder to third and the heretofore incomparable Nettles, playing with a slightly fractured left thumb, fumbled this one. The next hitter, Guerrero, hit a looper into left-center that fell for a two-run single and it was 8-1, and time to start printing up the apologies. Hooton left in the fifth, but Steve Howe pitched $3\frac{2}{3}$ shutout innings and the final Dodger comeback was over.

They had gotten this far only after trailing, 2-0, to the Astros in the best-of-five division playoffs, 2-1 to the Expos in the league playoffs, and 2-0 in this Series. The Yankees also had leads of 4-3 in Game 3, 4-0 and 6-3 in Game 4 and 1-0 in the seventh inning of Game 5.

The Dodgers also had resisted all provocations to complain about anything. When a bottle was thrown past Dusty Baker in the opener here, he said he understood, that it was a shame one person could embarrass so many good people. When the Series turned around, though, Steinbrenner complained that the Dodger infield was too hard. "A disaster," he called it.

Then, Sunday night, Steinbrenner said he had a fight in a Hyatt Wilshire elevator because, he said, "I was tired of hearing people dump on New York."

Several ex-employees, notably Billy Martin, who was taken down by Steinbrenner after he got into a fight, got a charge out of that. Martin, now managing the A's, sent his old boss a telegram. It said:

"George,
Just heard the bad news. You're fired."

The Dodgers, meanwhile, were having just a great time, waiting for Game 6. They have a veteran team and they had spent a lot of this season hearing about the young prospects in the minor league system. They could see one of them, Steve Sax, apparently being readied to compete with Davey Lopes for the second base job.

"There are some guys on this club who realize this might be their last year in a Dodger uniform," Jay Johnstone said a couple of days ago. "They're not winning it for management . . . They're winning it for themselves."

Johnstone, a member of those '78 Yankees, was also asked if this Yankee team compared to that one. "Not at all," he said.

And so they embarked on Game 6. The Dodgers started it with a six-game losing streak in Yankee Stadium that dated back to the '77 Series. There are good reasons for this. Yankee Stadium is built for lefthanded power hitters and eats up righthanded power hitters. The Yankees have a lot of lefthanded power and the Dodgers have a lot of righthanded power.

"Neither of those balls that went for homers today," Russell said after Guerrero and Yeager, both righthanded hitters, won Game 5, "would have been out of Yankee Stadium."

Hooton had already put together a big postseason, including victories in two games—Game 3 against Houston, Game 4 against Montreal—where a loss would have meant the off-season had begun. He worked two scoreless innings Wednesday, but then proved a righthanded hitter *could* get one out of Yankee Stadium. He threw something in the middle of the plate to the 166-pound Randolph, who jacked it over the left-field fence.

It was 1-0, but not for a long time. With one out in the fourth, Baker hit a looper over second base. With two out, Monday slashed a one-hopper at Yankee first baseman Bob Watson, who could only knock it down. Runners at first and second.

Up came Yeager, the "unlikeable hero," once more. There might be some Dodger veterans who think they might be gone soon, but Yeager wasn't one who was losing any sleep over it. He spent the season asking the Dodgers to trade him. Finally Vice-President Al

Campanis told him they didn't intend to, so tough.

For dimly understood reasons, however, Yeager has always hit well in the World Series, and he started this game with a .333 average and two homers in this Series. This time, he hit the ball through the shortstop hole and it was 1-1.

An inning later, John was gone. "I don't know if that was the turning point," Lasorda said later, "but we scored as soon as he left." Frazier's first hitter, Lopes, singled. Russell sacrificed. Garvey popped out.

Then Cey hit a weak ground ball up the middle. Cey isn't fast, and the Yankee second baseman, Randolph, has a lot of range, not to mention a terrific arm, so this looked like little more than a routine play. Randolph was in front of the ball, waiting for it in front of second base, but it seemed to hit the lip of the grass, It didn't come up and it rolled through Randolph into short center. Lopes scored exuberantly and the Dodgers led, 2-1.

Baker hit another bloop over second base that plunked into short center and there were runners at first and second. Guerrero then hit a three-wood into the gap in left-center, hooking away from the center fielder, Mumphrey. The ball rolled to the wall, Guerrero had a stand-up triple and the Dodgers led, suddenly, 4-1. Their dugout looked like the front row at a Beatles concert.

In the sixth, Lemon tried Davis, who got an out, then walked Hooton and Lopes. After that came the RBI single by Russell, the RBI fielder's choice by Thomas and the two-run single by Guerrero, and it was 8-1. The ninth run was Guerrero's line-drive homer in the eighth.

The Yankees had gotten a last run off Hooton in the sixth, which was when Howe entered. They should have had a third run, except the third base coach, Joe Altobelli, kept holding Rick Cerone at third base. He stopped Cerone there, after Lou Piniella singled to center with Cerone at second. He kept Cerone there while Randolph flied to Guerrero in medium-deep right field, a ball anyone could have scored on without a lot of trouble. It should be noted that the last time a Yankee third base coach got an important runner thrown out in a playoff, it was Mike Ferraro, and Steinbrenner tore him apart in the papers. Ferraro now coaches first base.

Anyway, the Dodgers coasted in. The fans contented themselves with booing Dave Winfield, who was in the process of finishing his first World Series 1 for 22. They cheered loudly for Reggie Jackson, who is now eligible to become a free agent and has been in Steinbrenner's roomy doghouse all season.

They also left the park in large numbers. By the ninth inning, the stadium was half empty and if Steinbrenner wanted to apologize to any of those people, he was going to have to chase them down, or run an ad. The first had become last, the last had become first and what goes around comes around.

Sometimes it takes a while, though.

The Stuff of Champions

GOLF

By *ART SPANDER*

From the San Francisco Examiner
Copyright © 1981, The San Francisco Examiner

It is the most individual of games, golf, a sport where a man can do what he chooses. Or what he doesn't choose. Dave Graham chose to be a winner—and he is.

He has a bit of arrogance, does David Graham, arrogance and ability and determination. It should be no surprise, then, that he also has the U.S. Open championship. Of such characteristics as arrogance, ability and determination are U.S. Open champions made.

You have to believe you can do it. You have to be able to do it. You have to work to do it. Most of all, since you may not possess the confidence or ability, you have to work.

David Graham worked. And yesterday the work was rewarded. Yesterday David Graham came from three strokes off the pace to win the 81st U.S. Open in the heat and hysteria at Merion Golf Club in the Main Line suburbs of Philadelphia. It is to smile.

Flash back to November 1967, the Dunlop International at Royal Canberra Golf Club. David Graham, back from residence in Tasmania where in effect he served his apprenticeship, had returned to mainland Australia, his home, to compete in a professional tournament for the first time. The shame was monumental.

A pair of 84s were Graham's scores the first two rounds. The world had crashed down around him. But he would attempt reconstruction, immediately. That evening after the second round, after he missed the cut, had embarrassed himself, David Graham went to the practice tee. He worked. And he worked.

"I was driving out of the club," recalls Tom Ramsey, the golf writer from the *Sydney Sun,* "and it was almost dark. And I see this figure practicing. I was so fascinated I stopped to inquire."

The inquiry was not unproductive. David Graham introduced himself to Ramsey, and then, almost as an afterthought, he added, "I'm going to become one of the great players in the world." This from a man who couldn't even break 80.

Now, in hindsight, we know that David Graham was correct. With his U.S. Open victory, with his win in the 1979 PGA Championship, with his earnings of nearly $1 million alone on the U.S. tour, with his dozen triumphs in events from Thailand to South Africa, David Graham has to be considered one of the great players in the world. But then, in 1967, after a pair of 84s, the statement seemed absurd.

Ramsey reached forward for a farewell handshake. In the fading twilight Ramsey glanced at Graham's other hand, his left, the one covered by a white golf glove. Blood was seeping through the air holes in the glove. David Graham had worked.

"I wrote the story for the next day," said Ramsey. It seemed a mistake. In the recreation room at Royal Canberra were eight Australian pros. Their decision was unanimous. A waste of space, the golfers contended. David Graham would never amount to anything.

"I checked on those eight pros a while ago," said Tom Ramsey. "Not one is playing today. Two are driving cabs. And David Graham ...."

Yes, and David Graham, at age 35 and now residing in Dallas, is the U.S. Open champion. If the pros in Australia of the late 1960s were surprised, the pros at Merion in 1981 were not. One of the least surprised pros was David Graham.

Saturday, Graham sat in the green-and-white striped tent where the press interviews are conducted. He then trailed George Burns by three shots. Was that differential, wondered a journalist, too much to overcome?

"Not at Merion," Graham had said. "You can start 3-4-3 here (birdie-birdie-par) just as well as 5-6-4 (bogey-bogey-bogey). You can make up three shots in three holes."

Yesterday, David Graham did not make up three shots in three holes. He made them up in four. He birdied the first two and George Burns, tough-luck George Burns, bogeyed the fourth.

Graham would bogey the sixth to fall back, but in the locker room, where early finishers watched on television, a trend had been detected.

"David is in very good shape," said Bruce Devlin, another expatriate Aussie. "He can do it." Gary Player, sitting a few feet away, would only nod his head in agreement. The tournament, they believed, was David Graham's. They were correct.

Graham is a natural lefthander. So, for that matter, is Johnny Miller. Miller always played golf as a righthander. Graham did not.

As a lefty, David Graham lowered his handicap to 2. He won a trophy that still rests on the mantel of his mother's home in Windsor, a suburb of Melbourne. However, in golf the idea persists that left-handers can never be outstanding. As a teenager, Graham made the shift to playing righthanded.

He did not shift his goals. Nor was there a change in attitude. Even now, after a few years of polish, there are some who do not fancy Graham. They perceive him as conceited, imperious. The words by which he is described are those heard in barracks.

Still in Australia, one day he saw entreprenuer Kerry Packer taking a lesson from the most famous of local teaching pros, Norman Von Nida. Later he haughtily told Packer that Von Nida was a jerk, actually something much stronger. For years, Von Nida refused even to say hello to Graham.

He thought he knew it all. He realized he didn't. This year, David Graham sent a first-class ticket to Norman Von Nida in Australia to attend the Masters and help him with his swing.

David Graham may be arrogant. But he isn't stupid. He chose to be a winner. And he is.

Prime of Coach Bum Phillips

PRO FOOTBALL

By *ROY BLOUNT, JR.*

From Playboy
Originally Appeared in Playboy Magazine
Copyright © 1981, Roy Blount, Jr.

"COACHING? Gosh, you can do it in a jillion ways," says Oail A. "Bum" Phillips, head coach of the Houston Oilers. "Coaching is the only profession that six or seven people can be right about, and they're all opposites."

Actually, there isn't that much diversity among National Football League coaches. They boil down to two broad categories: on the one hand, all the technocrats; on the other, Bum.

Bum is the only NFL head coach who chews thick-cut Tinsley's plug tobacco all the time except when he's sleeping or eating. He's also the only one who wears cowboy boots all the time except when he's sleeping or showering. Boots in a wide variety of leathers: "Oh, I've got lizard, alligator, crocodile, python, kangaroo, badger, 'course, calf and bull and . . . oh, hell, eel. Yeah, eel's pretty. Anteater. Caribou. I'm sure there's more. I've got a bunch of each one. Three colors of eel. Blue-and-white patchwork ostrich. Oh, and turkey. Beaver. Hell, I don't know. Ostrich *leg*, that's different from just ostrichskin, I've just got one ostrich-leg pair. In blond."

Bum is the only one who wears a cowboy hat all the time except when he's under a roof—including that of the Oiler's home stadium, the Astrodome. "Momma always told me to keep my hat off indoors. When it can't rain on you, you're indoors."

Bum is the only coach who would say about one of his players (5-foot-7, 195-pound Austrian place-kicker Toni Fritsch), "It looks like a whole Dutch family moved out of the seat of them pants." Or say anything so sympathetic about what his players go through as, "Football can't all be fun. Like weight lifting. Now, who likes to go-lift a bunch of steel?"

Bum is the coach who will tell you, "There are only four things I know anything about: barbecue ribs, gumbo, cold beer and pickup trucks," but who actually knows a whole lot about football and, well, friendship.

"Friendship," he says, "is nothing you can *take* from a guy. He has to *give* it. So you got to stop and smell the flowers every now and then. I mean, you got to take the first step." Any other coach would say, "When a guy stops and smells the flowers on you, apply the proper techniques." That is, knock his ass off.

Not that Phillips disapproves of good old head-on assectomy. After all, he acquired Jack Tatum from Oakland not long after the appearance of that free safety's concussion-hungry autobiography, *They Call Me Assassin*. "All I've ever seen Jack Tatum do is knock the *fire* out of you. Make the *sparks* fly," Bum says with feeling. But Bum spends more time talking about, and demonstrating, amicability than extolling perfectionist aggression. He actually likes amicability. Even about his nemesis, the Pittsburgh Steelers, he says, "If you get beat by somebody you like, at least you got *something* to feel good about."

No wonder he's a folk hero. No wonder he is so highly evident in Texas on billboards, radio and TV, endorsing boots, trucks, coffee and a cafeteria. (He turns down beer commercials—he says he doesn't want to influence a single teenager to have a car wreck.)

Furthermore, Phillips is the only NFL head coach who gets himself mentally prepared for a game by remembering Inspector Clouseau routines.

Your basic pro coach, during the hour or so before he goes to the stadium on Sunday, presumably practices his gamut of sideline facial expressions (blank to grim), runs everything one more time through the Fortran of his mind, makes sure all his assistants realize that they have every reason to fear for their jobs and reminds himself once again that there is no such thing as defeat.

What Coach Phillips will do is sit around with some good friends, who include his assistants—among them, his son, Wade—and tell football or rodeo or eating stories for a while. Sooner or later, the discussion will swing around to something Peter Sellers did as Clouseau.

Now, if your basic pro coach were ever to suffer the nightmare of finding himself in a *Pink Panther* movie, he would be the Herbert Lom character, the one who believes in doing things properly and whom Clouseau drives crazy. But Phillips *identifies with Clouseau*. You should see his face when he gets to remembering those movies!

To begin with, he has an amazingly untechnocratic head. Sort of a cross between aging bulldog and baby bird: ample jowl, huge jaw, jutting lower lip, possum mouth, pointed nose, squinchy eyes, goggly glasses and all-but-naked-on-the-sides burr haircut. A head that must be a real cowboy's head, because it looks so peculiar, and yet at home, beneath a cowboy hat. A head that goes well with his body, which seems to be jury-rigged out of heavy angle iron, burlap and old tires.

But it's what he permits to go on inside his head that is really distinctive. Here he is, remembering Clouseau: "He runs into the hoooo, the revolving door, and (*heave, heave*) gets his suitcase caught and, hoo, he's (*heave, heave*). . . . And then, finally (*heave*), he gets inside the hotel and he hands his coat and hat to somebody standing there (*heave, heave*) and . . . and . . . and the guy runs out the door with them. *Gets in a car and drives away with 'em!* Hoo, Clouseau thought it was (*heave, heave*) the bellboy! Hoo! Oh!"

All those heaves and hoos are Phillips dissolving in helpless laughter. The sumbitch is a human being! And yet he coaches one of the two or three best teams in the NFL! A team that he keeps improving with smart trades.

Bum's opponents like him; so do the press and the public. *Even his own players like him!* How can that be?

I had personal reasons for wanting to check out Bum Phillips. Maybe I'm 38 and a bad athlete, but that doesn't mean I have given up on finding a coach I could play for, if I could play. Not one of those totalitarian coaches who try to squelch your spirit. Not one who would want you to tear up other people's knees on purpose. Not one to whom you would be just a line item in his data bank.

A coach you could drink with and listen to Willie Nelson with; chew on some rib bones with; exchange fearless though respectful raillery with; talk about your folks with. A coach who would jostle your children and dogs and they'd enjoy it and who'd want you to do the same with his.

At the Oilers' Saturday practice, I had heard, wives and baby strollers and loose toddlers abounded, and players who weren't married brought the girlfriends and dogs. Players who had been *cut* by Phillips spoke of him with enthusiasm. He didn't know me from Adam, but I called him up and said that if he would let me come down and do a stop on him for *Playboy*, he wouldn't have to pose naked.

"Good," he said. "I don't think America would like that."

Well, Phillips and I drove around in his pickup (it has a certain amount of honest mud in it, and a Terrible Towel that some Pittsburgh fan sent him, which he uses to clean his boots and steadily drank beer and chewed and spat into cups.

We talked in his office, the decor of which is as follows:

On his desk, he has a plastic Charlie Brown statuette labeled WORLD'S GREATEST COACH and several horseshoe-and-wire cowboys and horses that a retired man and a couple of other people made for him at various times. On his wall he has something hard to categorize that his youngest daughter knitted for him in school and an unframed photo of himself with center Carl Mauck that Mauck stuck up there one day. On the floor leaning against the wall is a portrait of John Wayne.

Phillips and I went by the vegetable garden that he is starting, near his house in Quail Valley south of Houston. Friends appeared as if by magnetism and began to josh him, his garden *and* his new $1000 gasoline-powered Rototiller.

"You got a license for that thing?" asked Jerrel Wilson, one of the NFL's all-time greatest punters, who is now a scout for the Oilers. He might have been referring to the garden or to the Rototiller.

"What're these?" Bum mused, looking at an infestation of little green sprigs. *"Radishes?* Why have I got all these radishes? I don't *like* radishes."

"You've got 'em," said the man who had brought the Rototiller, "because you threw in radish seeds by the handful."

"I been around the world twice and seen two goat ropings and a preacher pounding," said Wilson. "But I never saw a man with that many radishes."

"I hated to cut Jerrel," said Bum, "back when he tried out with us for punter. Cliff Parsley could hang it higher, better for my purposes. And he was younger. But Jerrel could kick it farther.

"I told Bum there was one place I didn't want to go," said Wilson. "New England. And he sent me to New England. Just because I hit him with a punt."

"I was standing in the Astrodome," said Bum, "and the ball came down and hit me right between the horns. Broke my glasses, cut my face. I turned around, saw Jerrel come running up, saying, 'I told Parsley not to kick it over here!' "

"I'm going to come back here," said the Rototiller man, "and see that 'Tiller sitting here rusting and grass growing all over this garden."

Phillips and I went to the small spread he leases for his cutting horses. There were some excellent white beans and ham cooking in the barn, and we ate them around a table set with Jack Daniel's, hot sauce, pink sole dressing, veterinary enema solution, Scotch, meat tenderizer, salt and pepper. Present was Bum's cattle partner, Gene Denges (who once found Bum way out on the range, lying there immobilized with broken ribs after his horse had thrown him). There were several other folks around. People said things like, "That bald-faced horse looks just like his daddy, don't he?"

Phillips and I ate a tremendous amount of epicurean shrimp, gumbo and oysters in Cap'n Benny's Half Shell, a little counter joint in Houston where everybody stands shoulder to shoulder. Occasionally, somebody would yell across the room, "Hey, Bum Phillips!"

And Bum would answer calmly, "Ain't these some oysters?"

Then, too, we attended a banquet where Bum told a group of bank workers, "An expert is an ordinary fella away from home." And, "When I was a kid, our land was so poor we had to fertilize the house to raise the windows." And, "I believe people are human. If you're going to criticize them, compliment them first."

After he had finished, somebody in the crowd yelled, "We love you, Bum!"

Then a lady came up to him and said, "I thoroughly enjoyed your talk."

He answered, "That's good, because I was going to give it anyway."

You pronounce the name Oail to rhyme more or less with Lowell, but Bum doesn't know much more about it than that. A real cowboy doesn't have to give a lot of reasons for what he does, and Bum's grandfather, Joe Phillips, who named Bum's daddy Oail, started working at the age of 13 as a full-blooded panhandle range rider—"just a nice, plain old cowboy," Bum says—for the legendary cattle baron Charles Goodnight, back in the 1870s. "Two or three days, no water," says Bum. "I've drove enough cattle myself to know that ain't no fun."

Everybody called Bum's father Flip. Bum got his name when he was 1 year old, from the way his sister pronounced Brother. At least four times during the three days I spent with him, Bum told some new acquaintance or audience, "It's a name, not a description." He has a book out titled *He Ain't No Bum.* But maybe having such a name helps protect a man from intellectual arrogance.

Being from outside Orange, Texas, probably does, too. Orange is in east Texas, 25 miles from Beaumont. "Orange isn't the end of the world," Bum says, "but if you get up on your tiptoes, you can see it from there."

To keep the family from falling off, Flip Phillips drove a truck, dairied, worked as a mechanic, farmed "whatever the hell you could raise," Bum says. "We didn't have nothing. I thought Post Toasties was for *everybody's* supper. But both my parents could be very comical. Around a crowd, my dad would get a laugh." The family went to church hard, played dominoes hard, listened to country music hard. "Guy Lombardo didn't come through Orange. Even if I'd liked Guy Lombardo, I couldn't listen to him, because Daddy had the radio turned to country music. And there wasn't no such thing for a kid then as your own radio. If you got nothing to compare it with, country music has got to be the best you ever heard. And, of course, it was real good." Today, he knows Willie Nelson personally.

Bum didn't grow up determined to be a coach in pro ball. "I didn't know they *had* pro ball." So where *were* his aspirations? "I don't remember," he says. "I'm 57 years old.

"Well, you know, one day you'd want to be a trucker, one day a cowboy, one day a gangster. When you're a kid, you wake up every day in a new world." By the time he was good size and chewing Tinsley's, however, he was independent enough to insist on playing high school football.

"I don't know whether it was so much because I wanted to play or because Daddy didn't want me to. He never played football. Said he used to go down to Port Arthur and help them fight after a game, but he thought football was just a thing to get your leg broke. He told me I couldn't play. I told him I was, anyway. When I came home from practice, he told me to lay down on the bed and he wore me out good, and I went to practice again the next day and he wore me out again, and I went back and finally he let it go. But he didn't like it. Like a lot of country people, he thought all you were supposed to do was work."

Not even Bum thought he would ever get a job from football. He played well enough to win a scholarship to what was then Lamar Junior College in Beaumont, but he was preparing himself seriously for the future by working as a cowboy, and bulldogging for prize money, and roughnecking in the oil fields. He had married the redoubtable Helen Wilson, whose looks years later still make it obvious that he is joking when he says, "I take my wife with me everywhere because she is too ugly to kiss goodbye."

After his first year at Lamar, World War II arose. He joined the Marines and set out to take islands all over the Pacific. "I didn't see how we could win it without me. I got to where I didn't see how we could win it *because* of me.

"On one island, I came upon a Jap who had his rifle slung over his shoulder and one foot up on a palm tree, getting ready to go up there and snipe. No farther than 10 feet away. I had my rifle right out in front of me, and I had eight rounds in it, and I fired every one of them and I haven't hit him to this day. He took his foot down calmly started taking his rifle off his shoulder, and if I hadn't had people with me, I wouldn't be here. I never had seen a Japanese so close. I didn't know anything about Japanese. Except I wasn't supposed to like 'em.

"I went in the Marines as a private and when I came out after the war, they tried to put Pfc. on my discharge and I said no, private is what I am, that's what I want on there. I didn't like the Marines, because I didn't like being *pushed*. Didn't like being told there was only one way to do things, that I didn't have a choice. 'Cause I *did.*"

After the war, he remained choosy, though he didn't seem to have a wide range of options. He took a job at a Beaumont refinery, doing electrical work up on poles. The company tried to get him to sign a form allowing it to take a small amount out of his paycheck for the Red Cross, an organization he had taken a disliking to during the war when he'd seen some of its workers take money from soldiers for cigarettes that were supposed to be free. "I didn't even smoke, but that just aggravated me. I said I'd give to the Salvation Army, anybody but them."

The company was adamant, so, says Bum, "I said just get my check ready, I'll quit. And I left to go back to Orange. It's a lot shorter if you turn right leaving the refinery, but I don't know why, I went left. Drove by Lamar, where they just happened to be practicing football. I stopped to watch and the coach asked me if I played."

Bum won another scholarship, "and with the GI Bill, it turned out real good for me. Chances are, if I hadn't quit that job and then turned left, I'd still be right there in that refinery, high-lining. I'da prob'ly fell off a pole by now, or I'd still be up on one."

From Lamar, he went on to Stephen F. Austin, a teachers' college, where he was an all-conference tackle. "When I got out, I didn't know I wanted to be a coach, but my old high school coach, Elbert Pickell, was at Nederlands High then and he offered me a job coaching his B team. I figured it'd be good until I got me a good job, rough-necking. As it was, I had to work in the oil field three months so I could coach nine."

After a year, Pickell went to another job and Bum took over the Nederlands varsity and turned it into a perennial power. In 1957, Bear Bryant picked him to be one of his assistants at Texas A&M, and Bum was upwardly mobile.

Six years later, he was 40 and back coaching in high school. "Everybody knew that Bum was the best coach in Texas," says Oiler scout Bob Baldwin. "At all the coaching clinics, Darrell Royal and Bum would be there and it would be Bum everybody'd be crowding around."

But all the good college jobs were going to slick young guys who looked and talked like ad salesmen and therefore impressed university presidents. "I thought they were looking for somebody to coach, not model," recalls Bum with some asperity. The colleges apparently had the idea that they were founded to *break* people from looking country.

"I thought, the devil with it," he says. "A man ought never to get his plow stuck in hard ground." When an old friend offered him the head high school coaching job at Port Neches, Texas, he decided that was his place in the world. "I bought me a house and a cotton-picking boat. I was just going to enjoy life. I had my teacher's, principal's and counselor's certificates. I had quit chasing that rainbow.

"But then, while I was at Port Neches, I got interested in *pro football*. And I'm glad I did. In pro football, you got no flunk-outs, no *aloomni* and you don't graduate anybody. And I enjoy the companionship of 28- or 30-year-old men."

In 1967, Sid Gillman, then the San Diego Chargers' head coach and in need of a defensive coordinator, called Bryant, Royal and other eminent college coaches for recommendations. They all extolled a guy he'd never heard of named Bum. "Finally, Sid said the hell with it and called me. When I got off the plane in San Diego, I didn't know him and he didn't know me. I walked right by him."

Eight years later, after various shifts of employment (he has also coached for four Texas high schools, four Texas colleges and Oklahoma State), Bum moved past Gillman into the Oilers' top coaching job. Gillman had tried to set himself up as general manager and Bum as a puppet head coach, but Bum balked at the puppet part and when the dust had settled, Gillman was out of a job and Bum was running the show.

Running it according to a philosophy that can only be called heretical. "When I started out in coaching, I went along with the thinking that you didn't dare get friendly with your players. You could like 'em, but you couldn't let 'em know. But then I had my son Wade on my team in Port Neches. I had no difficulty in liking him. Hell, I loved him. And I found that I had fewer problems because I liked him and he knew it. Some coaches feel that if a player is too close to them, he will take advantage of them. Personally, I'd much rather have someone I like take advantage of me than somebody I don't like."

So Bum shows up at a party to help one of the Oilers move into a new apartment. On most teams, that would be like the Pope showing up to help set up the chairs for bingo. Bum hosts team beer-and-singing parties. He refrains from pitting his offensive and defensive teams against each other in scrimmages, because he doesn't want either of them to feel beaten. "Houston's not on our schedule, so why should we play us in practice?" He sets an extremely loose tone around the office: Coaches and scouts and guys who run movie projectors drift around, visiting with one another. They get things done and go home by 7:30, whereas most pro staffs grind away at their film analysis till all hours.

On the other hand. Bum tells his people, "I like effort and extra effort. If you don't like my attitude, see your friendly player rep." His practices are short but tightly focused. "I want players to have their habits down so they don't have to think about them. If you have to think about opening your mouth, you won't be a very good eater. And I know a lot about eating. *But* you don't have to do things over and over and over till you're sick of them.

"There are two types of coaches. Them that have just been fired and them that are going to be fired. I'm sure when I'm fired, people will say he'da been a better coach if he'd been harder on his players. But that's like saying a kid will be better if you beat him. The main thing is getting people to play. When you think it's your system that's winning, you're in for a damn big surprise. It's those players' *efforts.*

"When I was growing up, if you didn't say yessir and nosir, they hit you in the mouth. They whipped you till you got grown. Today, kids say yep and nope, and never get whipped, but they're still the same good kids. After this last war, people were fed up with discipline. And we'd had a good enough economy going that people had given their kids things. One of the things was freedom.

"So a coach has got to be able to change. Got to be able to nod and grin. Still, somebody's got to teach people to care about other people's feelings. So you give them something they like. And tell them, 'You can have this if you do right.' "

Of course, a lot of coaches employ positive reinforcement these days. But Bum puts more heart, affection and entertainment value into it. The result is that his players consistently perform above their heads. The Oilers are still overshadowed within their division by the greatly more talented, increasingly mechanistic NFL champion Pittsburgh Steelers, but Bum's personality lends itself so well to horse trading that he keeps coming up with big new fully developed chunks of ability. He has swapped wisely for his crucial middle guard Curley Culp, his distinguished offensive tackle Leon Gray and the draft rights to the great running back Earl Campbell. During the past off-season, Bum traded his dissatisfied quarterback, Dan Pastorini (they are still good friends), to Oakland for Kenny Stabler, who has beaten the Steelers more often than any other field general. Bum also acquired the head-hunting Jack Tatum, who claims that Steelers ball carriers are afraid of him. "I want a P.S. on my tombstone that I'd probably have lived a hell of a lot longer if I hadn't had to play Pittsburgh six times in two years," Bum says, but nobody can accuse him of letting himself be buried without a struggle.

That tombstone would be Bum all over: putting things in perspective from the grave. After a defeat in which his team was extremely slow to get going, Bum will explain to the press: "There was a time mix-up. The game was scheduled to start at 8 p.m., but our players thought it was 9 p.m." After a big win, he will tell his team: "You know when I told you before the game that this was just another game? I lied."

Last spring, Bum risked damaging his inimitable rapport with the sporting press by denying flatly that a Pastorini-Stabler trade was in the works when it was. He went so far, in fact, as to say, "There ought to be a law to prevent anybody from writing in a paper or saying on radio or TV something that's just a rumor." Then, at a press conference called a week later to announce the trade, he explained: "I'd rather have to come back and apologize to you for lying than let something get out before it's supposed to, something that would hurt a player or keep a deal from happening."

"PHILLIPS' FIB WORKED; OILERS THE BETTER FOR IT," read a headline in *The Houston Post.*

As a matter of fact, Bum says that the local press *knew* he was lying to them all along; he had told them the truth off the record. Well, that kind of thing is liable, eventually, to get sticky. Bum expects the media to work with him the way he expects everybody else to: as friends. "The guys who cover this team have free access and, in return, I expect them not to report anything that will hurt us."

That kind of arrangement, even with a man who provides as much good copy as Bum does, can make a hard-hitting journalist uneasy. I'm feeling uneasy myself, because, well . . .

A man with Phillips' flavor, you *know* he says "sumbitch" sometimes. Don't you? It stands to reason. But . . .

The trouble is that after the Steelers eliminated the Oilers from the playoffs last year, Bum went home to a consolation pep rally of 75,000 souls in the Astrodome, and he got up and exclaimed, "Last year we banged on the door. This year we knocked on the door. Next year we are going to *kick the sumbitch down!"* The Astrodome went wild. Bum had snatched rousing perspective from the jaws of defeat once again.

There were enough high-minded Houstonians watching on television, however, to produce a small flood of complaints about Bum's language. He answered each letter personally, saying he had apologized to every one of his six children and if his daddy had ever heard him say such a thing in mixed company, he would have slapped him.

The worst thing, though, Bum's mother—Mrs. Viola Phillips in Vidor, Texas, up the road from Orange—had been watching on television, when she heard him say "sumbitch," she called him up and gave him holy Ned.

"My mother is 81 years old," Bum says, "and she is still driving an automobile back and forth and doing whatever she wants to. She loves children and she's as bright as can be. And as long as her dad was alive, she would never let two weeks go by without bundling us kids up and taking us to visit him. The trend these days is to love your parents but not go to so much trouble proving it. I don't think she loved him more than I do her, but . . . ."

Anyway, Bum is grimly determined, for his mother's sake, not to be quoted as saying "Sumbitch" ever again. I honor that injunction. But I can't help quoting one unsanitizable thing Bum told me—there were no ladies or children present—when we were driving around in his truck. "The trouble with most coaches," said Bum, "is they start with the assumption that everybody is a turd. And that ain't right."

It *ain't* right. Be proud, Mrs. Phillips, to have raised a son who can coach predominantly victorious NFL football and still maintain that belief. I guess I have ironically enough acted like a turd myself in identifying Phillips publicly with that statement, but I think America ought to hear it, whether America will be shocked by it or not.

If I thought there were any chance at all that I could make Bum's team, though, I wouldn't quote it. I would embroider it on a sampler and hang it in my home. And it would help me knock the fire out of people for my downright, by God, love-oriented coach.

Correcting a Bum Steer

by Anacleto Rapping of the *Hartford Courant*. Mark Schricker pulls his own weight, and a few hundred extra pounds, during bulldogging action in a rodeo at the Hartford Civic Center. Copyright © 1981, The Hartford Courant.

Agony of Defeat

by Adrienne Helitzer of the *Louisville Courier-Journal and Times*. John Homes of Floyd Central High School tried his best to hide his feelings after his team's loss to Madison (Indiana) High killed all playoff hopes. Copyright © 1981, The Louisville Times. Reprinted with permission.

When Martin Sees Certain Writers, He Sees Red

BASEBALL

By *ERIK BRADY*

From the Buffalo Courier-Express
Copyright © 1981, Buffalo Courier-Express

Billy Martin leaned against the bar in his cowboy hat with the rattlesnake band, his pointed-toe western boots crossed in a casual pose.

The bar was in Yankee Stadium, but it looked like the scene from that television commercial—you know, the one where Billy looks up from the bar and deadpans, "I didn't punch that doggie."

The advertisement for light beer makes light of Martin's several famous barroom incidents in which he's been accused of punching any number of argumentative patrons, including a marshmallow salesman—an incident, you may recall, which led to Martin's dismissal from the Yankees.

But Martin wasn't arguing with anyone yet this night. His A's had just lost the first game of the best-of-five American League Championship Series. But that didn't seem to matter. Martin's a hero in New York, and he was the center of attention in the hospitality bar set up for the media and guests of the Yankees.

Billy chatted amiably with a group who gravitated around him at the bar, and he was gracious to people who interrupted him for autographs, to have pictures taken with him, or just to shake his hand and tell how much they admired him and what a pleasure it was to meet him.

Billy just leaned up against the bar and ordered another scotch and water—you didn't think he really drinks the light beer he pushes on those commercials—while cracking jokes and telling stories to an assemblage which included three grinning and nodding New York police officers.

But then Martin spotted Phil Pepe, the baseball writer for the *New York Daily News.* Martin likes to hold court in a barroom, but he's a guy who loves a good argument, too. He'll argue with anyone —umpire and sports writers alike.

Martin accused Pepe of writing in that day's paper that he'd been fired from the Yankees twice. Billy felt that was inaccurate reporting. He'd been fired only once, he insisted, and resigned the other time.

Pepe produced a copy of the story and told Martin the erroneous information was contained in the caption under Billy's mug shot— and that writers don't write their captions or headlines.

By this time Dick Young, the *Daily News* sports editor who writes a column called "Young Ideas" which is read by sports fans throughout New York, had approached Martin at the bar with Bill Madden, another *Daily News* writer.

Martin picked up with Young where he'd left off with Pepe. Martin had resisted badmouthing old adversaries George Steinbrenner and Reggie Jackson before the game, but he could not resist letting loose some verbal blasts at old adversary Young after the game.

The arguments went round and round for several minutes when Martin recalled a game his Yankees had lost badly and he refused to talk to the press.

"Didn't you ever get the feeling one day in your life where you didn't want to talk to anyone?" said Martin, looking Young in the eye. "That was my one day. But you crossed that line into my office when I told you to stay out.

"You told me I was a little boy and I should grow up. Never call a man a little boy, Dick, never do that. I never forgave you for that. I wanted to hit you that day, I really did."

Martin's eyes were flashing as he listed past grievances, most of them dealing with stories Young had written criticizing Martin.

"Take a look at the percentage of stories I've written about you," countered Young. "It's probably 80-20 favorable stuff. Look at it like a batting average. No one gets a hit every time."

Martin said all the favorable stories amounted to nothing when stacked against the hurtful things said about him.

"You guys write something nice when things are going right and then, with your first chance, you cut a guy wide open and leave him there to bleed in public," said Billy. "You guys wrote great things about Casey Stengel (Martin's manager when he was with the Yankees) and then he took over the Mets and you ridiculed him."

Madden cited the ovation Martin received before the game and said it was thanks to three things: the way he brought the Yanks back to prominence in 1976, his performance with the A's this year, and a story Young wrote about him which said Billy is loved in New York because he popped off to his boss, Steinbrenner, the way every fan would like to pop off to his boss.

"Are you kidding?" scoffed Martin. "Dick Young has nothing to do with it. I get standing ovations everywhere I go in this league where I've managed before—Detroit, Minnesota, Texas, here. You know why? They like what I do, and they like the way I do it. I brought the Yankees back to the World Series after 12 years."

Young said Martin had helped in that regard—that Steinbrenner was also the architect of the 1976 season in which New York entered the World Series only to lose four straight to Cincinnati.

"He wasn't even around that year," said Billy sharply. "I did that myself."

"Not around in '76?" cried Young, his eyes wide.

"That's right, and I'll bet you a hundred bucks to a penny," said Martin. Young puzzled over that for a moment when Madden told him that was the year Steinbrenner was forced to sit out of baseball by Commissioner Bowie Kuhn because he had been convicted of making illegal campaign contributions to Richard Nixon.

"Oh, come off it, Billy," said Young. "When you get kicked out of the game by the umps you're still in charge from the clubhouse. Are you going to tell me Steinbrenner was not in charge that year?"

"That's right," said Martin. "That was a beautiful year, 1976. It was the next year, even though we won the Series (beating the Dodgers in the 1977 Series) that I saw the worms starting to come out.

"George knows money, he's a genius with money. But he doesn't know baseball. He's an ignorant s.o.b. when it comes to baseball."

Lights began blinking in the bar to signal closing time. Martin introduced his farm director and told how many hours he spends building the A's for the future in addition to managing them in the present. The farm director nodded while Billy did the talking.

"Look at George's farm system," said Young. "The organization won six of seven pennants this year. And did you know what he did with the people who run the team that didn't win? Fired every one of 'em."

Billy Martin threw back his head and laughed. He gulped down his last scotch and told Dick Young he was in charge of his own clubhouse, which was more than Young could say.

"You're not in charge of your stories because you don't write the headlines," Martin said. "Do you?"

Young started to protest but Billy wasn't waiting for an answer.

"When you start writing your own headlines, then you come and talk to me about running a team."

Billy Martin loves baseball. And he loves a good argument almost as much.

The Mark of Excellence

COLLEGE BASKETBALL

By *JOHN SCHULIAN*

From Inside Sports
Copyright © 1981, Inside Sports

It was some big boat, all right—a '79 Lincoln Continental, long as a city block, blue with a white top and enough chrome to make it look like a rolling mirror. When it steamed out of Chicago's West Side last year, there wasn't anybody on the cracked sidewalks who didn't figure a heavy-duty gangster was lurking inside. But no, it was just Mark Aguirre driving over to play a little basketball at De-Paul University. Naturally, people started wondering what kind of budgetary provisions the good Vincentian fathers had made for the All-America whose jump shot told the nation about their gritty, little El-stop campus.

Aguirre tried to explain that the Continental was his mother's, that his family was better off than the public had been led to believe, that he wasn't a flashy outlaw risking an NCAA-sponsored flogging. But the basketball program kept getting muddy tire tracks on its image, so he finally pointed the big boat back to mama's and returned with the pearl-gray '77 Oldsmobile 98 he still drives. As a concession to the demand for modesty, it is only half a city block long.

No matter now, though. Aguirre has another concern as he warily circles the Olds in the parking lot behind DePaul's Alumni Hall. A dent in the right front fender is staring up at him, and he is glaring back at it. "Shouldn't never let my mother use my car," he murmurs. "Every car I ever had, she give it a wreck first. Uh-huh, that's what she did."

The promise of dinner—turkey with dressing, a julienne salad without the lettuce and a couple of tall 7UPs—gets him on the road. His destination is The Seminary Restaurant, where DePaul's training table is set nightly. When he hoofs the three blocks to dinner, he doesn't get a chance to prove how adept he is at finding parking places for his boat, and if there is one thing Mark Aguirre likes to do when he has an audience, it is put on a show.

"How 'bout that one?"

In one instant, he is pointing across Fullerton Avenue at a space a short jump shot away from the The Seminary's side entrance. In the next instant, he is making a frantic U-turn to ace out any competition that might be heading his way from the busy intersection up ahead. As he steps on the gas, he utters a brief prayer; "Please don't be any police around."

There are, of course.

The cop at the wheel of the squad car motions Aguirre back across the street—on foot. His partner does the talking through an open window. "You got a driver's license?" he asks.

"Yeah, sure, I got one," Aguirre replies hesitantly. "But I left it at home. I really did."

"Yeah."

"Okay, then tell me why you made the U-turn. You know it's against the law to make one 100 feet from an intersection, don't you?"

"I didn't know nothing about no 100 feet."

"Yeah, well, you're supposed to take a test about rules and regulations when you get your license. That is how you got yours, isn't it?"

Zipping up his DePaul basketball letter jacket, Aguirre laughs nervously and sits on the curb beside the squad car. Now he and the cop are face to face.

"What's your name?" the cop asks.

"Mark."

"Mark what?"

"Mark Aguirre."

The cop isn't impressed and when he notices a man with a notebook at Aguirre's side, his dispassion turns to scorn. "Who's this?" he asks. "Your lawyer?"

"No, man," Aguirre coos. "He's a writer. He's writing about me."

"Yeah?"

The cop looks as though he has just found a hair on his bacon cheeseburger.

"All right," he says, turning toward the writer and jerking a thumb back at Aguirre. "Maybe you can vouch for this guy."

DePaul—alma mater of George Mikan, spawning ground for seemingly every City Hall fat cat in Chicago, cornerstone of a neighborhood that has gone from street-gang treacherous to rehab chic—has never seen a basketball player like Mark Aguirre.

And you can read that any way you want to.

The good way is to imagine Aguirre on the court, muscling inside with the ferocity of Adrian Dantley, then floating in jumpers from the faraway places where Dantley never treads. Dantley, Dantley, Dantley. You hear that name every time one of the National Basketball Association's deep thinkers starts rooting around for a standard for measuring Aguirre.

It's an understandable comparision in terms of physique as well as talent. At 6-5, Dantley of the Utah Jazz has always had to look up at the NBA's other small forwards, and Aguirre seems destined to do the same; he was listed as 6-7 at Chicago's Westinghouse High and DePaul does likewise, but the pro scouts project him at 6-5½. Would that he could shed weight as easily as he loses inches. Unlike Dantley, who has shackled his appetite far from the nearest refrigerator, Aguirre's caloric intake remains suspect. Even though the rigors of playing for the Olympic team last summer helped trim 24 pounds from a body that once weighed 252, no one can forget that his high school coach nicknamed him Ziggy the Elephant. God, how that reputation for flab gripes Aguirre. And yet it may have underscored his startling grace on the court. "When Mark gives you that little Julius Erving swoop," says Pat Williams, general manager of the Philadelphia 76ers, "you forget about his bulk."

Aguirre has been mesmerizing people one way or another since he was the 5-9, 180-pound seventh grader the other kids called Laundry Bag unless they needed two points. Then they shut up and gave him the ball. "The only reason I was around," Aguirre says, "was because I could shoot good from the outside." With time, a sudden surge of genetic juices and the fierce counsel of his cousin Ricky Scott—"He told me he'd never speak to me again if I didn't keep playing"—Aguirre tied the rest of his game together with the gaudy bow now on display at DePaul.

On offense, the package looks complete. He can call on the soft 20-footer. He can take two hard dribbles and pull up with a 10-foot power jumper that bears testimony to both his strength and his accuracy. He can slant across the free-throw lane, double-pump in midair and drop the ball in the basket so gently you'd think it is a snowflake. He can bull underneath, bench-press anyone who steps in his path and throw down a dunk shot. He can even lead a fast break, and will as long as he gets to dribble the ball between his legs at least once while running full speed.

There are those who suggest this is everything there is to do, but Ray Meyer, the grandfatherly taskmaster of DePaul basketball, is not among them. "Points?" he says, as though the very word offended him. "I want something besides points. When Mark has six or eight assists and 14 or 16 rebounds, then I'll tell him he played a good game."

The implication is obvious: Aguirre is capable of more than he gives much of the time. Much more. Dave Gavitt, his coach on the Olympic team, realized just what a special case Aguirre is after watching him loaf. "He'd be getting back on defense, going down the left side of the floor," Gavitt says, "and he'd see his man over on the right side. Well, hell, he wasn't going to run way over there, so he'd holler for somebody else to take his man, even if that guy had to run just as far himself. God, that made me mad. But I'll tell you something: It takes a pretty smart player to figure that out on the fly."

For someone whose announced goal in high school was to become a carpenter, Aguirre plays with the wisdom of a talmudic scholar. He knows what defense his team should be in; he knows when he should have the ball and when he shouldn't; he knows because his natural instinct tells him so.

"I don't want to give anybody any ideas," says Joey Meyer, Ray's son, chief assistant and heir-apparent, "but Mark could coach this team."

There is a catch, though. He would have to want to be a leader, and so far in his three years at DePaul, he has rarely shown such inclinations.

"You can tell when Mark's not going to play," Ray Meyer says. "If he doesn't think the team we're playing is any good or if he has something else on his mind, he'll just go out there during warm-ups and fool around. And when the game starts, he won't say anything to pick the other kids up. He could make them jump through knotholes if he wanted to, but he just worries about Mark."

It is a tribute to the enormousness of Aguirre's skills that the other Blue Demons pretend they don't notice his sleepwalking routine. "If you need a bucket," says Clyde Bradshaw, the savvy point guard, "you just automatically throw the ball in to Mark, because you know he's going to get it for you." Such blithe confidence is a blessing when Aguirre is primed for action and a curse when he is either uninspired or triple-teamed. The classic example of the latter was last spring when fuzzy-cheeked UCLA upset DePaul in an NCAA West Region playoff in Tempe, Ariz., and sent Aguirre running from the arena in tears. "I got my pride hurt the way it had never been hurt playing basketball," he says. "It shook me up. It made me want to destroy UCLA when we played them again." True to his word, he shot down the Bruins 93-77 two days after Christmas, dunking savagely, mugging relentlessly for Al McGuire and a national television audience, and pulling out a nine-month-old T-shirt bearing the words "BEAT UCLA."

"I can wear it now," Aguirre announced proudly.

Once again he had been vindicated. He was free to revel in his teammates' unspoken adoration, a gift he had been receiving since he first wrapped his hands around a basketball for DePaul. He was on the baseline in Pauley Pavilion and David Greenwood, the UCLA All-America, was staring down at him imperiously, wondering what sort of trash this moon-faced freshman fatty was going to try. Aguirre dribbled once, twice, then took off for a dunk shot that still may be ringing in Greenwood's ears. Even Ray Meyer was impressed.

"We wound up losing by 23," says Meyer, "and other than that dunk, we really had Mark's hands tied the whole game. On the plane home, it all came to me. I thought, 'My God, this kid can give me the first team we ever had that could go one-on-one with UCLA and beat them. Why not let him go?'"

Meyer had been coaching at DePaul since 1942, and never before had he surrendered to talent, mainly because he never had much talent to surrender to. The legendary Mikan? A gawky giant who spent part of his career riding the bus in from Joliet so Meyer could untangle his feet. Howie Carl? A Jewish boy who made the Catholic All-America team, but hardly a franchise. Bill Robinzine? A trumpet player who never thought of basketball in high school. Dave Corzine? An almost 7-footer who spent half his career at DePaul in outer space. And they were the top of the line.

The rest of the time, Meyer made do with kids nobody else wanted, zealous ex-seminarians and candidates for the intramural league. You learn to coach that way—to coach and plot and scheme. Meyer could do it all. He even got his Blue Demons within one game of the 1978 Final Four. But surely he must have wondered if he didn't deserve some greater reward for his labors.

So it was that Aguirre descended on DePaul, a gift truly the result of providence. Joey Meyer was spending the winter at Westinghouse High four years ago putting the dog on a jump shooter named Eddie Johnson when he saw the glow of the future. Suddenly it didn't matter that he would lose Johnson to the University of Illinois. Joey had struck gold in Aguirre, the pudgy junior whose feathery shooting touch blunted worries about his dining habits. What's more, Aguirre fell in love with DePaul as soon as he realized DePaul was in love with him. Showed up at the Blue Demons' games, watched the Blue Demons practice, spruced up his wardrobe with Blue Demon T-shirts and sweatshirts. Oh, there was a scare when Aguirre went to visit Colorado because an assistant coach there had helped mold Adrian Dantley—that name again—in high school, but the scare was short-lived.

"I wanted to play at home," Aguirre says, "so I could get me a piece of Chicago."

Ray Meyer realized his sincerity after Aguirre came to a game with an unholy case of the blues, then left without saying good-bye. "Nobody thought anything about it," says Meyer, "but two days later, Mark called and apologized." It was both a sign of how charming Aguirre can be and a warning of future funks.

One day he would be hugging the little round man he calls "Coach Ray" the way he did when they upset UCLA to make the Final Four in 1979. The next day he would be clouding up and raining on everybody, coming late to team meetings, not coming at all to pregame meals, getting bounced out of practice for overwhelming sloth, even talking back to Meyer in front of overflow crowds. Last year, when the Blue Demons were packing to move to the spacious new Rosemont Horizon and Aguirre was trying unsuccessfully to break Howie Carl's single-game scoring record at tiny Alumni Hall, player and coach spent night after night screaming at each other and feeding bad impressions.

"The question has never been Mark the talent," says the 76ers'

Pat Williams. "It's always been Mark the person."

"The people in the pros, they put that label on me and I'll probably never get rid of it," Aguirre said. "But I've changed, man. I really have. Like last year, there were some games I wasn't ready to play. This year? No way. Sometimes I won't take a shot for five, six minutes, but that's not loafing on my part; I'm just trying to get my other players involved in the game. You know what I'm saying. I can play with anybody. When I reach the pro level, they'll understand. Go ask coach."

"I yell at Mark, sure," Meyer says, "but I don't treat him the same as the other boys. You can get by without the other boys, but you can't do without Mark. He's a superstar."

The old coach sighs plaintively.

"I don't know. We want to make Mark the all-around boy, but I don't know."

There are things that Meyer can't control. He is dealing with one of nature's children, and just as the right moves instinctively come to Aguirre on the floor, so do the off-court moves that perplex his elders. To them, he is almost alien at times, glowering, seldom speaking. Yet to the friends he confides in, this shell is nothing more than the natural by-product of fame. "He got to do this, he got to do that," says Bernard Randolph, who followed him from Westinghouse High School and became DePaul's sixth man. "Everywhere he go, he got to be Mark Aguirre."

Nobody will ever mistake him for just another DePaul junior schlepping to school on the El, then hurrying down to Kroch's & Brentano's to stock the shelves with best-sellers. He is the 1980 College Player of the Year, the shooting machine who shattered Corzine's career scoring record midway through this season. He is someone special, and being special is not without the price he has just begun to pay.

The first installment came due at DePaul last season when he fathered a daughter out of wedlock. "We have a very conservative faculty here," says one of its more liberal members, "and when they heard that Mark wasn't getting married, they were shocked." But Aguirre held his ground, debating the issue in a philosophy class and declaring loudly, "I'm not ashamed of my baby."

Erika Allen was the product of a short-term romance that perhaps was never destined for the altar, a romance that flowered amid the questionable ambience of a South Side summer basketball tournament. "Mark didn't even want to go at first," says DePaul guard Skip Dillard, a friend and teammate since the two of them were 12. "Only reason he went to the tourmanent at all was because I said there was going to be lots of girls there." Dillard quickly tired of the available leg, but Aguirre remained until he sealed the liaison that made him a father who visits his daughter on weekends at her maternal grandparents' home. While it doesn't sound like much, it is more than he sees of his child's mother.

"She's going to nursing school right now," he says. "In Peoria, I think it is. She just briefly told me about it."

He stares down at the record album he is carrying.

"We're real close," he says softly.

The name of the album is "At Peace With Woman."

There was never a word that Mark Aguirre's mother was pregnant. Maybe it was because everybody had the blues 21 years ago about daddy selling the farm in Arkansas, acknowledging at last that none of his sons wanted to stay home and work those 80 acres. Maybe it was because of the excitement over the move to Chicago, daddy in his faithful pickup truck, mama and the expectant Mary on the train. Who knows?

The verifiable answers didn't start coming in until December 10, 1959, when the three of them arrived in that strange northern city. At midday, mama called her eldest daughter, a strong-willed storekeeper who had already settled there, and said Mary was sick.

"So I took her over to Cook County Hospital," Tiny Dinwiddle Scott says, "and that's where Mary had little Mark."

He weighed 8 pounds, 11½ ounces and had the beginnings of the hands Ray Meyer would later compare to toilet seats. "When we got home," Tiny recalls, "I said, 'Lord, Mary, will you look there? Little bitty baby and big old hands like that.'"

Tiny can wax poetic on them or most anything else. "I'm a big talker," she says proudly. But on the subject of Mark's father, a slight postal worker named Clyde Aguirre, her expansiveness quickly shrinks. Clyde Aguirre did not stay long with his family and he is regarded now as if he never existed.

"You just have to put some spaces in there," Tiny says.

The spaces seem bigger than ever when you realize that Mark's mother isn't going to fill them in for public consumption. "She's hidden from us, she's hidden from everybody," says a member of the DePaul coaching staff. The response seems somehow childlike, yet it fits the way Tiny Scott thinks of Mary. "She's my baby sister; I'm 16 years older than she is," Tiny says. "Her, Mark, they both my children."

Tiny's children live in an inner-city stereotype that seems to be substantiated by the talk about Clyde Aguirre's shadowy fatherhood and his divorce from Mary about a decade later. It all appears as predictable as the vacant lots, boarded-up windows and abandoned automobiles on the 1300 block of South Karlov Avenue, where Mark Aguirre spent the first 15 years of his life.

They call the neighborhood "K Town" because of the street names—Karlov, Kedvale, Kedzie, Keeler, Kostner, Kilbourn. "It's a jungle," says Skip Dillard, who grew up there, too. And the jungle is ruled by the West Side's cruelest gangs. The Four-Corner Hustlers. The Vice Lords. The Souls. They used to chase each other through the pickup basketball games at Bryant Elementary School, which sat outside Mark's back door. They carried knives, chains, sticks, rocks.

And guns. You always knew they had guns. "One time we went out to play ball," Dillard says, "and we seen a guy that had been shot."

"You hear bang-bang," Tiny Scott says as she stares out the window at the emptiness across the street from her corner grocery store. "Okay, you hear, uh-huh. Where you going to run to? K Town, to me, is home. If there's something better, I don't know about it."

The stereotype stops at Tiny.

It was she who encouraged her four brothers and two sisters to come north. By the time she was finished, almost the whole block was family. And the family ate dinner together after church on Sunday, helped shoulder each other's burdens and watched out for each other's kids. "I guess we was pretty emotional," Mark says. "Whenever there was any kind of crisis, everybody would be there helping."

Time brought changes. Mark, so overweight and withdrawn as a child, sprouted into the giant who worked such wonders with a basketball that gang members gathered to drink wine and watch him. His grandmother, Cora Dinwiddie, died when he was 13 and, says Aunt Tiny, "He was surely his grandma's boy." His mother got married again, this time to Wesley Ross, the owner of a trucking company, a man who could put her and Mark and her three daughters in a big house a couple of miles from Karlov. The old house caught fire one night and burned to the ground, leaving yet another space in K Town.

"But, you know, that Mark, he still calls me every week. He still stops by and sees me whenever he can," Tiny says. "There's no snobbish in him. Now that's a miracle these days, isn't it?"

Perhaps it is testimony to the appeal of the corner grocery store that it has no name out front and greets its customers with this felt-tip proclamation: "You must buy at least $1.00 in all meat." Aguirre, Skip Dillard and Bernard Randolph scarcely notice the symbols of hard times, though. They are too busy taking advantage of Tiny's family discount (translation: no charge), charming the Hostess Cakes delivery man out of a box of Twinkies and astounding Terry Cummings, the gentle muscleman who plays center for DePaul.

When Aguirre goes to wash down his share of the Twinkies with a quart of milk, Cummings proves he's a stranger in K Town. "You're going to drink that by yourself?" he asks.

"Sure," Aguirre chirps merrily. "That's the way we do things around here.

Basketball is the No. 1 sport at DePaul University. Trying to figure out Mark Aguirre runs a close second.

He never shows anyone the same face two days in a row, and the result has been as many opinions about him as he has moods. The opinions range from the obtuse—"He's deep and he isn't"—to the cynical—"He's an actor; he wants to keep you off balance so he can have his way with you." Lately, however, there has been a tacit moratorium on the amateur psychoanalysis, primarily because in the town where you can see a man dance with his wife, you can now also see Mark Aguirre dive on the floor for a loose ball.

"That," says assistant coach Jim Molinari, "is a first."

The first of what, though? Of the changes that will turn Aguirre into the good soldier everyone thinks he should be? In Ray Meyer's office, with the thump-thump-thump of the handball court next door punctuating every sentence, the old coach is telling himself exactly that. "There's no sense in saying we made him into the player he is," Meyer says. "All we're doing is maturing him."

If that is indeed what is happening, Meyer's blend of screaming and back-patting is part of the story, but not all of it. The rest is rooted in the gauntlet Aguirre has been running for the past year.

He began his long, strange trip by flirting with the same sweet temptress who will be back this spring—the NBA draft. It would have been easier on the nerves to straight-arm the agents who came around eager to do his bidding. Instead, he enlisted one Charles Tucker to serve as his middleman—not his agent, mind you; and agent would have made him a pro. Tucker, the Michigan-based psychologist who held Magic Johnson's hand in similar circumstances the year before, screened the offers, rumors and gossip. And Aguirre listened, suffered and brooded, for no team could promise it would deliver on his dream of a five-year, $1.5 million no-cut contract.

Since the Celtics had the first pick last spring and, after failing to woo Ralph Sampson into the pros, expressed an interest in Kevin McHale, Aguirre would have been left dangling. Obviously, the Celtics were the only team with a guaranteed first-round pick. Any other franchise could have been cut off at the pass by another team which drafted ahead of it.

"I have decided," Aguirre announced after a sleepless April night, "that I have a love for more than money."

It may not have been the whole truth, but Aguirre had been force-fed enough reality for the time being. He realized that, as he says now, "you make yourself crazy if you wait till the last minute the way I did." And, although he didn't verbalize it, he seemed to understand that he had some work to do on his game and his image. "For the first time," says Rod Thorn, general manager of the Chicago Bulls, "I think Mark figured out that the sun doesn't rise and set on him."

Maybe that was why he played for the U.S. Olympic team last summer. He certainly didn't have to. Look at the ease with which Ralph Sampson of Virginia said no to the red, white and blue. "We weren't going to Moscow," says Dave Gavitt, the wise man from Providence who coached the Olympians, "but we were going to play a series of games against the best players from the NBA. I thought that ought to be a helluva thrill for any kid." It was enough for Aguirre, who willingly banged heads and bodies with teammates Michael Brooks of LaSalle and Danny Vranes of Utah, did his share of the rebounding and passing, and kept his mouth shut when he only played 24 minutes a game. "He did the dirty work," Gavitt says, "and he was still the greatest talent we had."

Only once did Aguirre act like he knew it. In Phoenix, with the NBA stars on the ropes, Gavitt's assistant, Larry Brown of UCLA, yelled at him to shake a tailfeather on defense and Aguirre responded with a snippy "Yes, sir!"

"I yanked him right there," Gavitt says. "Told him to clean up his act. I told him he wasn't playing for some Catholic boys' school in New Orleans where he could get away with that crap. Then he went back out and played like hell."

The fire and brimstone has stayed with Aguirre this season at DePaul. After Georgetown outrebounded the Blue Demons by 19, he tore into San Diego State for eight rebounds in the first half alone. When his teammates turned to stone on offense against Maine, he boogied for 47 points, hitting eight of nine shots from the field in one stretch and leaving Ray Meyer mumbling that only seven-foot centers are supposed to dominate games that way.

It is hard to believe that in DePaul's home opener, with Gonzaga down by 22, Aguirre was overcome by disinterest, threw away three straight passes and found himself on the bench next to Meyer engaging in acrimonious debate. The next day, Meyer kicked him out of practice for sulking while an assistant coach muttered, "He'll always be a shitass." A week later, they all resumed talking about how much Mark had changed for the better.

"So what are we going to do with you?" The cop is obviously enjoying a pliable audience. "Think we ought to take you to the station downtown and book you?"

"Ohhhh, man," Aguirre says, smiling as if he isn't sure he is being kidded.

"You broke a law, didn't you?"

"Yeah."

"Well, I got to do something, right?"

"Uh-huh. I guess."

"How about this? How about you spell the word DePaul for me? You do that and you walk, huh? How about it?"

"Sure. D-e-p-a-u-l."

"Wrong."

Aguirre's baffled smile suddenly reappears.

"It's capital P. Now get out of here."

Aguirre does as he is told, heading back across Fullerton Avenue, back toward The Seminary and some dinner. He pauses only long enough to take another look at his dented Olds, and when he does, his smile changes character, becoming strangely triumphant. "If the police seen that," he says, pointing to a temporary license sticker that expired three weeks ago, "I would've gone to jail for sure."

Mark Aguirre likes to think that nobody will ever catch him.

Judge's Comments

John Schulian likes to examine more than an athlete's raw numbers. He looks at the whole person, the good and bad, and with Mark Aguirre, he does it eloquently.

Aguirre was a phenomenal basketball player for DePaul University. Chosen as the 1980 College Player of the Year, Aguirre had more talent than many players who play professionally. But Aguirre also was human, and he suffered from the same problems that affect us all. Schulian doesn't let us forget it.

Born and raised a poor black in Chicago, Aguirre was able to escape the ghetto—with a basketball. He went to DePaul University, a small Jesuit school in his hometown, not to study physics or chemistry, but to play basketball.

A very emotional person, Aguirre often allowed his personal problems to interfere with his play on the court. He would sulk, pout, cry and engage in angry shouting matches with his coach, the legendary Ray Meyer, in full view of fans and teammates.

In recalling one of Aguirre's tirades, a DePaul assistant coach said of Aguirre, "He'll always be a shitass." That statement may or may not be true. But Schulian leaves little doubt to the reader that Aguirre is a unique, but troubled individual—with or without a basketball.

Love Letters?

GENERAL

By *HAL LEBOVITZ*

From the Cleveland Plain Dealer
Copyright © 1981, The Plain Dealer

Dear George,
   It's all over town that you signed Dave Winfield for $1.4 million. That's more than three times what I'm getting. Remember how you always said I'd be No. 1?

Your obedient right fielder,
(Signed) **REGGIE**

Dear Reggie,
   You're still No. 1 with me. I eat a Reggie Bar every day. You should thank me for getting Winfield. He'll bat behind you and that's going to make you a better hitter. You'll be greater than ever.

GEORGE
President, New York Bankees

Dear George,
   I've always been a better hitter than this guy. And don't avoid the subject. Am I or am I not supposed to be the highest-paid player on the Bankees?

REGGIE

Dear Reggie,
   Well, you're still second. Things happen. I didn't want to let Winfield sign with the Mets. You're still my absolute favorite. We'll make it up to you. We'll get you a few more personal appearances.

GEORGE

Dear George,
   Don't do me any favors. I can get my own personal appearances. Let's talk numbers. How can a man live on $412,000 in New York?

REGGIE

Dear Reggie,
   Have another good year and you'll be right on the top again.

GEORGE

Dear George,
    Promises, promises. I just read that the arbitrator gave Rick Cerone $440,000. That makes me No. 3 in the Bankees' salary parade.

REGGIE

Dear Reggie,
    You can't blame me for what some stupid arbitrator did. The guy probably never saw a game. Now Reggie, you know I love you. Today I ate two Reggie Bars.

GEORGE

Dear George,
    Today I just found out that Bob Watson made $537,000 last year, his first as a Bankee. How could you do this to me?

REGGIE

Dear Reggie,
    How did you find out?

GEORGE

Dear George,
    And today I learned that Graig Nettles makes $508,000. That puts me fifth on your list. So, I'm still No. 1 in your heart? Where am I in your pocketbook?

REGGIE

Dear Reggie,
    What about all your fringe benefits and the thrill of wearing a pinstriped Bankee uniform?

GEORGE

Dear George,
    I'll bet the other guys have all the same fringes and they've got the pinstripes, too. I can't believe you any more. Today I found out Tommy John is making $495,000. That makes me No. 6.

REGGIE

Dear Reggie,
    Who's the squealer?

GEORGE

Dear George,
    And I forgot about Oscar Gamble. He's making $478,000. Now I'm seventh.

REGGIE

Dear Reggie,
    Aw pal, you can't blame me for that one. Gamble got that deal when he was with the San Diego Padres. Ray Kroc gave it to him. Kroc must have a head like a hamburger to give Gamble all that money.

GEORGE

Dear George,
     Yeah, but you picked up Oscar's salary. Who's the real hamburger?

REGGIE

Dear Reggie,
     You know I'm in your corner. We have a meeting at my American Ship Building Company today. I'm going to ask them to name a ship after you. That's better than a candy bar.

GEORGE

Dear George,
     You know what you can do with your ship. If you promised me a canoe you'd charge me for the paddles. I found out today that Rick Gossage makes $480,000. That makes me No. 8. Me, the man who puts people in the park, and led you to a championship. Me, No. 8 in your money lineup. I can't hold up my head.
                    Your former obedient right fielder,
REGGIE

Dear Reggie,
     Aw, Reggie . . .

GEORGE

Dear George,
     What do you mean "Aw, Reggie"? If you don't give me more than a paltry $412,000 next year I'll go to the Mets.

REGGIE

Dear Reggie,
     How could you become a Met after all we've meant to each other? Have you no loyalty? I have proof of mine. Enclosed are three Reggie Bar wrappers. I ate them all myself. And, believe me, that wasn't easy.

GEORGE

Dear George,
     This is to notify you that as of today I have formed a syndicate. Winfield, Watson, Nettles, John, Gamble, Gossage, Cerone and myself are pooling our salaries. We have come up with an offer to buy the Bankees, one your partners can't afford to refuse. You can have all your shipyards, boats, race tracks, hotels and real estate. Without the Bankees you won't get a headline. You're nothing.
                    Future president of the Bankees
REGGIE

Dear Reggie,
     Please come into my office immediately. I'm tearing up your contract. Who's Winfield? You're my No. 1 forever and ever.
                    Affectionately,
GEORGE

Ilie Nastase:
The Tragic Twilight

TENNIS

By *PETER BODO*

From Tennis Magazine
Copyright © 1981, Golf Digest/Tennis, Inc.

"Is fantastic, no?" Ilie Nastase asked me, as he waved at the cluttered table that stood like a defiant gesture against the stark, contemporary furnishings of the hotel room high above suburban Memphis. Nastase's voice filled with wonder: "I never see nothing like it—never. I don't even know how it works." Nastase laughed and then added: "But it's fantastic, I can't stop looking at it."

Nastase was talking about a clock, one of the three he had purchased on an impulse a few days earlier in Chicago. The "fantastic" one was encased in a horizontal chrome cylinder about eight inches in diameter. The face of the clock lacked numerals. Instead, two lines—set at right angles like the crosshairs of a rifle sight—quartered the clock's face. The hour and minute hands were mere black slivers, and the second hand wasn't even a hand; just a disc as big as a silver dollar freely wandering around the clock's face. The most fantastic part of all was the way the clock's face changed colors, from passionate red to orange to magenta to melancholy blue.

Still dressed in his wet tennis clothes, Nastase flopped into a white wire chair. Just an hour earlier, he had lost in the first round of the U.S. National Indoor Championships, lost in straight sets to Jim Delaney, a qualifier who ranked 270th in the world. Nastase looked at the television, but he couldn't resist glancing over to the clock. "You should see it in the night," he said. "If I wake up in the dark and see the clock, it is really something—strong, like the sun. . . ."

Nastase popped out of his chair. The only two racquets he had brought to Memphis fell to the carpet. The racquets were different models. Neither of them had a cover. The room went dark as Nastase switched off the lights, leaving it illuminated only by the vivid, slightly disconcerting light of time passing in colors—time passing for the vibrant, unforgettable genius of a tennis player whose career, like his moods, has been a sequence of dramatic colors.

The clock slowly turned blue, deep blue as the days have been for Nastase for well over a year. In the darkness, I could hear the words Peter Fleming had spoken earlier in the day, in the locker room of the Racquet Club of Memphis: "Look, I know that everybody thinks Nasty's a big joke now, I know they say he's gone off the deep end. But I wish he'd get his stuff together. Physically, he can still play. Maybe he is a basket case mentally, I don't know. But I know he's better than No. 79 in the world. And there's no need to trash him, he's a good man."

Suddenly, the lights went on again. Nastase returned to his chair and began to strip off his shirt. His eyes settled on the television that is always on to ward off the loneliness of a hotel room. Besides, he was going to talk about his troubles. And if you are going to reveal some of your deeper feelings to a guy like me with a notebook, it is easier for both of you if there is something to look at besides each other.

"I lost a little speed, maybe a step or two, and I lost some confidence," Nastase began without benefit of a question. "When you lose your confidence, everything else goes. You eat bad, you sleep bad, you don't practice." Nastase paused. He continued in a quicker, anxious tone: "One day, I'll wake up and decide I won't play any more. I don't enjoy losing. But I would miss the tour too much. The tour is something inside me."

It was the fierce confession of a man who has spent almost two full decades playing tennis, playing more demanding, mentally debilitating tennis than any man alive. Many people feel he played too much, left too much of his fluid, poetic game on overnight flights between continents, and in cowtowns all over the world.

Nastase is 35 now, and critics whisper that his nerves are shot, burned to cinders like the elements of an overused appliance. Harold Solomon says he hasn't seen "competitive fire" in Nastase for about four years. But Nastase doesn't see the cost of his fame and wealth in those terms. To him, it is more painful, more desperate.

"Tennis is a very dangerous life," he said somberly. His tanned, youthful face grew old and sad. He let the wet shirt fall to the carpet. "Tennis cost me my family because it isn't a normal life," he went on. "To spend nine years with a person (his wife Nikki) and to have a child . . . to lose them because of a game is a big, big price to pay.

"But what can I do, kill myself? I am not the first person to go through this." Nastase's voice went flat. "So I am losing now, I have no confidence. I suffer when I lose, but I want to be where the show is . . . because tennis is my life. I know people say I should retire, but what do I do then? I don't care about opinions; it's my own life. To tell me to retire tomorrow is like saying I must die tomorrow. And I don't want to die."

The spark of defiance in Nastase's eyes died. He began to undo the laces of his shoes.

Some of Nastase's friends worry about his health. His frame of mind has been constantly colored by the divorce proceedings that have dragged on in the French courts for nearly a year. Despite the state of his game, the promoters of tournaments and exhibitions line up for Nastase's services because he is still a big name. And no matter how far his ranking drops, he can still get into tournaments as a wild-card entrant admitted at the discretion of the promoters. But the way he has been playing drives him deeper into himself. Earlier, Gene Mayer had said, "If Nastase stopped playing for awhile, he'd probably realize how unhappy he is. But the circuit, it's like a fantasy, like college—an escape from the real pressures of life."

Struggling with a lace, Nastase addressed his shoetops: "Tennis is the strangest game ever. It is all in your head. Little things can bother you, destroy your game. So think what a big thing can do."

The big things, like losing the companion of your best years. It was a storybook romance between Ilie an Nikki, a courtship played out across the verdant lawns and sun-dappled verandas of tennis clubs around the world, culminating in marriage when Nastase was at the zenith of his career. For a few years, Nikki was a delightful apparition at tennis tournaments, as cool and distant as Nastase was hot and close. After bearing their daughter, Nathalie, who's now 6, Nikki stopped going to tournaments. Her husband did not.

"Exactly how do the big things affect you on the court?" I asked.

Nastase threw a shoe over toward the middle of the room, where a suitcase lay with its contents exploded all over the floor. Nastase calmly replied, "I know I can't be on top anymore, but I know I shouldn't feel confused on a tennis court and I do. Sometimes when I'm playing I feel like the court is not my place anymore. It makes me sad and I just think, 'Okay, this is bad so just finish the match anyway.'"

After a moment he continued: "I don't feel the pressure before matches now. Now when I go into a match, I'm not so nervous like I used to be and I miss that very much. When I was playing my best, I was never aware of the people, the fans. All I want was to win, and I played well when I was down. I fight like hell, that's how I was. Now I am there just to be in the game. It is like a fashion for me. But I have to be there or else the people, they forget you."

I almost asked Nastase why he didn't just go home, but I remembered about the divorce. According to Nastase, the fickle French, who adopted him so eagerly years ago, have all but abandoned him. Yannick Noah, the top French player, had told me, "It's true, the French love you when you are winning but when you begin to lose, they have no more respect. But still, everybody knows him. Every time I take a taxi, the driver asks me about Nastase."

One of Nastase's lawyers, Peter Lawler of Donald Dell's firm, told me that his client was booked to play for 47 weeks this year. The figure is preposterous, the itinerary of a homeless man. But that's how Nastase wants it. He admits he's a "yo-yo" and claims that if he stops for two weeks, he gets sick.

Nastase's income will be enormous and the job of Dell's firm, as Lawler put it, "is to make sure he doesn't end up sitting on a bar stool when he's 70, without a penny to his name." Nastase has made some financial errors in his past. There were many "friends" who came along offering spectacular deals that only trimmed Nastase's bank account. For a while, Nastase was managed by his brother-in-law. But money never occupied Nastase's mind.

"Is it normal for me to go in the street and buy three clocks?" Nastase asked, laughing. "The people who work for me, they are more nervous than me about the future. In France, I have to pay a $25,000 fine because I have a Mercedes-Benz with German plates, a Ferrari with Italian plates and a pickup truck with American plates. So I am crazy, just like on court. But if my plane go down tomorrow, I don't want to be the richest guy in the cemetery. I want to go down in a good mood."

The atmosphere in the room momentarily lightened. In a drama on the TV screen, Evita Peron stood before a cheering throng. Nastase watched her, with the eyes of a man who knew the same intoxication. But like most professionals, the respect of his peers has a deeper meaning than the cheers of the crowd for Nastase. That's why he feels bitter toward John McEnroe, who often makes fun of Nastase, denying him the respect Nastase feels he deserves.

"The ones who understand me are the ones who saw me at the top, who knew how I could play," Nastase said. "Arthur (Ashe) understand me. So does Borg. Jimmy (Conners), too. You know, Jimmy invite me down to Florida to practice with him. Jimmy is a good man, he cares. But I know how I am. Maybe I am a little too proud. I never went."

Because of his pride, Nastase comes and goes at a tournament, shrouded in mystery. The other players whisper about the man who was once the best player on the planet. "Nobody considers him much of a factor anymore," Trey Waltke had told me. "Nasty's pretty much in his own world. He comes in, does his little routine, and then everybody lets him go off to his corner." Waltke's voice dropped, and when he continued, it was almost reverentially: "It's sad, because he's the most respected talent any of us have ever seen. I hate to say it, it's kind of weird, but everybody talks about him in a tragic sense."

The great moments, the titles, won't be forgotten, though. When I asked Nastase about them, his craggy, mobile features relaxed. The mention of his four Masters titles brought a sheepish grin to his face. "I don't know what I was doing to win four Masters titles," he said. "I can't say. For me, the nicest memories always are the jokes. How happy people were when I was in the dressing room.

"Wimbledon." Nastase paused. He was obviously haunted by his failures in his two appearances in finals there. "I can't think about Wimbledon," he continued, "because I had too many other good tournaments."

"What else are you proud of?" I quickly asked.

"That I am professional," Nastase answered. "In almost 20 years of tennis, I averaged about 35 tournaments a year. I played non-stop and I never defaulted from one tournament. I had one broken ankle and one kidney stone and that was all. I did my job pretty good, I think."

Pensively, Nastase picked up one of his racquets and began to heft it. He looked trim and fit, wearing just his shorts and the smile brought on by memories of better times—times when his nerves were like the strings of a violin and his game served as a bow to bring forth some of the most melodious tennis any mortal has ever witnessed.

"Everybody thinks it was easier for me with my attitude," he said. "But I don't think so. All the extra things took the energy out of me. When I was younger, I didn't realize it. I just go out to play. But I see it now, how much it hurt me in some big matches."

Nastase let the racquet drop. He muttered, "I know I can still win, but I'm not strong enough to say, 'Okay, tomorrow I will win the tournament.' Even when I was No. 1, I never thought I could win for sure. It was always maybe I can, maybe I cannot. I wasn't a killer, maybe I had too much fantasy. I had to feel how my game was going, then I could say, 'Okay, today I win.' "

I forgot what I wanted to ask Nastase next because a little incident that occurred just after he lost to Delaney occupied my mind. We were upstairs in the club, watching a match through a big window. Nastase had decided to skip the locker room; he was just cooling off before going back to the hotel. A ball girl reached through the crowd around us, hoping Nastase would autograph a ball. She finally had to touch him to get his attention.

"You work my match," Nastase said as he took the ball. "Were you scared?"

The girl bravely shook her head, pretending that she hadn't been scared at all.

"Good," Nastase said. "Sometimes they get scared. You don't have to be scared of me, I'm an okay guy."

A ball boy from the match stood nearby, munching a corndog, staring. Nastase grinned at him, saying: "You were so slow tonight because you didn't eat, yes? Next time, you eat a big dinner before you ball boy. Then you'll be the best." The boy shyly smiled.

Nastase's life is full of such vignettes. He has always craved communication, hungered for the touch of passionate feeling in his relationships with everyone, including umpires. Yet he has made very few close friends, as if such a relationship would inhibit his freedom, cramp his need to express his individuality on the stage that is both larger and smaller than life.

I remembered something Solomon had said: "Nastase always avoided real close relationships. That's probably been the chief thing missing in his life. Nastase's reaction was always to put others down. It was a way of keeping people at a distance."

Then I remembered what I'd wanted to ask Nastase. It was, "Do you think you'll ever marry again?"

"No, I don't think so," he replied. "It would be nice to have a child who likes to play tennis, I would like that." Crestfallen, he added, "My daughter, she is not interested in tennis."

"And the future, what do you want people to say about you in the future?"

Nastase pondered the question. The fantastic clock was silent, but the disc kept moving and the crosshairs were pointing right at the almost naked man sitting in the wire chair. "I was a crazy player, a fantasist," he finally replied. "I don't want them to say that I was the best, just how I really was—a complicated player. Now there is still the controversy, but I know that in some years all that will be gone. The titles, they will stay."

It seemed like the right time to go. Nastase saw me to the door. When it softly closed behind me, I had to beat back an impulse to knock again, to go back inside and throw all those clocks out the window, especially the "fantastic" one that kept turning blue.

One Man's Vote: Davey Lopes

BASEBALL

By *JIM MURRAY*

From the Los Angeles Times
Copyright © 1981, Los Angeles Times Syndicate
Reprinted With Permission

The World Series, the first one in history where the two teams were certifiably not the best in baseball, came to a merciful end in Yankee Stadium Wednesday. The Dodgers, who would have been second in their division and third in the league had a full schedule been played, beat the Yankees, who would have been third in their division and fourth in the league.

The game may have been lost in the dugout.

It is the bottom of the fourth inning in this Series where the DH, or designated hitters, are not permitted on this alternate year. The score is tied, 1-1, and the Yankees have a runner on second with two outs. The pitcher is coming up next, Tommy John, no threat to Stan the Man at the plate. Tommy Lasorda, the Dodger manager, hits on a stratagem. He will walk batter Larry Milbourne. This will force Yankee Manager Bob Lemon to an agonizing decision. Tommy John is pitching a masterful game. But Lemon needs that run on second. Or thinks he does. He sighs, sends up a pinch-hitter. Bobby Murcer pops out.

The Dodgers feast on the pitchers who succeed John. For only the second time in eight tries, they manage to win in New York.

It is an anticlimactic end to the most bewildering season in all baseball annals. Scholars will search the box score for a guy to give the gold watch and the scholarship.

I have my own candidate and it may be an exclusive. Bear with me while I make my case.

This Dodger team which finally broke through to a world championship was put together by the registered geniuses of the Dodger organization over a decade ago. This may be the last game they will play as a unit. They were Lasorda's boys, the little Boys Blue. He nursed them, nicknamed them, bragged on them, cursed them, prodded them and they won pennants but always came up a dollar short to the lordly Yankees and the sneaky-good A's in World Series.

The second baseman, a feisty little Portuguese-American from Rhode Island, made some of the big plays for them. He hit two World Series homers in one game, he played with the burning-eyed intensity of the self-made ballplayer, self-made infielder. He was part of the longest-lasting infield unit in baseball history. They weren't the most stylish, just the most durable. Nobody wrote any poems about them, but they threw in four pennants in eight years, and Tinker-to-Evers-to-Chance never did that.

Somehow, in this season when all baseball turned sour, it all turned sour for Davey Lopes. Management, turned off, followed by the fans and to some extent, the media, the town, the world. Davey's batting average plummeted. He began to get hit in the belt buckle by double-play balls. He got down on himself. He was in his twilight as a Dodger, maybe as a ballplayer. The word was out to hide the knives and forks if Davey came in the room and to nail the hotel room windows so he couldn't climb out on any ledges.

You saw him make an abattoir out of second base during this World Series. He set records that may never be broken. Records for ineptitude.

But come with me to the sixth inning of Game 4 of this year's World Series. The Dodgers have been battling back from 4-0 and 6-3 deficits. Jay Johnstone has just hit a two-run home run to bring the deficit to one run, 6-5. They are still one run shy as Davey Lopes comes to bat and lifts a high fly into short right. Outfielder Reggie Jackson has a bead on it. It's a "can o' corn," the ballplayers' term for a routine fly ball.

Davey Lopes does not treat it as a routine fly ball. Davey Lopes tears around first base and he is safely standing on second as the ball comes down on Reggie Jackson's chest.

Not five ballplayers, World Series or no, would have run out that pop-up as sincerely. Pete Rose would. And Davey Lopes did. On the next batter, he steals third base. When Bill Russell lifts a single to right, Davey Lopes ties the score and, eventually, the World Series.

In Game 6 in Yankee Stadium Wednesday night, in the fifth inning, the Dodgers again are tied, 1-1, when Lopes opens the inning with a ground single to left.

Russell sacrifices him to second. Lopes is on second when Ron Cey comes up and hits what appears to be a routine soft grounder behind second base. But Lopes doesn't believe in "routine" anything. When second baseman Willie Randolph unaccountably lets the ball go through his glove and roll dead on the outfield grass, Lopes has torn around third and scored standing up.

That may have been the key play of the game. If an out is made there, it is the third out and the score is still 1-1. But Dusty Baker keeps the inning alive with a single. And Pedro Guerrero triples. The Dodgers have all the runs they need. They have, at last, avenged past humiliations at this historic ballyard.

They awarded the gold watches and the scholarship to triple

MVPs: Guerrero, whose homer tied Game 5 and whose RBIs put Wednesday's game out of sight; Cey, whose bat and glove mocked the Yanks, and Steve Yeager, the overlooked catcher.

Davey Lopes will be remembered in the Series for making the most errors by a second baseman in the history of the Series—6.

They don't keep stats for running out pop flies to short right field or legging it for home on an apparently sure out to a sure-handed infielder.

Lopes won't get a watch, a car, a headline. All he'll get is "E-4" in the record book. No one will remember that none of his errors figured in the scoring.

In Inning 6 of the championship clinching game Wednesday, Lopes drew a walk. He reached second when Russell singled to left and pitcher Burt Hooton scored on a Little League throw from outfielder Dave Winfield. Then he lead a double steal, stealing third base for the second time in the Series.

They'll talk of the Dodgers' Kiddy-Kar infield around the watering holes where ball is remembered in the future. They'll be remembered not for their slick fielding but their robust hitting and the way they found a way to beat you. No one was any better at that than Davey Lopes. No one was any better at that in this Series. I don't care what the vote was. He can have my watch.

Judge's Comments

Jim Murray has that special knack of taking a minor occurrence or figure and transforming it, with his incomparable style, into something important. In this case, he's talking about a player, Davey Lopes of the Dodgers, who many observers called the "goat" of the 1981 World Series. Murray thought otherwise, and made a pretty convincing case for making Lopes the MVP.

Lopes apparently is on his way out as the Dodgers second baseman. Age and slowed-down reflexes are working against him. Where he once played "with the burning-eyed intensity of the self-made ballplayer, self-made infielder," he now relies on experience and know-how to get the job done. Forget his record-setting six errors in the Series. Forget his low batting average.

". . . come with me to the sixth inning of Game 4 of this year's World Series. The Dodgers have been battling back from 4-0 and 6-3 deficits. Jay Johnstone has just hit a two-run home run to bring the deficit to one run, 6-5. They are still one-run shy as Davey Lopes comes to bat and lifts a high fly into short right. Outfielder Reggie Jackson has the bead on it . . .

"Davey Lopes does not treat it as a routine fly ball. Davey Lopes tears around first base and he is safely standing on second as the ball comes down on Reggie Jackson's chest. Not five ballplayers, World Series or no, would have run out that pop-up as sincerely. Pete Rose would . . ."

What would seem to be a prosaic incident comes to life and plays on the reader's emotions with Murray telling the tale. He goes on to relate a similar incident in Game 6, in which Lopes scores a key run and keeps an inning alive by scoring from second on what started out as a routine grounder behind second before being fumbled by Yankee second baseman Willie Randolph.

Murray closes out the column by stating that nobody was any better than Davey Lopes in this Series. And nobody quite makes the case as well as Murray.

Muncey Killed in Crash

SPEEDBOAT RACING

By *JOHN ENGSTROM*

From the Seattle Post-Intelligencer
Copyright © 1981, Seattle Post-Intelligencer

The Old Man had 'em on his hip, and then the world blew up in his face.

Bill Muncey, at age 52 the patriarch of unlimited hydroplane racing, was killed as he attempted to reach back to his glory days. After a smoking start that had the Atlas Van Lines screaming at the front of a hot pack of five boats in the final heat of the World Championship yesterday, Muncey's magic slipped as he roared into the second turn.

It came at 5 in the afternoon, the traditional time of blood and death in a land of bullfights.

The chatter of the beach crowd cut short as the Atlas slowly rose into one of those horribly beautiful backward loops that left his boat hanging upside down for a stop-action moment before it tore into the surface of Laguna de Coyuca.

Muncey was pulled from the lagoon unconscious and barely clinging to life. Doctors worked for 45 minutes at a nearby airstrip to strengthen his pulse, but they couldn't get him breathing on his own.

Still unconscious and in critical condition, he was rushed by a light plane to a Mexican navy hospital in Acapulco some 10 miles to the south where doctors continued the attempt to save his life.

Muncey's blood pressure was stable and his heart was beating on its own but he still wasn't breathing without artificial help. When work at that hospital failed to bring any improvement, he was rushed to a nearby second hospital where, at mid-evening, he was pronounced dead.

Doctor Matt Houghton, a member of the three-man medical team for the race, said Muncey died of a completely severed spinal cord between the third and fourth vertebrae in his neck.

"It was a condition completely incompatible with life," he said. "His heart stopped three times on the way to the (first) hospital.

Each time we injected drugs and got it going again. As long as you've got a sign of life, you've got to keep trying.

"But he had flacid paralysis and was not breathing without artificial help. About a half hour after we got to the second hospital, the drugs just wore off and he was dead."

Houghton said Muncey died about 8:45 p.m. Acapulco time, nearly four hours after the accident.

The driver toll could have been much worse.

Two other boats were mangled as they tried to avoid the Atlas wreckage, but neither driver was badly injured.

Milner Irvin, driving the Miss Madison, threw his boat into a hard right turn, a direction the unlimiteds are not designed to go. The force of the skid twisted his boat and tore huge chunks from it but Irvin escaped with what was diagnosed as possible cracked ribs.

Chip Hanauer, driving the Squire Shop, was almost a full straightaway behind Muncey, but the glare from the lowering sun prevented him from seeing the Atlas debris until he was nearly on top of it.

"When I got to the corner, I saw what had happened and I turned to the right to avoid it," said Hanauer. "But my right side, about half my boat, went right over the Atlas."

Incredibly, Hanauer was not injured as the Squire slammed over the Atlas wreckage and coasted to a stop, so badly battered that it would later sink while being towed to the launching pier.

Race officials ruled against a restart of the final heat. Miss Budweiser, a victor in each of the two preliminary heats for the five fastest in the 10-boat field, was declared the winner, bringing the world championship to driver Dean Chenoweth and owner Bernie Little.

It was not the way they wanted to win. And when one of Little's employees was sent to pick up the trophy an hour later, only a dozen Mexicans were on hand to applaud politely when they noticed him pick the trophy off its stand and carry it to the Budweiser camp.

While Muncey was fighting for his life, Jim Harvey, a member of the Atlas crew, stared out onto the course, like many others, wishing his eyes had not witnessed the tragedy.

"You okay?" asked John Walters, driver of the Pay'N Pak.

"Not really," said Harvey, as tears rolled from under the sunglasses that hid his eyes. "All we can do is pray, just pray. He's a very strong-willed person and physically in excellent shape. . . ." But he kept the rest of the thought inside.

A day earlier, Scott Pierce, the circuit's most successful rookie, had praised Muncey as the greatest driver on the unlimited tour, an honor not unexpected for a man who had won 61 races, three times the number of any other driver, beginning in 1956 when he won the Gold Cup on the Detroit River in the Miss Thriftway.

Though he had raced unlimiteds for a quarter of a century, Muncey was ever-aware of the risks. Before every race, he prepared for the worst.

"I don't eat the day before or the day of a race," he told driver Ron Armstrong on Saturday. "Because they can't operate on you if you've eaten too much food recently.

"I want 'em to operate right away, glue me back together. Leave me unconscious but do it right away while I can't feel the pain."

In yesterday's first heat for the fast boats, the Atlas finished second, despite a punctured sponsor suffered when it struck "something mighty hard," as Muncey explained, "because it had to be damn hard to fracture that particular part of the boat."

A rush-patch job sent the Atlas back onto the course less than five minutes before the start of the second fast-boat heat. Muncey had his hydro in good position for a start when his nitrousoxide system failed.

"It was like going into an intersection, seeing other cars, putting your foot to the throttle and nothing happens," he said later. "It was my mistake. I shouldn't have been there, and I wouldn't have been there if the system hadn't failed.

"I took a bath from everybody and a pop right in the mouth."

The Atlas never recovered from the wash down of roostertails and finished fourth in the heat. That gave Muncey a total of 469 points, second behind the Bud's 800 and easily enough to put him in the winner-take-all final.

There were those in the pits who said Muncey was under a lot of pressure to win the race because of the presence of so many officials and friends of the Atlas firm, which does big business in Mexico.

"We're going to run," he said after the second heat troubles. "We'll do the things we have to do to race."

At the start of the final heat, with his nitrous system back in order, Muncey lagged behind the other four boats as the countdown began for the final minute. Running on near-perfect water, he suddenly roared up the backstretch, going high into the north turn and then down the inside at full power, robbing the Bud of first place as the hydros blasted across the starting line.

The Atlas, with Muncey doing his usual precision job in the first turn, held the advantage and carried it into the glare of the second turn, where the boat suddenly broke that thin dividing line between skimming and flying.

Walters, who was right behind Muncey in the Pay'N Pak, said the accident happened just as Muncey prepared to make the turn.

"I saw him start to set up for the turn when I was about a length and a half back of him," he said. "When I set up for the turn, I saw the boat come up over the roostertail. It tried to go all the way over, but hit real hard on the transom and then kind of rolled over until it was upside down."

Chenoweth and the Bud, in third place, were past the wreck before he could react but he quickly turned the boat around and cruised the area looking for his friend.

"I was going to cool it for that lap," said Chenoweth. "Bill wasn't that far out of reach, and I was going to pick him off later on. I was maybe 200 feet behind him when it happened.

"I turned around and was looking for Bill when the Squire Shop came along and ran right over the boat."

After the crash, Pierce, driver of the Oh Boy! Oberto, hunkered down on the dirt pier and looked toward the north turn, where small boats still crossed back and forth searching for debris.

"I tell you one thing," he said to a reporter who had asked nothing. "If we've lost him, we've lost him right where he belonged, out there in first place, going for it all the way."

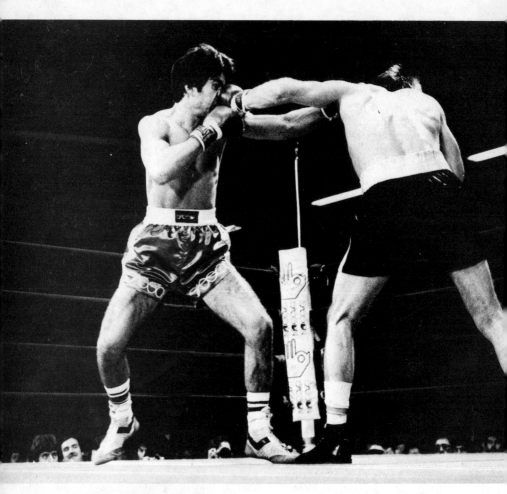

A Real Nose Job

by Will Cofnuk, whose photo appeared in *Suburban Trends,* a New Jersey publication. Andy Riccardi took a nose-bending jab from Rick Hamlisch (right) during a middleweight bout in Totowa, N.J., but came back strong to win the fight. Copyright © 1981, Suburban Trends.

Little Big Men

by Judy Griesedieck of the *Hartford Courant*. Seven-foot-five Andre the Giant stands tall in the topsy-turvy world of professional wrestling, dwarfing partner Rick McGraw and his latest victim after a tag-team victory at Bristol High School in Connecticut. Copyright © 1981, The Hartford Courant.

Why Jim Otto Faces a Life of Pain

PRO FOOTBALL

By *MURRAY OLDERMAN*

From Newspaper Enterprise Association
Copyright © 1981, Newspaper Enterprise Association, Inc.

He rolls out of bed gingerly in the morning. His legs start to buckle. He grabs for the night stand to keep from collapsing to the floor.

Jim Otto hates the idea of being a cripple, but that's what he is in his own mind.

Fifteen hard years of professional football left him this way—with one deteriorating artificial knee and the other knee so arthritic and unstable that he lives in constant pain. He is virtually immobilized to the point he is classified permanently and totally disabled.

The other day, he accompanied his wife, Sally, to a furniture store. As they left, she stepped off the sidewalk curb. Jim followed her. His knees wobbled, and he fell on top of her. Jim weighs 230 pounds. Sally is a slim, petite blonde.

The last time Jim Otto used his legs to run was in 1975 when he wore the silver and black uniform of the Oakland Raiders and trotted out on the field for the final game of his long and illustrious career, an exhibition against the Washington Redskins. He can't jog now. He can't lift weights or perform any other meaningful exercise. He can't even hold a job.

After his retirement, the Raiders, the only team for whom he played professionally, made him their business manager. He quit after a couple of years because of his legs.

"I don't want to fall down in front of those guys," he explains. "It happened to me twice, and it was embarrassing."

He could walk with a cane or what they call a Canadian crutch. He used a cane this past autumn once when it rained and he had to be in San Francisco on business. But he discarded it when he accompanied the Raiders to New Orleans for their recent Super Bowl game.

"Can you see Jim Otto around the team like that?" he asks.

Jim Otto, who was voted into the Professional Football Hall of Fame a year ago, recently passed his 43rd birthday. His hair is dark blond with no sign of gray. A couple of slight hollows indent his upper cheeks. His jaw line is firm. He weighs 25 fewer pounds than when he was an active athlete, so his stomach is flat and his jeans fit snugly. He shows very few signs of aging—other than those gimpy legs.

He is never without pain, which he controls with Clinoril, an anti-arthritic drug. Still, he can't stand in one spot for more than 15 minutes. And after an hour of standing he would topple over.

The problem is that Jim Otto virtually has no knees. During his 15-year career with the Oakland Raiders—from 1960, when the team was formed, through 1974, a period in which he never missed a game and made All-Pro 12 straight years—Otto submitted to nine knee operations. Those crucial leg hinges have turned completely arthritic from the wear and tear.

An artificial knee was implanted in his right leg, but it's tearing loose. So he walks with a perceptible limp. He should undergo further surgery, but he is hesitant because of the ordeal he has already been through.

Never drafted by a pro team when he came out of the University of Miami (Fla.), Otto signed as a free agent. He built himself up from a 205-pound center to a 255-pound immortal by lifting weights. He can't lift weights anymore because the bones in his shoulders have also become arthritic. The lack of exercise has atrophied the muscles in his once sturdy legs.

Yet Jim Otto doesn't regret one moment of his football career.

"I would do it all over again," he says. "Football was a means for me as a youngster to be recognized for doing something well. I wasn't a good student. Football did everything for me. So I can't be bitter."

He played his last three years under the greatest physical stress imaginable. Three days a week he would have his knee injected with xylocaine and then drained with a long needle. On Sundays, he would get it braced, lace himself with Darvon and go out and play. He finally quit during training camp in the late summer of 1975, when he was approaching 38, because he realized the pain would be too much.

"I could have played one more year," he says now, "though I wouldn't have been very effective. I had a bone graft before I came to training camp, but it came apart after two and a half weeks. Then I read about a player suffering a dislocated knee which also severed an artery, and they had to amputate his leg. That did it for me."

He was prepared for the abrupt severance from active football. After hunting during the off-seasons in the Yuba City area in central California, he had bought a 134-acre walnut orchard. He has a fast-food hamburger franchise in Auburn, Calif., in the Sierra foothills. He plans to open another near Sacramento.

"But I don't work at anything," he says. "My legs don't allow me to. I have nothing to look forward to in my legs. They're beyond help.

Four different doctors, independently, have examined me in the last two years and all have classified me permanently and totally disabled in the legs."

His worst period has been the last six months, when he experienced the first deep depression of his life. When he gets up sometimes in the morning, "the pain is so great I swallow five or six aspirin right away."

His son, Jim Jr., is 14 and plays tight end and defensive end on the high school team in Yuba City. His dad does nothing to discourage him.

"I've seen tears in young Jim's eyes when he sees me," says the father. "He's had to help me get in the house when I get out of the car. But he makes his own decision. My son doesn't have to play football."

What worries Jim Otto Sr. now is that he can't plant or flex his left foot, indicating some nerve damage. He faces up to the physical future uncertainly. But he knows he's not alone.

"Dick Butkus (the great Chicago Bears linebacker) lives in pain," muses Jim. "He sacrificed his body. E.J. Holub (a fine center-linebacker with the Kansas City Chiefs) destroyed his body.

"I knew what I was doing. I broke my ankle in high school and taped it up each week and played the whole season on that broken ankle."

The remembrance doesn't bother him as much as the fact that he couldn't help Sally decorate the family tree at Christmas.

Nothing Could Be Finer Than the 49ers, 26-21

PRO FOOTBALL

By *PAUL ATTNER*

From the Washington Post
Copyright © 1981, The Washington Post

The San Francisco 49ers defeated the Cincinnati Bengals, 26-21, today to complete a three-year journey from ineptitude to glory. Not even the fury of a second-half Cincinnati rally could prevent them from becoming perhaps the most improbable Super Bowl champion in history.

This was a moment the 49ers had been waiting 36 frustrating years to celebrate. Now they have a victory they can talk about for seasons to come, a triumph that produced the kind of drama and excitement that has been missing from so many other National Football League championship games.

Never has a team been 2-14 one season, 6-10 the next and the Super Bowl winner the third. But the 49ers have been accomplishing unlikely things all season, and they continued today as they won their first league title.

They built the biggest halftime lead in Super Bowl history, 20-0. Then they almost made more history by blowing it before deflating the Bengals' comeback by stopping 249-pound Pete Johnson on a fourth down at the 1 late in the third quarter.

But despite that defensive gem, this day still belonged to the offensive genius of Coach Bill Walsh and his quarterback, Joe Montana, the third-round 1979 draft choice out of Notre Dame who now can add the game's Most Valuable Player award to his trophy case.

It was their showing in the first half—Walsh's play-calling and Montana's execution—that provided the 49ers with the cushion they needed to hold off Cincinnati. And it was their combined talents during a fourth-quarter drive, setting up Ray Wersching's fourth field goal—tying a 14-year Super Bowl record—that finally ended the Bengals' comeback hopes.

"This was one rare moment when a team without great stars and experience rises up," said Walsh, who spent 22 years waiting for a head coaching opportunity in the NFL and then won Super Bowl XVI three years later. "No one could take us. It was the highlight of my life. Anything can happen now."

Cincinnati will wonder about its four turnovers, including two that wiped out potential scoring opportunities. The Bengals will wonder about that Johnson goal-line run. It was a play that had worked so many times before in the season (Johnson rushed for 12 touchdowns) but not today, not when Cincinnati needed it the most. And the Bengals will wonder about their dreadfully flat first-half performance.

"It was just beginning to look like one of those days," cornerback Louis Breeden said. "We couldn't do anything right, but we came out in the second half and we had a shot. Nobody wanted to be embarrassed and I don't think we were."

Yet why were the more experienced Bengals seemingly much tighter than the 49ers, a team that began this season with 20 new players? "We were loose in the locker room before the game, but for some reason, we were tense when we first came out on the field," said tight end Dan Ross, who caught a game-record 11 passes. "Stage fright, maybe."

Montana, in only his third pro season, and Walsh, the former Bengal offensive coordinator who was denied the team's head coaching position, had just as much reason to be jittery. But they were as steady as Starr and Lombardi at their best.

In a first half that could be used as an offensive training film, Montana completed 12 of 18 passes for 132 yards and one touchdown. He turned Walsh's don't-be-greedy calls into time-consuming scoring drives of 68, 92 (longest ever for a Super Bowl) and 61 yards to frustrate the Bengals.

And then when Cincinnati's Archie Griffin, the two-time Heisman Trophy winner turned fill-in pro player, fumbled away a squibbed kickoff at the Bengal four and Wersching kicked a 26-yard field goal with two seconds left in the half, the game seemed all but over.

But a defensive adjustment by Cincinnati at halftime changed the Bengals' outlook dramatically. They decided to revitalize themselves by turning to an all-out blitz on almost every play.

Suddenly, Cincinnati forgot about two devastating first-half mistakes: a Ken Anderson interception at the San Francisco 5 after the Bengals had recovered a fumble on the game-opening kickoff, and a fumble by receiver Cris Collinsworth at the 8.

Quarterback Anderson, once a Walsh protege, had been just off-target in that first half, missing open receivers by inches while trying to avoid the pressure of the 49ers' defensive rush. He was being clearly outplayed by his younger counterpart in the San Francisco uniform.

Now Anderson was a different man. He took the Bengals on an

83-yard touchdown march on the opening series of the third quarter, scoring himself on a five-yard scramble up the middle. No longer was Cincinnati playing like a team which was outgained, 208-99, in the first half.

Walsh decided to counter the Bengals blitzing by turning to running plays. The result was almost disastrous. San Francisco could gain only four yards in the period after trying only two passes. Cincinnati kept pounding and pounding, hoping for a breakthrough.

It almost came midway through the quarter. A stunning 49-yard Anderson completion to a speeding Collinsworth on a third-and-23 play gave the Bengals a first down at the 49ers 14. On a fourth and one at the 5, Johnson bulled for a first down, helped by San Francisco having only 10 men on the field.

But that would be the 49ers' last mistake in this dramatic sequence. Johnson, who has made a living producing in these situations, got to the 1. On second down, linebacker Hacksaw Reynolds slashed into the fullback, stopping him for no gain. On third down, an Anderson pass to halfback Charles Alexander in the right flat was stopped inches short of the end zone on a memorable open-field tackle by Dan Bunz. On fourth down after a timeout, Johnson tried right tackle. The 49ers defense overpowered the Bengals offensive line and Johnson never had a chance. No gain.

"We ran the same play a lot of times," Johnson said. "It's just one of those things that happens. I figured I could go under them. It just didn't work."

Even though Cincinnati refused to fold even after that letdown, the 49ers had the break they needed to regain their poise. When the Bengals finally did get their second touchdown on a four-yard pass from Anderson to Ross with 10:06 left in the game, San Francisco was able to respond with a back-breaking field goal.

To set up Wersching's 40-yard success, Montana first had to complete a 22-yard pass from his own 22 to receiver Mike Wilson for his team's first substantial gain of the half. Then the 49ers started offsetting the Bengal blitzing by calling trap running plays. Seven rushes later, Wersching gave San Francisco a 23-14 lead with 3:25 remaining, making another field goal and Anderson's second scoring pass to Ross incidental.

"In the huddle, we said, 'Let's think this is the last 10 minutes of our life,' " receiver Dwight Clark said about the pivotal 49er drive. "There was also mention of a $9,000 drive (difference in the winning and losing shares). Money is a big motivator in this type of situation."

Anderson had been magnificent in defeat, completing 17 of 20 passes after intermission for 217 yards. His 25-of-34 day set Super Bowl records for most completions and highest passing percentage. But this was also the first time that a Super Bowl loser has ever outgained the winner (356-275).

Walsh had confused Cincinnati by using an unbalanced line in the first half and he had almost broken the Bengals' defensive confidence with the ease in which his team had moved the ball. But his decision to be careful in the third period had almost neutralized his handiwork.

"We didn't know what to expect from them offensively because of Walsh, especially with two weeks to prepare for us," Cincinnati linebacker Reggie Williams said. "They just ran the ball better on us than we anticipated."

Inside the 49ers dressing room, the San Francisco players still were trying to believe that this long-sought championship finally was theirs. The veterans, the ones who had suffered through the lean years, probably were the happiest.

"I don't know how we are ever going to top this," tackle Keith Fahnhorst said. "I'm still numb. To grasp something like this, well, it's unbelievable."

Heaven Can't Wait
—Or Can It?

COLLEGE FOOTBALL

By *CALVIN FUSSMAN*

From Inside Sports
Copyright © 1981, Inside Sports

It is a standard publicity shot, the player holding a football out in front of him. The pose blunts the impact of the photo—until you realize that this is not a college or professional player. This is a high school kid, barely a senior. At 6-3, 215 pounds, he seems to be wearing shoulder pads. He is not. But it is not his size that is most striking. It's his hands, the long fingers and huge palms. When Remuise Johnson shook your hand, he would engulf it, and your wrist, too.

Coach Antoine Russell of Pahokee Junior-Senior High spent many spare moments staring at that photograph on his office wall, wondering about his star defensive end who graduated in 1976.

"Remuise, oh, Remuise. That joker could bust some headlights. One time he went to sing in the church choir and missed practice. I had to punish him. I put him on the second-string defense. That meant he was practicing against Rickey Jackson, who I had playing tight end. After a few plays, Rickey came back to the huddle and whined: 'Coach, please don't punish Remuise no more.' "

Two years later, his body 25 pounds lighter from labor and occasional religious fasts, Remuise Johnson stood at the altar of the Bible Church of God with his arms upraised, as if signaling a touchdown. Against a backdrop of slithering tambourines and a hoarse chorus of "Praise the Lord!," Remuise spoke to the congregation:

"I'm so glad to be living in Jesus' name.

"A lot of sports stars have fame and glory.

"But they need Jesus.

"I could be a millionaire if I played football.

"But I'd go to hell without Jesus.

"God comes first in my life."

In three years, Forbes Avenue in Pittsburgh had become a haven of "What's happins" and "My mans" for Rickey Jackson, who was preparing for his senior season with the Panthers.

"You on an expense account?" he asked his visitor. "You don't need no expense account to do a story on Rickey J. I don't want you to ever come to Pittsburgh and say that Rickey Jackson didn't show you a good time."

Rickey stepped into a restaurant owned by a man who fancies himself a big booster of the team. A preseason bash was in progress. Players, fans, alumni and a media type or two were bustling around a buffet table.

Rickey, only nine months from being a second-round draft pick of the New Orleans Saints, got an ample helping for himself and his visitor and sat down next to quarterback Dan Marino.

"Rickey, please pass me a tomato," Marino said.

"You see, that be the difference between Pittsburgh and Pahokee. I ain't never heard nobody use the word 'please' until I got to Pittsburgh. If I had a plate of food and you wanted that tomato in Pahokee, you'd say, 'Gimme that!' "

"What's Pahokee like?"

"Pahokee be so small you could put the whole town in one of those U.S. Steel buildings downtown. But I think we got more whorehouses in Pahokee than there be in all Pittsburgh.

"See, I look at Pittsburgh as an up-to-date city. People come up to me in Pittsburgh and shake my hand. In all my years in Pahokee, I never once shook my daddy's hand. Pahokee's years from civilization. Back home, I be eatin' rabbit three times a week. In Pittsburgh, I be eatin' steak three times a week. Pahokee's a town of losers. There's 600,000 people in Pittsburgh. Not one ever told me I'm not gonna make it. There be 6,000 people in Pahokee. Not one ever said I'd make it. People down there get jealous. I be the top athlete to come from that area."

"What about Remuise?" the visitor asked.

"Remuise could play. We was like brothers in high school. The things I dreamed of me and Remuise doin', me and Hugh have done. God just put Hugh in Remuise's place. Hugh a winner. Remuise a loser. He just don't have that winner inside him."

Hugh Green walked by to say hello. "Hugh and me be best friends, just like brothers. Hugh got a car, I got a car. I got money, he got money. Hugh got his chance first. I didn't get to play. It made me try harder. But maybe people will recognize me this year. I put 111 licks on somebody last year. They'll know who I am this year."

Rickey drifted away from the crowd. It was getting late and a number of toasts to the season had lowered his eyelids to half-mast.

"I get to feelin' sad about Remuise. The only way I could help him is to make it and open a business and let him handle it. My success will be Remuise's success. I wear his number under my jersey. I be playin' for both of us."

There was a long silence.

"Remuise Johnson," Rickey said slowly, as if reading the name off a tombstone. "He could play."

"Do you think he could come back if he wanted to?" the visitor asked.

"I know he can do it if he feel like it. He was the same as Hugh and me. He was just as big as we are. He was just as fast, just as strong. He could hit just as hard. I'll tell you somethin' not too many people will believe. I be just as good as Hugh."

"What about Remuise?"

The answer did not surface for a long time.

"Lot of people say Remuise was better than me."

The small city of Pahokee is roughly 45 miles and 100 years from the southeast coast of Florida, separated from West Palm Beach by a grid of cane fields and telephone poles. The northern portion of Pahokee is inhabited by whites, the more wealthy of whom reside in plantation-style homes resting behind magnificent columns of palm trees. The south side of the city is populated by blacks who work the fields and sugar mills.

Colored Quarters: Wood shacks and two-story plasterboard apartments litter Rardin Avenue. Ripped screen doors. Busted wood doors. No doors. People congregate on porches. "We just sittin' 'round tellin' lies. That's all there is to do 'round here." Greater New Hope Baptist Church. A roof is collapsing into a brick building. The open door of the abandoned apartment reveals a carpet of trash. A group of men tucked into a tight circle howl as dice scrape along the sidewalk. St. James AME Church. A rooster plucks at a scalp of watermelon in the center of a garbage heap. Two barefoot boys stand at the opposite ends of the street, giggling as they hurl rocks at each other. A poster at Big Jim's Servall Cafe advertises a boxing card at the El Ranchito Club. Main events: Mihon Towen vs. Sparkman. Coke Eye vs. Billy Cunningham. House of God #2. Angry shouts over a pool game drift from a bar down the street. A police car stops. The officer pulls over a white stranger. "What are you doin' here?" Two blocks away, there is an open exchange of reefer and cash in the laundromat on the side street called Jamaica Avenue by some because of its drug traffic. Bible Church of God.

The bench in front of Daddy Add's pool hall has been holy wood for three generations. Charlie Roach, Love, Eddie Mo, Little Bro and a few of the latest crop sit under a sweet cirrus cloud of smoke. Time dawdles and talk prods it along.

"First thing you got to know is this town be a big family. Hardly nobody leaves and, with everybody messin' with everybody else, everybody be related somehow. We all come up hard here. The people be tough just from workin' the fields. That's why we got such good football players. Man, you see dudes out in the sandlots hittin' each other with their heads and shoulders. But hardly nobody gets to use their natural abilities."

"Lots of dudes had the talent. But they say, 'I can't make it. Me? On TV?' Poor people don't want to leave their family and try to make it at somethin' they don't know nuthin' about."

"There be two roads a man can take in Pahokee. You come up through the Daddy Add or else you come up through the church."

"See, man, that be the difference between Rickey and Remuise. Rickey had the killer instinct of the street. Remuise didn't have no killer instinct."

"No killer instinct! What you talkin' about, nigguh! I seen Remuise smash a helmet with his forearm. I'd take Remuise over Rickey 100 times."

"Remuise didn't have no drive that Rickey did. Rickey wanted to prove to the world and Pahokee that he be somebody."

"Has nuthin' to do with it. I seen that Hugh Green play on TV. He wasn't as good as Remuise. If Remuise was at college in Pittsburgh, he starts over Hugh or Rickey. Remuise wants to live his life in church. That be his business."

"What I'm talkin' about, nigguh, be makin' it."

The land jolts the senses: Stalks of green sugarcane stand straight out of soil absolutely black. Plant and earth exhale an aroma so sweet that a slight breeze offends the nostrils. The rays of the sun lean fiercely on flesh and muscle. Corn, celery, lettuce and radishes rise in huge patches from the soil the folks call the Muck. "If you got somethin' goin' for you, you get out of here," explains a man on a street corner in Pahokee, sucking survival from a beer bottle. "Ain't no hope for a black man here. But it ain't so easy to get out. Walk down this street. Take a left turn down any of these side streets. Gotcha self a dead end. Can't see nuthin' but a wall of sugarcane. We boxed in by a wall of sugarcane."

The sun has come up in a burning orange tint and a steamy mist rises from the fields. It is six in the morning and everyone is easing into work on the mule train. The mule train is what the workers call the corn-packing assembly line built onto a long, tractor-like machine. Men rustle ahead through the fields, plucking the corn and tossing it into the loading bin. Some of the women softly sing the gospel as they stuff the corn into boxes. The lighter boxes weigh 40 pounds. The belt carries the boxes toward ninth-grader Remuise Johnson at quick intervals. Remuise lifts each box over his head and hurls it onto the trailing truck, his body blurting out the only word in the cornloader's gutteral language: "Hnnnt! . . . Hnnnt! . . . Hnnnt! . . . Hnnnt! . . . Hnnnt! . . . Hnnnt! . . . Hnnnt! . . ." He will lift more than 2,000 boxes before the day's work is done.

"We don't have a summer weight program here," coach Russell would say years later. "We really don't need one. We just send the kids to work in the fields."

The leaves have been burnt off the cane, leaving gnarled stalks in the field. The rabbits have lost their cover. Nine-year-old Rickey Jackson spots one. Sensing danger, the rabbit begins to glide through the field, jutting left and right at acute angles, each stride sprying soft soil into the air. "Gonna get your ass." The rabbit cannot get solid traction in the Muck. The race has gone on for 25 yards now and Rickey is close behind. He swoops down, snatches the rabbit with his left hand and breaks the rabbit's neck with his right.

Rickey smiles. He ties the rabbit to the handlebar of his bike. When the handlebar is covered with fur, he will ride into town and sell the rabbits for 50 cents each. A few will be brought home to mama for dinner.

"A lot of people in Pahokee can run down regular rabbits," he says. "That ain't nuthin'. You know you quick when you can run down a cottontail."

There were eight children in the Johnson family and Remuise (pronounced Ree-muss) was the only one who refused to attend church on Sunday. That day was sacred in the fall: Football on television.

Football is the town's salvation. The game flourishes from the sandlots through the high school level. Remuise Johnson and his friend Rickey Jackson spoke about little else as adolescents, even after a blend of boredom and curiosity lured them to the bars and pool rooms.

"At first, we'd never drink or smoke 'cause we was body freaks," says Robert Banks Jr., a former Pahokee High basketball star who spent time on the streets with Remuise and Rickey. (Banks' speech, like Remuise's, is not as heavily influenced by the street as Rickey's is.) "We was concerned about our bodies 'cause we thought that's how we was gonna make it out. But then someone said, "Well, if we have a beer, we can run it off tomorrow.' Then we be drinkin' a quart a day. Then we be gettin' real drunk. Then it was constant. Same thing with reefer.

"Pahokee's such a small town that everythin' spreads. Once that fire catches you might as well jump in it 'cause the flames gonna get you anyway. At the time we was comin' up, everyone wanted to whup everyone. Someone would be standin' on the corner and someone else'd walk over to him and without a word hit him in the head and start beatin' him from one side of the street to the other. Then everyone wanted to be a lover, to have three or four women. Now, everyone wants to be a pusher, a hustler. You go out on the street and you hardly see no young fellas workin' no more. They all out there sellin' dope."

It wasn't long before Banks, whose father is the reverend of the Bible Church of God, turned to Christianity. Remuise was shocked when he learned of his friend's conversion. They first talked about the change on a summer afternoon after Remuise's sophomore year in high school.

"Remuise, I been saved. Why don't you learn about Jesus?"

That evening, his friend's father explained the doctorines of the church.

He attended prayer sessions, and decided to clean up his life. "Guys who I saw doped up and lookin' like trash on the streets a few months before had a new look to them in church. I began to wonder where I would end up. I might have gotten hooked on drugs. Then you start stealin' to support your needs. Somethin' came over me. I stopped drinkin'. I didn't have no desire to go to dances. I started watchin' Oral Roberts and Christian programs on television. All I wanted to do was pray, to serve the Lord. I didn't even want to play football that much anymore."

When Rickey Jackson was in fourth grade, he showed up at East Lake Middle School for the first day of football practice and asked the coach for a tryout.

"You can't play on this team."

"Why?"

"This is a junior high team."

"I know."

"How old are you?"

"10."

"The players are 13 and 14."

"So?"

When the season began, Rickey was the starting nose guard. Palm Beach County school officials, alerted to the prodigy after a few games, ordered him off the team.

The experience etched an indelible image of winning on Rickey's mind. The chances of a 10-year-old making the junior high team were ridiculously remote. He believed he had achieved the impossible. For as long as he lived in Pahokee, Rickey would be told that his ambitions were beyond his means. He would pursue his goals with a fury, seeking not only the satisfaction of accomplishment, but also of belittling those who doubted him. From fourth grade on, he dreamed of making it to the National Football League. As he grew older, he avoided the ragtag sandlot games, because he was afraid his career might end with the twisting of a knee, the snapping of an ankle, the poking of an eye. Rickey was maligned on the street corners for his refusal to play, for sandlot football is a rite of manhood in Pahokee.

He responded by bragging. There is a sign at the entrance of the city welcoming visitors to the home of country singer Mel Tillis. "Someday," Rickey would say, "there be a sign on the other side of the road. 'PAHOKEE. Home of Rickey Jackson.' "

"I didn't like braggin'," Rickey says. "Pahokee be a town of losers. To get out, you got to tell yourself over and over that you a winner. I didn't want to end up like them wineheads in the streets. I didn't want to get stuck in the fields. All them old dudes you see on the streets—they ain't so old. Their bodies just be torn down. You work in the fields for 10 years—if you 30, you look 60. I convinced myself that I was goin' to be the best around and that nuthin' could stop me. Everythin' I did was a surprise to the people down there."

Folks on the street, accustomed to idle boasting, were unable to distinguish Rickey's talk from the banter of the city's previous athletic casualties.

"Lots of dudes talk that trash and lots of dudes go to college and flunk out and come back to the Muck," says Charlie Roach, the street-corner sage who played on the 1974 and 1975 Pahokee High teams with defensive ends Remuise and Rickey. "Rickey be smokin' and drinkin' and jivin' with the rest of us. He like a good time. He be talkin' about makin' the pros, but you figure he was gonna end up like the rest. If Rickey didn't make it, he probably be in front of the Daddy Add right now. Hustlin'. In high school, nobody even knew Rickey be that good. Remuise got all the publicity."

"I didn't want to play football the summer before 11th grade," Remuise says. "I stopped workin' out because it took time away from readin' the Bible. I asked God if He wanted me to play and the Lord said He could use me to help other players on the team. As long as I didn't take no cheap shots it was all right. So I went out and got a pair of squeezers. I'd squeeze them all day long until my forearms got so tight they felt like iron. That's why I didn't feel nuthin' when I cracked that guy's helmet into pieces. Once I hit a man on the side of his helmet so hard the ear cushion popped out and the screw put a hole in his head."

A tale is told about the coach of Atlantic High in Delray Beach who had developed a disciplined offense that relied on strength and execution. It was virtually impossible for his running attack to function in games with Pahokee because not one—or two—of his players could handle Remuise. Frustrated, the coach ordered a sweep to be run at Remuise. Linemen on the opposite side were instructed to pull and help bludgeon Remuise. A blocking back was dispatched to finish him off. Between four and six players (depending on the quality of the storyteller) were assigned to the demolition. "Remuise beat the hell out the whole Atlantic team and still made the tackle," says a street-corner raconteur.

He once made so many successive tackles in a game that safety James Burroughs, now a senior defensive back and preseason All-America at Michigan State, admonished him in a huddle: "Remuise, let a runner pass you. I wanna get in a hit."

Says coach Russell: "Remuise was the best prospect I've seen in the last 10 years. To give you an idea of how good he was, the other teams would leave him alone and run at Rickey. It's the same thing that happened at Pitt, when teams would run away from Hugh Green and Rickey would pick up the traffic."

Remuise was an all-Florida defensive end and tight end in 1974 and 1975, when those Pahokee teams reached the state AA championship games.

"During every game, my mind was on gettin' to church," Remuise says. "There were services every Friday night and I knew they were havin' a good time. After the games, I shook hands, got dressed real quick and caught the end of church."

Unable to attend after road games, Remuise conducted an abbreviated service on the team bus. He loaded his travel bag with Bibles and passed them among players and led the team in the pregame prayer. Many teammates—including Rickey Jackson—would follow him to the Bible Church of God and join the Christian Club that Remuise helped organize to discuss the Bible during lunch and free periods.

Perhaps the ultimate testimony to Remuise's talents came from the church's congregation, which once canceled a Friday evening service to watch him play. That was the night, it was said, that Remuise beat out God. After he caught a pass and dodged a defender, Remuise waved to church members in the stands as he sprinted for a touchdown.

The recruiting in Palm Beach is intense on the coast, primarily because of population density but also because the county's lowest functional-literacy test scores historically come from the inland Pahokee-Belle Glade (migrant worker) area. For whatever reason, Pahokee is woefully neglected by recruiters, considering the wealth of talent in the city.

The word spread about Remuise Johnson, though. Notre Dame, Michigan, Michigan State, Pittsburgh, Georgia Tech, Florida and Miami were all interested.

A Georgia Tech scout came down with a stopwatch and asked Remuise to run the 40-yard dash. He ran a 4.5 in street clothes.

"Can you do that again?" the astonished coach asked.

"Coach, I was just gettin' warmed up."

An assistant coach from Michigan stopped by to see Remuise. Rickey was nearby and jumped into the conversation.

"Can a freshman start on your team?" Rickey asked boldly.

"It's a possible," the coach said. "But to be honest with you, it's rare. It takes some time for a player to work into our system."

Rickey turned to Remuise with a scowl on his face. "I wouldn't go there," he said.

Remuise did not want to go anywhere. He preferred to remain in the Bible Church of God. He met a girl he liked in the church's sister congregation in the coastal city of Boynton Beach and he wrote to her frequently. Many people in Pahokee blamed the girl, Debra Andrews, whom Remuise would later marry, and other church members for holding him back. Coach Russell, whose life is devoted to lifting the town's talent out of the Muck, often argued with church members, imploring them to leave Remuise alone.

"If I could have got Remuise off by himself everything would have worked out," Russell says. "I thought I had Remuise cornered once and convinced to go to Michigan State. He said, 'Okay, I'm gonna sign.' So I called a coach from Michigan State and he flew all the way down from East Lansing and Remuise went into hiding. His mother didn't even know where he was.

"I think Remuise just became too attached to the people in the church. He didn't want to lose them. If Remuise really wanted to serve the Lord, all he would have had to do was play college football on Saturday afternoon and the school's entire alumni would have followed him to church on Sunday morning."

Robert Banks insists that church members did not persuade Remuise to stay. "I encouraged him *to go* to school," Banks says. "He didn't know what to do so I told him to consult God and let the Lord make the choice."

Remuise would enter church alone, drop to his knees and pray for hours, asking the Lord for direction. He once walked out of church shocked to see the sun rising. He had started to pray at six the previous evening.

He was worn down by the constant inquiries of schoolmates and townsfolk and the pressure from his family and coach Russell. A compromise was reached. Remuise would go to the University of Miami, where he could play football and remain within a two-hour car ride of the church. He signed a letter-of-intent grudgingly, saying, "Coach, I'm not gonna go. I'm tellin' you, I'm not gonna go. The only reason I'm signin' is to get everyone off my back."

Recruiting coordinator Bill Proulx was waiting at the bus station in Miami for Remuise to arrive at noon on August 15, 1976. Remuise was with Robert Banks and a few other church members in upstate New York harvesting potatoes.

"I got so sick after Remuise didn't go to school I had to go to the doctor," says Remuise's mother, Hattie, who expected Remuise to be the first of her children to attend college, though she didn't object to Remuise's working the fields during school vacations. She often recalls the day her son, then a sophomore, came running into the house rejoicing over the first signs of recruiter interest. "I'm gonna make it, mama!"

Remuise's decision shook Rickey. "I used to go to church with Remuise all the time. We was even baptized on the same day. But after he didn't go to college, I had people comin' up to me day-in and day-out, sayin', 'You ain't gonna go to school! You gonna be just like Remuise!'"

Although he attended services frequently, Rickey found it difficult to adhere to a few of the church's laws, especially the teaching against premartial sex. He had a daughter, Tomorrow, while a sophomore in high school. His son, Rickey Jr., was born two years later to his current girlfriend, Penny Brown.

"That didn't matter," says older sister Brenda. "I tell you, that church had Rickey on strings. You just couldn't reach him. He was all wrapped up in it. We had to keep at him and then all of a sudden he pulled away."

"I don't have nuthin' against the church," says Rickey's mama, Lelia Lawson, "but the church ain't gonna pay your bills, buy your food. You've got to make a good livin' to serve the Lord best. And you got to get an education to make a good livin.' "

Lelia Lawson and her husband divorced before Rickey entered elementary school, and she supported her family by driving a school bus. She is a strong, bosomy woman with a wonderfully rich laugh. She speaks with the inflections of a preacher, her voice reaching out and grasping the listener's attention.

"I was raised in Pahokee and I packed corn. I'd be out there in the fields tellin' myself, no way am I gonna let my kids do this. The main point in my life was to send my children to school. My baby didn't have to pick no corn for mama. Like I always said: You feed him, sleep him and when he is in need of a dollar or two, you give it to him. I didn't want him to know the feel of a $100 bill in his hand. I wanted to make sure he'd get out and go to school."

There is a proud smile that ought to be framed and mounted in a museum. "All five got high school diplomas. Four went to college."

Rickey played his final season as if he were out to expunge the city's collective memory of Remuise Johnson. "Remuise made Rickey," says Russell. "Everyone talked so much about Remuise that Rickey would drive himself as hard as he could to do better." But he would never be granted mythic stature on front porches or in high school hallways. The player who inherited Remuise's number, 89, would say a year later: "It gave me chills just flipping that man's jersey over my shoulder pads."

The movie camera used to film Pahokee games was damaged in Rickey's senior year and coach Russell did not have film of Rickey or safety James Burroughs to show recruiters.

Rickey waited for offers. Coaches called wondering about Remuise. Russell had to travel to a convention in Miami to persuade recruiters from Pitt and Michigan State to take his two current stars. Burroughs, wanting to play immediately, opted for Michigan State, which was on probation. Rickey assumed he would play anywhere and selected Pitt, which had just won the national championship, figuring exposure would be the best route to the NFL.

"Rickey? Goin' to Pittsburgh?" a man in town said to mama amid the excitement of the signing. "He be lucky just to wear a jersey up there."

Mama, Penny and not-yet-one-year-old Rickey Jr. accompanied him to the airport in West Palm Beach that August. "Rickey will never admit it, but at the last minute he didn't want to go," says Penny.

"He was crying."

What that be? The hole in the street with the fog comin' out. A manhole? Why they call it that? . . . Banana ice cream? Never heard of that before. . . . Anything a person ever wanted you can get on this street. Anything. . . . Got up at four in the mornin' and went down to Forbes Avenue and got me another scoop of that banana ice cream. Can you believe it? Banana ice cream.

"I don't think he'd ever seen a parking meter or a sewer before he came to Pittsburgh," says Pitt football coach Jackie Sherrill. "A lot of people have props as they come through life. Rickey had to do everything by himself. He started to mature in his junior year. Physically, he was ready to play the day he got here."

Rickey confronted his worst fears upon arrival at Pitt. He didn't start and was granted minimal playing time. Two factors inflamed his frustrations: The experienced starter was, in his opinion, an inferior player. He was envious of the emergence of a freshman defensive end named Hugh Green, whose performance in the Panthers' opening game, a nationally televised loss to Notre Dame, elicited raves. Rickey had traveled 1,200 miles to leave the shadow of Remuise Johnson, only to step under one far darker, far larger, far wider.

A team member recalls the day when Green, a second-team All-America as a freshman, uncharacteristically boasted of his success in Jackson's presence. "Rickey pushed Hugh into a corner of the locker room and told him that he was just as good, that the coaches wouldn't give him a chance to prove it and, if he kept on talking like that, he was going to kick his ass. Hugh is big, but Rickey is almost as big—and a lot crazier. Not too many people would want to mess with Rickey Jackson. Hugh didn't." Rickey and Hugh deny the story. They are close friends.

A few weeks into his freshman season, Rickey asked Sherrill for a day of judgment. He was told to be patient.

Rickey's mood swung between depression and anger. He phoned Pahokee coach Russell and said he was coming home. The land, the people, the fear of getting stuck in the Muck kept Rickey at Pitt. He got more playing time. He scored after intercepting against Tulane, and he was on television in the Gator Bowl, where Pitt beat Clemson, 34-3.

When he came home for the holidays, Rickey brought Remuise a Gator Bowl shirt. But he rarely saw his friend during summer vacation because Remuise interspersed construction work with migrant sojourns to northern farmland, and Rickey didn't bother much with the Bible Church of God.

"They don't let you have no sex before you get married," Rickey said. "I already got a daughter and a son and I ain't about to stop now. I ain't no hypocrite."

He shrugged. "That's okay. I'm not saved now, but I look at it like this: After I make it in the NFL, I'll get married and go back to church and I'll be saved again."

Rickey Jackson is walking to the Cathedral of Learning for class
Religious Studies 148. He leads his visitor on a winding tour through
the Gothic archways with an air of proud ownership, as if this castle
were his home.

"If Remuise could see this, I know he'd come here. There be more
to religion than just Jesus. You can hear about Calvin and Martin
Luther and all them dudes.

"I don't like where Remuise at. God don't want you tearin' down
your body for nuthin'. Me and Hugh visited a children's hospital and
I saw a lot of kids in there who would pray to God for the talent Remuise got.

"Remuise could be in church more in Pittsburgh than he was in
high school. I be real tight with the Lord. He got Christ. I got Christ
Who is to say who got more Christ? How can a person tell you to live
for heaven? That the flesh ain't nuthin'. That only the spirit counts. I
can't live for when I die. Remuise be livin' his life. I be livin' my life.
Whatever it takes, I'm gonna survive.

"He already got people sayin', 'Remuise used to be.' When you
used to have a million dollars but now you broke—you ain't got
nuthin'. 'Used to be' is like death to me. In a few years, Remuise will
be all hunched over like an old man 'cause of what all that hard work
does to your back. You wait and see."

Remuise Johnson isn't sure if he's going to get to the street-corner revival later on. He just got home from work and he's tired. He
quit his job putting up walls for a less-demanding one laying the
foundation for floors in a condominium. "My back was gettin' to
me," he explains.

The revival is purposely situated near a rabble of people drinking tonight into tomorrow. The choir serenades the neighborhood in a
rich harmony, enticing people from blocks away.

The preacher wails about the glories of Christ, haranguing the
hazards of the bottle, the dice, the needle and cheating.

A man wearing a rumpled gas station attendant's shirt with the
name "Buck" stitched over the pocket comes swaggering toward the
preacher, contemptuously tearing the brown paper bag from around
a beer bottle.

"What you talkin' that trash for?" Buck shouts. "Man, if you
read the Bible, you find out that the Lord say it all right to have more
than one lady. That's right. I knows, 'cause I's a learned man."

A large man quickly strolls over to Buck and politely requests
that he lower his voice tone to a whisper. Another congregation
member shouts, "Shut up, you crazy old man!"

"Crazy! I knows the Bible from Deuteronomy to Leviticus. If you
so smart and holy," Buck calls out, his voice lifting above the preacher's, "tell me who be the wisest man in the Bible?"

There is no response.

"You see, you don't know nuthin' about the Bible. Well, I'll tell

ou. Solomon. And Solomon be a black man. That's right, wisest man
n the Bible be black. And that nigguh had hisself one thousand
vives!"

"The Devil!" lashes out the preacher. "Right here on your front
porch! Pay the Devil no mind!"

The scene is not out of the ordinary. Such antics shadow the re-
vivals, forcing Remuise to examine his religious beliefs and weigh
heir importance. "Even if there is no such thing as God and if Jesus
never lived, I'd still live my life this way," says Remuise in his
apartment in Boynton Beach, less than two blocks from the church.
"I have my son and my wife and my family and my friends and I'm
a happy man. How many people you know can say that they truly
happy?

"The people, they don't understand why I stayed to serve the
Lord. A lot of people wish I went to college and Rickey stayed home.
They figured out of all the players, I had the best chance to make it.
But Rickey's like a brother to me and I'm behind him 100 percent.
People come back to me and say Rickey said, 'Everyone say that
Remuise was better than me in high shool. Well, where is he now?'
He may say I'm a loser, but he don't mean it. He just got to say it so
he can think he took the right road. What did I lose? Money? I
wouldn't mind makin' $200,000 a year. But if I did, I'd give it to the
peoples who are down. The poor peoples. Who is society to tell a man
he's a loser if he don't make all kinds of money and want to be a star?
want to live a normal life and make heaven my home. I know I
could live a moral life and play football. But I'm happy here. Rickey
was a Christian once. He may say he's a Christian now, but in his
heart, he knows he straddlin' the fence. You got to accept Jesus 100
percent. Rickey ain't no Christian."

The blue jersey is smoothed by the hands over the stomach and
tucked inside the pants. *They'll all know the name Rickey Jackson
by the time this game ends. I'll show them who I am. I won't just
tackle people. I'll slaughter them.* The tip of a white washcloth is
folded inside the top of the pants, allowing the body of the towel to
unfurl. On the cloth are the initials R. J. and the number 89. Rickey
Jackson wore the number 87 as a defensive end for the University of
Pittsburgh between 1977 and 1980. During that time, he was not
asked why he played many games with the number 89 beneath his
jersey. Nobody noticed.

The fists are pressed against the forehead, the mind is in harmony with the almighty chords of the organ, the eyelids are clenched
and the lower lip is quivering as Remuise Johnson stands before the
altar in the Bible Church of God praising the Lord. Remuise will not
forget his friend up that cold road in Pittsburgh. He prays that Rickey Jackson will have a good game, that Rickey will not be injured,
that Rickey will make it to the National Football League. *I know
that if Rickey makes it, I could have made it, too.*

PITT 36, TEMPLE 2
September 27, 1980

Evidence of the sore rib cage is seen on the face of Temple tail-back Kevin Duckett. His cheeks wince as he removes the shoulder pads. "Everybody was saying, 'Watch out for Green! Watch out for Green!' All I kept seeing was 87, pounding me all day. He was crazy. After I was down, he'd grab my ankle and try to twist it off."

"Rickey, Duckett says you tried to twist off his ankle."

He laughs. "I wanted to send Remuise a souvenir."

The media have dispersed from around Green's locker and a ring of kids surround the empty stall, waiting for Hugh to return from a shower for an autograph session. Rickey, whose locker is next to Green's, moves out of the way.

A man approaches 87 with the hope of procuring a star signature without waiting 10 minutes.

"Who are you?" he asks.

"I be a walk-on tryin' to get me a scholarship."

"Oh."

The man moves to Green's locker.

"I lead the team in tackles, sack the punter, break up passes and still get no pub. What do I got to do to get people to know me?" Jackson shakes his head sadly. "I'm gonna kill somebody next week."

He phones his mother and Penny afterward to report his heroics and to check on life at home. The conversations are brief. Twice, he asked Penny about little Rickey.

"Penny be a special girl," Rickey says as he walks to his dormitory. "After I make it in the pros, I'm gonna marry her. There be so many different kinds of women here. Some gonna be doctors, lawyers. But I still stick with Penny. I know it be hard for her to stay down in Pahokee while I'm up here. I'll make it up to her someday."

A stunning woman with a caramel complexion appears as the dorm elevator opens.

"Good game," she says, sliding by him with a smile.

Rickey nods and steps inside. "That be my old girlfriend," he says.

In Rickey's room, a woman with the tender mocha features of a model is slightly annoyed. She had come over after the game as instructed and had been waiting for some time, doing homework.

"How come it took you so long?"

"Interviews," Rickey says, laughing at his joke.

He placates her with talk of a party later that evening. In the meantime, there is someone he wants to see upstairs.

"I be back in a little while," he tells her. "Wait for me."

"C'mon, Remuise, let's run home," father says to son as they exit the church. He backpedals, laughing at the tiny steps of a one-year-old as the mother jogs along. She looks at the furious little strides and can't help but laugh. The child, glancing up at his parents, giggles happily as the three run down the street through darkness under a sky powdered lightly with summer stars.

PITT 41, LOUISVILLE 23
November 8

The publicity pumped out of Dave Billick's office helped Tony Dorsett win the Heisman Trophy in 1976. Billick's task in 1980 is far more difficult: to influence sports writers to select a purely defensive player for the first time in the Heisman's 45-year history.

He wages a magnificent campaign, capping it in November by mailing a three-foot poster of Green to 4,000 writers around the country. The sports information director is asked if he thinks Rickey Jackson is being denied due publicity.

"We haven't neglected Rickey. We know how good he is. Maybe he is an All-America. But, let's face it, I'm pushing Hugh Green for the Heisman. Do you think people would believe me if I told them that Pitt had the best *two* defensive ends in the country?"

Louisville punter Mark Blasinsky stands on his five-yard line surveying the defense. The snap is ordinary. The initial movements in Blasinsky's technique reveal no excessive motion. The unusual aspect of the play is the blue blur that whips in on the punter at a sharp angle. A cottontail wouldn't have stood a chance. "I took one step and 87 was all over me," Blasinsky would say later. "If I tried to kick it, he would have blocked it, so I just took the hit. I've never seen anyone rush that fast. It was amazing."

But no amount of lightning will steal the thunder of Green on this day. The crowd stands and applauds for a minute as the number 99 is retired in a halftime ceremony that might have touched Rickey had he not been so tormented by his own lack of recognition.

"If they won't retire my jersey, then I'll retire it myself," he said the day before. "I'll take it home and hang it on my own wall."

Remuise has lived on the coast for three years now. He visits Pahokee, walking the corridors of the high school, pointing to the bench where he and Rickey used to sit between classes. Students, some of whom were 10 years old when Remuise made hallow the number 89, encircle him.

"Remuise! Remuise! When you comin' back, Remuise?"

"You thinkin' of playin' again?"

"Yeah, I been thinkin' about it," he tells them with a smile, not wanting to hurt anybody's feelings.

He walks down Rardin Avenue. "Yep. When Remuise played defensive end," says a man, the words accented by a slight chuckle, "Rickey could hardly find a place on the squad."

Children, ladies, old folks cluster around him. "Remuise! Remuise! When you comin' back?"

PITT 45, ARMY 7
November 15

Rickey sets up two touchdowns in the first quarter by intercepting a pass and blocking a punt. He would also make 12 tackles, three quarterback sacks and cause a fumble before the game ends.

"Maybe," Billick says in jest, "I put the wrong guy on that poster." The humor does not appease Rickey, who is beginning to worry about the NFL draft. "I won't get noticed if I don't do things like that. I make 20 tackles and they give me 15. I make 15 and they give me 10. Nobody appreciates me in Pittsburgh. I be tired of Pittsburgh."

Three men struggle to free the back of a Cadillac, stuck on a ball of concrete rising out of the street in front of Remuise's apartment. The concrete sits under the rear axle, propping the right wheel off the ground. The men frantically lift and push while the driver steps on the gas pedal. Loose dirt sprays from under the wheels. In the distance, Remuise is walking home from work in dusty work clothes.

"Remuise will take care of this."

Remuise looks at the car as if he has the idea of hoisting it free by himself. He is tired, though, so he steps into his own car, pulls behind the Cadillac and, with a nudge of the gas pedal, slides it off the concrete.

"Thank you," says the driver. "Let me give you a couple dollars for your troubles."

"Oh, no."

"Don't be like that," the man says, holding out a few bills. "With the price of gas these days, it costs this much to start up your car."

"No," Remuise smiles, waving off the money. "You have a good day, now."

PITT 37, SOUTH CAROLINA 9
Gator Bowl

The outcome is decided early, the second half's only attraction being Heisman Trophy winner George Rogers' struggle to gain 100 yards against the nation's best defense. In the third quarter, Rogers takes a handoff at the South Carolina six-yard line and collides savagely with Rickey, the impact of the blow briefly jolting the runner to attention. Officials whistle, but Rickey doesn't feel the play is dead enough. He locks the backpedaling Rogers in a bear hug and pushes him into and out of the end zone.

"I knew all about Hugh," Rogers says. "But they didn't tell me nuthin' about you."

"They just kind of slipped me in on you."

"Well, you are the toughest thing out here."

The game had been hyped as a confrontation between Rogers (113 yards) and Green (five tackles), but Rickey makes his final case for publicity with 19 tackles.

The reporters are oblivious, flocking around Green to find out why he *didn't* have a good game. A stray writer meanders over to Rickey.

"I didn't get the pub of Hugh Green. But the fans know what I did. You can't tell me I'm not the best."

Remuise is wearing the blue Pahokee jersey with the number 89
as he plays defensive back in a three-man game on the playground
near his apartment. Fred, a superb athlete himself, is the receiver.
He runs down the field and cuts sharply to the left, his eyes following
the flight of the pass, which appears to be perfectly timed. Remuise
accelerates with smooth strides and snares the ball with one palm.
"What kind of pass was that?" Fred screams. "I had him beat.
Bad!"

Fred sprints downfield on his next pattern. Remuise moves as
fast backward as the receiver does forward. The pass is overthrown.
While Fred gets the ball, the quarterback calls to Remuise: "Let him
get it this time and then tackle him."

Fred takes three steps, turns around and catches the ball with a
mammoth grin creasing his face. He tries to juke Remuise, who
laughs, picks Fred up and plunks him down.

"I told you I could beat you."

"Man, I let you beat me so I could tackle you."

"I don't want to hear no 'scuses."

"No 'scuses. I play this game for pride."

The inside of the home, a trailer with cement steps set out in
front, is devoted to Rickey. Sunlight splashes off plaques and tro-
phies, granting an ordinary living room a regal touch. Family and
friends are stuffed in a horseshoe around the television, awaiting the
NFL draft. Rickey sits on the floor, leaning on his mama and cra-
dling his four-year-old son in his arms. Penny is not far behind.

The room rejoices as Hugh Green is picked by Tampa Bay. Green
and a few other Pitt players had visited Pahokee earlier in the
spring. Rickey is hoping that his play in the Gator Bowl and East-
West Shrine game convinced scouts he, too, is worthy of a first-round
selection. The round passes. Anxiety replaces eagerness. The second
round is almost over and Rickey looks uncomfortable. He stands up
and begins to pace the living room. His back is to the television when
his name finally is flashed. The New Orleans Saints, the worst team
in the league, have made him the 51st overall pick in the draft.

"What was the Saints' record last year?"

"I think they won only one game."

"Out of how many?"

"Sixteen."

"Whoa! Rickey got his work cut out for him now."

The phone rings.

"SHHHHH!" Rickey hushes the havoc, holding his palm over the
mouthpiece. "The coach, Bum Phillips, be comin' on."

"Hello, Mr. Bum. How you doin'?"

The conversation is brief.

"What he say, Rickey? What he say?"

"He say he knew I be a leader and that I would lead the defense.
He got that right."

George Rogers, the Saints' first-round pick, calls. Rickey's agent phones. (Later, he would negotiate a reported $225,000, three-year contract with the Saints—including a $75,000 signing bonus—not bad for an unknown rookie, even one who would start at linebacker.) A newspaper reporter calls. A radio station in New Orleans conducts a live interview.

"I just need a chance to play," Rickey says. "That's all I ask. I'll try to bring New Orleans from the bottom to the top. Just like I done the rest of my life. From the bottom to the top, I be used to that."

Remuise is sitting on the back porch of his apartment after work as the sun sets. He gazes into the distance, beyond the yard cluttered with weeds, beyond the flipped shopping cart, the discarded motor-oil cans, shattered glass, crumbled cinderblocks. "Sometimes I get to thinkin' about playin' again. If I did, I'd cut my hair real close to my head and I'd go back home to mama and eat some neckbone and collard greens and all that good food and I'd drink a quart of milk and orange juice every day like I did in high school. I could put on 25 pounds in a few weeks without addin' an ounce of fat. It wouldn't be hard for me to get back in shape.

"I was thinkin' of playin' some semipro ball. You know anything about that? Do the pro scouts ever look at semipro teams?

"You know what I'd really like to do. I'd like to be a grandfather and go to church and see all my grandchildren sittin' in a row, clappin' and singin' and praisin' the Lord. I'd like to tell them how to have a good life. That would be joyful.

"Hey, Debra!" he calls to his wife inside. "You and little Remuise ready to go to church?"

The argument rages on in front of Daddy Add's pool hall, as it always had, as it always will.

"Rickey made it, that's all I got to say."

"In his own way, Remuise made it, too."

"Don't you see what Rickey did? Ever since he went to Pitt, he showed everyone else they could make it. Ronnie Osborne, he up at Iowa State. Joe Brown, he up at Iowa State. Nate Hannah, he at Michigan State, Clint Wilson goin' to Pitt this year. Rickey their example."

"I be all for Rickey, don't get me wrong. I be as happy for him as anybody else in Pahokee. All I be sayin' is that Remuise was better in high school. And if he woulda gone on, he woulda made the pros, too."

"You can't say that 'cause you don't know. Rickey proved hisself with desire."

"Remuise has the same desire. Only it be for prayin'."

"But, man, he coulda made it to the NFL. If I had my choice, I be a star on TV before I be sittin' in church and prayin'."

"Why don't you be more respectful of God?"

The dispute intensifies, until it is halted by one statement, punctuated by the slapping of palms. "Listen here! Remuise may be a Christian. But Rickey, he a Saint."

Mudder's Day

GENERAL

By *HUGH MULLIGAN*

From the Associated Press
Copyright © 1981, the Associated Press

Mud wrestling, the latest spectator sport sweeping the country, or oozing across it, made its first big splash in our area the other night.

On the whole, it beats bear baiting, pig sticking and cock fighting and is not nearly as violent as Italian soccer, in which during my European experience a referee had his nose bitten off.

The sport made its local debut at the Cuckoo's Nest, an aptly named sometime discotheque that has been trying to broaden its psychedelic horizons with more exciting, from the audience viewpoint, forms of groping in the dark between the stabs of the strobe lights.

In keeping with the hallowed hyperbole of professional wrestling, the contestants, all female, had names like Killer Kim, Hurricane Heidi and Mad Duck Marcia. Or was it Mona? Monica? My notes are a bit mud splattered. I'm not much on remembering names, but I never forget a leotard.

Ballerina-style black leotards were the uniform of battle, although the figures they attempted to contain were a good deal more lush than one observed among the Royal corps de ballet at Covent Garden or the Bolshoi. The decorum was a bit less decorous, too.

"No biting, no hair pulling, no eye-gouging," the referee, known as Mr. Clean, intoned the rules as the gladiatrixes entered the arena: a 12-by-15 foot pit of mud about a foot deep on the site of what a few hours before had been the dance floor.

Mr. Clean, wearing an immaculate white T-shirt and matching clam digger shorts, detailed for the contestants several sensitive areas of the anatomy that were not up for grabs "under federation rules." He never did specify which federation, but there was no challenge to his authority.

Indeed, there were no managers, seconds, handlers or cutmen in the respective corners to file a protest or throw in the towel. If any of the girl grapplers had a husband or boyfriend in the house, he kept a low profile throughout the evening. But there was no shortage of fans, both male and female, urging on the combatants once the bell sounded.

Actually there was no bell. The referee just said "Go at it" or words to that effect and they did, for three two-minute rounds. The match began with each Leotarded Lioness facing the other in a kneeling position, hands on the opponent's shoulders. The object of the game hasn't changed since Ajax got a half-Nelson on Ulysses back in the primordial ooze, with a Greek scribe named Homer in the press box: attempt to pin your opponent to the mat, both shoulders touching, with a series of holds, locks and grips.

In the first match of the evening, a slender, long-legged blonde named "Killer Kim" slithered and sluiced through the slime trying to come to grips with a slippery compact brunette simply named "Mad Dog," but never was able to get a handle on her. By the time the third round was over, the blonde wasn't very blonde anymore and the eel-like Mad Dog had got the upper hand or at least was sitting on the other's face.

"A revolting, dehumanizing spectacle, I'm leaving," said a young lady in the front row, whose jogging jacket paid allegiance to the University of Connecticut.

"I'm not," answered her boyfriend, or former boyfriend, emptying his beer into the pit to lubricate the mud bank, a custom that seemed to win encouragement from the management, which after all was also in the beverage business.

The house, for the local debut of this new exhibition sport, was an odd mixture of young college kids and middle class blue-collar types, several of whom wore the intitals "B.P.O.E." across their backs. The predominance of sports cars and pickup trucks in the parking lot seem to bear out this random analysis of the audience. Men outnumbered women, but not overwhelmingly.

The audience was strangely sedate until Hurricane Heidi and Mad Duck entered the lists. Then even the boys in the back billiards room deserted their cue sticks for the main event.

Heidi was a generously built baby-faced blonde with a Bo Derek braided coiffure, who according to the announcer tipped the scales at 165 pounds. This gave her a 40-pound weight advantage over the taller, rather elegant looking Mad Duck, who affected a sort of Theda Bara hairdo and the same bee-stung lips, soon to be buried in the muck.

Although this was opening night and her first bout, Heidi already had a noisy claque who cheered her on with resonant bovine mooings. An instant Mad Duck faction responded with vociferous quackings. Still, the ladies went about their slithery scuffling in a rather demure fashion, despite the barnyard overtures from the gallery, most of them now on their feet, moving around the pit to follow the action. Mad Duck was quick and wiry, inclined to use her height as leverage to overturn the other, but Heidi had the ability to roll her-self into a ball, a large mud ball that didn't present any shoulders to pin. Both seemed to lack the killer instinct, although Heidi several times rolled over on top and seemed to be squashing more than her opponent's hopes.

At one point the referee tried to separate them, since neither seemed able to break the other's grip or escape her bulk. For his troubles, he wound up with two embarrassing handprints on the back of his previously pristine shorts.

I can't recall whether Hurricane or Mad Duck won the featured event of the evening. Near the end of the round, someone at the cor-ner of the bar intoned, "Here's mud in your eye," and as if on cue the interlocked combatants obliged by plopping over in a huge splash of slime. The local dry cleaner cheered the loudest.

As if in sensitivity to any women's rights issues that may be at stake here, the management urged the patrons to "remember Mon-day nights are ladies nights with an all-male review."

Role reversals or something are involved here.

A Long-Playing Hitter Copes With Loneliness

BASEBALL

By *STEVE JACOBSON*

From Newsday
Copyright © 1981, Newsday, Inc.

"I'm glad the Series is going back to New York," Joe Garvey said softly. "This way, he's going to get to see the kids a couple more days. Aren't those nice pictures?"

He guided his listener to the locker stall of his son in the Dodgers' clubhouse. There were two large color photographs of Steve Garvey's daughters, the bills of their baseball caps turned up, their eyes bright and smiling. There was another in black and white of Garvey crouching in his Dodgers uniform, the two girls on his knees, his arms around them.

The pictures were taken in spring training, such a long time ago. And high up on the stall, suspended from a coat hook, was a large painting some parents call refrigerator art. It was in orange and black Halloween colors on newsprint, just the kind of thing a 5-year-old would send to her father.

The stall had a wistful look. Garvey, the father, 32 years old and the most significant player on the Dodgers for a decade, spoke with long pauses, his eyes narrowed, and he seemed to be pinching back tears. "It's the hardest part," he said.

At midsummer, the storybook marriage of Garvey, the embodiment of athletic myths—a junior high school was named for him—and Cyndy, the beautiful, aspiring West Coast television personality, came apart after nine years. Cyndy left him for composer-piano player Marvin Hamlisch. Krisha, 7, and Whitney, 5, are living with her on Long Island, not far from the Rockville Centre home where Joe Garvey lived before Steve was born. "Pure and simply," Steve Garvey said, "I am no longer married to a wonderful wife and mother."

It was a shattering event for him. It is a cruel fact of public life that Garvey is not permitted his private sadness. It's a measure of the man that he was able to maintain his professional standards. He continued building his consecutive-game streak, to 946. He is hitting .450 in the World Series, .366 in the Dodgers' 15 postseason games. Over the long season, when a man can't direct his thoughts so completely, Garvey was more remarkable. His run production was as good as ever. He made only one error in 119 games. His batting average fell to .283, his lowest in a decade, 20 points off his career average.

"I try to block out everything but the task at hand," he said. "Fortunately, I've always had that ability." With runners on base, with the game in the balance, Garvey believes he was more aggressive with his oversized forearms, able to turn the emotional screws tighter. He relates his ability to concentrate to that of Bjorn Borg, but Garvey still is not impervious to his personal pain. "It obviously had some effect, probably in average," he said. "I would have thought less of myself if I had hit .300 and continued as if nothing had happened. There's no way you block it all off. I wouldn't be the person I think I am."

Garvey always has tried to be the person he thought he was, and it wasn't that difficult. He goes back in Dodgers tradition to the time he was 6, his father drove the Greyhound bus in spring training and Steve was their batboy. He rode the bus and sat in the dugout, and the words he heard burned his ears. "That shattered some images for me," he recalled. "I thought, I'm not going to do that when my time comes. Somebody had to set an example sometimes."

For a lot of years, a lot of Dodgers believed the example Garvey and his wife set was of how to cultivate a self-serving image. He was generous with his time, cordial to polite fans and courteous, a virtual island in a sea of selfishness. He says his consistency eventually convinced teammates and critics of his sincerity. He is certain, however, that others gloat over his misfortune. Another thought is that his vulnerability has brought him closer to his teammates.

Irrepressible teammate Jay Johnstone teases with obscenities. Garvey concedes that he has those words in his private vocabulary, "but you will never hear me say them." It is not an attempt to create image, he says, it's the way he is, and the image has followed.

Since the separation, Garvey says he has heard from all of the women he ever has known, telling him where they could be reached. "Most of them say, if I need someone to talk to, they're available," Garvey said. Some of them clearly want a piece of a major celebrity who suddenly appears available. "I try to be as private a person in my life as I am open as a professional," he said. "There is no privacy for me now."

He has directed his wit to cope with some of the insensitive questions. He likened his ability to perform professionally while his private life was being torn to "separation of church and state. State is my profession; church is my private life."

He closed his ears to outrageous catcalls from fans in San Fran-

cisco, New York and Montreal by never acknowledging that h
heard anything. "Nothing a fan can say will ever affect me in a sta
dium," he said. He was stung by a gossip-page item in San Francisc
and a brutal anonymous wisecrack in New York suggesting tha
Hamlisch play the National Anthem at Yankee Stadium. The un
washed fans have no monopoly on bad taste.

He is as proud that he has coped as he is proud of his record fo
longevity. The consecutive-game streak is a kind of allegory
"There's the durability, of going out there day after day," he said
"There's the consistency; in order to play, the manager has to wan
you out there every day. And, three, there's a certain amount of lead
ership involved when you do play with some minor injury, to be hur
and still get a hit."

During his last eight seasons, beginning at age 25, Garvey ha
been the All-Star first baseman, batting .311 with an average of 2:
home runs and 104 runs batted in. He is in the last year of a contrac
which pays him $335,000 and probably makes him the most under
paid player in baseball. He thinks 85 or 90 players are being paid
more.

In a year he will be free to play the marketplace, if he chooses. H
says the thought that his daughters live in New York and that a big
spender here, Yankees Owner George Steinbrenner, is an admirer i:
in his awareness, but he wants to stay in Los Angeles. "Sometimes,"
he said, "it's like my name has three extra words: 'Steve Garvey, Lo:
Angeles Dodgers' . . . My whole career from the age of 6 has beer
with the Dodgers."

This season when the loneliness of the road was intensified by the
absence of family at home, Garvey made the Dodgers more his family than ever. He plunged himself into reading and studying issues
with a thought of politics in the future. He speaks of the Senate. He
reads about foreign policy, abortion, gun control.

He seeks reinforcement and support from his Catholicism; but
does not try to inflict his beliefs on others or back away from the responsibility to make his own decisions. He is determined to guard
what is his own, and is not public, as jealously as possible. "I'm
aware that my public performance makes my private life of interest," he said. "I have two lovely daughters. I will no longer subject
them to the sports pages."

At World Series time, there is more public scrutiny, but there is
less time for intrusion into his privacy. It's easier to focus on the
game. "I try to raise my concentration higher," he said. "I try to
eliminate as much extra input as possible. I will continue to live my
life as a baseball player; this is something that occurred in my private life."

Joe Garvey, 32 years a Greyhound driver, listened quietly. "I
miss my granddaughters, too," he said.

Judge's Comments

Many writers have a talent for discovering and bringing out the human side of athletics. The George Steinbrenners, Billy Martins, Reggie Jacksons and Muhammad Alis are always in the spotlight and ready to talk. Others go about their quiet way, handling themselves with dignity both on the field and off.

Steve Garvey, the outstanding first baseman of the Los Angeles Dodgers, is such a player. Divorce, separation from his two lovely daughters and national exposure of the personal side of his life put him through a tortuous 1981 season that few fans could understand. Steve Jacobson picked Garvey as his subject and dealt with Garvey's sadness with sensitivity and understanding.

Through it all, Garvey survived, devoting himself to baseball and performing at the same high level that Dodger fans have become accustomed to seeing. He maintained his high personal standards, treated fans with respect and understanding, and suffered in silence.

But, as Jacobson so capably points out, fans and writers throughout the country wouldn't even allow the man one important luxury. They wouldn't allow him privacy in his torment.

Child Psychology?

by Eric Mencher of the *St. Petersburg Times and Evening Independent*. There's no room for mistakes these days, even in the supposedly easy-going world of little league football. The coach takes his player to task for missing a tackle. Copyright © 1981, St. Petersburg (Fla.) Evening Independent.

Born With One Leg and Tremendous Heart

by Bill Serne of the *St. Petersburg Times*. Carl Joseph, a Florida youngster who made headlines as a one-legged high school football star, looks out toward the practice field at Bethune-Cookman College. Joseph, listed as a linebacker, sees action in extra-point and other defensive situations. Copyright © 1981, St. Petersburg (Fla.) Evening Independent.

Indiana Wins NCAA Title

COLLEGE BASKETBALL

By *JOHN FEINSTEIN*

From the Washington Post
Copyright © 1981, The Washington Post

On a night when basketball seemed unimportant, Indiana won the most important college basketball game there is. In doing so, the Hoosiers denied North Carolina Coach Dean Smith the one honor that has escaped him during his 20 years as a head coach.

Led by the brilliant Isiah Thomas, who scored 19 of his 23 points in the second half, Indiana put together an overpowering second half to blitz the Tar Heels, 63-50, tonight, winning the national championship for the second time in six years.

But there was almost no game tonight. Because of the shooting of President Reagan this afternoon, the NCAA waited until less than an hour before tipoff to decide the contest should be played.

The tipoff was nine minutes late because of the events in Washington and the public address announcer in the Spectrum informed the crowd of 18,276 that the President had come through surgery successfully and was in good condition.

The game started and, for two hours, reality stopped and a group of college kids played a game. None of the players expressed any regret over playing, with Thomas summing up the general feelings of the two teams:

"We were happy the President wasn't dead. A lot of people get shot. We were just happy that he could still think with his brain, that's the most important part. We were just trying to win a ball game tonight."

Thomas may have been trying too hard during the first half. He shot one of seven from the floor and was outplayed by Carolina point guard Jimmy Black. As a team the Hoosiers, who won their last 10 games to finish 26-7, could not get untracked offensively, shooting just 38 percent.

But offense does not make or break Indiana teams. It is defense that has made Coach Bob Knight a national champion twice. Tonight was no different. For the first 20 minutes the Indiana defense kept it in the game. The second 20 minutes the Indiana defense took North Carolina out of it.

"They played more aggressively on defense tonight than the two times we played them in the regular season the last two years," said Smith, who refused to show any emotion at the end. "They played about as good a second half as anyone has played against us all season."

It was during the first half, though, that Carolina had its chance to win this game. Al Wood, who had destroyed Virginia Saturday with 39 points, started well, hitting three of his first five shots, making it clear to Knight that Landon Turner could not stay with him.

Into the game came Jim Thomas. At 6-3, he gave away three inches to Wood. But he made up for it with quickness. Wood finished the night with 18 points, but many of them came in the final three minutes when Indiana was in control as Thomas dogged him all over the court.

"I knew I had the quickness and I knew I would get help from my teammates," said Thomas. "I tried to deny him the ball, keep him from getting that first step to the hoop."

With Wood quiet, the Tar Heels struggled offensively. They also had problems because Smith was forced to rest Wood, Sam Perkins and James Worthy. "I was getting a lot of tired signs out there," Smith said. "I think we're in shape. We might have been too excited."

The tired signs and Thomas kept the Tar Heels from building on a 16-8 lead midway through the half. Indiana crept back, Randy Wittman doing most of the offensive work from outside. On the final play of the half, Wittman hit his fourth outside bomb and it gave Indiana a 27-26 halftime lead.

"That shot was important because it meant we were forced ahead even though we knew we hadn't played a good half," Isiah Thomas said. "It may have been the turning point of the game."

Not so, said the two coaches. "I thought the key for us were the two quick steals Isiah got at the start of the second half," Knight said. "That got us going."

Smith agreed. "If there was a turning point, those two steals were it," he said.

For Thomas the turning point may have come during intermission. He sat in front of his locker listening as Knight told his team, "Patience, be patient. We can play much better. Just think patience and remember there are only 20 minutes left in the season."

Quickly, Thomas made certain this season would end for Indiana the same way it did the last time the Final Four played here, in 1976. On the first possession of the second half he stole the ball from Black and went in for a layup and a 29-26 lead. Perkins and Turner traded baskets, then Thomas did his magic act again. He dashed into the middle, flicked the ball from Perkins and was gone again for another layup and a 33-28 lead.

Carolina, which almost never gets rattled, was rattled. Worthy, who made just three of 12 shots before fouling out, threw another bad pass and Wittman, who finished with 16 points, hit another jumper. Black finally hit but Thomas made a jumper and went backdoor for a layup. In just 4:28 he had eight points, two assists and two steals. Indiana led, 39-30, and Carolina never got closer than seven.

"Isiah getting going that way is the way it's been all season," said center Ray Tolbert, who had 11 rebounds. "He's our catalyst. He makes us roll."

The Hoosiers rolled this entire tournament, winning their five games by 113 points, a record. They shot 63 percent tonight, compared to 43 percent for the Tar Heels (36 percent the second half). They made an excellent team, one that finished its season 29-8, look bad.

"They took us out of our offense completely," said Wood, who wept during the award ceremonies. "They're a lot like us, only more patient. That may be the big difference, patience."

Carolina's impatience was created by Indiana's in-your-face, help-at-every-turn defense. The Hoosiers overplayed everywhere, forced 19 turnovers and only lapsed once, letting Carolina creep within 55-47 with 2:22 left on a Mike Pepper jumper.

But just when it appeared, as Smith put it, "that we might have a great TV finish," Indiana nailed the lid shut. With Carolina trying to close the margin to six, Tolbert stole the ball from Perkins and fed Steve Risley, who was fouled and made both shots.

That sealed it. Indiana, which had been 7-5 at one time in December, had won a title even Knight never imagined it could until the last month of the season.

For Knight and his players, the events in Washington did little to dampen that joy. Knight said nothing to his players about the shootings, knowing they were aware of them. Instead he brought Quinn Buckner, captain of the 1976 team, and John Havlicek, his teammate on the 1960 Ohio State championship team, in to talk to the players about what winning a national title meant.

For Knight and the Hoosiers it meant joy and ecstasy. For Smith and his players it was another bitter pill, an almost horrifying letdown after being so close.

Denied the national title in the ultimate game for the third time, Smith remained stoic. He applauded his players as they received their awards and showed them no emotion during their brief time alone in the locker room.

Only once did Smith betray his feelings. When someone asked if he felt frustrated by feigning happiness.

"I guess we'll be like Penn State football," he said. "They finish second sometimes, too. I'm thrilled to be second. Ask Digger (Phelps) how he would feel about being second. He's only been to the Final Four once. Ask my great friend Looie (Carnesseca). He's never been here.

"I'm thrilled to be No. 2."

Less true words were never spoken.

For Boyish Rose, It's All Fun

BASEBALL

By *HAL BODLEY*

From The Sporting News
Copyright © 1981, The Sporting News Publishing Co.

Several hours after a recent game, Pete Rose picked up the telephone and called Cincinnati.

"Had two hits, slid on my belly to score a run and we win 6-1," Rose said, sounding like a little boy giving his dad a report. "Yeah, I'm swinging pretty good right now. Closing in on the record. How you swinging?

"No, that's not good. I don't want you to play with older boys. It's bad for your confidence. Play with guys your own age. Don't forget. A hundred percent is not enough. Got to give 110. Give you a call when I get close to the record."

Every week or so Pete Rose gives his 11-year-old son, Petey, a progress report. When you really want to know how Rose thinks he is doing, the best way to find out is to eavesdrop on one of these conversations.

Petey is his No. 1 fan and the rapport between the two is incredible. The son understands the father better than most adults do. Maybe it's because Pete's enthusiasm to play a little boy's game has never changed since he was Petey's age.

Peter Edward Rose was expected to pass Stan Musial and become the National League's all-time leader in hits during the Philadelphia Phillies' home series against Houston, June 8-10 at Veterans Stadium. Rose needed just four hits to tie Musial's total of 3,630 and five to become the new leader.

The Musial record has been one of the most important items on Rose's checklist of future accomplishments for years. The fact that it was within sight was one of the main reasons he signed with the Philadelphia Phillies after playing out his option in 1978 with Cincinnati. He could have received more money from the Kansas City Royals, but they are in the American League.

"Somebody pointed out to me the other day there have been something like 13,000 players in the National League so far," said Rose. "To think I am about to become the No. 1 player in hits from a group that large is obviously quite an accomplishment.

"But, to me, what this means is I have been consistent. You cannot get 3,600 hits if you do not play. You cannot get that many hits if you have bad years. You cannot get that many hits if you have other things on your mind. You have to be consistent, you have to be durable. That's what I am most proud of."

So, when they stop the game to celebrate Rose's 3,631st hit, it will be a tribute to longevity, determination, hustle, and the fun of playing a game that no longer is enjoyed that much by many of its briefcase-carrying participants.

"Peter has never stopped being a little boy at heart," said his mother from her home near Tampa, Fla., recently. "His father was just like that. He played (semipro) football until he was in his 40s and if I hadn't threatened him with divorce, he probably would have played even longer."

Pete's dad, Henry Francis Rose, died on December 8, 1970.

"I just wish he could be here for this great moment," said Peter's mother, now married to Robert Neth, a close friend of her first husband. "He always stressed consistency. I remember when Peter was a little boy. He would get four hits and come up to his father, obviously proud. His dad would only tell him he could have done better. I would be waiting in the car and want to cry. Each night before Peter would go to sleep, his dad would make him swing a bat nearly 100 times, first from the right side and then from the left side.

"His father is the reason he has been such a great player. He just kept pushing him, but at the same time he made playing sports a lot of fun. I know that is why Peter has maintained his enthusiasm all these years. And he is teaching his little boy the same way."

"You have to have fun at what you do to get the most out of it," says Pete Rose. "The way you become good at anything is to practice. My father taught me how to practice and have fun. That's why I go to the ballpark so early, that's why I have so much fun taking extra batting practice. But the one thing I learned at an early age was to practice the things you are not good at. Not many people do that. If you're weak at fielding, you should take ground balls. If you're weak at hitting, you should practice hitting. Most people, however, practice what they do best."

"Peter was only 2 years old when his dad bought him a glove, bat and ball and took him out in the back yard for the first time," said his mother. "From that time on, Peter loved sports. His dad would be tired from working all day at the bank, but Peter would beg him to play with him and he did. When he was young, he was a mama's boy, but as he got older he spent all his time with his father. Most boys his age were interested in other things as they were growing up. Not Peter. All he cared about was sports.

"He didn't go to dances and other things at school. He didn't even like girls. I'll tell you something else, though, he was a spoiled brat, a little stinker. . . . But aren't they all? He never got in trouble, but always got his own way, except with his father."

"The only time I can remember crying after I grew up was when my dad died," said Pete. "He and I had a great relationship, much like the one Petey and I now have."

Petey has not been able to spend as much time with his dad as he would like because Pete and Karolyn Rose were divorced a year ago and the son lives with his mother in their native Cincinnati.

"But Dad calls me and when we are together we make up for lost time," said Petey. "He has taught me everything I know about baseball. We watch a lot of television together. And, you know, I love basketball, too."

Rose was not a good student. His marks were not high enough for him to graduate with his class at Western Hills High School in Cincinnati and school officials asked him to go to summer school. His father wouldn't have it. "No," said Henry Rose. "If you do that, you won't be able to devote the whole summer to baseball." So he made Pete repeat the 12th grade the next school year.

"The entire time I played for the Cincinnati Reds my father was in the clubhouse only once," said Pete. "That was a day when he posed for a picture with me for a magazine article. And the only time he would wait for me outside the clubhouse was when he wanted to have me meet someone—or chew me out.

"He was a great football player. He had poor eyes because of all the detail work he had to do at the bank, but he was excellent. He played until he was 42. He was a nicer man than I am; I have done some things he would not be too proud of."

Rose has led the National League in batting average three times, in runs scored five times, in hits seven times, in doubles five times, in games played five times and in at-bat three times. He has appeared in every Phillies game (over 350) since he signed a four-year, $3.2 million contract with them in December of 1978. He is officially the all-time singles hitter in league history and considered the best leadoff hitter in baseball history.

He admittedly lacks great natural physical ability, but makes up for that with his enthusiasm, desire and dedication. When you talk about Pete Rose, you keep coming back to those words.

People in Cincinnati said he had little chance to make the Reds or any other major league team when he was finishing high school. They said he was too small.

"Everybody on my father's side of the family matured late," said Pete. "My dad was only 105 pounds when he was 20 and I was only 155 when I was 19. Nobody was much interested in signing me, but I wanted to play for the Reds. I grew up in Cincinnati, so my uncle, Buddy Bloebaum, talked them into signing me because he knew I would mature. He's dead now, but he was a good minor league player, especially after he learned to switch-hit. He told my father I should learn the same thing, so that's why I had to swing the lead-weighted bat every night. That also helped build up my arms and chest."

Rose got his chance with the Reds and has caught Musial in 19 years.

"The thing that gives me a lot of self-satisfaction in catching Musial is the time it's taken me to do it. I'm the youngest in terms of years, not age," Pete said. "Most of the guys with 3,000 or more hits played over 20 years.

"I was the youngest player to get 2,000 hits, 2,500 hits, 3,000 and then 3,500 hits. I've averaged 198 hits a year. If I played 24 years, like Ty Cobb did, I'd be near 5,000 hits."

People keep asking Pete Rose what it's like to be 40 years old and he says that's just another number.

"When I play baseball, I feel younger than teenagers," he said. "The difference between me and other 40-year-olds is that I don't take days off. I never do. Once you start taking days off, at this age, you lose the momentum to play the way you should. Sure, I get up tired some mornings, but there were days when I got up tired when I was 25."

Except for a stride or two, age hasn't worn Pete Rose down. He still plays with the same enthusiasm he brought to the game in '63 when he was National League Rookie of the Year. He still slides head-first, he spikes the ball after the third out most innings and he just grins when the fans boo him in opposing parks.

"I'm hitting over .330 and having fun, so why talk about retirement," he said the other day. "If you can still play the game, have fun, why should I quit? The game's fun for me and I'm playing on a team that can go all the way again.

"I've still got a lot of enthusiasm. Enthusiasm comes from winning. I'd like to feel I would play the same way no matter what, even if I was on a club that would lose 100 games a year, but I don't know if I could honestly say I would. There's a winning attitude and a losing attitude and I've been able to develop a winning attitude."

Rose does not feel the years have taken their toll.

"I'm a lot better now," he said. "The longer you're a hitter, the more you learn the pitchers, the better you are. I've had my lowest strikeout totals in the last three years. That has to mean something."

"The thing about Pete Rose is he takes care of himself," said Sparky Anderson, now the Detroit Tigers' manager, who piloted the Reds in 1975 and '76 when they won world championships. "We had a long chat in spring training one year and I told him when your reflexes go, there's nothing you can do about it. But I also told him players who do not drink and smoke and get their rest keep their reflexes a lot longer."

Said Rose, "I've always followed that advice. I never drank or smoked and didn't plan to, but it was good advice. Something to keep in mind."

Dallas Green, the Phillies' manager, said of the Rose situation, "The Musial thing is almost over now. Then, they will start talking about the Ty Cobb record (all-time major league hits record of 4,190). Don't sell him short when it comes to that. Don't ever sell Pete Rose short on anything."

"The Cobb record is not something I think about," said Pete. "That's down the road. It's the type of thing that might happen. You have to give it time.

"You know, I don't really fear age. I only worry about losing my enthusiasm. I'm not worried about my legs going, about my arm going, about my eyes. It would kill me not to have the fun I have playing baseball.

"Look, I am a baseball player, a sports nut. Until I find something that pays me as much money as baseball, I am not going to get a lot of side interests. I am not going to worry about something that pays me $50,000 a year at the expense of something that pays me as much as I make from baseball."

That is the reason Pete refuses to get involved in much other than baseball during the season. He is a good businessman, but leaves his financial dealing to Reuven Katz, a prominent Cincinnati attorney.

"I know I make more money than the President of the United States, but I don't see it," said Pete. "My advisers handle my money, my investments."

"Sparky Anderson probably said it best," commented Katz. "He said Pete Rose has more street sense than anyone he ever met. I have to agree. People think I merely pull the strings. That is wrong. Pete makes a lot of his own decisions. I merely help."

The one thing that still troubles Rose is that the Reds turned their backs on him after 16 years.

"I try to get along with people," said Pete, who at times is accused of being an intense, talkative, sharp-tongued, ambivalent man. "I took a lot of heat from the fans for leaving the Reds. It's amazing the number of people who called me a traitor—they called my kids traitors in school. No one knew the situation or the circumstances. Here's a guy who slid on his belly for 16 years for them and played just as hard as he could for them, and all of a sudden they (the Reds) decided they didn't want him anymore and he's the villain. But how can one guy, even Pete Rose, take on an organization like the Cincinnati Reds? No way.

"I use to sit and wonder why Dick Wagner (Reds president) didn't like me because I know one thing about Dick Wagner. He likes games. He likes people who work hard, and he likes people who play every day. Now, sure, I do some things off the field he didn't like, but he does some things I don't like.

"One thing is for sure. When I was on the field, I produced. And from that standpoint, I didn't quite understand. I did anything the

Reds ever asked me to do. Go here, promote 'em here, go there, go to the Caribbean—anything the Reds asked me to do, I did. I guess that was just their way of saying thanks. Thanks, but no thanks.

"I guess what disappointed me most about leaving the Reds was the fact I never had an opportunity to talk to the team's owners, Mr. and Mrs. (Louis) Nippert. They are really nice people, down-to-earth people. It didn't make sense to me people that smart and that rich could let something like that happen without ever saying yes or no—or, wait a minute, we'd like to talk. They just gave Dick Wagner all the authority."

That is all behind and Rose has found a fortune and new home with the Phillies, not to mention a third World Series ring to add to his collection.

Rose comes into full, fiery bloom as the media gathers to chronicle the historic moment of him passing Stan Musial.

"Maybe I haven't sat down and considered how big a deal this really is," Pete mused. "Maybe it will hit me after I do it. But I came into the season knowing I had to get 74 hits (to break the record). I knew I'd get them sooner or later. I want to get 200 hits this season, not 74.

"I'm not gonna stop there. I never met a ballplayer who was happy with 74 hits in a season. If I finish with 74, then I will be hitting like a 40-year-old baseball player."

And that's not Pete Rose.

Judge's Comments

Pete Rose knows what he must do on the field. He resorts to that desperate belly slide to get himself out of a tough situation. He notes the way he's being played and drops a looper into a vacant spot. He lunges at the foul pop as it drops from the catcher's mitt to save the sixth game of the World Series. Give Pete Rose a uniform and he will give you 110 percent in return.

Hal Bodley, the talented writer of this story, captures the essence of the man, beginning with a telephone conversation with his son, Petey, after a game. "Had two hits, slid on my belly to score a run and we win 6-1," Rose said into the receiver. The rapport between father and son is incredible, writes Bodley. Rose constantly hungers for his son, who now lives with Rose's former wife Carolyn.

But there also is sadness in the man's life. Rose's father, his lifelong baseball tutor and greatest fan, died in 1970.

Rose already holds many hitting records and is considered by many to be the greatest leadoff hitter in history. Before he's through, a major chunk of the baseball record books will belong to him. This compelling, lucent study from The Sporting News evokes the feeling that if baseball can create a Pete Rose, it's got to be doing something right.

Gossage Gives Yanks Edge in Any Ball Park

BASEBALL

By RICK BOZICH
From the Louisville Courier-Journal
Copyright © 1981, The Louisville Times
Reprinted With Permission

This may be cause for debate in the Los Angeles clubhouse, but there are moments when Rich Gossage knows not what he does. Moments when the catcher's glove becomes a red light in the smog, moments when Gossage realizes he's still crazy after all those fastballs, fastballs, fastballs.

"Sometimes it's a scary feeling out there on the mound," said Gossage. "Like I'm out of control or really don't have any control over my emotions. Like I'm standing on the edge of a cliff about to fall. At times I get so high I don't even know what happens.

"I don't like the feeling. I don't know what I'm capable of doing."

As Gossage talks with reporters, droplets of beer collect on the corners of his furry mustache, tying down the corners of what can be an engaging smile. His cheeks have the chubbiness of somebody whose wisdom teeth have just been yanked. His stringy hair is in retreat all along the forehead. His thick fingers, the nails chewed away, surround the can of brew.

No smile here, only worry lines making waves across his brow. The raging bull within him frightens the New York relief pitcher, a 10-year veteran and only 30 years old. "I'm tellin' you, it's scary," said Gossage. "Absolutely frightening. I feel like I'm almost on the end of the world."

As the scene of the 1981 World Series shifts to the City of Angels tonight, it is the urgent, satanical Gossage glare that requires more examination.

In search of their 23rd world championship, the Yankees have won the first two Series games. Both nights Gossage, a Rocky Mountain man at heart, recorded the final six outs. He has pitched to 15 batters when the minimum would be 12. He has allowed two hits and one walk. Five batters have struck out.

So has Gossage. Twice out of the bullpen he has been incapable of generating the maniacal concentration for which he is known. Relief pitching is as much intimidation as it is a fastball running high and inside, and Gossage does not believe the intimidation has been there.

His heart has not fluttered, his mind has not buzzed. When the feeling festers as it should, a certain surliness overcomes him in the bullpen through the middle innings. The Yankee hat is pulled over his eyes. His bending back puts his body in a crouch. His facial muscles tighten.

"When I'm really psyched I tell them to give me the ball and let me pitch," said Gossage. "If the catcher comes out to the mound, I'll tell him to get the hell behind the plate.

"One time Barry Foote (Yankees' reserve catcher) said, 'Go to hell yourself.'

"So I said it back to him. We stood out there for about 10 seconds cussing back and forth."

Those are the nights that Gossage's fastball will outrun a speeding bullet. The nights that he stands on the mound and sees only the catcher's glove. The nights he says things he later laughs at. In his words. "The nights that really scare me because I'm not in control of my emotions," he said.

Those emotions have not surged within him during this World Series. He is only this emotional: After the first two games he has been unable to eat for two hours after the game. He has bypassed the post-game pasta and returned to his New Jersey flat. There is no stove at home. His wife, Corna, his former Colorado Springs hometown sweetheart, fixed him a tuna fish sandwich.

"There are fastballs and then there are fastballs," said New York Manager Bob Lemon. "Gossage's is just extraordinary. It's up there with Bob Feller's."

The analogy with Feller, the best pitcher ever seen in Cleveland, is a stretch mark in baseball history. Feller started. Gossage relieves. With the mustachioed assistance of Rollie Fingers, Gossage has done for relief pitchers what Japanese autos have done for Detroit: restructured the industry, giving glamour to a product that once drew scorn.

Even a Little Leaguer understands the predictable cadence of the Yankees' approach to the game. The starter goes six innings; the bullpen (Ron Davis and Gossage) goes three. In 10 post-season games no Yankee has pitched a complete game. Of New York's seven victories, Gossage has saves in six. He has not been charged with a run in his last 13 innings.

"The thing is," said catcher Rick Cerone, "is that in the Series, Goose hasn't pitched like he can. He's been tough, but he hasn't been Goose."

Goose is the nickname a former Chicago White Sox teammate, Tom Bradley, gave the then gangly righthander seven summers ago. Until then he had a nickname unbefitting the game's best reliever.

"They called me, 'Gos,' " said Gossage, emphasizing the short "o." "Tom Bradley didn't like that."

For five seasons the White Sox shuttled Gossage between the bullpen and starting rotation. He was the American League's leading reliever in 1975 and perhaps its worst starter in 1976. He lost 17 of 26 decisions and had an earned run average of nearly four. He asked to return to the bullpen.

Chicago, instead, sent him to Pittsburgh for Richie Zisk. A year later he moved to New York, signing a six-year contract for the now-impoverished sum of $333,000 a year. He turned away the Dodgers in the 1978 Series. As he once said to a batter who belittled his fastball, "You swung at what you heard."

Throughout this Series, the Dodgers have professed no fear of the Gossage fastball, claiming they have gotten their cuts but not their breaks. "That's all right," said Gossage. "I'm not afraid of any hitter."

Such is the Goose, still blazing after all these years.

Brooklyn No Longer Place to Be When Dodgers Win

BASEBALL

By *JOE SOUCHERAY*

From the Minneapolis Tribune
Copyright © 1981, Minneapolis Tribune

It is New York and it is late at night, and from all you have ever heard and read on the subject, you should go to Brooklyn in the hours after the Dodgers beat the Yankees in the World Series.

It used to mean something, a World Series in Brooklyn when the Yankees were the other guys; it used to mean real despair and real hope and once, in 1955, it meant real joy because that autumn the Bums beat the Yankees in seven games in the tournament between subways.

You have read somewhere, something by Roger Kahn probably, that after the 1955 Series victory by the Dodgers the Brooklyn Eagle blocked out new type for its traditional banner headline. "Next Year Is Now," it said. In 1941, 1947, 1949, 1952, 1953 and back again in 1956, the Eagle always set the same type, "Wait Til Next Year," after the World Series. And it was always the Yankees who had done the Dodgers in.

Maybe they have remembered that in Brooklyn. Maybe they have gotten over the broken hearts they suffered after the 1957 season when Walter O'Malley neatly packed his club into a carpetbag and fled to Los Angeles, all the way across the world. Maybe there are a few of them still, Brooklyn Dodger fans dancing in old saloons and honking their horns up and down the avenues in 1981.

"Maybe in your imagination," Danny said.

This is Danny from Brooklyn, Danny the hack driver. This is Danny at the wheel of an automobile that has a life expectancy of perhaps two more hours before it falls into a heap on the street, like some jalopy from a Bowery Boys film. This is Danny who can't possibly risk having his last name appear in print, even in Minneapolis. But this Danny is perfect for the trip to Brooklyn because this Danny hates the Yankees the way a real Dodger fan should, this Danny was one of the shocked when the Dodgers evacuated westward.

"It ain't the same, rooting anymore," Danny is saying. "It ain't the same rooting for any of the sports. It's just a feeling that none of it is the same."

He is rattling uptown through Manhattan along the FDR Expressway, to the Brooklyn Bridge, which is beautiful, its suspension cables glowing like harp strings on a dark stage, its lights reflecting off the black waters of the East River below.

From the bridge, off to the right, you can see the towers of the World Trade Center and the Wall Street district and the Statue of Liberty in the harbor and the whole city of Manhattan lights in the background. Yankee lights to a Brooklyner, as Danny calls his people.

"The Brooklyn Eagle is gone," Danny says, "and so is Ebbets Field. It's a housing project now on Bedford Avenue."

He is going up the Brooklyn Heights side of the East River, up the Brooklyn-Queens Expressway. The clock on the tower of the Bon-Ton Potato Chip factory reads 2:59 a.m., but in some spots they have forgotten to turn back the clocks in Brooklyn. Danny pulls off finally and motors the heap into Bay Ridge. It is quiet. O'Sullivan's is closed. So is Hobnails and the Golden Dove and Manar's. And there is no honking of horns or dancing in the wide streets. The real, modern Dodger celebration was taking place at that moment on the team's jetliner at 30,000 feet. But there is a joint that Danny knows of and there will be people there who remember the Dodgers from Brooklyn.

Irish music is spilling out the doors of Danny's place, a joint called Peggy O'Neill's, which actually is a very new place and not full of much memory except for the people inside. A guy named Timmy O'Donnell is behind the bar and when you mention the Dodgers and the kinds of feelings that his patrons must have on a night like this, he points to his friend at the bar. It is like a beam of light has come on this guy, Bob, a policeman, 45, working on a drink and a cigarette and 25 years worth of sorrow over his absent Bums.

"It broke my heart when the Bums left here," Bob is saying, "and I will take it a step further. You will never find fans in your life like Dodger fans. The Dodgers were bums."

"Why?"

"Because they were bad and they let the Yankees beat them," Bob says. "But I will take it a step further. The Dodgers were the hope of all the people that were struggling in Brooklyn. It used to be this way: People thought New York State was New York City and they thought New York City was Brooklyn. The team made us."

They were all taking it a step further now. It seems that when the Dodgers beat Montreal for the National League pennant, and folks in Brooklyn knew the Dodgers would be coming to Yankee Stadium again, a petition drive was started to ask the Dodgers to change their name in Los Angeles, that the O'Malleys had no business hanging on to that name.

"The name comes from people in Brooklyn having to dodge trolley cars," Bob says. "What are they doing with our name in Los Angeles?"

Bob did not root for the Yankees on this night. But he didn't feel cheer for the Dodgers, either. Most Brookliners have retained allegiances in the National League and bestowed a cautious affection on the Mets when that team was born in 1962. But it isn't the same, the Mets aren't tucked into the burrough the way the Dodgers were. The Mets aren't family the way the Dodgers were.

"And I will take it a step further," Bob is saying now. "Look at all your old war movies. When they really wanted to test a guy's loyalty, who do they bring up? They bring up the Dodgers. The Dodgers were the hope of all the people who were struggling in Brooklyn."

Part of that image, of course, was the work of script writers and comedians and those of us who find affection for the underdogs on the sporting fields. Part of that image is real, if for no other reason than the nostalgic memories that the pairing of the words Brooklyn and Dodgers creates in all of us.

A fire burned in the hearts of men for a baseball team in Brooklyn. That much is certain. It made no difference that the club was considered "hapless" more often than not. The club belonged to Brooklyn and in a few hearts the longing still exists, but there can be no cheer in the longing.

"That's what's different," Danny is saying, retracing the route back toward the lights of Manhattan. "Teams don't seem to belong to a place anymore. Not the way they did. The teams now, they belong to themselves."

At Foxboro, Fans Good at Drinking It All In

PRO FOOTBALL

by RANDY HARVEY

From the Los Angeles Times
Copyright © 1981, Los Angeles Times
Reprinted by Permission

Half an hour before game time Monday night, Dennis Crowley was enjoying the calm before the storm.

Inside the dressing rooms, coaches Tom Landry of Dallas and Ron Erhardt of New England were giving their players last-minute instructions, but Crowley's team already was in action. Now, all he could do was wait for the results and hope there wouldn't be any records broken. Or heads.

"We've got a game plan," Crowley said, pausing to wait for someone to ask him what the plan was. Someone did.

"Stop 'em at the gates," Crowley said. "Don't let trouble inside the stadium."

As a vice president of the security firm hired by the Patriots, it is Crowley's resposibility to prevent a night at Schaefer Stadium from turning into X-rated entertainment. It sounds like a joke to tell people they can't carry alcoholic beverages into a stadium that is named after a brewery, but that is one of the duties of Crowley's men. Anyone carrying bottles, cans or other containers filled with alcohol is barred. So is anyone who appears to have had too much to drink. It's no joke. Leave peacefully and there won't be a punch line.

Crowley had 190 men working the Dallas-New England game. An additional 100 men, mostly police officers from surrounding boroughs, were there for the city of Foxboro. It's not a large enough army to prevent the Russians from invading Poland—but it could stop them from bringing bottles and cans.

By comparison, the National Football League employs 45 security guards for a Super Bowl game at the Rose Bowl. But then, no one questions the need for such a large security force at Schaefer. It has a reputation for attracting the rowdiest crowds east of the Mardi Gras.

A Boston Globe reporter who sat in the stands for a game here last season wrote a detailed account of "lewd remarks made to women in the parking lot, sodden men urinating into restroom sinks, people vomiting in the aisles, shirtless celebrants with sagging bellies, beer being spilled on neighbors, obscene shouts at Patriot players and gynecological suggestions directed at their cheerleaders, drunken brawls in the parking lot and beer-swilling males packed six to a car knocking down highway cones on the way home." And that was on a Sunday afternoon.

Under the cover of darkness, the place really goes up for grabs. In what has become known as the Monday Night Massacre, more than 60 persons were arrested during a Patriots-New York Jets game in 1976. During a Monday night Patriots-Buffalo Bills game last year, 49 persons were arrested. Because the paddywagons couldn't haul them away fast enough, some were handcuffed to the chain-link fence surrounding the stadium while awaiting transportation to jail.

Foxboro, a bedroom community of 14,000 with only 23 policemen, finally began to defend itself this summer. Concerned that the town was becoming the East Coast's Dodge City, the Board of Selectmen appointed a committee to study the situation.

It mailed questionnaires to team owners, police chiefs and sports editors in the other cities with NFL teams to find out if Foxboro's experiences with Monday night games were unique.

"They weren't," said Committee Chairman Jim Sullivan, no relation to the Sullivans who own the Patriots. "Of the responses received, 85 percent said they would rather not have Monday Night Football in their cities. Why? Because Monday Night Football presents more problems for the police."

Crowley, whose security firm has been employed by the Patriots for four years, could have told the committee that without a questionnaire.

"The profile of the fan who comes to Monday night games is different from the average fan," he said. "You don't get the families on Monday nights. My 8-year-old son goes to the Sunday afternoon games, but a lot of people don't bring their children to Monday night games because they're over so late and the wives stay home with the kids. So hubby gets to come with his friends.

"They buy tickets in groups, and then they get together after work and party it up until it's time to come to the game. Now the situation isn't the same on the West Coast as it is on the East Coast. The games here don't start until 9 o'clock. That gives these guys four hours to drink before the game starts. If the game isn't close, they get bored and start looking for excitement.

"You know, if you split these guys up, they wouldn't say 'boo'. But together, they want to show off. Some of them, if they could see themselves the day they've sobered up, they would feel like damn fools."

But while that type of fan is by no means peculiar to the Patriots, there are extenuating circumstances that contribute to the atmosphere here. One is purely esthetic. Schaefer Stadium is totally utilitarian. Completed in 1971 for only $6 million, it has none of the amenities of other recently built stadiums.

"If you walk into a nice bar where everyone is wearing sport coats and ties and drinking martinis, you act one way," Boston Globe columnist Leigh Montville said. "If you walk into a bar where people are wearing T-shirts and spitting on the floor, you act another way."

Schaefer Stadium is a place where you spit on the floor. And sometimes on the person sitting in front of you.

Location is another problem. The stadium is 30 miles south of Boston, 25 miles north of Providence, with only one four-lane road either way. Traffic jams are notorious. As a result, many fans leave for Monday night immediately after work to beat the rush. Cars were lining up outside the stadium at 5:45 p.m. Monday. There is nothing to do until kickoff except sit in the parking lots and empty the cooler. Tailgate parties were never like this before the Harvard-Yale game.

After completing its study, the Foxboro committee recommended that the Dallas-New England game be played Sunday afternoon, adding that if it had to be part of ABC's Monday night package, that it should begin no later than 7. The selectmen voted, 3-0, for Monday night at 8.

That was unacceptable to the NFL and ABC, which feared that an 8 p.m. start would be too early for West Coast audiences. ABC has experimented this season with 8:30 p.m. East Coast kickoffs for two Thursday games but was not willing to alter its Monday night routine. The selectmen relented and voted, 2-1, for the Monday night game as scheduled. If they expected cheers for their change of heart, they were disappointed.

Some critics thought the selectman never should have introduced the issue.

"They embarrassed the town," said Ben Igo, assistant publisher of the Foxboro Reporter. "Now because of the attention, the wire services will run the magic number, the arrest count, all over the country." Indeed, the Associated Press did just that Tuesday afternoon.

"The whole situation was unnecessary," said Pat Sullivan, who is in charge of stadium operations for the Patriots. "They were making a statement that we can't control our organization and that our fans can't control themselves. That kind of annoyed me."

But others thought the selectmen should have stood fast.

"In order to accommodate the NFL and ABC, the city of Foxboro is hosting a 9 o'clock game that is unfair, unsafe and ridiculous," said Eddie Andelman, co-host of a Boston radio talk show and owner of a harness racing track that is next to Schaefer Stadium. "It's like asking to have a punk rock concert in the Los Angeles Coliseum at 1 a.m.

Whatever happens Monday night should be on the conscience of Pete Rozelle and the NFL."

It will not be on the conscience of selectman Pete Stanton, who cast the minority vote. "I had been assured by the other two select- men that if there are serious problems Monday night, they will never again vote to allow a night game at Schaefer Stadium," Stanton said last week.

The Patriots got the message during the offseason. They spent $60,000 to improve security inside the stadium, even though they don't own it. They ruled that beer sales must stop 15 minutes by the clock after the third quarter begins. They had eliminated beer ven- dors and prohibited customers from buying more than two cups of beer at a time at the concession stands before last season. When the contract with the concessionaires runs out after next season, the Pa- triots probably will end beer sales.

"I'd say that 85 percent to 90 percent of our problems are directly attributable to alcohol," Crowley said Monday night. "Everyone who is arrested is under the influence."

He was stationed in the security booth on top of the press box and peering out over the sellout crowd of 60,311 like Roy Scheider watch- ing for sharks in "Jaws."

Crowley, 44, has softer features than Scheider but the same de- termined look. He had $5,000 worth of electronic equipment at his disposal to focus on trouble spots, primarily the cheap seats in the end zones. He occasionally left his perch to visit the front lines, once finding two policemen escorting a drunk and disorderly teenager outside the stadium. When they turned him loose, the teenager slugged one policeman and took a swing at the other. They wrestled him to the ground and were handcuffing him when the television cameras arrived.

Crowley sighed. "That'll look bad on TV," he said. "Where were they when the cop got slugged?"

By the end of the third quarter, Crowley was breathing easier. There had been only a dozen or so arrests, only one fight and the game was still close.

But a couple of Cowboy interceptions, a safety and three field goals later, all hell broke loose. The telephone rang. When Crowley hung up seconds later, he was visibly shaken.

"We may have lost it all," he said. "There's been a report of a stabbing. That's all anybody will talk about tomorrow." Ambulance sirens wailed in the background.

On Tuesday afternoon, Crowley reported that there were 42 ar- rests inside the stadium, 20 arrests on the access road outside the sta- dium, 20 persons taken into protective custody. No broken heads. The man who was stabbed—a Dallas fan who was gloating too ob- viously in the late stages of the 35-21 victory by the Cowboys—was released from Norwood Hospital Tuesday morning.

There are two ways to look at it when that many persons are arrested. Either the crowd was unruly or the security was efficient. According to local press reviews, the security was efficient.

Crowley relaxed. "We survived," he said.

He said he would watch the game between the Rams and Bears on television next Monday night until the third quarter or so, and then he'll go to bed. Monday night football is the problem of someone in Chicago now.

The 'Hard Bastard' Theory

GOLF

By *PETER DOBEREINER*

From Golf Digest
Copyright © 1981, Golf Digest/Tennis, Inc.

They gave David Graham the silver cup for winning the 81st United States Open Championship, but he did much more than win a golf tournament during those four sweltering days in Philadelphia in June. This was a triumph over years of adversity, a victory over the fates that had been stacking the deck against him ever since he chose golf as his life at the tender age of 14. It was the final step in a conquest over the most dangerous adversary a man can face—himself.

The fates struck early when his first set of golf clubs, which he found in the garage of his home in Windsor, Australia, turned out to be lefthanded. Although a natural righthander, Graham played as a lefty for more than two years, well enough to earn a 2-handicap at Wattle Park, a short nine-hole layout in another Melbourne suburb of Burwood. When he finally converted to the right side, it took him two more years to return his game to its previous level.

By then he was assistant to George Naismith, a well-respected professional at Riversdale Golf Club in Melbourne. It was Naismith who convinced him to make the change, and of such decisions is history made.

Graham's decision to quit school at the age of 14, before he had finished what would be the seventh grade in the United States, was a wrenching one. It drove the final spike into his parents' already ailing marriage and prompted David's father to sever his relationship with him. Graham remains close to his mother, but except for a brief meeting at Hazeltine during the 1970 U.S. Open, he has not seen or spoken to his father since their split more than 20 years ago.

Why such a choice so young?

"I had a great love for the game," Graham recalls, "but I also felt it was about the only choice I had. In my early days I used golf as a vehicle to accomplish what I wanted out of life, not necessarily as a golfer but as an individual. I wanted success, to better myself."

The task was not easy. At 18, after finishing his three-year apprenticeship with Naismith, Graham set up on his own account as the professional at a small nine-hole club in Tasmania, a backwater island off the southeastern seaboard of Australia that was settled originally by convicts exiled from England. Innocent as a babe in business and not blessed with a supportive membership, he ran up debts of about $6,000 during his 2½ years there.

Convinced by Eric Cremin, a noted figure in Australian golf, that he had some possibilities as a player and should leave Tasmania, Graham went to Sydney and took a job with Precision Golf Forgings, Australia's biggest club manufacturer. It was there that he learned the skills of clubmaking and acquired his lasting interest in club design, an apprenticeship that was later to lead him to an advisory association with Jack Nicklaus and MacGregor in the United States. (This may be the appropriate moment to recall an incident in 1976 when Nicklaus said to Graham, "Look, David, why don't you concentrate full time on club design? Let's face it, you are never going to be a great player." In the next few weeks Graham won the Westchester Classic and the American Golf Classic. Never has Nicklaus been so wretchedly underclubbed.)

For the 2½ years that Graham labored at PGF, doing promotional work and clinics as well as learning the clubmaking business, his wages were garnished to help settle his debts. It is perhaps a measure of the man that, because he was less than 21 and legally a minor when business dealt him a foul blow, he could have declared bankruptcy and had his encumbrances erased. But he chose instead to pay off his creditors. Eventually, with further aid from pro-am winnings, he did.

Graham won the Tasmania Open of 1969, which paid peanuts but which gave him his first taste of blood. The following week he won the Victorian Open and the week after that was beaten in a playoff in New South Wales. The wiry youngster was like a greyhound puppy that had sunk its teeth into a live rabbit. At last he was running free.

Taking advantage of a PGF sponsorship, really only an airline ticket, Graham embarked on the Asian Tour in 1970. His first week out, he was beaten in a playoff in the Singapore Open, later won the Thailand Open and finally the Yomiuri International, then Japan's biggest tournament. He earned a $2,500 bonus as the best performer on the Asian circuit, and later in the year won the French Open.

Some of the rabbits eluded him, notably his U.S. player's card on his first attempt in 1970, but the next week he teamed with Bruce Devlin to win the World Cup for Australia.

Early in his career Graham acquired the reputation of a loner—an assessment he considers incorrect but probably justified—and a rebel.

"I was extremely frustrated and very rebellious toward the system," he recalls. "Golf in Australia in those days was nearly impossible for a young player. All the courses were private and assistant

professionals were considered second-class citizens. It was unbeliev-
ably difficult for a young player to get any help.

"So I was very, very frustrated because I was very ambitious
and I felt the system was making it so difficult to get ahead. There
were not many tournaments to play in, so competitive golf was at a
minimum. So I became the black sheep of the golfing family.

"I had a violent temper, because I was destitute and nobody
really gave a damn. I was a young guy with the bloody ass out of my
pants trying to make ends meet, trying to get ahead. The less I socia-
lized with the establishment and the more I practiced, the more of a
black sheep I became. I felt that rather than people understanding
my situation, all they ever did was criticize, because I wasn't one of
the group. I tried to create attention by being overly opinionated, but
I don't think my friends who have known me for a long time would
ever say I was a loner."

In those days, however, he was admittedly a very private person,
hard to get to know and, for most people it must be said, not easy to
like. He also had an undoubted air of arrogance, emphasized by his
drill-sergeant walk, straightbacked and displaying no hint of human
emotion. There is still a hint of disdain in his face, which comes part-
ly from within but also accidentally from his turned-up nose, a ski-
jump of a nose that might give Bob Hope cause for an action for
breach of copyright.

The remodeling of David Graham, the person, began in November of 1968 when he married Maureen Burdett, a bank teller
whom he met while playing in a golf tournament in Cairns, the black
marlin fishing area in northeastern Australia.

"She has done everything for me," David says softly. "She has
given me confidence. She has taught me to enjoy life. She has borne
my two sons, Andrew and Michael, the pride and joy in my life. She
taught me to like myself in those days, when I don't think I did because I was so frustrated. She has taught me composure. She has
taught me how to dress. She taught me to be less abrasive, to be a little more reserved and keep my opinions to myself a little bit."

The redoing of Graham, the player, he owes to Devlin, who
urged him to try again for his U.S. card, which he earned in late 1971.
He won the 1972 Cleveland Open, but the next year he was playing
badly and went to Devlin for help. Cursed with the short, flat, wristy
swing that is spawned by the Australian winds and the small ball, he
was advised that he must stand closer to the ball and make his swing
plane more upright if he were to achieve the height and accuracy
needed in America. It took six months, but he did it. Not a piece of
cake, of course, but hardly daunting to a fellow who had changed
from one side of the ball to the other.

By this time, however, fate again had crept up behind him and
swung its loaded cosh. He was playing in the 1971 Dunlop Masters in
Melbourne. Lee Trevino, rising in golf like a rocket, was winning.
Trevino's manager, Bucky Woy, offered Graham a contract. What

could be better than to be allied with such a stablemate? Besides, it was the only such offer he had ever received and he was desperate for help. Graham signed, without examining the conditions too closely. "He gave me $200 a week, which didn't pay for my bloody food, and he got 50 percent of my gross income after his expenses were paid back," Graham growls. "I think it would be fair comment to say David Graham was given a snow job."

Both Trevino and Graham came to regret their contracts, of course. In Graham's case, it took years to disentangle himself. Buying out the contract, in his words, cost him an arm and a leg, actually around $200,000. Not until he won the Westchester in 1976 after years of struggle and bitterness could he raise the money to free himself. Nobody can say whether he might have won more tournaments during those years under different management, but there is no doubt that Graham was deeply scarred by the disputes and legal wrangling. "It destroyed me for two years," he states flatly.

Despite his flash flood of success in 1976—he eventually won $176,174 and finished eighth on the money list that year—he played erratically the next two seasons, plagued by self-doubts and trying to justify the wisdom of spending half the year away from his family pursuing an income that seemed, at best, insecure. He was torn between playing golf and doing other things for a living, which in part led to his signing with MacGregor as a club designer and consultant. It wasn't until he won the PGA Championship in 1979 that his attitude changed.

"I came to a very quick assessment of the fact that I was selling myself short as a player," he says. "I think if a player wins a major championship, he has to feel he can play. There aren't many miracles ever performed in winning a major championship, simply because the competition is so great."

That assessment was not immediately shared by others. Nicklaus was not alone in seeing a limit to Graham's potential. There are two schools of thought about how to pick a future champion. The method of the golfing establishment might be termed the Sound Chap Theory. If a young player is clearly a Sound Chap (well mannered, respectful) and has a sound method (classical swing), then he is marked for greatness. Ben Crenshaw epitomizes the Sound Chap Theory, having been tapped for golf's highest honors ever since he was a freshman at the University of Texas. Besides, he knew who Joyce Wethered was, and that clinched it.

The other way can be called the Hard Bastard Hypothesis. Under this system, if you see a kid who is undoubtedly tough, selfish, aggressively ambitious, egotistical, ruthless and has the guts of a fighting dog, then it does not matter how he swings the club. You can be sure that he will find a way of getting the ball round the course in fewer strokes than the others.

David Graham would approve of that Hard Bastard tag, for among Australian sportsmen there could be no greater compliment, suggesting as it does both admiration and affection. He has never been remotely in the Sound Chap category. It made no difference when the Hard Bastard beat the Sound Chap in a playoff for that PGA Championship at Oakland Hills, because the PGA was not to be compared with the Open championships of the United States and Britain. That fellow Graham was still a first-class second-rater, a good money-winning professional but not to be considered among the elite of true champions.

The swing is not classical, except to the aficionado who can appreciate its technical virtues. But Graham has been working on it. Acting on the advice of Gary Player, he has spent the last two years lengthening his swing by swinging a weighted club dozens, sometimes hundreds of times a day. Once no more than a three-quarter swinger, he now can get the club back almost to parallel, even under pressure, with the result that his shots are traveling higher and farther.

Graham conveys the impression that he learned his golf out of a book, and that as he sets up for a shot he's mentally reciting a checklist from a technical manual. His movements are precise and deliberate and follow an unvarying routine. Nearly everyone grounds the clubhead square behind the ball and then sets the stance, but with Graham the ritual is accompanied by this idea that he is counting how many knuckles on the right hand are visible and setting the angle of each foot. His stiff, straightbacked stance is as rigid as a guardsman standing to attention and quite alien to the impression you receive from Sam Snead, for instance, who looks like a fast middleweight preparing to throw a jab.

Again, it is with almost military precision that Graham takes the club back in an upright plane and then reverses its direction at the same, deliberate tempo. Inside Snead, as he tells us, there is a voice that advises him: "Just swing at her real smooth, Sam baby, and think slice." Inside Graham, one imagines, there is a drill sergeant snapping out orders: "Target at 200 yards partially blocked by large tree. Adjust right-hand grip two degrees for deflection. On the command fire. Take club back to count of three. Fire! 1, 2, 3. . . . Don't rush it, lad! Down! 1, 2, 3. . . . Finish with hands high and clubshaft parallel to the ground. Shot on outer ring of target. Well done, but we must get closer next time."

No, not the classical swing, but it is an effective one—and when you add up the strokes at the end of the round, that is just as good.

In recent years Graham has labored even harder on his mental processes, operating on the simple premise that "before you can control the ball you have got to control yourself."

There may never have been a better example of such control than his final round at Merion. Those who ascribe human characteristics to golf courses, as many do, would probably see Merion as a little old lady in bombazine and high-buttoned boots, a very pillar of rectitude and unforgiving Victorian values who lived in a village with a companion and seven cats. However, dear Miss Merion also has an ugly streak in her, and when provoked, the prim Sunday school teacher can turn into a vicious, vindictive bitch, raining double and triple bogeys on contenders all around.

Graham would have none of it. Three shots behind George Burns at the start of Sunday's play, he marched through the day with his drill-sergeant's stride, his deadpan facade broken only occasionally by a smiling reaction to the gallery's huzzahs. Watching him, the outstanding impression was the unvarying rhythm of his swing, seemingly at the same measured tempo on upswing and downswing, like a metronome.

Within, Graham's emotions were human enough and turbulent enough. Half of his mind was rehearsing the gracious speech of a good loser, congratulating the winner the way a sportsman should. The other half was saying, "Hey, concentrate on what you are doing. You can win this thing."

Win it he did, with a rare and remarkable closing 67 for a seven-under-par total of 273. Bill Rogers, finishing in a tie for second with Burns, had to make the speech of the sporting loser, and he did so with grace: "Graham hit 18 greens in regulation, and in the last round of the U.S. Open that is unbelievable."

Give or take an inch or two, that is exactly what Graham did. After he missed the first fairway he didn't come within yards of missing another. Golf lore has it that the finest single round of golf ever played was the 66 scored by Bobby Jones in the qualifying round for the British Open at Sunningdale in 1926. He took 33 strokes to get to the greens and 33 putts; 33 on the front and 33 on the back. However, that round was marred by one trip to a bunker and other small blemishes.

Perfect rounds from tee to green are blue-moon events, to be savored perhaps once in a lifetime by a great player. Peter Alliss had one in the British Open at St. Andrews of all places, seven 3s and eleven 4s and not one recovery shot among them. Neil Coles had one earlier this year, the first in his long career, in the British PGA Championship. But to hit every shot flush, with the right club, in the right direction, must surely be unprecedented in the winning last round of a major championship.

Bob Toski, who saw Ben Hogan's final round at Merion in 1950, rated Graham's round as the superior technical performance.

Better than Hogan? That single round must kill forever the label of first-rate second-rater. Graham must be regraded and acknowledged as a member of the elite category of multiple championship winners under the stern dictum laid down years ago by Walter Hagen: "Anybody can get lucky and win the Open but it takes a real champion to do it twice." With the PGA Championship and the Open, Graham has passed the test and his record shows another important qualification for a player of the highest quality in that his record has been largely compiled on golf courses of the highest quality. Wentworth in England (1976 World Match Play), Oakland Hills (1979 PGA Championship), Muirfield Village (1980 Memorial Tournament) and Merion are all severe tests of a man and his game. Good golf courses search out flaws in a player, and unless he has a full armory of strokes and capability to produce them under pressure, then the championship courses will expose his shortcomings. That is one good reason why the world esteems champions above tournament winners, why Jack Nicklaus (19 championships and 68 tournament wins) is a greater player than Sam Snead (seven championships and 84 tournament wins).

David Graham, the man and the champion, came to the fore in the waning daylight hours that day at Merion. He had not planned to play in the British Open this year because he objected to its policy of exempting the U.S. PGA champion for only one year. Indeed, he would have been forced to prequalify for the championship proper, a circumstance he considers humiliating to a player of his stature. But as the U.S. Open champion he was reserved a spot, and two weeks later he was to be on his way to England.

"I now hold an honored title," he told the press that evening, "and I do not think it would be right to use it as an instrument of rebellion."

The rebellion is gone now. The world that treated him so harshly is gone, too, and Graham is at peace with himself. He speaks articulately and knowledgeably on many subjects, belying his lack of formal education. And he has a diversity of interests. He has invested wisely in recent years and is, by his own count, a millionaire. He lives a life of casual affluence in his half-million-dollar Dallas home, drives a $40,000 Mercedes, wears a $12,000 Rolex watch and belongs to three expensive golf clubs. One of those is Preston Trail, an ultra-exclusive, men-only Dallas establishment that provides Graham with a sanctuary for practice when he is home. His membership there cost him $30,000, but he considers it the best investment he ever made.

"I'm comfortable there," he says. "I don't impress anybody there. They are all super-nice, successful people in their own right and they weren't in awe of the fact that a professional golfer was going to join their club. They were more concerned that I was the type of member they wanted."

Graham is totally committed to America and the American way of life and does not disguise his disdain for overseas players who take what they can get from the U.S. tour and then return to the international circuit when the going gets tough.

"I shall always be grateful to America and to American golf for what they have given me," he said after winning the Open, "and I have no intention of ever leaving this country." His resident alien status gives him all the privileges of citizenship except the right to vote or work for the government. The latter seems an unlikely necessity at the moment.

I have known David Graham for many years and know and like the real person under that prickly, defensive shield he has occasionally put up. Just as Nicklaus won the affection of the golfing public after years of grudging respect, so I believe that the real David Graham will now allow himself to emerge and that he will enjoy a deserved popularity.

With the Greatest of Ease

by Paul Chinn of the *Los Angeles Herald Examiner*. Like the man on the flying trapeze, Southern Cal star running back Marcus Allen took to the air against Oklahoma for some short yardage during a 28-24 victory over the Sooners. Allen rewrote the NCAA record books in 1981, rushing for 2,342 yards. Copyright © 1981, Los Angeles Herald Examiner.

Back Arches to Triumph

by William Meyer of the *Milwaukee Journal*. The backstrokers uncoil into the water after coming off the starting blocks in a heat during competition in the AAU Junior Olympic Swim Meet. The meet was held at the Schroeder Aquatic Center in Brown Deer, Wisconsin, a suburb of Milwaukee. Copyright © 1981, Milwaukee Journal.

At 19, Thomas Makes His Decision

COLLEGE BASKETBALL

By *IRA BERKOW*
From the New York Times
Copyright © 1981, The New York Times Company
Reprinted by Permission

It was Draft Day in the ghetto. That's what everyone there called it. On a few days each year, chieftains of the notorious Vice Lords street gang appeared at certain homes on the West Side of Chicago to take recruits.

On this summer night in 1966, 25 Vice Lord chiefs stopped in front of the home of Mary Thomas. She had nine children, seven of them boys, ranging from Lord Henry, 15 years old, to Isiah, 5. The Thomases lived on the first floor of a two-story red brick building on Congress Street, facing the Eisenhower Expressway.

One of the Lords rang the bell. Mary Thomas, wearing glasses, answered the door. She saw behind him the rest of his gang, all wearing gold tams and black capes and some had guns in their waist bands that glinted under the street lamps.

"We want your boys," the gang leader told her. "They can't walk around here and not be in no gang."

She looked him in the eye. "There's only one gang around here, and that's the Thomas gang," she said, "and I lead that."

"If you don't bring those boys out, we'll get 'em in the streets," he said.

She shut the door. The gang members waited. She walked through the living room where the rest of the family sat. Isiah, frightened, watched her go into the bedroom and return with a sawed-off shotgun. She opened the front door.

She pointed the gun at the caped figure before her. "Get off my porch," she said, "or I'll blow you 'cross the Expressway."

He stepped back, and slowly he and his gang disappeared into the night.

Isiah Thomas never joined a gang, and was protected from the ravages of street life—the dope, the drinking, the stealing, the killings—by his mother and his brothers, even those who eventually succumbed to the streets. Two of his brothers became heroin addicts, one was a pimp, a couple would be jailed and one became a Vice Lords chief.

Isiah, though, was the baby of the family, and its hope.

He became an honor student in grade school and high school, an All-America basketball player in high school and college, and, as a 6-foot 1-inch point guard, led Indiana University to the National Collegiate Athletic Association championship last month. After only a few weeks out of high school, he was a standout on the United States team that won the gold medal in the 1979 Pan-American Games, and was a starter on the 1980 United States Olympic team.

The pros liked what they saw. "He's a terrific talent," said Rod Thorn, general manager of the Chicago Bulls. "Not only physically—and he seems adept at every phase of the game—but he has a charisma, an ability to inspire confidence in his teammates that only a few players have, like Larry Bird and Magic Johnson and Julius Erving."

Last weekend, Isiah Thomas, a 19-year-old sophomore and B student majoring in forensics, with an eye toward law school, made an important decision. He passed up his last two years of college basketball to declare his eligibility for the National Basketball Association's draft on June 9. Thomas said that three teams—New Jersey, Detroit and Chicago—had been told he could expect an offer of at least $1 million to sign.

Thomas had wrestled with his decision all season.

"Don't do it," said Bobby Knight, the Indiana basketball coach. "You can still improve in basketball. You could be worth more."

"Stay in school," said Quinn Buckner, a former Indiana player and now with the Milwaukee Bucks. "The college experience at your age is valuable and can't ever be repeated."

"What's left for you to prove in college?" asked his brother, Gregory.

"Go only if the price is right," said his former high school coach, Gene Pingatore. "Don't sell yourself short."

"Son," said Mary Thomas, "do what makes you happy."

The idea of turning pro had been with Isiah for as long as he can remember, instilled by his brothers who had their own basketball dreams squashed.

"There was a lot to consider," said Thomas. He sat on the arm of a couch in his small apartment in the Fountain Park complex on the Indiana campus in Bloomington. He wore a red baseball cap, a blue USA Olympic jacket, jeans and yellow sneakers. He speaks softly, thoughtfully, with careful articulation. Sometimes he'll flash that warm, dimpled smile that has become familiar from newspaper photos and national magazine covers. Behind that smile is also a toughness and intensity—twice last season he was involved in fights in games.

"I know I'm a role model for a lot of people back in the ghetto," said Thomas. "Not too many of us get the chance to get out, to go to college. If I quit school, what effect would that have on them?

"And I had said I wanted to be a lawyer, and one day return there and help the people. They need it. I've seen kids who stole a pair of pants and they get a five-year prison sentence. Literally. Because there was no adequate legal help for them. I know that I'll get my law degree. I know you can only play basketball for so many years. Then you've got the rest of your life ahead of you.

"And I have to think of my family. My mother worked hard all her life and for not much money. My father left when I was 3 years old, and my mom kept us together by herself. She worked in the community center, she worked in the church, she did whatever she could. She's got a job with the housing authority in Chicago now, and she shouldn't be working. Her eyes are bad, and her heart's not good. I'd like her to quit."

He feels that with the connections he makes in basketball he can help his brothers. He has already opened a few doors. Larry has a job with city housing and Mark is with the police department.

"I can always go back to school," Isiah said. "But I can't always make a million dollars. I won't always have a chance to provide stability for my family. And I'm doing it at basketball, a game I love."

He was a prodigy in basketball the way Mozart was in music. At age 3, Amadeus was composing on a harpsichord; at 3, Isiah could dribble and shoot baskets. He was the halftime entertainment at the neighborhood Catholic Youth Organization games. "We gave Isiah an old jersey that fell like a dress on him, and he wore black Oxfords and tossed up shots with a high arc," said Ted Kalinowski, who was called Brother Alexis before he left the order. "Isiah was amazing."

By the time Thomas was in the fourth grade, he was a standout on the eighth-grade team at Our Lady of Sorrows.

His mother and brothers watched him closely. Mary Thomas made sure that he went straight home from school, and did not dawdle in the streets. "If I did," he said, "my brothers would kick my butt."

From the time he was in grade school, his brothers lectured him. The seven of them sat in a bedroom and closed the door so that their mother and two sisters would not hear the horror stories of the street. They would take him for a walking tour and point out dangers. "They told me about the mistakes they had made, so that I wouldn't have to make them," said Thomas.

Lord Henry, for one, had been an all-city basketball player at St. Phillips; people in the neighborhood contend that he was the best basketball player in the family. He still holds the Catholic League single-season scoring record. But he had problems with discipline and grades and was thrown out of school. He went into the streets, and became a junkie. Isiah could see for himself the tortures his brother went through and the suffering it caused his mother.

As an eighth-grader, Isiah sought a scholarship to Weber High School, a Catholic League basketball power. The coach turned him down—too short. He was 5-6. "Look, I'm 6-4," Larry Thomas argued to the coach. "My brother will grow just as tall."

Gene Pingatore, the coach at St. Joseph's in Westchester, a Chicago suburb, was convinced. "He was a winner," said Pingatore. "He had that special aura."

At Westchester, a predominately white school in a white middle-class neighborhood, Thomas endeavored to learn text-book English. At one point his brother, Gregory, was confused. Isiah recalls his brother saying: " 'You done forgot to talk like a nigger. Better not come around here like no sissy white boy.' "

"Hey," Isiah said, laughing, "pull up on that jive."

But the brothers, like Isiah, understood the importance of language, and the handle it could provide in helping to escape the ghetto, a dream they shared.

"What I was doing," said Isiah, "was becoming fluent in two languages."

Isiah would rise at 5:30 in the morning to begin the one-and-a-half-hour journey by elevated train and bus to Westchester.

"Sometimes I'd look out of the window and see Isiah going to school in the dark and I'd cry," said Mary Thomas. "I'd give him grits with honey and butter for breakfast. And felt bad that I couldn't afford eggs and bacon for him, too. He sure did like to eat."

Although he excelled in basketball, Isiah neglected his studies and nearly flunked out of high school after his freshman year.

"You're a screwed-up kid," said Larry. "You can go one of two ways from here. I had a choice like this once. I chose hustlin'. It's a disgustin' kind of life. You got the chance of a lifetime."

Pingatore emphasized that without a C average he could not get a college scholarship, under NCAA rules.

"From that point on," recalls Isiah's sister, Ruby, "he was a changed kid." He made the St. Joseph's honor roll in each of his next three years.

He also led his team to second place in the Illinois state high school tournament, and was chosen All-America. He had his pick of hundreds of college scholarships. He chose Indiana because it was close and because Bobby Knight played it straight. "He didn't try to bribe me," said Mary Thomas. "Other schools offered hundreds of thousands of dollars. One coach promised to buy me a beautiful house. Another one said that there'd be a Lear jet so I could go to all Isiah's games. All Bobby Knight promised was he'd try to get Isiah a good education and give him a good opportunity to get better in basketball. He said that I might not even be able to get a ticket for a basketball game. I liked that." She also got tickets, and went to all of Isiah's games, sometimes traveling to Bloomington by bus.

He made all-Big Ten as a freshman. Last season he was a

consensus All-America. Despite this, he and Coach Knight had conflicts. Thomas appreciated Knight's basketball mind, and knew that the coach relied on his ability as a floor leader, but Thomas had trouble swallowing what he considered Knight's sometimes insulting behavior.

Once, Thomas, who had been appointed team captain, decided to talk with Knight about the team's poor morale. Thomas believed that Indiana—going poorly at the beginning of the season—had some of the best players in the country, and could win the championship if they could pull together and not fight the coach. "There's a problem here, coach," said Isiah.

"There's no problem here," replied Knight.

Indiana, however, did improve and made it to the final of the NCAA tournament against North Carolina at the Spectrum in Philadelphia on the night of March 30.

Amid the blaring of the school bands and the waving of pom-pons and the screams from the crowd—the Indiana rooters were sectioned on one side of the court in red and white, the school colors, and the North Carolina fans on the other side wearing blue and white—the game was tightly played. North Carolina led by 26-25 as Isiah Thomas took the ball from under the Tar Heels' basket, and dribbled slowly upcourt. There were only 12 seconds to go in the half and tense Indiana fans wondered if the Hoosiers would get another shot off, especially with Thomas' casualness.

"I didn't want the team to press, I wanted them to relax, and if they saw I wasn't rushing I hoped they wouldn't either," Thomas said later. With two seconds to go he hit Randy Wittman with a pass in the corner, and Wittman connected, giving Indiana its first lead of the game, and a terrific lift as it went to the locker room.

Starting the second half, Thomas stole two straight passes from North Carolina and scored. Indiana went ahead by 31-26 and went on to a 63-50 victory. "Those two steals," said Dean Smith, the North Carolina coach, "were the turning point in the game," Thomas scored a game-high 23 points, and had five assists and four steals. He was named the outstanding player in the championship tournament.

As soon as the game ended, Indiana fans rushed on the court. One of them, Thomas saw, was a black woman in a red suit jacket with a button on her lapel. The button read, "Isiah Thomas's Mom. Mrs. Mary Thomas." Near the center of the court they embraced. She was crying and it looked as if Isiah was holding back tears.

"Thanks, mom, thanks for everything you've gone through for me. I hope I can do something for you."

"You done enough, honey," she said.

Reporters and camera men were all around them. And Isiah whispered in his mother's ear. "Well, you can do one more thing for me," he said.

"What's that, baby?"

"I heard you in the first half when I threw a bad pass. You

hollered, 'What the hell are you doin'?' Don't cuss at me on the court. I was fixin' to get it together."

Then Isiah was scooted off to receive the winner's trophy. And the woman who wore the button proudly saying she was Isiah Thomas's mom took out a handkerchief and wiped her eyes.

Clutch Pass Closes Door on America's Team

PRO FOOTBALL

By *LARRY FELSER*

From the Buffalo Evening News
Copyright © 1981, The Buffalo Evening News

A generation from now, football anthologies will feature the photograph. . . Dwight Clark, extending his body as fully as it could be extended . . . leaping, grasping . . . thrusting the San Francisco 49ers into Super Bowl XVI.

"The first day of training camp last summer, Bill Walsh drew that play on the blackboard," said Sam Wyche, the ex-Bills quarterback who now coaches that specialty for San Francisco.

"Six months later, it put us in the Super Bowl. No, that's wrong. Joe Montana and Dwight Clark put us in the Super Bowl by executing that play."

That Play.

There were volumes to talk about after the 49ers had beaten Dallas, 28-27, in one of the greatest playoff games in National Football League history, but the conversations and monologues kept returning to That Play.

The 49ers weren't down to their last gasp, just their semi-last—third and three on the Cowboys 6-yard line. There were 59 seconds on the clock when San Francisco broke the huddle. Dallas led, 27-21.

Montana took the snap from center Fred Quillian and rolled to his right. He bellied back to give himself more time.

"As slow as I am," says Clark, "it takes a long time to develop."

D.D. Lewis, playing his final game after a 13-year career as a Cowboy, rumbled toward Montana. Too Tall Jones, extending his arms like some angry condor, rumbled even more menacingly.

Montana waited another split-second and then threw his pass. It was thrown high, very high. In fact, it looked to those unfamiliar with the 49ers that it was being thrown away, beyond the end zone.

It wasn't.

"We scored a touchdown with that play earlier this season," he says. "It has to be thrown high."

The primary receiver on the play was to be Fred Solomon. Clark was to turn back to the right, once he got to the rear of the end zone, in order to lure some of the coverage away from Solomon.

That didn't work, so Montana selected Clark.

Up went the 6-foot-4 receiver, like a strong forward snatching a rebound in basketball. Only this rebound was worth six points, and $13,000 a man to Clark and his teammates.

"The funny thing is that when I played basketball, I didn't rebound," says Clark. "I was a guard. I used to take long jump shots."

That Play culminated an 89-yard drive, which pitted the coaching skills of San Francisco's Bill Walsh against those of Dallas' Tom Landry.

There were four minutes, 54 seconds left in the game when San Francisco took possession of the ball at its 11-yard line. Landry sent his pass-defense specialists into the game. On first down, Montana threw a long pass, too long in fact.

Then the 49ers crossed up Landry by running, something they had not done very well throughout their excellent season.

Lenvil Elliott ran around right end for 11 yards and a first down. Elliott ran up the middle for another first down. Finally, Solomon put the Niners deep into Dallas territory with a 14-yard reverse.

The Cowboys were totally off-balance during the climactic drive.

For a few brief moments it seemed as if That Play might become anti-climactic.

With 39 seconds to play, Danny White passed 31 yards to Drew Pearson on Dallas' first play after the ensuing kickoff. It put the ball on the San Francisco 44. If the Cowboys could reach the 25, Rafael Septien, who had kicked a 44-yard field goal early in the game, would have an excellent opportunity to kick the winning points.

"I was on the phone to the bench, giving instructions for Montana to get his two-minute offense ready in case we had to get out on the field and come from behind again," said Wyche.

The Niners had reason to be frightened.

Pearson nearly broke for a touchdown on his catch. Rookie Ron Lott played the ball too much on the play and it took a diving tackle by another rookie, Eric Wright, to save the touchdown.

As it turned out, it would be the last shot Dallas fired.

On the next play, Lawrence Pillers, a New York Jet castoff, made a thunderous sack of White. The Dallas quarterback fumbled, Jim Stuckey of the 49ers recovered and San Francisco, which won only six games the season before, had a date with the Cincinnati Bengals in the Pontiac Silverdome on January 24.

Colleges on the Razor's Edge?

GENERAL

By *JIM SMITH*

From Newsday
Copyright © 1981, Newsday, Inc.

College basketball players, coaches, athletic directors, educators, agents and even tout-sheet publishers agree that the recruiting process—in which ethics often are abandoned—contributes to an atmosphere in which point shaving can, and does, take place.

Whether or not allegations of point shaving two seasons ago by three Boston College players are true, those involved in college basketball suggest that recruiting is the root of such problems. They offer a wide range of solutions including tightening NCAA rules, de-emphasizing college sports, and professionalizing college players.

The Boston College scandal has prompted educators and university officials to examine college sports, their own athletic programs, the win-at-all-costs mentality that seems prevalent in American society, and illegal betting. What many have found is a system at least in need of repair. Others see it as out of control, possibly headed toward self-destruction.

"Point shaving is a logical extension of the way money and greed have taken over big-time college athletics, just a further means of milking the system," said David A. Jones, an associate professor of history at North Carolina Wesleyan College who teaches a course called "Sports in America." "There is pressure to produce winners. The athletes have become hired guns, mercenaries. There's no such thing as amateur sports. Nobody believes it."

"It's a matter of business, no doubt about it," said University of Texas basketball coach Abe Lemons. "They dangle the TV money in front of you, the big arenas, $300,000 for making the Final Four. In the old days everybody would play and the two teams would shake hands and go to a school dance together. That doesn't happen anymore.

"Most coaches don't have tenure," Lemons added. "The pressure (to win) is tremendous. When you recruit a kid, you ask him, 'how many illegal offers did you get?' How can you expect your players to stay straight when everybody around you is doing things? Since

many players don't have money, it leaves them open to enticement."
University of Michigan athletic director Don Canham said that
his school spends $100,000 a year to send coaches on recruiting trips.
He says the trips are necessary to remain competitive nationally.
"It's nonsense," Canham said. "Completely ridiculous. We recruit year-round. It leads to all the problems we have in intercollegiate athletics, including point shaving. We tend to overglorify the
athlete. The recruiting process spoils the kids. When Bear Bryant, Bo
Schembechler, Joe Paterno and Johnny Robinson all visit a kid, his
sense of values gets screwed up."

In the early 1970s, current Brigham Young University basketball coach Frank Arnold was a UCLA assistant and chairman of the
National Association of Basketball Coaches (NABC) recruiting
committee. Arnold said a survey his group conducted over three
years showed that 12 percent of the nation's big-time basketball colleges offered illegal inducements to recruits and 40 percent of the top
high school players said they had been offered illegal inducements.

"If a young man feels he's being bought in the recruiting process," Arnold said, "why wouldn't he justify illegal actions in other
areas? Not many schools cheat, but cheaters still reach a high percentage of kids. We need to do that survey again."

Mitch Kupchak, who went to North Carolina and is now a Washington Bullet, remembers being offered $50 for "cab fare" by college
coaches he visited who knew his parents were to meet him at the airport. "I know my family was approached by one institution. My
mother still won't tell me which one," Kupchak said. "Either my
family was going to get money or my father would get a better job—
if I went to that school."

Princeton senior Steve Mills said, "Basketball is pretty easy to
manipulate at some colleges. You can get a guy to come to your
school who might not graduate. You keep him eligible for four years
and then you don't have to worry about him. It isn't that way here
(Princeton gives no athletic scholarships). If I don't want to play
basketball anymore, it doesn't affect my financial aid."

At most colleges, it would. The recruiting process, critics argue,
is the beginning of a dehumanizing and a programming of student-
athletes which sometimes leads them to quit school.

"You go through a grammar school and high school and basketball's fun up until your junior and senior years," senior forward
Frank Gilroy of St. John's said. "Then you start being recruited.
Then you go to college and it's a job. It's the money. The coach is putting food on the table."

"With all the people looking to make big money and fill the
arena, it's easy for a kid's values to get distorted," Gilroy added. "He
can say, 'They're using me to make money. Why shouldn't I get
some?' I could understand why a guy might do it (shave). I've felt
that way sometimes. What do you get? Some sneakers and warm-
ups, a handshake at the end—and a senior watch."

"As long as you can justify it (shaving) in your own mind," Mills said, "you could do it. If the money is right, it wouldn't be hard to convince yourself that you're still winning the game and the odds are that you probably won't get caught." Mills added that he would not consider shaving points himself.

Several coaches and players pointed out that players on athletic scholarships are worse off financially than athletes getting Basic Educational Opportunity Grant (BEOG) aid. The NCAA prohibits scholarship athletes from working during the school year. Those on BEOG can work. If a scholarship athlete comes from an impoverished background, the temptation to accept illegal payments from alumni or school officials—or to shave points—increases.

"From the time they're in high school," Cincinnati-based agent Ron Grinker said, "they are told how marvelous they are. If you cheat a little, you're still cheating. Whether you buy them a pair of sneakers or a suit, a player's values get confused."

"You put a coach in a bind," Lemons said, "when you say, 'win or else.' He'll say, 'I'll give a run at it.' I don't think the whole system's that bad, except the recruiting. That's degrading. It's ridiculous."

"The pressure to win comes from alums," Arnold said.

"They're the ones with the bumper stickers that say 'fire the coach,' " Lemons said.

"It's the same as it was 30 years ago," long-time St. John's sports information director Bill Esposito said. "Then kids stayed home and played college ball in New York City because they were taken care of. They got fat jobs at hotels in the Catskills and played ball all summer."

Thousands of players have filtered through the system, gotten degrees and entered the job market without being exposed to the lawlessness of college basketball. Mills said financial aid covers about $6,500 of his $9,000 yearly cost for tuition, room and board and books. He takes a bank loan to cover the rest. He has worked summers at Hempstead's Percy Jackson Youth Center and as a management trainee for Chemical Bank at the World Trade Center in Manhattan. He probably is not typical.

"I've heard about other schools giving money under the table and I think about it sometimes," Mills said. "It's funny. They're getting something and I'm not. But I figure it'll even out in the long run."

BYU's Arnold has recommended to the NCAA that those who qualify for BEOG aid should receive it "on top of" their athletic scholarship money. The way the system works now, if a student athlete qualifies for $4,500 worth of BEOG money based on financial need and his tuition, room, books and board are $5,000, he may receive only the difference—$500—from the athletic department.

"That's a good idea," Kupchak said of Arnold's proposal.

"Right now," Gilroy said, "the guy who's working after school is going to make twice as much money as I do, and he doesn't have to work with 6,000 people watching him."

"The main thing," Gilroy said, "is that it (involves) a lot of money. Guys come to college and have the impression that a scholarship is a big thing; that cheating goes on. It's easy to get disillusioned and feel it isn't worth the work. Guys who see they're not going to continue in the pros say, 'This diploma is only going to get me a $15,000 job. Why not take something with me?'

"But you can make that work for you. You play your role, get your education, hold your own values. I grew up with simple values: God, family, country. I would never have considered it (shaving). I wouldn't sacrifice myself or my team. I have my standards. Even though they say you don't have to lose, I have to look in the mirror in the morning. You get caught, you're ruined. I wouldn't sell myself for a couple of thousand dollars. I've got the rest of my life to make money."

Why do players shave points, that is, take money to influence the outcome of a game to coincide with the way a fixer bets?

Hale McMenamim, a former FBI agent who is an NCAA enforcement official, said, "We do have a gambling task force we set up a year ago to see if we can come up with a profile as to why kids do it. We're seriously concerned with the situation. What the underlying psychological reasons are, I'd like to know."

"Kids do it for money," Esposito of St. John's said. "There's an atmosphere of breaking the law in recruiting. It's taught by coaches who don't give a damn about anything but winning. In effect, the kids are being paid to win. So if they're asked to win by not as much (as the published betting spread), they figure it's all right."

"It probably reflects the morality that as long as nobody gets hurt, you can bend or break general rules of conduct," said Jeffrey Nevid, a Hofstra psychology professor with an interest in sports. "It's just like ripping off an insurance company or cheating on your income tax return. And there's the old idea that the end justifies the means. If some 'responsible' person (gambler) tells me it's all right, I don't have to question it individually.

"I see students quite openly cheating (on tests). I think it pervades virtually every aspect of life. There's an increased acceptance of cheating as regards social institutions. There's a post-Watergate mentality. Even the most respected institutions are not to be trusted. Educational institutions, oil companies . . ."

"Credibility and believability are a sparse commodity in America right now," said Gregory Sojka, assistant professor of American studies at Wichita State who has lectured on point shaving. "Everybody's looking out for No. 1. Tom Wolfe called it the 'Me Generation.' Christopher Lasch writes about the same thing in 'The Cult of Narcissism.' "

"America has a neurotic personality based on competition," said Mike D'Innocenzo, a Hofstra history professor who lectures on sports history. "The rationalization some people use (for shaving) is, 'We're not being disloyal, we're just affecting the margin of victory.' Except, it violates basic ethical considerations. There's a predatory mentality in America. 'I'll get mine; if you don't get yours, too bad.' "

"It's like anything else, like white-collar theft," said Ray Wilson, basketball coach at the University of Massachusetts. "What factors cause somebody to steal or to do something wrong knowing it's wrong? Look at the college kid. We bring him often out of a (depressed) area to a 'clean' environment. Often he can't rely on money from home. We move him from one society without money to another society without money. We don't let him work. We tell him, 'unless your folks sustain you, you have to survive on your own.' "

"Corrupt people are always looking to beat the system," said Mort Olshan, owner of the Los Angeles-based bettor's guide The Gold Sheet. "Greed, the acquisition of unearned money, that's what motivates it (shaving). Why should college basketball be sacrosanct? Any area's vulnerable to corruption—banks, the stock exchange."

Many college basketball observers believe that people like Olshan are part of the problem. Taking bets on college sports events is a federal crime. And yet daily newspapers publish "the line" from Las Vegas on college games and tip-sheets like Olshan's feed the sports-betting public. There are papers that even offer the top 40 college teams' records vs. the point spread.

"People always like to point the finger at those who wager on sporting events," Olshan said. "One always looks for scapegoats in these matters. But the people who bet on these games often are in the top echelon of the community. They enjoy the sport of trying to analyze sporting events. It seems the more logical scapegoat is recruiting malpractices. There are kids playing college basketball today who have no business being in school.

"Bookmakers say there's not much interest in college basketball," Olshan added. "They can't keep up with the volatility of it. They feel vulnerable. Some feel the players have an edge."

Just how much betting is done on college basketball is a matter of debate. Brigham Young's Arnold reported that the two major wire services reported different scores for the same game involving his team recently. The same day, Arnold said his secretary received 15 long-distance telephone calls.

"The spread was nine," Arnold said. "One guy told the secretary, 'If you won by eight, I lost $600. If you won by 12, I won $800.' That tells me there's an awful lot of people gambling on a game and they've never even seen our players."

University of Nevada-Reno athletic director Dick Trachok said Nevada colleges have not been included on "the line" since 1946. "We, being in the only state where gambling was legal, were always suspected (of shaving) by you outsiders," he said. "We're pleased they never put us on their cards. I think it would be easier on all the kids if there were no lines printed at all."

"I asked every sports editor in the city in 1952 to take the line out of their sports sections," said former Manhattan College coach Ken

Norton, now retired and living in Palm Beach, Fla. "These things sell papers. Max Case of the Journal told me, 'If you can get the rest of the guys to do it, I'll do it.' Nobody would be the first."

"You ask yourself, 'Why do they publish the line?' " Wilson of UMass said. "They suggest that gambling is all right, if you don't get caught."

"If they broke it (college basketball) down so there were no money in the programs, no fans in the gym and no line in the papers," Seton Hall coach Bill Raftery said, "there'd still be a line (in Vegas). There'd still be betting. Where there's greed, avarice, a chance to turn a dollar, it's gonna happen.

"Sure I can (understand why shaving occurs). Some of these kids have seen their mothers die. Some have alcoholic fathers. There was no money in the house or their parents worked. These kids don't understand why it's wrong. They say, 'Nobody gets hurt.' We know some kids like the easy way. I'd be naive to think it can't happen here. But eliminate the cancer, don't kill the body."

Most colleges bring in an FBI official or somebody familiar with the history of the fixing scandals of 1950-51 and 1960-61 to lecture players on avoiding contact with bettors and bookmakers. The players are told not to give injury reports to friends or predict the outcome of any games.

"Players today are educated not to get involved (in shaving)," Kupchak said. "Twenty or thirty years ago, when the game wasn't on national television, the FBI was not monitoring it and it wasn't in the papers every day, I could see it (shaving). I think the blame (now) goes to the kids. They did the wrong. Why they did it goes back to their upbringing. People are products of their environment."

Many educators say the environment is part of the problem. "There's been a legitimization of institutionalized gambling in America," Hofstra's Nevid said. "There are state lotteries, casino gambling, the traditional acceptance of gambling on horse races. Jimmy the Greek's a regular announcer (on NFL pre-game telecasts)."

"Say I have 10 alums who are very into the BYU-Utah rivalry," Arnold said, "and they bet $10, $50, $100 on our game and we lose. Then I have 10 alums mad at me and mad at my players. They might eventually threaten to withdraw their support for the program. It's a bad situation."

How much point shaving goes on today?

Defenders of college basketball point out that there have been few proven incidents of point shaving. There was a nationwide scandal in 1951 involving CCNY, NYU, LIU, Manhattan, Bradley, Kentucky and other schools. In 1960-61, the last major scandal broke involving 47 college players, all banned from the NBA for life because of the league's by-laws concerning association with known gamblers.

"The rarity of it means there might be some hope for a decent structure of college athletics," David Jones said.

"People are deceiving themselves if they think it's not going on now," Norton said. "I definitely think it's going on and has gone on through the years. What can you do? Keep up surveillance? Tell the kids to report any questions from suspicious people about injuries or other information?"

Norton said that in the late 1960s and early 1970s, he knew of "three or four" investigations of dumping and point-shaving involving Eastern teams or officials. "It's very hard to prove," Norton said. "If you don't catch 'em, you can't do anything about it. We went 20 years between exposes. That doesn't mean things weren't going on."

Are there solutions?

"I think we shouldn't subscribe to basketball publications which feature gambling information," BYU's Arnold said, "and we shouldn't discuss it on our coaches' television shows. Too many guys would like to touch (set up) college kids and probably a lot of college kids have been touched in the last few years. I know gambling is the great cancer. The people who are gonna ask for point shaving are local people, those who can get to the players."

Sam A. Banks, a social psychologist and president of Dickinson (Pa.) College who lectures on sports in America, said, "Basketball lends itself to point (shaving) by the very nature of the sport. The key lies not in de-emphasis but in setting the standards by which players are recruited more clearly. I think it's part of a deeper national malaise, though. We have told generations of our people about the American Dream. Play it cool, take care of yourselves. No institution, including a college, is impervious to national trends. The attempt to achieve immediate gain by giving up a principle is part of the malaise."

"I think there's got to be more internal policing," Sojka said, "and being more realistic about money for college athletes."

"College athletics have become so big and business-oriented," said Angela Lumpkin, an associate professor of physical education at the University of North Carolina, "that they will either have to cease to exist or become uncontrollable. I think we're headed to self-destruction. Many schools are doing away with so-called 'non-revenue-producing' sports. The others just grow bigger."

"I don't see how we can de-emphasize college athletics," Leverett Smith, who teaches a "Sports in America" course at North Carolina Wesleyan, said. "How do we do it?"

"The idea of de-emphasizing is almost impossible," Mills said, "because too many people are benefitting. I read where the Louisville basketball team brought in $1 million last year. Any university would be crazy not to want to bring in money like that."

"De-emphasize?" Lemons said. "Most places have 80,000-seat stadiums. Kentucky seats 23,000 for basketball. How do you de-emphasize? What do you do, tear down the stadium and use it for the rodeo? They've found a way to make money at it."

Retrospect: A Tip of the Cap

BASEBALL

By *JERRY SPINELLI*

From Philadelphia Magazine
Copyright © 1981, Jerry Spinelli

"Look at you. You're dirty again. Your friend is here."
The nun hauled me to the nearest sink and scrubbed my face
nearly raw. She took scant care to keep the soap out of my eyes. It
was from the soap that I cried. The rough treatment I was used to. I
expected it.

I lived in an orphanage. I was therefore known to the kids in
town as a "homie." That alone was enough to make me feel different,
but even among the homies I seemed to be an outcast.

For one thing I was a wet-the-bed, a status that caused me to be
paddled every night as I emerged dripping wet from the shower. At
night I would stay awake as long as I could, only to be betrayed by
sleep. In the morning, with the inevitability of eternal judgment, I
would waken to the damp, faint mustiness of my sin.

For another thing, I was smart. I could read in the first grade.
My hand was forever waving wildly in the air. Sometimes a whole
day seemed to pass with no one volunteering answers but me. Time
and again the nun would scan the seats in vain for another hand. She
would try to coax answers from slumping heads. Then, with a sigh,
she would finally turn to me and, flicking her forefinger, release me
from my bondage of silence. Though my answers were invariably
correct, the nun never seemed as happy to receive them as I did to
give them.

Then one day during recess in the playground, three of the bigger
(and dumber) kids in class came up to me. As usual I was in the dirt
near the roots of a huge old tree, playing marbles against myself.
One of the big kids said, "Stand up."

I stood up.

"How come you always raise yer hand?" he asked.

I shrugged.

"How come?"

"I know the answers."

"Well don't raise yer hand no more."

I squealed. "What?"

"You deaf?" he snarled. Then he placed my biggest marble on top of my shoe, and with the heel of his shoe he ground the marble into my foot.

I was too upset to appreciate the befuddled look on the nun's face the rest of the day as she kept glancing at my hand which, since recess, had become firmly desk-bound.

Then there was the great three-day mystery. It took place in the classroom. On the first day it started with the nun turning from the blackboard and sniffing into the space above our heads, rabbit-like. Her chalk hand was still pasted on the board, stopped in the middle of a word. Several more times she sniffed that day, and once, while we were doing our spelling, she bent over and ran her pointer along the black, dusty space beneath the radiator.

On the second day she turned from the blackboard, chalk hand and all, and announced, "Alright—out. Out!" We filed outside, the head nun went in, and a half hour later we returned. All windows were open, as was the door.

On the third day she came stalking down the aisles. My eyes were fixed on my spelling, but I could trace her movement by the soft rustle of her skirt. It stopped right behind me. Then came the most horrible shriek: "Eeeeeey ahhhh-HAH!"

It was me. It seems I had an unconscious habit of slipping out of my shoes while sitting in class. And it seems, as I was to learn later, that I was afflicted with a condition in which a perspiring foot, however clean, gives off an overwhelming odor.

Of course, I was thenceforth forbidden to go anywhere unshod outside the shower room. And kids I never knew found it impossible to pass me without pinching their nostrils. "Feet," they would honk.

These things made me feel I was the fly in every pie. Apparently I had been born with a terrible power: I spoiled everything around me.

I had forgotten that a friend would be coming for me on this particular Saturday. ("Friend" was the home's word for anyone who came to visit you or take you out. A friend was usually a perfect stranger, but could also be a relative or even a long-lost parent. Some of the homies had a long string of friends. This was to be my first.) Why a friend would want to visit me, I couldn't imagine.

He was a fat little man, shorter than the nuns. He held a straw hat in front of him with both hands.

He smiled. "How would you like to go to a ball game?"

"Okay," I said.

It turned out to be a baseball game in the city. It might as well have been Rumaninan rugby. I had heard of baseball, but I had never played it and knew next to nothing about it. Except for marbles, I was woefully unathletic.

The game was at Shibe Park. A sign said, HOME OF THE

PHILADELPHIA A'S. Now it began to make sense: the A's were orphans, too. They were playing the Boston Red Sox. The man (Mr. Coleman was his name) took me by the hand, stunned and docile, through dusty, hawking, mustard-sweet catacombs, up endless iron stairways, finally to emerge onto what I was told were the bleachers. We were beyond what was known as left field.

It was the most beautiful sight I had ever seen—a vast, fan-shaped, emerald-green lawn. I had never known the earth could be so immaculate. It was all so ordered, so perfect. Two utterly straight and pure-white lines diverged from a point called home plate and created the borders of this perfection, along with the tall green fence that they intersected. I was vaguely comforted that the white lines did not diverge forever.

Men toting rakes and other implements came out of nowhere and swarmed over the field.

Mr. Coleman saw my puzzlement and chuckled. "That's not baseball. That's the grounds crew. Watch the tractor."

And sure enough a little blue tractor came putting out from under the grandstand, dragging what looked like a large window screen. It headed for the tawny, half-moon-shaped portion of the field where no grass grew. From first base to third base it traveled, tracing exquisite loops, and what the screen passed over, it left in a condition so smooth and flat and unmarked that it could not possibly be called dirt.

Meanwhile, the men with rakes were smoothing the field around the bases where the tractor screen could not reach. And other men were smoothing out the pitcher's mound and the home plate area, or painting home plate itself, or repairing the white lines where someone had stepped.

Then, as if by signal, the men began leaving the field. The rakers trailed their rakes behind, to erase their own footprints.

"Now the water," said Mr. Coleman.

Two men were wheeling a large hose reel to near the pitcher's mound. They pulled out two hoses and began to spray the dirt portion.

"Keeps the dust down," said Mr. Coleman, answering my unspoken question.

Dust or no dust, I did not like the water men. I found myself urging them to pass over the dirt lightly, but they insisted on wetting it down so thoroughly that in a few minutes the infield had turned from yellowish to dark gray.

There was a lilt of expectancy in Mr. Coleman's next announcement, and an almost conspiratorial whisper. "Now—the bases."

What's wrong with the bases, I wondered, looking at the three gray squares on the infield. Then, to my amazement I discovered I had not been looking at the real bases at all. They were just covers which a man was removing one by one. Now the true bases were revealed—spanking snow-white cubes that had never been touched.

And I saw now the real reason they had made the infield so dark with water—to dramatically set off the gleaming bases.

The base man left the field. There it was, more beautiful, more perfect than when I had entered. The grounds crew, before our very eyes, had done as much a miracle as man could do.

I leaped to my feet. I clapped and cheered. What a performance!

A few seconds later I was crushed. Men in baggy flannel knickers were springing onto the field, scattering to all points. I felt on my own skin every footprint they left on the immaculate infield.

Until that moment Mr. Coleman had been a man of smiles. Now he was out-and-out laughing, his eyes watering. "These are the players," he said, nodding toward the field. I felt his hand cup my shoulder and pull me a little toward him. "Now the game's ready to start."

Then he drew his face near to mine and whispered. "See him?" He was pointing to a player jogging across the grass toward us. He didn't stop till he was almost to the fence. Then he turned around and faced home plate. He simply stood there. He was almost directly beneath us, so there wasn't much to see except his blue cap and his shoulders and a large blue number on his back. "That's Gus Zernial," Mr. Coleman told me.

"Who's he?" I said.

"The left fielder."

"What's he doing?"

"He's playing left field."

"He's just standing there."

"Well, that's right. He doesn't have much to do out there. But wait'll he gets to bat." Here Mr. Coleman put his lips right to my ear. "Maybe he'll hit a home run."

I turned to him full face. "Is that good?"

Mr. Coleman said nothing. He simply closed his eyes and smiled and nodded profoundly, and I knew that a home run, whatever it was, was a very, very good thing.

The game as I recall it was a series of whispered prophecies come true, few of them having to do with the actual action of the game.

Mr. Coleman told me to keep an eye on the third-base coach. And for inning after inning the third-base coach kept me enthralled with his antics and contortions and twitches. He seemed plagued by either poison ivy or a particular insistent mosquito. Even the batters seemed distracted, for they kept turning away from the pitcher to look at the third-base coach.

"He's giving the signs," said Mr. Coleman.

"Oh," I said.

When the hot-dog man came down our aisle, Mr. Coleman raised his arm and shouted. "Two!" Then, as he leaned across me to pass along the money: "Watch the mustard. Watch."

I watched. Like that of the grounds crew it was a virtuoso performance. Two hot-dog rolls in the same hand—up goes the lid of the white carton and into the rising steam with gleaming silver tweezers

—a slight hesitation (he's fishing for the best!)—then they're out, two reddish, dripping morsels—deftly laid in their rolls. "Waaatch . . ." came my last warning. Into the giant mustard jar with a tongue depressor and . . . and . . . it was done. Before my eyes could digest the sight, the hot dogs were being passed down the row to us. All I had seen was a lightning flicker of the tongue depressor over the rolls, and yet when they reached us, sure enough, anointing each hot dog was a neat strip of creamy, bright yellow mustard.

Even as I chewed, my eyes never left the lightning-handed hot-dog man until he disappeared into the crowd.

A player slid. Home plate vanished under a layer of dust. Mr. Coleman nudged me. "Watch the umpire." The umpire pulled something from his hip pocket—it was a little whisk broom. With brisk, assured ceremony he squatted in the dust and whish, whish, whish—home plate reappeared. I decided then and there I wanted to be an umpire.

There were many other prophecies. That everyone would boo at such and such a time. That the manager would spit every time he left the dugout. That when the manager and umpire argued they would touch noses. That it would become very hot in the bleachers. That in the seventh inning everyone in the ball park would stand up and stretch.

And they all came true, every one. I relished the predictability of it all. My favorite was the seventh-inning stretch. "Now?" I kept asking. "Now," he finally said. I shot up, determined to be first. I looked around. Slowly they were rising, all around me, by the thousands, rising for the seventh-inning stretch. Not a single soul was left sitting. I honestly did not feel stiff or tired, but I'm sure no one could tell by the great, long stretch that I did.

Inning after inning Gus Zernial trotted back and forth from left field to the dugout.

"Did he hit a home run yet?" I kept pestering.

"Not yet," said Mr. Coleman. The confidential glee was gone from his voice. He sounded a little like a priest. "It's not for sure, now. All he can do is try. Don't get your hopes up too high."

I guess my hopes were up too high, for Mr. Coleman stared worriedly at me for a minute. The smile returned. "But I'll tell you one thing," he whispered, "if he *does* hit a home run, do you know what he'll do?"

"What?"

"He'll tip his cap."

"He will?"

He placed his hand over his heart. "Promise."

It was in the last inning of the ball game when a sudden commotion erupted around me. Everyone in the bleachers seemed to shout in unison and bolt to his feet, including Mr. Coleman. Then I saw it—the baseball—dove-white, like the bases, falling from the sun-squinting sky, angel-white against the murky girdered ceiling, engulfed at

last in a mass of frantically straining arms several aisles away.
I didn't have to be told. It was a home run.

"Gus Zernial?" I screamed up at Mr. Coleman. "Gus Zernial?"
The way he hugged me, I knew that it was.

What a wonderful thing is a home run, I thought. The joy that it
brought. The ecstasy. I could think of it only as a gift, a kind of salvation. It was a religious thing, a home run, something sacramental.
I thought of the priest offering the wafer, and of the Magi bearing
gifts, and of the archbishop who came every Christmas and we knew
then that we would get ice cream. Now there was the home run, delivered unto the bleachers. Now there was the priest and there were
the Magi and there was the archbishop and there was Gus Zernial.

I shaded my eyes so as to see most clearly the man trotting
around the bases. I saw him touch every bag. I saw him shake the
hand of the third-base coach as he passed by. I saw him step decisi-
vely upon home plate and shake the hands of the next batter and the
batboy and I saw him received into the welcoming arms of the dugout. But I did not see him tip his cap.

I kept silent, not wanting to show disappointment. All of Mr. Co-
lemn's other prophecies had come true, even the "not for sure" home
run. Who was I to quibble over one unfulfilled detail? I—a wiseacre,
wet-the-bed, stinky-footed homie.

But inside I couldn't help quibbling. Something was longing for
the tipped cap even more than for the home run. Without the tipped
cap the home run was incomplete, tradition was left dangling. I
couldn't help wondering: *Is it me? Does Gus Zernial know I'm in the
bleachers?* I tightened my shoelaces.

The answer came a few minutes later. Gus Zernial was trotting
out to take his place in left field, and again the bleachers erupted.
They flailed their arms. They screamed and whistled. "Gus! Gus!
Gus!" they chanted.

But Gus Zernial did not seem to hear. He merely stood there facing the infield, while just behind and above him 5,000 people were
going mad.

I dared not join the crowd. Oh, I wanted to. I wanted to chant his
name, wave my arms and cheer him. I wanted to go mad, too. But I
was afraid he might see me.

Suddenly the cheering shot to a deafening pitch. Down below Gus
Zernial was turning—not all the way, just his head and shoulders, so
that the brim of the blue cap was now facing the bleachers and you
could see the fancy white "A" in it. And now his head was tilting upward and there was the face of the great Gus Zernial and he was
looking right up into the bleachers—*he was looking right at me*—and
with a delicacy I would never expect, he took the blue brim between
his thumb and forefinger and briefly, briefly and forever, tipped his
cap.

Fisk Enjoys Red-Letter Days, Ways

BASEBALL

By *PHIL HERSH*

From the Chicago Sun-Times
Copyright © 1981, Chicago Sun-Times

Of course he is a catcher.

Carlton Catcher, son of Cecil, brother of Calvin, Cedric and Conrad, father of Carlyn, Carson and Courtney—Isn't that just like a Yankee? Why waste time playing around with the whole alphabet when C is a perfectly good letter—and kinsman of Cotton Mather.

Cotton Calvinism, godfather of the Puritan ethic, preaching hard work as the sure way to salvation. His terrifying vision of the alternative molded souls scattered across the New England wilderness, the forebears of the Fisks of Charleston, N.H., and the Hawthornes of Salem, Mass.

The sermons were still vivid 200 years later to Nathaniel Hawthorne, the customs inspector who lost his job and made himself a writer. He would protest the dogmatism of the Puritans' unflinching moral code and yet find it the maker of men, just and true:

"There was one thing that much aided me in renewing and recreating the stalwart soldier of the Niagara frontier—the man of true and simple energy. It was the recollection of the memorable words of his—'I'll try, Sir!'—spoken on the very verge of a desperate and heroic enterprise and breathing the soul and spirit of New England hardihood, comprehending all perils and encountering all."

—Hawthorne, the Scarlet Letter

"What position do you want to play?" the scouting questionnaire read. Carlton Fisk, the high school shortstop and pitcher answered catcher, the most demanding position in baseball, the one he had not played since outgrowing the equipment in Little League. Damned if he didn't make himself one of the best.

His better sport was basketball. Fisk played that so well he had 40 points and 36 rebounds in a high school tournament game. Not good enough, said Cecil Fisk, his jaw set like New Hampshire granite. You missed four of six foul shots. Mankind may be imperfect, but perfection is the only worthwhile goal.

"A disciplined man and a disciplined catcher. An old-line catcher," says Bill Freehan, once Fisk's peer, now a crewcut Tigers coach. Nine years ago, only five years after he began to work at catching, Fisk was a unanimous rookie of the year. In nine years, he has been seven times an All-Star. In his 10th, he is the White Sox' $2.9 million Moses.

Fisk made his money the old-fashioned way. He *earned* it.

He has played with broken ribs, a badly pulled groin and a chronic sore elbow. He squats 200 times a game on a left knee damaged so badly that the doctor who reassembled it told Fisk he might limp the rest of his life. He has felt the sting of foul balls off his shoulders, arms, hands, legs, feet, even his nose. Fisk broke his nose in several places with the tipped ball from his own checked swing. He dug in even harder on the next pitch.

"A lot of that has to do with stubborness, unwillingness to give in an inch, to let someone else get an edge through intimidation, finding a weakness or the fear factor," Fisk says. "I won't compromise myself physically and give someone an edge."

It would be Mather over mind, if only the body were as willing as the spirit. Such is the weakness of mortal flesh: separated shoulder in 1971; groin injury in spring, 1974; knee destroyed when Cleveland's Leron Lee crashed into him at home plate in June, 1974; arm broken by a Fred Holdsworth pitch in spring training, 1975; two ribs broken diving into stands for foul ball, 1978; elbow injured by favoring the broken ribs for the final six weeks of the season. "If I hadn't been so stubborn, I would have said I'm hurt. No one is supposed to play with two broken ribs."

"I looked into his eyes," said former Boston pitcher Bill Lee. "He looked like a raccoon. You could see he was playing in pain and it was just sapping his body. His eyes were sunk back in his head, with dark rings around them. I told him not to play. Some guys like days off, some guys don't. Some guys like to gut it out. Some guys like to have governors on them. Fisk is a guy you've got to put a governor on. He's just going out there because of his puritanical upbringing— you know, staunch, quiet, archconservative, play-with-an-arrow-in-your-heart type of thing."

Fisk demands that of himself and expects it of others. Shirkers, real or perceived, are pilloried with his whip of a tongue. Therein lies a curious New England paradox: the same pilgrims who fled religious persecution in England were intolerant of anything but Puritan orthodoxy in the New World.

Jim Lonborg was coming off his Cy Young Award season when he asked Fisk, who would be going back to the low minors, to catch him one day in spring training. When Fisk was ready, Lonborg started talking to friends. "Hey, big shot," the catcher said, "you're standing around on my time."

"I don't have much patience for people who approach the game with less than all-out effort," Fisk says. "I want people to play the game the way I do. If you have a pitcher who is on the mound every four or five days saying he's tired in the fourth inning, I'll tell him, 'Hey pal, I'm out here every day for nine innings and catching everything you're bouncing up here.' Some have to be coaxed and some have to be kicked when you go out to the mound."

The Red Sox have long needed a swift one. They are New England's team, providing a collective catharsis for six states as their not-so-tragic flaw—insufferable smugness—is revealed every season. Of course they know not the way to salvation: too few of their players are New Englanders; they have no moral fiber, no toughness. They have not endured a climate that deigns to let high schools play 11 baseball games a spring. New Hampshire is a state of mind.

Tourist to New Englander: "What's the best way from here to Chicago?"

New Englander: "You can't get they-yuh from he-yuh."

—Variation on an old Yankee joke.

Carlton Fisk, the native who played for the Old Town Team, does not epitomize the Red Sox; he is, instead, what the Red Sox should be. That they would accuse him of malingering is what led Fisk to to change his sullied Sox for clean, white ones.

The Red Sox are the team whose idea of a rehabilitation program after Fisk's knee surgery was to tell him, "See you at spring training. Hope you can catch." But indifference is one thing; insult another. As Fisk deferred to his elbow by sitting out early exhibition games in 1979, he was blasted by owner Haywood Sullivan, an ex-catcher, of all things.

The problems between them had begun when Fisk, Fred Lynn and Rick Burleson held out in 1976. Fisk eventually signed a five-year contract that paid $200,000 in its final season, making him the 17th highest-paid catcher in baseball. The Red Sox had renegotiated other contracts; why, Fisk asked, not his?

It was then Sullivan said the reason Fisk wasn't playing in spring training was that he was more worried about his contract than his elbow. "That opened the wound," Fisk says. It festered until this winter, when the Red Sox (purposely?) mailed Fisk's new contract just late enough that baseball's basic agreement was violated. After a two-month wait for arbitration, he was suddenly a free agent; after a month of negotiation, he was suddenly a White Sox.

"There has been a gradual breaking away mentally for the last two or three years, not so much from New England itself, but from the ingrown feeling, the loyalties," Fisk says. "I've spent 15 years of my life in that organization; they've known me since I was a baby. And then to have the things that happened the last two years."

"The things they said about Fisk are wrong," says ex-teammate Stan Papi, now a Detroit infielder. "He was hurt by those remarks."

Fisk rarely showed it. Stoicism comes with the territory. "There's a saying in New Hampshire that when you get into a dung-slinging contest, everyone comes out smelling like it," he says. "But it was hard to bite my tongue sometimes."

"Be true! Be true! Be true! Show freely to the world, if not your worst, yet some trait whereby the worst may be inferred."

—*The Scarlet Letter*

If there is an "A" embroidered into Carlton Fisk's character, it could stand for arrogance. There is a fine line between confidence and arrogance, and he does not tread it lightly. Fisk, 33, has swaggered publicly since he was a rookie.

"I don't think anyone catches any better than I do," he says.

Or perhaps the symbol means aristocrat. Nearly everything about Fisk suggests nobility—the Christopher Walken handsomeness, the elegance with which he strides to the mound. Only a long-outlived nickname, Pudge, and the cup he carries as a repository for snuff spittings are incongrous.

He is the lord of the foul flies. The field is his fiefdom. Pitchers and opponents are his vassals.

Fisk was only a couple days out of Class AAA when he blistered veterans Carl Yastrzemski and Reggie Smith for not hustling. The team immediately fought back into the pennant race, and that year he helped turn around the falling career of Luis Tiant. The Red Sox have had a much better record with Fisk catching; they did not take first place in the pennant-winning season, 1975, until he recovered from the broken arm.

He heads for the mound on the slightest provocation, even though his first big trip drew a retort from veteran pitcher Gary Peters.

"Here I was, a rookie, trying to take charge—that's what catchers are supposed to do—and Peters is asking me, 'What the eff are you doing out here?' I thought to myself, 'Is that the way pitchers are supposed to talk to me?' and walked away."

Fisk hasn't backed off since. A pitcher who shakes off his signs better have a reason. A baserunner who collides with him better be ready to fight. He dares pitchers to throw at him; Fisk was hit 13 times, the league high, in 1980.

"I know I annoy people and I don't care," he says. "I don't do it on purpose, but I know it irritates people. All my actions serve a purpose."

He is painstakingly deliberate about everything—walking to the mound, getting dressed after the game—but especially about hitting. Thus the routine each time he bats. He puts the bat between his legs, leans over to get dirt for his hands, stands up to rub the dirt into the bat, which he stares at, as if it were an unfamiliar object. Then, if he gets distracted, the whole song and dance repeated.

"I am deliberate at the plate to have a singular thought process," he says. Use the left shoulder. Hit line drives. Be the stalwart soldier: "I'll try, Sir!"

He had a lot of trouble hitting anything in the minors. A .229 average in Class AA had Fisk on the verge of quitting. The Red Sox first called him up only because he could catch.

Of course. He is Carlton Catcher.

Master Golfers Respect and Fear Corner With the Name

GOLF

By *GARY VAN SICKLE*

From the Milwaukee Journal
Copyright © 1981, The Milwaukee Journal

Amen Corner looks like something that fell from heaven, but it plays like something straight out of hell.

It is beauty, and it is beast.

You know it's something special by its distinctive name. There were Hell's Kitchen, Devil's Island and Spanish Harlem. All were places to get out of.

In golf there were Hell's Half Acre, the Road Hole, the Blue Monster and The Quarry. And there was Amen Corner.

Those, too, were places to get out of.

Amen Corner is made up of the 11th, 12th and 13th holes at the World's Wonder Inland Course, as Alister Mackenzie called the Augusta National Golf Club after he and Bobby Jones had designed and begun building it in 1931. When the course was finished, the Masters Tournament was born in 1934.

Mackenzie died a year after the course was completed. Did he know how many prayers he would cause to go unanswered with Amen Corner?

Tom Weiskopf stood at the 12th hole at last year's Masters, watching his tee shot on the 155-yard par-3 hole land in Rae's Creek in front of the green. He dropped a ball in the fairway and hit again. It, too, landed in Rae's Creek.

He threw down another ball. Another splash. The next one splashed, and the next one, too. His sixth ball made the green and he two-putted for a 13.

Facing an unsympathetic press corps, Weiskopf was asked how he could possibly take a 13 on the hole.

"I missed a short putt for a 12," he said, not smiling.

The next day, before missing the cut, Weiskopf did much better.

He hit only two balls into the water at 12 and made a 7.
Amen.

A golf magazine's recent poll of pro golfers rated No. 11 the hardest hole at Augusta National. No. 12, perhaps the most famous par-3 in the world, was rated the eighth-hardest. And No. 13, a par-5 on which the 1979 field averaged 4.56 strokes, was voted the easiest, and the best hole.

"The whole back side is where the excitement starts," said Tom Kite. "I've played those holes pretty well. I guess my time is coming, but hopefully, it's no time soon.

"I birdied 10, 11 and 12 one year and then didn't get a birdie at 13. That really burned me."

To refresh your memory before this weekend's telecast of the Masters, No. 11 is a long par-4, 445 yards, with a pond to the left of the green.

The 12th is the par-3 over the creek, with the stone-fashioned Ben Hogan Bridge on the left. The green is a narrow target, with bunkers in front and back.

The 13th is a 485-yard par-5, reachable with two good shots. It is a dogleg left, but a creek runs along the left side and then cuts in front of the green, offering danger to those trying to reach it in two.

Some players consider No. 10 part of Amen Corner, because of its difficulty and awesome beauty. It is a 485-yard par-4 that is flanked by rows of trees as it drops down a considerable hill. There is a large bunker short of a somewhat elevated green.

"The holes play defensively," said Ben Crenshaw. "Everyone is tickled to get pars there, except at 13. I've never had any real disasters there.

"I take that back. I made an 8 on No. 10. Is that part of Amen Corner? You're darn right it is. It's sure tough enough."

Ben Hogan reportedly didn't shoot for the pin whenever it was cut behind the pond on No. 11. Instead, he played to the right of the green and hoped he could chip up and sink his par putt.

"If you see me on the green, you'll know I missed the shot," he said then.

In the last round in 1954, he went for the flag anyway, hit his ball in the water and took a double bogey 6. He eventually lost to Sam Snead in a playoff.

Amen.

All the holes at Augusta National have names—largely ignored—based upon the flora to be found along each one. The 11th is called White Dogwood, the 12th is Golden Bell and 13 is Azalea. They sound sweet, and smell even sweeter.

But No. 11 is best known now as Fuzzy's Heaven. That's where Fuzzy Zoeller sank an eight-foot birdie putt to beat Ed Sneed and

Tom Watson in a playoff in 1979, and when the putt dropped, Zoeller heaved his putter high into the air.

"I hope my putter stays in the sky," Zoeller said Wednesday. He admitted that No. 11 isn't a birdie hole.

"If the pin is on the left, you've got to stay right," he said. "Unless you're hitting an 8-iron, like I was in that playoff. But you're usually using a 3- or 4-iron.

"I only play for the par. If you get a birdie, it's a plus."

Jack Nicklaus said: "It's the hardest hole. You rarely shoot at the pin. You almost never have a birdie putt unless you hit a bad, but not too bad, approach shot."

When Sam Snead won in 1952, the crucial moment occurred on No. 12. He was the final-round leader, but he hit into the creek. After dropping another ball—it came to rest in a depression—he hit into the deep grass of the embankment below the green.

He faced at least a six. Instead, he chipped in for a bogey and breezed in for a four-shot victory.

Amen.

The 12th hasn't yielded only disasters. Claude Harmon aced the hole in 1947, and William Hyndman did it in 1959.

In 1937, Byron Nelson birdied 12, then eagled 13 in the final round. That helped him catch and eventually beat leader Ralph Guldahl, who had a double bogey and bogey on the same holes.

"At 12, it's just pulling the right club out of your bag," said Bill Kratzert, last year's Greater Milwaukee Open champion. "In the practice round today, I hit a 6- and a 7-iron. I hit the 7-iron further."

At the southeast corner of the course, the winds swirl and change constantly. That's what makes No. 12 even trickier.

"It's a great par-3, and the hardest thing is the wind," said Andy North of Madison. "It swirls in there. I've seen one guy hit a 5-iron short and the next one hit a 7-iron over 40 seconds later."

You've probably never heard of Toney Penna. Here's why:

In 1938, his tee shot at 12 was headed for the pin—straight for it. But the ball hit the flagstick and ricocheted into the creek. It supposedly happened to Gay Brewer once, too.

But Penna's story is more interesting. The next year, in 1939, on the same hole—yes, you guessed it—it happened again.

Amen.

There have been plenty of hits and misses at No. 13. Someone named Tsuneyuki Nakajima took a 13 there in 1978. Cary Middlecoff made an eagle 3 in 1955, sinking a 75-foot putt to do it.

"It's the greatest par-5 that's ever been built," said Jim Colbert.

North agrees. "The guys who design courses ought to come up with more of them like it," he said. "You can reach it in two and it's an easy birdie, but it's a tough second shot. And if you lay up, your third shot isn't easy."

When Byron Nelson won in 1947, he scored two eagles and two birdies on the 13th. But it was at 13 where the amazing saga of Billy Joe Patton ended in 1954.

Patton, an amateur, led after two rounds, but trailed by five shots going into Sunday's round. A hole-in-one on the sixth regained the lead for him.

The crowd was going wild. Well, until he went in the creek and took a 7 on 13. He added a bogey 6 on 15 and finished third. Sam Snead beat Hogan in a playoff.

A tale straight from the official Masters record book: During the third round of 1953, Count de Bendern (better known as Johnny de Forest) found his ball lodged in the bank of the brook in front of the 13th green.

Although the stream was running rather full, he decided he could play the ball. He stripped off his left shoe and sock and rolled his pants leg above the knee. Then he very carefully planted the bare foot on the bank and stepped into the deep water with his well-shod right foot.

The spectators long remembered the look of incredulity on the affable Count's face as he realized what he had done.

Amen.

Amen Corner would not have come to its notoriety if not for a major change in 1935, three years after the course was opened. Would you believe the nines were originally played in reverse order? They were switched to their present order in time for the 1935 Masters.

That's a bit of forgotten trivia. And other Masters lore is fading out.

Why is it called Amen Corner? The noted golf writer Herbert Warren Wind was listening to an old jazz recording while writing a story and trying to think of a name for the stretch of holes. The recording was, "Jumping at the Amen Corner."

Crenshaw, noted for his interest in golf lore and history, didn't know that.

"I should, but I don't," he said.

Neither did Fuzzy Zoeller. "Because you pray after you play, I think," he said.

Nor Andy North. "I don't follow that junk," he said. "I've got enough other things to think about."

Amen.

The Scooter's Life and Times

BASEBALL

By *VIC ZIEGEL*
From New York Magazine
Copyright © 1981, News Group Publications, Inc.
Reprinted With Permission of New York Magazine

Phil Rizzuto is 62 years old and continues to be called Scooter. Wait—it gets sillier.

This is his 25th season as a Yankee broadcaster and cheerleader, a quarter of a century of listening to him call the Yankees "we," as if he were still playing shortstop for them. Asking him to be an impartial play-by-play announcer would be no different from sending Captain Ahab after bay scallops.

When a play on the field dazzles or surprises him, Scooter responds by shouting, "Holy cow!" His reaction would be the same if the sun moved behind a cloud. After 25 years, very little in that corner of the Bronx has failed to earn a "Holy cow!"

Somehow, it all works. Rizzuto's provincialism is from the heart. Just as much of the rest of what he delivers is from the hip.

Consider the time a foul ball was lined into the seats behind first base and the Yankee Stadium customers scrambled out of the way. Rizzuto commented, to the horror of his employers, "Holy cow, it's a wonder more people don't get killed coming to the ball park."

On the road, the guileless approach continues. The Yankees were making their first trip to Seattle when Rizzuto decided to tell his listeners about this new American League city. It was an unusually long game, and the Yankees were losing. "It was almost 4 a.m. back in New York, and I figured, what the heck, who's listening?"

One person staying up past his bedtime was Michael Burke, then president of the Yankees. Imagine his surprise when Rizzuto's on-the-air tour of Seattle included a description of his hotel room. "We're staying at a new hotel," Rizzuto informed his audience, "and the rooms are all round. My wife, Cora, isn't with me on this trip, but if she was, there'd be no cornering Cora tonight."

Quick like that, Burke went from the radio to the telephone. "Phil," he snapped, "keep in mind that you're doing a Yankee game, not Floogle Street."

Burke, who says he still listens, has fallen under Rizzuto's spell. "For him to pretend objectivity would be phony," Burke points out. "He was a Yankee and he'll always be a Yankee. I never tried to tone down that part of him. His lack of self-consciousness, to curb that would be to harm a genuine product."

Four years ago, Fran Healy, an articulate and light-hitting catcher, moved from the Yankees' bench to the radio booth. His rapport with Rizzuto is uncanny. The two are at their best, if that's the word, during their three mutual innings behind the microphone. They're liable to chatter about anything, even the game in front of them.

When Rizzuto left his chair for a few minutes during a game against the Chicago White Sox, this is how Healy greeted his return:

"Here's Scooter, back from the men's room."

"Healy, you huckleberry, you're not supposed to tell people that," Rizzuto said. "Tell them that I went to see Bill Veeck (then White Sox president)."

"Okay, Scooter."

"Besides, Healy, I've been drinking coffee all day. You know what happens when you drink coffee all day."

"What's that, Scooter?"

"You go see Bill Veeck."

Their patter is ridiculous. "The real baseball fan, it must drive them bananas, and I can see why," Rizzuto says. But the producers keep asking for more. And Rizzuto's delighted. He was never comfortable hanging out in the clubhouse, securing bits of information to deliver on the air. ("Yogi thinks the players in his day were much better tap dancers.")

More often than not, Rizzuto arrives at Yankee Stadium just before the game, leaving only enough time for the free meal in the media lounge. And he is always the first one to hustle out of the booth, considering it a long night if he is still working after the sixth inning.

"I've got the fewest complete games," Rizzuto admits. "Some of the sponsors, the director, they weren't happy about it. I tried to miss as many trips as I could because I hate that traveling, hate flying. But I'm not as bad as I used to be."

It was easier to play hooky before the Yankees signed a cable-TV contract. Now all the announcers have their innings. "I'm just glad we're winning," Rizzuto says. "It makes a difference. That's why I feel so sorry for the announcers with the Mets."

The Yankees wandered in the desert for 10 years, Rizzuto concentrating on his golf game and his fast exits. "It always seemed like we were dragging into another town at 4 a.m. I'm glad I'm not playing in this day and age."

At 5-foot-6, 150 pounds, he was the wrong size for major-league baseball. But he was a splendid shortstop for most of his 13 seasons, and was voted the league's Most Valuable Player in 1950 on a team that included four Hall of Famers. Rizzuto should be in the Hall of Fame himself, but he made the mistake of hitting fewer than 500 home runs, the yardstick currently in fashion. He was without peer as a bunter—his finest moment the squeeze play that brought home Joe DiMaggio and broke a first-place tie with Cleveland in September of 1951.

Scooter was released by the Yankees, those sentimental so-and-sos, on Old Timers' Day 1956. "You weren't set like the ballplayers today," he says. "You didn't have a nest egg. Those days, it was like the end of the world."

The Baltimore Orioles and the Giants—moving to San Francisco —needed announcers. But both teams wanted Rizzuto in their cities on a year-round basis. Scooter, born in Brooklyn's Ridgewood section, went to high school in Richmond Hill, just across the Queens line. He lives in New Jersey now, as far west as he ever wanted to travel.

While Rizzuto wondered about life away from the infield, he played golf. Carl Badenhausen, who played golf with Rizzuto, happened to be chairman of the board of Ballantine beer, the Yankees' sponsor. "I played golf with Mr. Badenhausen's sons, too," Rizzuto says. Uh-huh.

The Yankee broadcasters at that time were Mel Allen, Red Barber and Jim Woods. "If I may say so, a crackerjack team," Barber told me. He remembered standing at the bar at Toots Shor when Woods joined him. "Jim had come from a meeting with George Weiss (the Yankees' general manager) on what he thought would be a routine renewal of his contract. Weiss told him, 'Jim, Mr. Badenhausen wants Rizzuto to be a broadcaster and so you're out.'"

That's Red's story. Another version is that Ballantine was afraid of losing Rizzuto to the beer company in Baltimore that owned the Orioles.

"I'm sure the golf had something to do with it," Rizzuto says. In any case, Mel and Red have long since departed, and Scooter's the one we hear every day.

"Well, I don't want to say it's like stealing," he says, "but after you've been a player, this is so much easier. When I played, I took the game home with me, worried about the next day. Who am I batting against? Which guys slide hard into second? Certain guys might knock you down, spike you. Up there, in the booth, it's a picnic."

Mexican Blowup

by Terry Bochatey of *UPI Newspictures*. Dodgers pitcher Fernando Valenzuela dazzles National League hitters with one of the most wicked screwballs in baseball and photographers with his major league bubbles. Copyright © 1981, United Press International.

Peek-a-Boo Golf

by John Long of the *Hartford Courant*. That's Chi Chi Rodriguez blasting his way out of a sand trap on the 16th hole on the first day of play in the Sammy Davis Jr. Hartford Open. Copyright © 1981, The Hartford Courant.

Cross-Country in the City

RUNNING

By *DAVID ZINMAN*

From the Runner
Copyright © 1981, Ziff-Davis Publishing Company

I am thinking back to the fall of 1947. I am 17 years old, wearing the sky-blue colors of Columbia, toeing the line with 120 runners in the IC4A Freshman Cross-Country Championship. The gun fires and off we go, streaming across the plains of Van Cortlandt Park in the Bronx like a troop of charging cavalry. Even before we cross onto the bumpy terrain leading to the back hills, I am far behind. Up front, Larry Ellis, a gangly black runner from New York University, is showing the way over the park slopes, his purple jersey fading out of sight as I try to cope with the fatigue numbing my body on this bright autumn day.

My coach, Carl Merner, is at a bridge crossing. "Stretch out those legs, Zinman," he calls. But his exhortation is so much wasted breath. Ellis and the others are running a different race, the NYU lad winning in 15:39 for the three-mile course. Long after he has re-trieved his sweats, I reach home in 110th place in 19:27.

Humbling though it was, that experience is the first that springs to mind when I think of Van Cortlandt Park. The struggle. The hurt. The hills. The relief when it was over. The realization that there was much work to be done. That day in '47 remains one of my fondest teenage memories.

Van Cortlandt does that to you: It opens you up a little, helps you to grow, gives you a point of reference to share with almost every runner you'll ever come across. At this time of the year, with the last of the county fair fun runs going off and the fall semester about to commence, Van Cortlandt Park is busy again—the cross-country season is under way.

What Churchill Downs is to thoroughbred racing and the Indi-anapolis Speedway is to auto racing, Van Cortlandt Park has be-come to the world of cross-country running. It has served a critical role in this regard since cross-country, even in these running boom days, remains the stepchild of American running. You wouldn't suspect it, though, on a crisp Saturday morning in October when thousands of runners from all over the East and even points west gather for a full day of training and competition.

"I think Van Cortlandt is one of the finest, if not the finest, cross-country courses in the nation," says Fred Dwyer, the great miler of the '50s who is today the coach at Manhattan College. "Many colleges run on golf courses. But to me that doesn't represent cross-country."

To Joe Fox, longtime track and cross-country chairman of the city's Catholic High School league, Van Cortlandt's five-mile college layout has everything a challenging cross-country circuit needs: grassy flats, rough terrain, undulating trails that wind through a thick woodland, and a steep, craggy bluff in the final mile. "If you can run good time at Van Cortlandt," Fox says, "you can run any place."

The last gut-straining climb is called Cemetery Hill. It got its name not because the egos of many runners lie buried there, but simply because it is the site of the old, now forlorn burial grounds of the Van Cortlandts, a wealthy 17th-century Dutch family who made their fortune as traders, merchants and shipbuilders. The family's 233-year-old fieldstone mansion, where some history buffs say George Washington once slept, still stands near the starting line used for high school competition.

Despite Cemetery Hill and environs, some say Van Cortlandt is not the most difficult of courses. "Belmont Plateau (in Philadelphia's Fairmont Park) is tougher," says David Merrick, formerly of the University of Pennsylvania, whose 23:51 in 1975 is the Van Cortlandt five-mile college course record. "It is a minute slower than Van Cortlandt with five or six major hills. It will eat you alive if you don't know what you're doing."

Matt Centrowitz, a two-time Olympian who grew up within blocks of Van Cortlandt and attended Manhattan College and the University of Oregon, says Stanford University's course in Palo Alto, Calif. is the toughest he's run. "It's much hillier than Van Cortlandt and the hills are longer. I've been more spent after running there than any other place." To Centrowitz, Van Cortlandt is somewhat overrated. "If you measure Cemetery's actual climb, it's only about 40 yards. The course has uneven footing that makes it hard. And those sharp downhills can hurt the legs. But it's really a fast course. Look at those flats. You run them twice."

If there is not unanimity about Van Cortlandt's toughness, there is agreement as to its popularity. More harriers pound over it than over any other cross-country course in the nation, and probably the world. Access is easy—its 1,146 acres lay in the north Bronx, in the heart of the heavily-populated Northeast.

It is easy for city kids from Bedford-Stuyvesant and Elmhurst to reach by subway because it is at the shank end of the Broadway line, the same Broadway of street hustling 10 miles to the south. Once there, you get into the park by walking past a string of delis and bars. One of them, the Terminal Bar & Grill (also known as the "Dutchman's" because its previous owners were Dutch), is a traditional watering hole for coaches. Race scoring is often done here, and decisions to cancel meets because of hazardous running conditions caused by heavy rain are usually fought out at the Dutchman's as well. "You can find some bloodstains on the wall," says Joe Fox.

The Van Cortlandt neighborhood is a mixed one. Not far to the south are welfare slums. Closer by, bordering the parade grounds, are middle-class homes, modest but neatly kept houses and apartments that soon give way to the elegant spreads and posh high rises of the chic Riverdale section, where John F. Kennedy attended Riverdale Country Day School. Riverdale is also home to other prep schools and Manhattan College, for whom the park is, in effect, a home course.

With such community diversity, Van Cortlandt is the quintessential urban melting pot on fall weekends. While thousands of runners scatter about the park for their respective meets, young people shouting in half a dozen tongues stakes territorial claims for their games of baseball, football, soccer and rugby. A few furlongs away, the more genteel natives play golf, tennis and ride horseback—the latter in occasional interference with the procession of runners looping the footpaths.

Still, Van Cortlandt offers something unique to the distance runner. "Road running and cross country suffer from one common problem," says Marty Liquori, Villanova's former star miler who once held Van Cortland's 2.5-mile high school course record (12:23.2 in '67). "The times from various courses aren't comparable. But many of the variables are reduced by Van Cortlandt. It's one place where you can compare your times with great athletes of the past. Ten years from now, I can be talking to another runner from anywhere on the East coast and we'll know what our times meant at Van Cortlandt."

Van Cortlandt is the site of the nation's oldest cross-country meet, the Intercollegiate Association of Amateur Athletics of America (IC4A), which includes most of the major eastern colleges and some from the South and Midwest. The IC4A began cross-country championship runs in 1908 and held its first meet at Van Cortlandt in 1913. With few exceptions—the most recent being 1979 when financially-plagued New York City let the course deteriorate and the IC4A temporarily moved to suburban Long Island—it has been staged there ever since.

Since 1927, the Metropolitan Intercollegiate Conference—composed of New York area colleges like Manhattan, St. John's and Fordham—has also held its meet there nearly every year. So has the Heptagonal Games conference—the Ivy League plus Army and Navy—which began its meets in 1939. In addition, hundreds of high schools and colleges compete there every week, joined by clubs active in events sponsored by The Athletics Congress and even the New York Road Runners Club.

Sometimes, so many races go on at once at Van Cortlandt, they cause a human gridlock. Roy Chernock's Baruch College team was favored to win the City University title in 1974. It was not to be. At a critical point in the race, high school runners converged with the college harriers. "They wiped us out," said Chernock. Brauch missed the title by one point.

Simultaneous racing is not the sole hazard. Van Cortlandt Park has a stable, and its bridle path runs through the cross-country course. On more than one occasion, runners have had to dodge horseback riders, and vice versa. Though these encounters are rare nowadays, they were fairly common in the past and sometimes bitter. Once, after a particularly heated confrontation, a rider picked up a runner and tossed him off the course.

But such incidents only serve to color Van Cortlandt's lore, passing from one generation of runners to another along with stories of the nation's most celebrated cross-country events. In 1968 alone, the NCAA, AAU and USTFF all held their national championships at Van Cortlandt.

Old-timers still talk about Gerry Lindgren, then a Washington State senior, making his farewell appearance as a collegian in the 1969 NCAA run. He turned in a record performance, winning the six-mile race over defending champion Mike Ryan of the Air Force Academy in 28:59.2. An Oregon freshman named Steve Prefontaine was third.

The most famous runner to test the course may have been Frank Shorter when he ran for Yale. Still far from his early '70s peak, he was runner-up in the 1968 Heps, turning in his best time of 24:52. Twenty-five minutes is considered the mark of excellence for the five-mile college course, a standard only 143 runners have bettered.

But perhaps it is more common for Van Cortlandt veterans, when pressed for a memory, to recall, as I do, the tough times. Chernock, now track coach at William and Mary, remembers riding the subway to Van Cortlandt when he ran for Flushing High School, in Queens. "All the high school runners changed clothes on the train. There were no girls running then, so the train was our dressing room. . . . We were in awe of the course. We never trained, and Saturday, we'd go up to empty our stomachs."

Larry Ellis recalls NYU needing a strong race by a fifth man to win the Mets one year. "He showed up sick from food poisoning. But he ran. Then, in the middle of the race, he got diarrhea. He couldn't hold back. The poor guy let loose all over himself. But he kept going. He smelled so bad and looked so awful that none of the runners behind him wanted to come near. Nobody passed him. He was the key to our victory."

Marty Liquori remembers that one of the most difficult races came at Van Cortlandt when he ran for Essex Catholic High School in Newark. "It was in the Eastern Champs. I was getting over bronchitis. I'd been on antibiotics, and I was running neck and neck over the last 600 yards with Dave Pottetti (of Fox Lane High). Fifty yards from the finish, he ran me right into the ground. It was the only time I ever passed out in a race."

Dennis Fikes of Penn was the target of a blockade when he ran for Rice High School, Manhattan. "Power wanted Tony Colon, their No. 1 man, to win," Fikes said. "Right after the start, six Power runners surrounded me. I found it amusing because I knew they couldn't stay with me. By the middle of the cowpath, they had all faded. By then, Colon had a lead of about 30 to 40 yards. But I was a good downhill runner. I had no trouble catching him in the backhills."

The history of the park is being debated to this day. The Bronx Historical Society proudly claims that Washington used the flats as camping grounds, and old history books say that the general used the Van Cortlandt estate as his headquarters several times during the Revolutionary War.

But this is disputed. "People like to boast that Washington slept there," says Lloyd Ultan, a vice president of the historical society and a professor at Fairleigh Dickinson who is writing a history of the Bronx. "But there is no documentary evidence. It is not mentioned either in Washington's diaries or in the Van Cortlandts' correspondence." Nevertheless, historians agree that Washington started his postwar victory march into New York City from the park. So it is not unreasonable to believe he slept in the house on the previous night.

What is not disputed is that Van Cortlandt Park went on to have many uses not usually associated with a park. In the 1890s, it became a stamping ground for a small herd of bison. Though they failed to thrive and were later moved to the Bronx Zoo, it is reported that some were shipped to western ranges to propagate the rapidly vanishing herd.

Today, the Van Cortlandt mansion is a museum that attracts about 20,000 visitors each year. Operated by the National Society of Colonial Dames of New York, it is furnished with high canopied beds, a cavernous kitchen fireplace and many original colonial pieces. Despite the lack of documentation, one second-story room is called the "Washington Chamber." The three-story house, built in 1748, remains an imposing structure, recreating the atmosphere of the gracious life of colonial gentry. The same cannot be said of the once proud family burial plot on Cemetery Hill, or Vault Hill as it is known to historians. It lies weed-strewn and neglected behind a broken iron gate, its tombstones cracked and toppled over by vandals.

Most of this heritage is, understandably, unknown to the runners. What a coach wants his athletes to carry in their heads is a knowledge of the course's tricky layout, poor strategy having lost many a race. But there are as many theories on how to run the course as there are coaches.

"You are running close to a mile on flats," says Fred Dwyer of Manhattan. "So you have to get out fast." In the big college meets, the athletes sprint to establish position as they cover three long straightaways—making about 90-degree turns each time—before they reach the undulating, sandy stretch called the cowpath.

The cowpath—it was, in fact, a path for cows on the Van Cortlandts' farm—requires careful footing. "If you're not in the first five or so," says Dave Merrick, "it's difficult to see ahead and pick your path around sandy holes, boulders and what have you."

The mile comes up about three quarters of the way through the cowpath. "There is no mark," says Ed Bowes, coach of Brooklyn's Bishop Loughlin High School. "But there is a flat rock and people know where it is. Someone is usually standing there calling out the time."

Scattered through the cowpath are bands of cheering schoolmates. Cross country requires a mobile breed of spectator. If you stay at the start, you see only the beginning, middle and end of the race. The more adventuresome go out on the course and move ahead of the pack, climbing hilltops or dashing from vantage point to vantage point.

Many coaches exhort their runners to charge out because once in the woods, passing is difficult. In major meets, the lead pack will cover the first mile around 4:25. "Some kids can take it out that fast and have the ability to maintain," says Ellis, whose Princeton teams have won the Heps five out of the last six years. "It's not our traditional way. We go out relatively fast. But we want to be comfortable. We attack the back hills and Cemetery. That's where the race is won and lost."

After the cowpath, the runners turn up a short steep incline called Freshman Hill, then cross a short bridge spanning the Henry Hudson Parkway. From there the runners forge ahead into dense woods, which wind through roller coaster hills for a mile and a quarter. Some runners think there is not much change of position here and don't push hard. For this very reason, experienced runners use this part of the race to advantage.

"It's easy to get away from people back in the paths," says Merrick. "You get out of sight, and people think you're just around the bend. But I'd just haul cookies for the next half mile to a mile and then relax a little in the last half mile coming out of the woods.

"It's all psychological. Because if someone can see you coming back to them, their adrenalin flows and they will push themselves. And so they don't have to work as hard to catch up to you. But if you're out of sight, then they come out onto the flats and see you far ahead and say, 'Holy Cow!' "

For most runners, the back hills are not as easy as Merrick makes out. Though the hills are not long, they are steep and winding and pockmarked with crevices and stones. On rainy days they can be treacherous, particularly one dubbed Roller Derby Turn that has a hairpin change of direction—a chain-link fence protects wide-running harriers from toppling into a ravine.

It is in these forest trails and later at Cemetery that the hill runners try to make up ground. "Many high school runners come to a hill and figure now they have to put out hard," says Liquori. "But that's not really the right way. It's an even effort uphill. If I were going to increase my effort, I would do it on the downhills. I would increase my stride and just bound down them."

Once out of the hills, the harriers go through a rising picnic grounds and concrete walkway, their clattering spikes signaling their return to the bridge. Then, it's down a short hill to a cinderpath that runs alongside Broadway the length of the plains. The best runners hit the three-mile mark under 15 minutes.

The most fabled part of the course, Cemetery Hill, lies ahead. Many face it with fear and trepidation. After a quarter mile along the bumpy base of the rise, runners turn sharply and go up a steep, fast-rising bluff. It comes just after the four-mile mark, adding to the fatigue of the climb.

"It's like the third quarter in a mile run," says Fred Dwyer. "You have to dig down to the bottom of the well. If you don't, you can give up everything you have accomplished up to that point."

Cemetery is deceiving. After you have chugged up to a big boulder, you think you have reached the peak. But the boulder is blocking sight of the real top. There is still another chunk of ground to cover. "That incline at the very top can kill a lot of runners," says Ed Bowes, who knows it as runner, coach and race director. "A lot of them are crawling there. If you can forget about sucking wind and accelerate, you can pass a lot of people."

Because of its critical point in the race, some coaches come here, stopwatches dangling from their necks, to urge on their runners. "You're in 17th place. Pick up your arms and knees. . . . Go with your teammates. . . . Work together." In frustration, they sometimes yell: "Dammit, get moving."

After Cemetery is negotiated, a downhill section takes runners back to the flats. All that is left is the 600-yard cinderpath to the finishing pole. By then, the race is usually decided. But occasionally runners battle down to the tape. And once in a while, there is physical contact.

Such an incident occurred in the 1976 Mets when Jay Vickery of Rutgers and Duncan Brown of Columbia came together after skirting a puddle in the last 300 yards. Vickery felt Brown was cutting him off. He shot an elbow into Brown's ribs and went on to win in 25:02. After the race, reporters went over to Brown. "It made no difference in the outcome," he said honorably. "I was fading and he was coming on."

The high school course is an abbreviated 2.5-mile version of the college layout. It covers the same cowpath area and backhills section, but it eliminates Cemetery and a second traverse of the flats.

Runners start with a quarter-mile run straight across the plains to the cowpath. They go up Freshman Hill across the bridge into the backwoods. Then, after coming out on the flats, they branch off onto a shorter cinderpath stretch to the high school finish.

Some coaches feel the high school course favors a particular kind of runner. "The strong, mature kid has a distinct advantage," says Dwyer. "There isn't enough flat terrain. If you don't get out fast, you are locked in."

Luis Ostolozaga of Bishop Loughlin, and later of Manhattan, set the record, 12:16.4, in 1975. Only 17 runners have bettered 12:30; breaking 13 minutes is considered the mark of excellence.

"Any coach who talks to a high school distance runner in the East wants to know what the kid ran at Van Cortlandt," says Larry Byrne, an IC4A official and the course's unofficial historian. "Van Cortlandt is a common denominator. When I tell a coach a kid ran 12:45, he can relate exactly to the boy's capability."

Cross-country addicts love to speculate on what times world-class runners could do on the high school course. "When I was close to the world record at 5,000 meters," says Liquori, "I wanted to go back and run the course and see how fast a time I could get. I would think someone could run it in 11:30."

Van Cortlandt Park veterans are not so sure. Joe Fox, who says he hasn't seen anyone go under Ostolozaga's mark, remembers a day when Denis Fikes, 27, came back for a high school alumni race. A 3:55 miler and 8:38 two-miler for Penn, Fikes set out to break 12 minutes. Fikes finished in 12:18, barely faster than he ran in high school.

Runners come and go. But Van Cortlandt stays the same, challenging the best and the pluckiest with its melange of hills, flats and rough terrain. Yet, even an also-ran can dream of setting records. Last year, the Heps held an alumni run before their meet. At 50, I returned to the scene of my better running days. But the race was delayed and while I was out on the course warming up, officials suddenly got organized, called the runners to the mark and sent them off.

Since I missed the race, I decided to run the course alone after the meet. While the sun faded, I stripped down and ran through the straightways, across the cowpath, up Freshman Hill, over the bridge and into the hills. There was nobody around. But I could imagine myself sliding past runners on the narrow paths, catching Ostolozaga at the crest of a hill, bounding past Liquori at Roller Derby Turn.

Sweat smeared my forehead like rain on a windshield and I rushed by Centrowitz on a hill leading down to the flats. I was running well within myself at the three-mile mark and I stayed loose as I picked up another runner on the way to the cowpath. There were just two ahead.

I turned sharply at the base of Cemetery and kept a steady drive up its tortuous climb. At the top, I pumped hard to maintain momentum as I descended to the flats. There was Merrick just ahead, but as I rolled passed him on the cinderpath, I knew it was not he whom I was aiming for. It was the tall, slender black runner who had showed me the way 34 years earlier.

In another 100 yards, I was even with Ellis and we matched strides until the finishing pole was in sight, I glanced over quickly. He had not changed. He was the same spindly youth I remembered from that fall day in 1947.

Though I was now gray and balding and my face lined, I had no doubt things would be different this day. Slowly, I drew away. Step by step, I increased my lead. There were only a few more yards to the finish.

And though the shadows were long and there was no one left on the great greensward, I smiled with anticipation because in a moment I, too, would know—as Ellis and Merrick and Landgren and Liquori had known—what it felt like, if only in my dreams, to break that red worsted string at Van Cortlandt Park.

Add It Up: Ex-Jocks Bowl 'em Over

GENERAL

By *RON RAPOPORT*

From the Chicago Sun-Times
Copyright © 1981, Chicago Sun-Times

Now I know what it must have been like to be living in the 1780s and receive an invitation to a rehearsal of *Don Giovanni*.

Now I don't have to wonder how it must have felt to be around in the 1880s and suddenly be handed the manuscript of *The Brothers Karamazov*.

It was with a sense of pride and humility that I received my invitation to be present at the creation of one of the works that will long be remembered as having defined our times.

I am referring to the making of a Lite beer alumni commercial.

Surely, I am not overstating the magnitude of what is happening here. Surely, when the cultural history of our generation is written, we will find ourselves explained by the fact that we responded so completely to "Even when you're just showing off." And "I didn't punch that doggie." And "Practice, practice, practice." And "Says here the winner's Bubba Smith."

Tell me the truth now. When the crazy coach commercial comes on, you try to determine the precise moment when the beer in the glass stops bubbling before John Madden breaks through the screen. When the cowboy commercial comes on, you can't understand why you didn't pick out Billy Martin easing up to the bar with his back to the camera until the 10th time you saw it.

If it is true that art is what makes brothers of us all, then Lite beer is as great a patron of art as the Guggenheim Foundation.

Who is to say that what emanates from a flat in Prague or a prison camp in Siberia is intrinsically greater than the product of a bowling alley in Teaneck, N.J.? No, when future historians equate the cultural artifacts of the first two centuries of American independence, my money is less on "Call me Ishmael" than it is on "Hey, you're Boog Powell."

It is said that art does not exist in a vacuum, that it must fulfill one of man's inner needs. But perhaps that is the most amazing thing about the Lite beer commercials. They took a product for which there was no demand, one that had failed miserably in a previous incarnation, and single-handedly thrust it upward through one of the most competitive markets in the United States.

"Without the right campaign, there might be no Lite beer," says Bob Lenz, the originator of these commercials, a man who moves through waves of his fellow admen with the easy grace of one who has long since learned to receive unceasing adulation with becoming modesty.

Yes, that is it. That is why a watered-down drink, which had once been marketed as something for ladies on diets and genteel men carrying rolled-up umbrellas, has become the third largest selling beer in the country.

And that is why we have come to Teaneck.

Deacon Jones has rehearsed his poem about 10 times before the firemen come and throw everybody out of Feibel's Bowling/Bar.

Once he was the greatest defensive lineman in professional football, but even when his notoriety for having invented the headslap has faded, Jones will be remembered for lines like, "Deacon's my name and bowling's my game/When I come around the pins all go down."

This is how the Lite alumni bowling tournament commercial begins. Jones recites his poem and bowls while John Madden rushes up to him and shouts, "Gutter ball! Gutter ball!" Somehow, the pins in three alleys fall, causing mass confusion among both the men in the red bowling shirts (the "tastes great" team) and the group in yellow ("less filling").

"Where I came from, three strikes and you're out," complains Billy Martin. Nobody knows what to do.

"OK, OK," interrupt the firemen, "everybody out till we find out what it is."

"I can tell you what it is," says Bubba Smith, pointing to the ceiling. "It's right over there."

These last two lines are not in the script. Real life has intruded on the production. The 22 performers, dozens of technicians and assorted observers, relatives and friends are out in the street. Four trucks from the Teaneck Fire Department have responded to the call that was issued when a shower of sparks flew from the bright television lights that have recently been installed.

Feibel's has been chosen as the commercial's location precisely because it is not a modern plastic and chrome family recreation center, the kind that comes with television lounges, nurseries and Space Invaders. It is a no-nonsense family-owned bowling alley—eight lanes upstairs, eight lanes down, snack counter, bar, shoe-rental concession. Nothing else.

"My dad built it in 1941," says Louis Feibel. "Somebody from the ad agency just happened to come in for a drink one day and he said, 'This is perfect. It's old.' I said, 'Thanks a lot.' "

When Lite asked to rent the entire building for three days, Feibel was willing. But first a meeting of the presidents of his bowling leagues had to be called. Many were excited about the prospect, but others were not impressed: They wanted to bowl their regular schedules. Not until Lite agreed to make up the prize money that would be lost did these holdouts go along with the sacrifices that are sometimes necessary for the creation of art.

The firemen come tramping out of the building. The problem with the lights has been solved. Production can resume.

Tom Heinsohn has his arms around the shoulders of two actresses who look as if they had made it to the final casting call for "Laverne and Shirley." One of them, a blonde named Willie Tjan, goes from this job to an off-Broadway production of "Orpheus Descending" by Tennessee Williams.

"Hey!" shouts Heinsohn as he propels the waitresses down the stairs, "we just won another round of Lite beer from Miller!" Watching him closely and writing down these immortal words is Frank Deford, America's finest sports writer.

"Maybe I'm a whore for doing it," says Deford between takes about whether he is violating journalistic ethics by appearing in commercials. "And maybe *Sports Illustrated* is a whorehouse for letting me. I understand people's concerns, but I don't have any problems with it. If I was advertising for the National Hockey League, maybe it would be different."

Heinsohn's lines lead to the inevitable "tastes great-less filling" argument between the red shirts and the yellow shirts. The fight is suddenly interrupted by Boog Powell, who notices that Jim Honochick is advancing from the alley onto the group and preparing to bowl into its midst.

"Hey, Jim!" Powell yells. "You're going the wrong way!"

The logistics of this scene are complicated, and Powell is having a hard time giving his line the required delivery. After dozens of takes, the words are given to Don Carter, who, since he is the only professional bowler in the group, is made to keep score.

There is great consternation over the possibility that Powell and Honochick, who are Lite's Abbott and Costello, may be broken up, but eventually Powell gets another chance and gives an acceptable performance.

"I thought I was doing all right," Powell says of almost being benched. "I guess every artist needs an inspiration."

Bubba Smith is having trouble. His scene with Dick Butkus is brief and relatively uncomplicated, but it is trying everybody's patience.

Butkus hands Smith a bowling ball and says, "Hey, Bubba, this ball doesn't have any holes." Smith crushes his fingers into it and says, "Now it does."

But the director wants Smith to say the line first and then hit the ball. Smith continually gets the sequence reversed. The takes mount up and so do the gibes from the others.

"What you should say," Deacon Jones tells Smith before he finally gets it right, "Is, 'Now it *do.*' "

Smith is one Lite alumnus who has made the most of his appearance in the commercials. He attributes getting a part in the new television series "Open All Night" directly to his new-found fame. When he and Madden, the coach-turned-television announcer, sit down today, they talk not about football but the time slots and audience shares.

The two others whose lives have changed the most significantly are pool player Steve Mizerak and former baseball player Marv Throneberry. Mizerak quit his job as a seventh-grade geography and American history teacher to go on the road full-time for Lite. Throneberry left the Nashville, Tenn., insulated glass plant where he once worked.

"There's more people who drink beer than play ball," Throneberry says by way of explaining the sort of popularity that has made him grand marshall of this year's Christmas parade in Natchitoches, La.

Not everybody is happy with the way things have worked out, however. Only the most dedicated Lite commercial buffs remember that it was former New York Jets fullback Matt Snell who appeared in the first spot in 1975 after Bob Lenz first saw his picture on a billboard advertising Off Track Betting.

"Everybody forgets where it started," says Snell, who has appeared in very few of the 72 subsequent Lite commercials. "I endorsed it when nobody knew what it was. For that first commercial, I got $3,500. For this one, we all get $11,500. It didn't come to where I thought it should come. I want to sit down and talk, find out what's in it for Matt."

The irony is that the Miller corporate executives profess to be extremely proud of the loyalty of their performers. In speeches that resemble locker-room enhortations, they openly sneer at their competitors who have tried to steal their athletes away and laugh at the fact that Busch's Natural Light, which did induce a few to make the switch, is now adopting a new campaign.

It is late in the afternoon and a hush has settled over Feibel's. The last major scene is being shot over and over and the audience is hanging on each bit of action.

Lee Meredith, the improbable blond who has become a fixture in the Lite commercials, looks at the score sheet and giggles, "Look, the score's all even."

"Last frame," glowers Ray Nitschke. "Who's up?"

"Rodney," replies Don Carter.

"RODNEY!!??" the company cries in unison. And sure enough, out from behind the bulk of Buck Buchanan and Bubba Smith comes

Rodney Dangerfield, grabbing his collar and trying to stifle his mournful facial tic in his quintessential version of the hopeless square trying to act hip.

"Are you kidding?" Dangerfield says as he goes to the ball rack. "It's a piece of cake."

Ben Davidson, the biggest and most ferocious-looking person in the building, thrusts a ball into Dangerfield's stomach and growls, "All we need is one pin, Rodney."

During one take, the ball drops and Davidson ad-libs, "All we need is one broken foot, Rodney."

At last, everything seems to be working right. The director calls for the last shot of the day. The spectators freeze in their places. The sound man announces that he is rolling. So does the film man.

"Action!"

Dangerfield bowls . . . the rest of the company menacingly follows him out onto the alley and closes in around him . . . the ball goes straight down the middle . . . and . . .

The fourth annual Lite beer alumni commercial will be shown on television beginning the middle of March.

Troy is No Trojan

by Mike Andersen, of the *Boston Herald American*. Troy Phauls of the New York All-Star Team looks apprehensive as 7-foot Patrick Ewing slams home a dunk shot during the Boston Shootout. This high school all-star game attracted players from eight states in the Northeast and was highlighted by the dominating Ewing, who recently completed his freshman season for nationally-ranked Georgetown University. Copyright © 1981, Boston Herald American.

Ribbon-Shy Racers

by John H. White of the *Chicago Sun-Times*. And the winner of the 50-yard dash is. . . . The closed-eyed grasps, the straining, the stretched hands with fingers extended to touch the ribbon all add up to an exciting race in which more than 2,000 youths from 18 Chicago Housing Authority projects took part. It's an every-kid-can-win affair. Copyright © 1981, Chicago Sun-Times.

PRIZE-WINNING WRITERS IN BEST SPORTS STORIES 1982

Joe Gergen (The Hit Man Became the Target) is in his 14th year at the Long Island-based *Newsday*. He has spent the last seven of those years writing a sports column. Gergen was graduated from Boston College in 1963 and spent five years on the sports desk of United Press International in New York before moving to *Newsday*. Gergen, who won the National Headliners Award for sports writing in 1971, is making his eighth appearance in *Best Sports Stories*.

Roger Kahn (He's a Yankee Doodle Dandy) shares the magazine prize with Thomas McIntyre. Kahn also won the *Best Sports Stories* magazine prize in 1960, 1969, 1970 and 1980. He began his newspaper career at the *New York Herald Tribune*, first as a copy boy, then as a sports reporter. He made stops at *Newsweek* as sports editor, at the *Saturday Evening Post* as a senior editor and at *Esquire* as a columnist. He currently free lances and writes books, the best known of which, *The Boys of Summer*, was published in 1972 and became a best-seller. The New York University graduate's newest book, *The Seventh Game*, will be published June 29 and has been selected by the Literary Guild as the featured alternate for July.

Thomas McIntyre (Buff) makes his debut in *Best Sports Stories* by sharing the first prize in the magazine category with Roger Kahn. The 30-year-old Californian left Reed College in Portland, Ore., after only three years, without a degree and "with no friends left among the faculty in the English Department—my major." But he quickly displayed his writing talent by selling his first story for $35 in 1972 and another in 1976 before *Sports Afield* took notice and hired him as a contributing editor.

OTHER WRITERS IN BEST SPORTS STORIES 1982

Nelson Algren (So Long, Swede Risberg) makes his first appearance in *Best Sports Stories* posthumously. Algren, a free-lance writer and novelist who often was called "The Poet of the Sad Metropolis," died in May of 1981 at the age of 72. Algren, who was born in Detroit, spent much of his life writing about the down-and-out, such figures as prize fighters, petty criminals, drug addicts and prostitutes. His best-known works are *The Man With the Golden Arm, A Walk on the Wild Side* and his prose-poem *Chicago: City on the Make*.

Paul Attner (Nothing Finer Than the 49ers, 26-21) has been a member of the *Washington Post* staff for 12 years. He moved to Washington after graduating from California State University at Fullerton in 1969. He has written two books, *The Terrapins: A History of Football at the University of Maryland*, and *The Fat Lady Sings for the Bullets*. His articles have appeared in numerous national publications. His *Post* jobs have included Super Bowls, NBA Championships and other major sporting events. He is making his second appearance in *Best Sports Stories.*

Phil Berger (The Yankees' $20 Million Gamble) has been a free-lance writer for 15 years. He once served as associate editor of *Sport* magazine and has been published by such publications as *Playboy, Penthouse, New York, Look, TV Guide* and *The Village Voice,* among others. Berger has written many books, including *The New York Knickerbockers' Championship Season* and *The Last Laugh: The World of Stand-up Comics.* He shared the magazine prize in 1979 and is making his third appearance in *Best Sports Stories.*

Ira Berkow (At 19, Thomas Makes His Decision) is a feature writer and columnist for the *New York Times.* He is a former sports editor and columnist for *Newspaper Enterprise Association,* who holds degrees from Miami (Ohio) University and Northwestern, and has written six books, including *Maxwell Street* and *Beyond the Dream,* a collection of his sports columns. He has appeared several times in *Best Sports Stories.*

Furman Bisher (Memories of a National Resource) is the sports editor of the *Atlanta Journal.* He has been honored by *Time* magazine as one of the outstanding sports columnists in the country. His stories and columns have merited inclusion in this annual anthology numerous times and his work is in great demand by many of the national magazines. He is a weekly columnist for *The Sporting News* and has written numerous sports books, the latest of which was *Arnold Palmer.*

Roy Blount Jr. (Prime of Coach Bum Phillips) is a highly regarded humorist and reporter. Blount has written two books: *Crackers,* a collection of essays about the Jimmy Carter presidency, and *About Three Bricks Shy of a Load,* an account of a year he spent with the Pittsburgh Steelers. In addition to his frequent contributions to *Playboy, The New Yorker* and numerous other periodicals, Blount has served as a staff writer for *Sports Illustrated* and has written columns for *Esquire,* the *New York Times* and *Inside Sports.*

Hal Bodley (For Boyish Rose, It's All Fun) has been sports editor of the *News-Journal* papers in Wilmington, Del., since 1971. He joined the company in 1960 as a sports writer and later served as a night sports editor and assistant sports editor before assuming his present position. The 44-year-old Bodley has been selected *Delaware Sports Writer of the Year 12 times. His column Once Over Lightly,* which has won numerous awards and has been included in *Best Sports Stories* four times, has been syndicated since 1978. Bodley, who is a weekly contributor to *The Sporting News,* where his Rose story appeared, has held office in such organizations as the Pro Football Writers Association, the Baseball Writers Association of America and the Associated Press Sports Editors Association.

Peter Bodo (Ilie Nastase: The Tragic Twilight) lives in Manhattan, N. Y., and is making his third appearance in *Best Sports Stories.* Bodo writes frequently about tennis and soccer and is a contributing editor of *Tennis* magazine. His work has appeared in such publications as *New York, Sport,* the *Star,* the *Australian* and the weekly magazine of the *New York Daily News.* Bodo is co-author of a book about soccer great Pele entitled *Pele's New World.*

Rick Bozich (Gossage Gives Yanks Edge in Any Ball Park) became a sports columnist for the *Louisville Times* in 1981. Previously, he covered high school football and basketball at the paper. He is a 1975 graduate of Indiana University who still dreams of being selected in the next NBA draft. His post-graduation experience was earned at papers in Anderson and Bloomington, Ind.

Erik Brady (When Martin Sees Certain Sports Writers, He Sees Red) is a sports columnist for the *Buffalo Courier-Express*. He joined the paper after graduating from Canisius College with a history degree in 1976. He became a columnist in 1981 after spending his early years as a general assignment reporter on the paper's city desk. This is his first appearance in *Best Sports Stories*.

Pat Calabria (The Human Side of a Soviet Goalie) began working for *Newsday* as a part-time high school sports reporter during his junior year at Hofstra University in 1971. He became a full-time employee the next year and continued his work toward a degree. After covering high school sports for two years, Calabria moved up to college football, college basketball and pro hockey. He has covered the New York Rangers and New York Islanders in addition to writing feature stories for the past seven years. This is his first appearance in *Best Sports Stories*.

Peter Dobereiner (The Hard Bastard Theory) is one of the world's top golf writers. The Oxford graduate began writing 20 years ago for the *London Observer* and now has expanded his golf writing to the pages of the *Manchester Guardian*. His stories are syndicated around the world. The author of five books on the game, Dobereiner is familiar to Americans through his monthly column in *Golf Digest*. He lives south of London in Kent and is making his first appearance in *Best Sports Stories*.

Dave Dorr (One Year Since the 'Miracle') is a staff member of the *St. Louis Post-Dispatch*. He was born in Colorado, raised in Iowa and is a 1962 graduate of the University of Missouri. His writing career began at the *Des Moines Register*, where he worked until 1966. His specialties are college sports, with an emphasis on football, basketball and track and field. He is a former president of the U.S. Basketball Writers Association and has covered three Olympic Games. He was selected Sports Writer of the Year in Missouri in 1981 and is the author of a nonfiction book, *Running Back*. This is his second appearance in *Best Sports Stories*.

John Engstrom (Muncey Killed in Crash) works on the city desk of the *Seattle Post-Intelligencer*. He began his career with United Press International in 1962 and spent the next 15 years in such jobs as political editor and columnist for UPI's Massachusetts bureau and Washington State sports editor where, based in Seattle, he covered a wide range of professional and college sports. Engstrom joined the *Post-Intelligencer* sports staff in 1977 as an NBA beat writer and covered the Seattle SuperSonics for three seasons. He moved to the sports copy desk in 1980 and became sports layout and news editor in 1981. He was covering the World Championship unlimited hydroplane race in Acapulco on vacation when Bill Muncey was killed in a crash. He was the only daily American reporter on the scene. This is his first appearance in *Best Sports Stories*.

John Feinstein (Indiana Wins NCAA Title) grew up in New York City and received a degree in history from Duke University in 1977. After serving as sports editor and managing editor of the student newspaper at Duke, he was selected as a summer intern at the *Washington Post*. He was hired by the *Post* as a metro staff reporter and served two years before moving to sports in 1979. He is making his first appearance in *Best Sports Stories*.

Larry Felser (Clutch Pass Closes Door on America's Team) is a sports columnist for the *Buffalo Evening News*. He began writing sports in 1953 with the *Buffalo Courier-Express* and became a pro football writer in 1958. He moved to the *News* in 1963 and covered the Buffalo Bills until 1976, when he began writing his column. Felser, a former president of the Pro Football Writers Association and one of a handful of writers to cover all of the Super Bowls, also writes a weekly column for *The Sporting News*, writes a pro football column for the *Toronto Star* and does free-lance work for different magazines. The Canisius College graduate has written four sports books.

Calvin Fussman (Heaven Can't Wait—Or Can It?) is a free-lance writer out of New York. He followed the lives of his subjects, Rickey Jackson and Remuise Johnson, for more than a year before writing their story for *Inside Sports.* Fussman, a University of Missouri graduate, worked for the *Miami Herald* and the *St. Louis Post-Dispatch* before going free lance. He currently is working on a collection of short stories. This is his first appearance in *Best Sports Stories.*

Jerry Green (Not Every Day a Kid Loses All) has been a sports columnist for the *Detroit News* since 1973. Prior to 1973, Green covered football for the paper after working seven years with the Associated Press, two of those years as the AP's Michigan sports editor. His other newspaper experience came from the *New York Journal-American* and *Long Island Star-Journal.* He also has written two books, *Year of the Tiger* and *The Detroit Lions—Great Years, Great Teams.*

Denis Harrington (Watson Masterful) is a well-traveled columnist-sports writer for the *Pensacola News-Journal.* He has worked as a sports writer-illustrator for newspapers and magazines throughout the United States, Europe and the Far East. Harrington, who was born in Oak Park, Ill., attended Butler University and holds graduate degrees from Washington University in St. Louis and the University of Illinois. This is his first appearance in *Best Sports Stories.*

Randy Harvey (At Foxboro, Fans Good at Drinking It All In) covers pro basketball for the *Los Angeles Times.* Harvey, born, raised and educated in Texas, worked at the *Tyler Morning Telegraph,* the *Austin American-Statesman* and the *Dallas Times Herald* before moving to the *Chicago Sun-Times* in 1976. He went to the *New York Daily News* in 1980 and moved to Los Angeles in September of 1981. Harvey, who holds a journalism degree from the University of Texas in Austin, is making his second appearance in *Best Sports Stories.*

Mark Heisler (It's Champagne with a Twist of Lemon) covers the Dodgers for the *Los Angeles Times.* Heisler began his journalism career in 1967 with the *Rochester Times Union,* moved to the *Philadelphia Enquirer* in 1969 and joined the *Philadelphia Bulletin* staff in 1972. He started working in Los Angeles in 1979. Heisler received History and Journalism degrees from the University of Illinois, his home state. This is his first appearance in *Best Sports Stories.*

Phil Hersh (Fisk Enjoys Red-Letter Days, Ways) covers baseball and handles special assignments for the *Chicago Sun-Times,* which hired him after the demise of the *Chicago Daily News.* Hersh is a 1968 graduate of Yale who came to Chicago from the *Baltimore Evening Sun.* He has twice been honored by the Associated Press as the top sports writer in Illinois and is making his second appearance in *Best Sports Stories.*

Steve Jacobson (A Long-Playing Hitter Copes With Loneliness) has been covering a wide range of sports for *Newsday* since 1960. He has written a column for the past three years. Jacobson is a graduate of Indiana University and lives on Long Island with his wife, Anita, and two children, Mathew and Neila. He has a book to his credit, *The Best Things Money Could Buy,* and was a 1977 winner in *Best Sports Stories.* This is his fourth appearance in the anthology.

Dave Kindred (A $35 Ride Bought a Nightmare) has been a sports columnist for 12 years, the last five with the *Washington Post.* He won the Kentucky Sports Writer of the Year Award five times during his years as sports editor of the *Louisville Times* and the *Courier-Journal* and was named winner of the National Headliners Award in 1971 for his general interest columns. He has written two books on basketball and is making his seventh appearance in *Best Sports Stories.*

Tony Kornheiser (The Rozelles: PR and Pizzazz at the Super Bowl) has been

272   *Writers in Best Sports Stories 1982*

with the *Washington Post* for the last three years, writing sports on a part-time basis. Before joining the *Post*, Kornheiser worked as a staff reporter at *Newsday* and the *New York Times*. His work has appeared in such publications as *Esquire, New York, Rolling Stone, New Times* and *Cosmopolitan*. He won the feature competitions sponsored by the Associated Press in 1977 and 1981 and currently is working on a screenplay. In 1979, his story on Reggie Jackson won the *Best Sports Stories* news-feature category and this story represents his ninth consecutive inclusion in the anthology.

Hal Lebovitz (Love Letters?) is a graduate of Case Western Reserve University who started his career as a high school chemistry teacher. But because of his avid interest in sports, he began writing for the *Cleveland News* and later moved to the *Cleveland Plain Dealer*, of which he currently is sports editor. His popular column, "Ask Hal," has earned him numerous honors and established him as an athletic arbiter on complicated questions about the rules of sports events. Lebovitz is a past president of the Baseball Writers Association of America and a weekly contributor to *The Sporting News* and the Gannett News Service. Lebovitz has written two books, *Pitchin' Man, the Story of Satchel Paige,* and *Springboards to Science,* a school textbook.

Mike Littwin (The Shot and the Dynasty Come Up Short) is a sports feature writer, specializing in baseball and professional basketball, for the *Los Angeles Times*. The University of Virginia graduate began his career in 1969 for the *Newport News (Va.) Times Herald*, moved to the *Norfolk Pilot* in 1974 and joined the *Times* staff in 1978. His book, *Fernando*, was published by Bantom in 1981. This is his first appearance in *Best Sports Stories*.

Leigh Montville (The Tube That Won't Let You Up) has been a sports columnist for the *Boston Globe* for eight years. Before joining the *Globe*, Montville covered the misfortunes, he says, of the New England Patriots. His previous experience came on the sports desk of the *New Haven Journal-Courier*. He is making his third appearance in *Best Sports Stories*.

Malcolm Moran (Picking Up the Pieces at Indiana U.) covers college sports for the *New York Times*. Moran was graduated from Fordham University in 1975 and joined *Newsday* on a part-time basis. He became a full-time member of the staff in 1977 and joined the *Times* sports staff two years later. Before taking the college assignment, Moran wrote features and covered the New York Giants. He is making his first appearance in *Best Sports Stories*.

Hugh Mulligan (Mudder's Day) is a columnist and far-roving reporter for the Associated Press who has covered cricket at Lord's, camel racing in Abu Dhabi and the Pope at Galway racetrack. His assignments have taken him to 110 countries and include wars in Vietnam, the Middle East, Ulster, Biafra and Angola. He even made it to the North Pole—in a Navy blimp. When not on the road, Mulligan resides in Litchfield, Conn., catching up on his column, "Mulligan's Stew," which appears in more than 500 newspapers around the country. This is his second appearance in *Best Sports Stories*.

Jim Murray (One Man's Vote: Davey Lopes) writes a daily syndicated column that is distributed by the *Los Angeles Times*. His perceptive and humorous thrusts resulted in a string of eight consecutive awards as national Sports Writer of the Year. Murray was born in Hartford, Conn., graduated from Trinity College and started his writing career with the *New Haven (Conn.) Register*. In 1944, he started working for the *Los Angeles Examiner* and later was one of the founders of *Sports Illustrated*. In 1961, he returned to the *Los Angeles Times* as sports columnist and won the National Headliners Award in 1965. He is the author of two books, both anthologies of his own writing. This is his fourth appearance in *Best Sports Stories*.

Gary Nuhn (Courtside Microphone John McEnroe's Worst Enemy) has spent the last 13 years at the *Dayton Daily News,* writing mostly college sports and golf. The New York native was graduated from Ohio State University in 1966 and spent two years at the *Middletown (Ohio) Journal* before moving to Dayton. Nuhn has won 13 national writing awards and is making his second appearance in *Best Sports Stories.*

Murray Olderman (Why Jim Otto Faces a Life of Pain) is a nationally syndicated columnist and cartoonist for Newspaper Enterprise Association. His work is distributed to 700 daily newspapers. Olderman holds degrees from Missouri, Stanford and Northwestern universities and has written seven books on sports. He has won the Dick McCann Award for professional football writing and is a former president of the Pro Football Writers Association. He also has done 12 murals for the Pro Football Hall of Fame. The New Yorker, now stationed in San Francisco, has appeared in *Best Sports Stories* many times.

Ron Rapoport (Add It Up: Ex-Jocks Bowl 'em Over) is a sports columnist for the *Chicago Sun-Times.* Before moving to Chicago, Rapoport worked for the *Los Angeles Times* and the Associated Press. He has written three books and is making his second appearance in *Best Sports Stories.*

John Schulian (The Mark of Excellence) writes four columns a week for the *Chicago Sun-Times* and is syndicated nationally. Schulian won the 1980 National Headliners Award and was voted the country's top sports writer the same year by the Associated Press Sports Editors. A graduate of the University of Utah and Northwestern University, he has worked on newspapers in Salt Lake City, Baltimore and Washington and has written for *Sports Illustrated, Inside Sports* and *Sport.* He has been nominated twice for a Pulitzer Prize.

Blackie Sherrod (The Ump Bump Has Gone a Little Too Far) is the executive sports editor of the *Dallas Times Herald.* Sherrod has captured most of the important sports writing prizes in the country. To name a few: The National Headliners Award, seven citations as the outstanding sports writer by newspaper, radio and television colleagues, and more than a dozen inclusions in *Best Sports Stories.* He also has made a big reputation as a master of ceremonies and banquet speaker and has his own radio and television programs.

Jim Smith (Colleges on the Razor's Edge) covers the New York Giants for Long Island-based *Newsday.* Smith started working for *Newsday* in 1966 covering high school and college sports. He moved to the city desk in 1973 as a news reporter and returned to sports in 1975, covering the New York Cosmos and local college sports. The Hofstra University graduate is a football correspondent for *The Sporting News* and free lances for such publications as *Football Digest, Sport* magazine, *Football Illustrated* and *Saga.* This is his second appearance in *Best Sports Stories.*

Joe Soucheray (Brooklyn No Longer Place to Be When Dodgers Win) has been a sports columnist for the *Minneapolis Tribune* since 1976. Soucheray worked his way through the College of St. Thomas (St. Paul, Minn.) first at a brass foundry, then as a rock musician and a delivery truck driver. He was graduated in 1971 with a journalism degree and worked for a publisher of airlines magazines before joining the *Tribune* in 1973. Soucheray has written two books, *Sooch,* a collection of his columns, and *Once There Was a Ballpark,* a history of Metropolitan Stadium, former home of the Twins. This is his fourth appearance in *Best Sports Stories.*

Art Spander (The Stuff of Champions) took over as the lead columnist for the *San Francisco Examiner* in 1979, filling a position that had been vacant since the death of Wells Twombly 2½ years earlier. After his graduation from UCLA,

Spander went to work for United Press International in Los Angeles and later worked for the *Santa Monica Evening Outlook* and the *San Francisco Chronicle* before moving to the *Examiner.* He contributes to *The Sporting News* and various other magazines, has co-authored a book with Mark Mulvoy, *Golf: The Passion and the Challenge,* and formerly wrote a wine column for *San Francisco Magazine.* Spander, who earned the 1980 National Sports Writer and Sportscaster Award, was the coverage prize-winner for 1970 in *Best Sports Stories.*

Jerry Spinelli (Retrospect: A Tip of the Cap) is a features editor for an industrial magazine who spends most of his spare time writing. His first novel, *Stuff,* will be published in 1982. Spinelli, who makes his home in Havertown, Pa., is making his first appearance in *Best Sports Stories.*

Gary Van Sickle (Master Golfers Respect and Fear Corner With the Name) has been a member of the *Milwaukee Journal* sports staff since 1976. His current assignments include golf, college football and college basketball. Van Sickle is a graduate of the University of Wisconsin. This is his first appearance in *Best Sports Stories.*

Vic Ziegel (The Scooter's Life and Times) is a contributing editor and columnist for *New York* magazine. Ziegel served as sports writer and columnist for the *New York Post* for 16 years and has written for numerous publications, including *Inside Sports, Readers Digest, Sport, Look,* the *New York Times,* and the *Washington Post,* among others. Ziegel co-authored the 1978 best-seller *The Non-Runners Book* with Lewis Grossberger and was co-creator of the CBS television series *Ball Four* in 1976. Ziegel has appeared several times in *Best Sports Stories.*

David Zinman (Cross-Country in the City) is a self-acknowledged sports buff who works for Long Island-based *Newsday* as a science writer. The 51-year-old Zinman runs every morning before work and occasionally enters marathons, leading to his association with *The Runner* magazine, in which this story appeared. Before coming to *Newsday,* Zinman worked for the *Norfolk Virginian-Pilot* and the Associated Press' New Orleans bureau. This is his first appearance in *Best Sports Stories.*

PRIZE-WINNING PHOTOGRAPHERS IN BEST SPORTS STORIES 1982

Richard Darcey (Pas De Two) has been photographing athletes and the games they play for the *Washington Post* for nearly 35 years. His action winner makes him a three-time champion in *Best Sports Stories*. He garnered a first prize in the old *Look* magazine Best Picture of the Year contest once and is a four-time winner (including 1981) in the White House News Photographers Association competition.

Norman A. Sylvia (Journey's End. The Trophy is Ours!) is making his second appearance in *Best Sports Stories*, this time as the feature photo winner. Sylvia is a staff photographer for the *Providence Journal-Bulletin* and spends much of his time shooting pictures for the Bulletin's Massachusetts edition. This suburban section is made up at two offices, one in Fall River and the other in Attleboro.

OTHER PHOTOGRAPHERS IN BEST SPORTS STORIES 1982

Michael Andersen (Troy Is No Trojan) is making his 10th appearance in *Best Sports Stories*. He won the anthology's feature award in 1977. He is a two-time Boston Press Photographer of the Year and has won more than 150 other awards during his distinguished career with the *Boston Herald American*, where he started working in 1960. His previous newspaper experience was in Lawrence, Kansas; Waterloo, Iowa; Casa Grande, Ariz.; Beaumont, Texas, and Lexington, Ky., his hometown. He is a former officer in the National Press Photographers Association.

Bruce Bisping (Punchoff After Faceoff) has been a staff photographer at the *Minneapolis Tribune* since 1975 when he was graduated from the University of Missouri. Bisping was named National Photographer of the Year in 1977 by the National Press Photographers Association and Regional Photographer of the Year the same year. Bisping, who does free-lance work for *The Sporting News*, is making his first appearance in *Best Sports Stories*.

Terry Bochatey (Mexican Blowup) began his career with United Press International *Newspictures* in New York after graduating from Colorado State University in 1972. He transferred to Columbus, Ohio, as *Newspictures* Bureau Manager in 1973 and has since opened a new photo bureau in Cincinnati.

Paul Chinn (With the Greatest of Ease) has been a staff photographer with the Los Angeles *Herald Examiner* since January of 1981. He attended San Jose State University and currently is finishing his education at Cal State University, Long Beach. Chinn, who grew up in the San Francisco Bay Area, is making his first appearance in *Best Sports Stories*.

Will Cofnuk (A Real Nose Job) was born in Caracas, Venezuela, and was graduated from the College of Environmental Science and Forestry in Syracuse, N.Y., with a degree in Landscape Architecture. Cofnuk has traveled extensively throughout Europe and has studied in Spain. He currently is Director of Photography for *Running New Jersey*, free lances for the *Passasic Herald* in New Jersey and works as a part-time photographer for *New Jersey Newsphotos*.

Dan Dry (Public Depression) works for the *Courier-Journal* and *Times* in Louisville, Ky. During his undergraduate years at Ohio University, Dry won the William Randolph Hearst National College Photojournalism Award and more than 50 regional, state and national honors. As a college senior, Dry was named Photographer of the Year by the Atlanta Southern Seminar on Photojournalism and has since won numerous awards as a professional. He was named National Photographer of the Year for 1981 by the National Press Photographers Association. He is making his third appearance in *Best Sports Stories*.

Judy Griesedieck (Little Big Men) is making her second appearance in *Best Sports Stories*. The St. Louis, Mo., native was graduated from Pitzer College in Claremont, Calif., and moved to Washington, D.C., where she worked for the Washington Diplomats soccer team. She now works for the *Hartford Courant*, but has freelanced for the Associated Press, *New York Times, Soccer America* and several dailies in Virginia.

Stormi Greener (Tongue Not in Cheek) is making her second appearance in *Best Sports Stories*. She joined the *Minneapolis Star* in 1977 after working for the *Idaho Statesman*. She attended Boise State University in Idaho and combines an art background with her photography.

Adrienne Helitzer (The Agony of Defeat) is a staff photographer for the *Courier-Journal* and *Times* in Louisville, Ky. She was graduated from the University of Vermont in 1979 with a degree in mass communications and went on to study photojournalism at Ohio University before going to Louisville. This is her first appearance in *Best Sports Stories*.

Jayne S. Kamin (Annual Fall Frolic), making her debut with *Best Sports Stories*, is a staff photographer for the *Los Angeles Times*. A New Yorker by birth, she received a photojournalism degree from the University of Miami in Florida. She began her career with the Associated Press in Miami and worked a year for the *Miami News* before moving to Los Angeles.

John Long (Peek-A-Boo Golf) is a staff photographer for the *Hartford Courant*. Long, who is making his fifth appearance in *Best Sports Stories*, is a former president of the Connecticut News Photographers Association. He lives in Manchester, Conn., with his wife and three daughters.

Eric Mencher (Child Psychology) is a staff photographer for the *St. Petersburg Times*. He was born in Enid, Okla., but grew up in Tampa, Fla. He attended the University of South Florida in Tampa, where he earned a political science degree. He began working with the *Tampa Tribune* upon graduation and moved across the bay three years later.

William Meyer (Back Arches to Triumph) is a staff photographer for the *Milwaukee Journal*, where he has worked since his graduation from the University of Wisconsin-Milwaukee in 1971. He has been named Wisconsin News Photographer of the Year twice and is appearing in the eighth consecutive edition of *Best Sports Stories*.

Anacleto Rapping (Correcting a Bum Steer) is a staff photographer for the *Hartford Courant*. Before moving to Hartford, Rapping worked as chief photographer for the *Thousand Oaks News Chronical* in Thousand Oaks, Calif. He received a journalism degree from San Jose State University in 1977 and has freelanced for such magazines as *Soccer World, Soccer America, Soccer Corner* and *California Today.*

Bill Serne (Born With One Leg and Tremendous Heart) was the winner of the action photo award in 1974, his first appearance in *Best Sports Stories.* After his graduation from Kent State University in 1972, Serne became a staff photographer for the *Tampa Tribune*, where he has worked for nine years. He now is employed by the *St. Petersburg Times.* This is his fifth picture to appear in the anthology.

John H. White (Ribbon-Shy Racers) is a staff photographer for the *Chicago Sun-Times.* His photographic work with children led to his action photo winner in the 1972 *Best Sports Stories*, a picture of a young girls' race. He attended Piedmont Community College in North Carolina, joined the U.S. Marine Corps in 1969 and began his newspaper career with the *Chicago Daily News.*